The Story began in...

The Kind of a Girl...
as Lorraine Innis, a man in disguise trying to avenge the death of his girlfriend, accidentally foiled the assassination attempt on Russian president Kropotkin.

It continued in...
The Girl in the Diamond Studded Heels...
as Lorraine became an international symbol of peace!

Then came...
The Girl in the Aubergine Sandals...
where we met Lorraine's Aunt Elinor and started to learn about the tragic flaws in Lorraine's past.

Which led to...
The Girl in the Lime Green Wellies...
and the star-crossed love affair with Verity Goodhue.

Next came...
The Girl in the Saffron Espadrilles...
where we learned the final pieces of the puzzle that resulted in the creation of Lorraine.

The story accelerated in ...
The Girl in the Blood Red Stilettos...
As Lorraine tried to step away from her unwanted fame, only to be drawn further into it.

Now, the story reaches its exciting climax in...

The Girl in the Sky Blue Plimsolls!

ALSO BY G.C. Allen

The Kind of a Girl

The Girl in the Diamond Studded Heels

The Girl in the Aubergine Sandals

The Girl in the Lime Green Wellies

The Girl in the Saffron Espadrilles

The Girl in the Blood Red Stilettos

The Girl in the Sky Blue Plimsolls

G. C. Allen

Daley•into•Print LLC

Mundus Est Vestra Locusta

For All Those Who Enjoyed This Series,
Especially:
Judy Berge
Tena Bremmer
Jama Conner
Sherry Cremer
Sheila Drebenstedt
Beatrice Followill
Bambi Rathman
Brandi Pearl Reynolds
Jodie Roberge
Jennifer Lynn Roche
Jimette Ross
Sandy Smith
Renee Simmons
Karina Thibodeau

and For Cyndi

As for you, you meant evil against me, but God meant it for good in order to bring about this present result..."

- Genesis 50:20

And we know that in all things
God works for the good of those who love him,
who have been called according to his purpose.

- Romans 8:28

The Girl
in the
Sky Blue
Plimsolls

-1-
The Time Before Time Runs Out

Lorraine Innis was dreaming again. Or was she? If so, it wasn't like any other dream she'd had before, and Lorraine was an experienced dreamer.

She was in an oddly luminescent place. A mist seemed to shroud her, though without reducing visibility, and unlike any other fog she'd ever seen, this one provided its own glow.

The last thing Lorraine recalled was being in a London courtroom, and then the judge said something, and she fainted. And now, here she was. Lorraine looked around. It certainly wasn't any London fog. Aside from it being so clean and bright, there weren't any buildings around. Lorraine felt warm, almost cozy, and wonderfully light and vibrant. It was almost as if she were…

She stopped, not daring to complete the next thought, though, of course, she already had.

…Dead?

"Am I dead?" she said. But as soon as she said it, she realized that if this were death, there was no fear, no hesitation, no foreboding. If this is death, she thought, I'd gladly take a second helping, please.

Then, as if to reinforce the notion of the hereafter, a recognizable form materialized, not out of the fog but from it. The form first appeared as a glowing pair of eyes of different colors. It could only be one person.

"Aunt El," cried Lorraine.

It was indeed the dearly departed Elinor Potoski, the aunt of Lorraine's alter ego, Chesney Potts. She looked marvelous, ageless, and vibrant as if her inner personality was exhibited in its full glory on her outer body. Aunt Elinor squinted for a moment at Lorraine and then shook her head.

"I haven't needed glasses since I came here, and I haven't seen a mirror in that same span," she said. "But I almost could attest I'm seeing my own twin."

"Aunt El," said Lorraine, "it's me!" Lorraine pulled back her hair to provide a clear view of her face. "It's me! It's Chesney."

Aunt El shook her head again. "No, young lady, Chesney's a boy, well, a fine young man. There is a resemblance, I'll admit; you could be brother and sister. And to be perfectly frank, you bear more than a passing likeness to me."

"But I am Chesney!"

Aunt El shook her head again. She looked Lorraine in the eye, and then her eyes wandered down to Lorraine's breasts.

"For one thing, or, rather, two," said Elinor, nodding at Lorraine's chest, "my nephew was not accompanied by such a healthy set of twins."

"But..."

"Are they yours?" asked Elinor.

"No, well, that is, yes, they're mine. I own them," said Lorraine.

"Are they real?"

"No, I mean, yes, of course, they're real," noted Lorraine pedantically. "They have form, weight, they occupy space, they're not imaginary in the least, now if you want to know if they're part of my body, grown by me in the natural course of human puberty, then no. But still, they are real."

"Chesney!" cried Aunt Elinor as she hugged Lorraine. "It is you! Only you could give such an arcane, nitpicking answer to a question when you obviously knew what I meant!"

Aunt and nephew enjoyed a prolonged embrace until Elinor pushed Lorraine back to arm's length.

"Let me look at you," said Aunt El, "oh, my, you have changed. I won't be as egotistical to say you look wonderful since I thought I was looking at myself. And I won't be so rude as to ask you how you went bonkers. Well, just leave it at that; you've changed."

"Only temporarily," assured Lorraine. "But it's wonderful to see you, Aunt El, and looking so alive. Death, I mean, well, this all suits you."

"Very sweet of you to say," said Aunt El, "but I can't really take any credit. But you still haven't explained why you've decided to honor me, not only with your presence but this living memorial...temporarily."

"Don't you know about Lorraine Innis here?"

"Who's that?"

"That's me; I'm Lorraine Innis...temporarily."

Aunt Elinor shook her head.

"Don't you get the news of Earth here?" asked Lorraine.

She shrugged her shoulders. "I suppose we could, but really, there's little interest in it. The notion that we all sit around on clouds, peering down at the world, is just too boring, no offense. Once you're here, there really isn't much allure to what's gone before. Time is terribly mundane.

Eternity is much more exhilarating and satisfying. I suppose it's like moving out of a hovel into a palace. You don't really want to go back to the old neighborhood."

"Oh," said Lorraine, "I never thought of it that way, but I suppose you're right."

"Thank you for understanding," said Aunt El. "I didn't want to sound like a snob about it."

"I've missed you terribly, Aunt El," said Lorraine.

"Thank you, dear," she said before sheepishly adding, "I know it's polite to say 'I've missed you, too, but...'"

"You haven't?" said Lorraine, crestfallen.

"Again, it's nothing personal. You're still fixed to the idea of time. I'm out of time now. Eternity's so much different, different as night and day. I haven't missed you because I haven't had time to miss you. I really can't explain it much better than that. It's like describing the aroma of a rose to a fellow without a nose or the colors of a perfect sunset to a blind man. Oh, but come now, just because I haven't missed you doesn't mean I'm not delighted to see you. If anything, I love you more than before, certainly in a much purer way. Everyone here does that. It really is delightful company."

"Have you seen..."

"Oh, please, don't start asking me about who's here. Have I met Aristotle, or Isaac Newton, or Harpo Marx..."

"But Aunt El," cried Lorraine, "I need to know, especially about two girls."

"Oh, yes?" she said skeptically. "Two girls, is it?"

Lorraine looked down and shuffled her feet nervously. "I supposed I want to know if they've met. I'd hate for some heavenly row to break out on account of me."

Aunt Elinor waved her hand. "Wouldn't happen here. Again, don't take offense, but I wonder if they've had much chance to think about you, let alone squabble over you."

"I suppose they didn't have the time," smirked Lorraine.

Aunt El smiled. "Exactly, now you're starting to understand."

Lorraine nodded. "Don't know if it would do much good to ask, but have you seen Martina?"

"Who?"

"Martina Fergus? Oh, yes, well, she died after you...."

"Here, we don't use the term 'died,'" said Aunt Elinor, "we're all much more alive than we were in time."

"Sorry, still, I doubt you'd know her," said Lorraine. "You don't seem to go around with nametags."

"No, it's hardly necessary."

"Well, you know Verity."

"Of course," said Aunt El. "Lovely girl. How is she?"

13

Lorraine was taken aback. "She died, I mean, she came here, the same day as you. I thought you might have arrived together."

Aunt Elinor laughed, causing her whole form to glow even brighter. "There isn't a shuttle or a Number 87 bus."

"Still, she, that is Verity, got here the same time, or lack of time, as you."

Aunt Elinor's smile faded, as did her luminosity; for the first time, she seemed almost corporeal. "No, dear, I'm sorry, but Verity's not here."

"Not here? But she has to be here. She died, or passed on, or transferred, had her ticket punched, or whatever term you want to use. She's got to be here, Aunt El."

Aunt El shook her head. "No, she's not here, Now, if you'll excuse me...." She turned and started to wander back into the light. "Oh," she said, turning around, "good luck with whatever this escapade is you've got yourself involved in. I would say that I'm flattered that you've chosen to imitate me in it, but we don't really care much about flattery here. I'm sure I'll see you soon enough, in fact, before I know it."

"But Aunt El," cried Lorraine, "can't I go with you?"

"With me," she laughed. "Why certainly not, my boy, you'd be terribly out of place."

"Do I have to go to some sort of orientation first?"

She shook her head. "Chesney, you can't come here, not yet."

"But, Aunt El, why not?"

"Because," she said with a shrug before misting away, "you're not out of time yet."

- 2 -
A Misinterpretation
of Mumbles

Her companion was regaining consciousness. Though her hands were tied behind her back, her mouth was taped shut, and the windowless room was totally dark, Clodagh Clott could still hear. The sounds emanating from Nikolai Kropotkin were difficult to bear.

Kropotkin was knocked cold by his political rival. His hands and feet were bound. Then their captor left them in the dark after locking and bolting the only door.

Kropotkin growled something in Russian; at least Clodagh guessed it was Russian. She doubted he had another Slavic language he reserved for such occasions. She also assumed that whatever he was saying wasn't a commentary on the weather or the reciting of his favorite poem but rather the saltiest curses he knew. That came through in any language, at least enough to make Clodagh feel the blush rising on her cheeks.

"I'm right here. You're not alone," said Clodagh, but through her gagged mouth, it sounded more like: "MFHGDKSSDFHLKAHPH."

Kropotkin muttered something else, still in Russian but decidedly more polite sounding. Then he obviously recalled why he came there. To rescue Lorraine and not be hit on the head, though circumstances turned out to be the reverse of that plan.

"Lorruska," whispered Kropotkin, "it is I. It is Nikki."

"I'm not Lorruska. I mean, I'm not Lorraine," explained Clodagh. Though this too sounded like she was reciting the Gettysburg Address with a mouthful of mashed potatoes.

"They have put a gag around your mouth, Lorruska."

The gag's on you, buddy, thought Clodagh. I'm not Lorraine. Again she tried to reply, though unsuccessfully.

"I understand," said Kropotkin.

15

"What's the use," said Clodagh, this time sounding like a constipated barn owl.

"Do not worry," said Kropotkin. "At least you were not blown up."

"Yes, not getting blown up is one of my favorite things," mumbled Clodagh. "In fact, I prefer it to just about everything, including being bound and gagged in a Russian bunker."

"I think I understood that, my Lorruska," said Kropotkin. "You say they brought you here against your will."

"No, but that's a good guess, Sherlock."

"Ah, and that you tried to warn me that it was a trap."

"Wrong again," mumbled Clodagh, "I didn't even know where I was or why. You've got to stop making these stupid guesses. Quit while you're ahead, pal."

"Yes," he said. "I feel the same way. At least we are together."

"Actually, I'd forgo the pleasure of your company if I could get out of this concrete Motel 6."

"Yes, you are right. At least we have each other," said Kropotkin. "With our love, we will overcome any difficulty our adversaries throw at us."

Clodagh rolled her eyes. Our adversaries? Unless his crackpot rival had enlisted the help of her sisters, Rhoda and Caprice, Clodagh Clott doubted she had any adversaries in this game. She was just a mistaken participant, a spectator forced onto the field of play. Not wishing to have any more of her mumbles misinterpreted, Clodagh just let out a long sigh.

"Do not despair, my dear. Nikki is here now."

"Oh, yes, that's no end of comfort," she muttered unintelligibly. "All the way here on that boat, I kept thinking: everything will be fine if a famous dumbbell comes to rescue me and he gets captured, too."

She could feel Kropotkin nudge closer to her, his warm breath in her ear.

"Please," he whispered, "save your strength. I will get you out of this, even at the cost of my own life, if necessary. I am almost certain the room is bugged."

"Not as much as me, bub," she said.

"Shh, my dear one, get some rest. You sleep. I will think."

"Taking up a new hobby, huh."

"Hush," whispered Kropotkin. "Sleep, and when you awake, I will have a plan."

Clodagh was about to reply when she was interrupted by a soft kiss on her cheek.

- 3 -
What Goes Best
Without a Pork Pie?

W hat a dump to be stuck in," bitched Valerie Fierro as she stared at the four walls of the budget hotel. When she fled from Lorraine and her entourage back at Heathrow Airport, she thought anywhere was better than at Lorraine's side. It was only a matter of time before someone accused her of blowing up Lorraine's car. Of course, she hadn't. But that rat, Robert Valvano, her later-day cousin, had rigged the evidence to make it look like she had. And her other cousin, her former fiancée, Michael Valvano, didn't do anything to help, aside from dumping Valerie when he found out they were related. Oh, yes, Michael did tell her that Robert was framing her. But that was of little comfort to her now, especially as she was alone on a lumpy mattress in a crumby hotel with rising damp.

Valerie couldn't very well stay in America with a villainous cousin. Nor could she stay at the side of Lorraine, her phony cousin, as Lorraine went to trial, especially since Valerie had left Lorraine holding the bag. Valerie had run out of options. It just wasn't fair..

With no other options, Valerie snuck out of the airport in a blonde wig, grabbed the first taxi available, and had them drive her as far as possible. It turned out that wasn't very far at all. Who knew England was stuck on an island with another weird little country named Wales? And now she was stuck there, too. All she knew about Wales was they had a prince who was in line to be king. That meant it had to be a pretty posh place, right? They had their own prince.

So, when the cabby dropped her in Caerphilly, Valerie was understandably disappointed, and that letdown quickly grew to total annoyance. If she ever ran into that prince, she'd tell him what she thought of his two-bit country.

17

Of course, staying at a nicer hotel might have made the town seem better, but she had to be careful with her resources. Her corporate credit card from Robert's bank was probably canceled. And even if it wasn't, using it would alert him to her location. Similarly, the card she held from The Cross of Lorraine charity may not have been stopped, at least not until Lorraine or someone figured out what was going on. But the use of it would also reveal where she was. That left her with her personal credit card, nearly maxed out, and the cash she had on hand. Welcome to poverty.

As she sat in her dingy room, Valerie thought back to just a few months before. She was shopping at upscale London boutiques and dining at the finest restaurants. Now she couldn't even afford a decent meal in the town's best restaurant; if Caerphilly even had a best restaurant.

With the sun setting on another annoying Welsh day, Valerie decided it was safe to get out for some fresh air, or at least fresher air than in her room. She started to put on the blonde wig but then decided against it. Even though she looked good with any hair color, Valerie's full Sicilian glory needed her shining brunette locks. Besides, the wig was getting itchy. She probably didn't need the disguise any longer. Despite her placement on just about every worthwhile magazine cover in the past year, Valerie hadn't seen any Welshlings, or Welshites, or whatever these boring people were called, who looked like they'd ever seen a copy of *Vogue* or *Elle*. And she didn't think Lorraine would be looking for her. After all, she'd sent a postcard to Lorraine saying she was off doing a bit of sightseeing and good luck with your trial. So, the coast was probably clear.

Valerie brushed her hair, not that any of the Welshawareans would appreciate it, counted the cash in her wallet, and headed out the door. A stroll around Caerphilly was almost as depressing as staying in her room. Near her hotel, there was a small square containing a park and a statue of a weird-looking man wearing an equally weird hat. She shook her head at what obviously passed for Welshy pride, then moved on to the nearest pub.

The hanging sign over the entrance proclaimed: "The King's Arms."

Valerie entered, looked around, and muttered: "More like the King's armpit!"

"Yes, Miss, what can I get you?" asked the man behind the bar.

"What?" said Valerie.

The man repeated himself in the same sing-songy lilt she'd heard everyone in town use. Valerie figured they must speak like that to impress the tourists; either that or she stumbled into a community of congenital idiots. Based on the fact that he was a bartender, Valerie guessed he was asking for her order.

"Give me a Cosmo."

The barkeep used the same puzzled expression on Valerie she'd just used on him. She feared that if she stayed here much longer, they'd vote her honorary membership in their imbecile's club.

"A COS-MO," said Valerie slowly and loudly, as one had to do when speaking with foreigners, even in their own county.

The man looked at her with a mixture of puzzlement and frustration. A woman came up beside him to assist.

"What can we get you, Dearie?" said the woman. She was slightly more intelligible but with that same irritating lilt in her speech.

Valerie sighed. "I just wanted to get a Cosmo."

The woman looked at Valerie and then looked at the man, and then back at Valerie.

"Oh, a Cosmo..." she repeated, though with little assurance.

"Yes, please," said Valerie.

Then the woman and the man began jabbering at each other in some weird language that Valerie was sure they were making up as they went along. After thirty seconds of this gobbledygook, the woman looked back at Valerie.

"I'm afraid we don't have that brand of beer," said the woman.

"It's not beer," whined Valerie.

"Ale?" offered the man.

"No, it's..."

"Stout?" said the woman.

Valerie threw up her arms. "No, it's the simplest drink in the world! It's a Cosmo! It's vodka, cranberry juice, um, well, it's got other things, too, and it's simple. Even in Delaware, they practically come out of the faucets. If you can get one in Delaware..."

It was no use. The couple were back to jabbering in their fake tongue. When they stopped, the man held up a nearly empty bottle of vodka.

"This is all the vodka we have," he explained. "I don't think we have cranberries..."

"Cranberry juice," said Valerie.

The man looked at the woman. "Well, you've got to have cranberries to get cranberry juice, and as we don't have the one, we can't make the other."

"It's just juice," said Valerie, "it comes in a bottle."

"We've got orange juice," said the woman holding up a plastic container. "Will that do?"

"That's a screwdriver," said Valerie. "It's not the same! Don't you watch *Sex in the City*?"

The man's eyes grew wide, and his face turned red. "Don't get to the city much."

"It's a television show," said Valerie, before adding with a totally justified sarcasm, "You know, television? That box with pictures that all civilized places have."

"Oh, we've got telly," said the woman missing the sarcasm. "I can turn it on for you."

"*Match of the Day*'s my favorite," added the barman.

"It's Football," said the woman.

19

"I wish I had a match," said Valerie, adding under her voice: "I'd burn down this entire town!"

"Don't allow smoking in here anymore, Dearie," said the woman.

"Never mind," said Valerie, "just give me a glass of wine. And what do you have to eat?"

"We've got some pork pies," said the woman.

Valerie had never eaten a pork pie but thought it was her best option under the circumstances. At least she recognized both words: "pork" and "pie." The woman pointed to a glass-covered tray with a round compact pastry underneath.

"Are they fresh?"

The man and woman stared at each other.

"The one I had day before yesterday was," said the man, "it was fairly fresh."

"Just the wine," sighed Valerie. Besides, she reasoned, drinking on an empty stomach would enhance the effects of the wine.

"Red or white?" asked the barman.

"Oh, I'll rely on your expert recommendation," she said with renewed sarcasm. "Which goes best without a pork pie?"

"I'd say either goes good without a pie," he said sincerely. "But I remember someone saying white goes with pork, so I say red would go better without pork."

"White," said Valerie with resignation. The barman poured a glass of wine. Valerie thanked him, barely, and started raising the glass to her lips but stopped, eyed the nearby pork pies, and decided to move away from them.

The barman turned on the television. The news from the BBC was just coming on.

"...a dramatic turn of events today in Queen's court at the Old Bailey, in London, where Lorraine Innis was facing dozens of bearded women who asserted their hirsute conditions were the direct result of using Mrs. Innis' trademark scent: *Quandry*..."

Valerie looked up. Would they mention her? Would they show her photo? Would she have to flee even the King's Armpit and find a hiding place more remote than Caerphilly?

The news anchor turned the coverage over to a field reporter.

"It was a day of remarkable events at the trial of Lorraine Innis," began the woman reporter. "The climax of which came when Mrs. Innis took the stand. She assumed full responsibility for the product, despite evidence from her own attorney that she was in no way culpable for the creation or marketing of the perfume."

Valerie sat with her mouth agape. She wasn't mentioned. She wasn't blamed. Lorraine took the rap. If Valerie had been in the same spot, she would have thrown anyone under the bus to save her own skin, but Lorraine didn't. Valerie would be free and clear to rush back to Lorraine's side. Good old Lorraine, good old Chesney. In her hurry to flee the impending disaster, Valerie hadn't considered Lorraine's odd way of thinking. Lorraine wouldn't look for someone to blame. She would look to help the people who'd been injured, in this case, all those stupid bearded women. If Lorraine was willing to blindly accept responsibility, she would surely welcome her favorite cousin and best friend back to her side. After all, Lorraine probably believed Valerie had just gone on a little vacation. That's what Valerie had said on that postcard. Yes, return to London, where she'd help Lorraine settle her legal matters with those hairy chicks. Lorraine would be so relieved she'd no doubt give Valerie whatever support she needed, mainly monetary, so Valerie could settle the score with all the Valvanos. Then Valerie would grab their wealth, which was rightfully hers. After that, it wouldn't matter what happened to any of them.

This strategizing took all of two seconds in the mind of Valerie Fierro, the same amount of time it took for the BBC reporter to pause between sentences.

"As remarkable as Mrs. Innis' generous offer was, the real stunning development occurred next..."

No, Valerie thought, she didn't. Don't tell me stupid Lorraine gave away all the money.

"...for just after she had promised full restoration to the plaintiffs, and the judge was commending Lorraine for her decency and goodness, Mrs. Innis went into a swoon and collapsed on the witness stand..."

Oh, that was okay, Valerie thought. Lorraine passing out was no big deal.

"...she was taken from the courtroom. Then in a final act to a day fraught with drama, Lorraine Innis disappeared from the Old Bailey. At this hour, her condition, or indeed her whereabouts, are a complete mystery."

"SHIT!" shouted Valerie, slamming her wine glass on the table with such force that it shattered.

The bartender and his wife turned around from watching the television. But before they could utter a word, Valerie Fierro was out the door and into the Caerphilly dusk.

Wasn't it just like Lorraine to go and do something inconvenient like disappearing just when Valerie could use her? Her options were quickly dwindling. Still, she needed to be in London in case Lorraine turned up. Stupid Lorraine, what did...

Valerie's furious ponderings came to an immediate halt in the small square, the one with the statue of the weird-looking guy. There she ran into a man with such force that it knocked them both on their backsides.

"Look where you're going, you idiot," snapped Valerie. "You stupid Welshies are really getting on my..."

"Oh, excuse me," said a man's voice in the darkness. "It was my fault entirely, at least I think it was."

From those few words delivered without that annoying accent, Valerie could tell she wasn't dealing with a local. He did sound British; still, it could have been worse.

The man helped Valerie to her feet. He was of average height; she could tell that much.

"Excuse me, young lady," said the man. "Assuming you are a young lady. Oh, I wasn't referring to your gender. But I didn't want to call you young if you weren't. And as to being a lady, well, in this dim light, I can only go by the sound of your voice. So, if you're a boy soprano, I apologize for slighting your manhood."

"What?" was all Valerie could manage.

"I was saying, in this dim light," the odd-sounding man reinforced his oddness with each word. He paused and laughed.

"What's so funny," asked Valerie.

"Oh, no, it's just that phrase dim light," he said with a bemused sigh. "It's almost an oxymoron, though not quite."

"Takes one to know one," muttered Valerie.

"Still, it's entirely my fault," he continued.

"You won't get any argument from me."

"I won't? Oh, good," said the man. "Still, I should have been here earlier, but I took a wrong turn. I'm not used to driving. And I should have waited until morning."

"Yeah, you would have had a good shot at me in full daylight . You might have broken my arm."

"But," he continued, ignoring Valerie's latest comment, "I just had to see the statue, or given the gathering dusk, not see it as the case may be."

"What statue?"

"Why…" he sounded totally mystified, "the reason anyone comes to Caerphilly, of course."

– 4 –
To Where the Fuzzy Gals Are

Patsy Einfalt sat in the small kitchen at The Cross of Lorraine offices. Her elbows on the table, her head in her hands. A heavy pall overhung her life. Even the twirls of her spiral perm seem to have lost their bounce. It was in this state that her fiancée, Purvis Twankey, found her.

"How do, love of me life," said Purvis exploding into the room.

Normally, just the sight of Purvis would put a smile on her face and a flutter in her heart. Today, she could barely nod in his direction.

"Oh, no, pet of me pulse," he said, noting her condition, "you look like you've got a bad dose of the Monday blues."

"It's Thursday," she muttered.

Purvis put down the paper sack he was holding and counted the days on his finger. "You're right; that makes it even worse." He sat down across from her. "It must be more than the day of the week, then, unless they've moved the weekend to Wednesday. That's not a terrible idea, though, two weekends a week."

"Oh, Purvis," she sobbed, "it's not because it's Thursday. It would be just as bad if this was Saturday, or Christmas, or my birthday."

He studied her face, then brightened. "I've got just the cure." He held up the paper bag. "I brought you lunch. Your favorite!"

"Double bacon cheeseburger," she said with nary a molecule of enthusiasm.

"Aye, but you forgot," he noted, "with extra pickles."

Patsy barely grunted in reply.

Purvis' face sank. "This is bad. What's the matter, flower of me heart?"

"It's all going horribly wrong, Purvis," she cried. "Everything is a mess."

"Now, now, me dimple dumpling," he said, patting her hand across the table. "Me mum said nothing's as bad as it may seem; even when it is. It just seems overwhelming 'cause it's whelming all over you. Just take it in turn and sort it out."

Patsy looked at him, took a deep breath, and nodded. "Okay, let's see. How about when Lorraine's car blew up with Miss Clott in it?"

"Aye, but then the foreskin guys…"

"Forensic."

"Aye, them, they said it couldn't have been Miss Clott because the bloke in the car was a bloke."

"But, then where is Miss Clott?" said Patsy. "She's missing."

"Aye, but not dead," said Purvis, "she's just been mislaid."

"Mmm," said Patsy casting a dubious eye, "okay, then Lorraine got sued over that perfume that made all those women in England grow beards."

Purvis adopted a sheepish look. Given that his regular expression started at sheepish, this one was positively ovine. "Aye, well, that was my fault, being that the perfume was me brainchild. But, I've figured out a way to make that right, or at least better. But, more on that later, go ahead."

Patsy's doubtful eye grew even more so at Purvis' declaration. "Okay, well, then, so Lorraine and Valerie went to England for the trial, and now they've both disappeared. What about that?"

Purvis shook his head. "I lived in England for years and hardly disappeared at t'all, but when I did, I always showed up again."

"So, you think they're all right?"

"Of course," he said, "they're as safe as houses."

"Safe as houses?"

"Aye, mind you, they're houses with mislaid addresses. If you want, I'll even look around for them next week."

"Next week? Purvis, don't tell me you're going to England," she cried.

"If I don't tell you, how else will you know that I haven't disappeared, too," he said, scratching his head.

Patsy wrung her hands. "Oh, no, another person disappearing into the black hole."

"More like Blackpool," he said. "That's one of the places I'm going. I've got to go to London, then I got to see me mum, and Blackpool's on the way." He grinned. "They've got champion roller coasters at Blackpool. I like roller coasters." Purvis saw the worried look on her face and adopted a more mature expression, one more like a ten-year-old. "But I'll be careful, like I said, I got to go to London to help Miss Lorraine. It was my idea what got her in the perfume business and made them female women sprout hair where there warn't none previous."

"Oh, no," said Patsy, "you haven't invented a hair remover, be careful, Purvis. Your brainstorms have a way of causing flash floods."

Purvis stroked his chin. "No, but that's an idea…" He took note of the panic in her eyes. "Well, we'll leave that to the barbers. Not to fret, me little pudding. I was thinking more of raising money. Before she passed out and evaporated, Miss Lorraine said she wanted to settle with them hairy birds momentarily."

"Monetarily?"

"Aye, that, too," he said. "So I wrote a song. Like when all them singers sang about them all being the world, for charity. Any road, I wrote the song and showed it to Mr. Slouch, you remember, Parvo Slouch."

"Your manager..."

"The very same," agreed Purvis. "I wrote a song to raise money to set up a payback to all those women. Only, I gots to record and release it in England, 'cause that's where the money will be distributed, 'cause that's where all the fuzzy gals are."

Patsy's knitted brow unraveled a few stitches. "Well, I suppose that makes sense. And it would help Lorraine, and it was you who started it. And you're sure it will raise money. Will it really be a hit?"

Purvis Twankey laughed. "It can't miss! At least, that's what Mr. Slouch said. He said that right now, my career's hotter than an armadillo passing a jalapeno! Mr. Slouch said I could up-chuck into a microphone and make a hit."

"Valerie said that's how you make most of your records," Patsy muttered.

"Pardon?"

"Nothing, dear," said Patsy.

"Champion," he said, pulling a piece of paper from this breast pocket. "I've got it right here. I can sing it for you archipelago."

Patsy nodded her head. She was a sucker for a serenade, especially from Purvis.

"Oh," he said after clearing his throat, "this isn't about any girl, in particular, you see. I'm mean, I learned my lesson from the time you put your foot through your telly screen."

Patsy grimaced. "There aren't any TVs in here, and I doubt my foot could reach the door of the microwave. But thank you for being so considerate."

He nodded and began to warble.

I've noticed a change, dear, there on your face.
The hair on your head is in a brand new place.
When we go out, the passersby all stare,
At my sweetheart, my gal with a face full o'hair

It was overnight that it started to sprout.
And when I tuck you in bed, your beard's hanging out.
It's grown, and it's grown; it t'ain't never stopped
You've gone from peach fuzz to your own bumper crop

And when we get married, as my vows are made
I'll ask you, dear: 'do you have enough blades?
Still, it doesn't matter to me; I hardly will care,
'Cause I'm madly in love with my gal with the face full o'hair

I'll stay by your side; we'll never breakup
I'd even buy you your own mustache cup
All of my razors I gladly would share
With my own little gal with the face full o'hair

Purvis finished and scratched his head. "That's most of it. It still needs a bridge, like, to get to the other side."

Patsy blinked several times. "Purvis, you know I think all your songs are wonderful but are you sure that these women, the ones with the beards and mustaches, won't find this upsetting?"

Purvis stared at her. "Upsetting? I'd hope not. Every penny from the sales will go for hair removal. Lasers just ain't for spaceships anymore."

Patsy smiled. Even if his ideas sometimes missed the mark, Purvis' heart was always in the right place. "I just wish you didn't have to go to England."

"It's all set," he said, "Mr. Slouch has the recording studio ready, and he's even set me up to debut the song on the telly, on *Slop of the Pops*."

"Well," she said, "I guess that'll be a good thing. I only wish a song could fix this mess!" She lifted the binder from the table and let it drop. "With Lorraine and Valerie missing, and Mr. Valvano gone, all the decisions of the whole charity have fallen on me. There are decisions to make: investments, money transfers, contracts, and more. They left me with quite a mess."

Purvis scratched his head. "Well, me mum always says when you've got a mess, the best thing to do is clean it up. She'd just grab a broom and start with one thing at a time. But first, you've got a delicious bacon cheeseburger with extra pickles that someone has brung you."

He handed her a burger wrapped in grease-stained butcher's paper. Patsy unwrapped it and lifted up the bun.

"Oh, I'm sorry, Purvis," she said, "it's grown cold. You were so nice to surprise me with lunch, and I've spoiled it."

Purvis scooped up the burgers. "Not a'tall. Cold food's nowt a problem, not while you've got a zapper gizmo!" With that, he placed the sandwiches in the microwave oven, punched in the time, and turned it on.

"Another problem solved by modern technologicals!" beamed Purvis.

Patsy pointed at the binders. "I wish you could get me some technologicals to straighten out this mess."

"For one thing," noted Purvis with a toothy grin, "them plastic covers would melt if you put them in the microwave."

The microwave oven beeped; Purvis removed the reheated sandwiches and placed them on the table.

"Things will look better after a bit of lunch," he said, nodding at her bacon cheeseburger.

Patsy picked up the burger and took a half-hearted nibble. "Thank you," she said.

"Hot enough?" he asked.

"Just right," she said, then took another bite and let out a cry.

"What's to do?" asked Purvis. "I thought it was okay."

"The burger and the bun are fine," she said, taking a gulp of soda, "but the pickles are too hot."

Purvis lifted the top of his burger, studied the contents, and then took a bite. He seemed to be chewing with judicial intent. After nodding his approval, he took a second bite and immediately winced. After a quick drink, Purvis lifted the bun again, felt the meat patty, and fingered the pickles. His brow furrowed, deep in thought, and stayed pondering for at least thirty seconds. Finally, his eyes opened wide, and he snapped his fingers.

Patsy recognized that look. She'd seen it before. The last time he was eating potato chips and got the idea for the genetically based perfume that was the source of one of their current problems.

"By gum," he said, staring at the topless burger, "that could change the world. 'Eck! That could change everything!"

"Purvis, please, be careful," she cautioned. If ordinary dining experiences kept stimulating him to wild ideas, she'd just have to stop feeding him.

"Why, it's there, as plain as the pickle on me beef burger," he said to no one in particular. "I gotta test that…" Purvis Twankey rushed out the door before quickly returning to plant a quick kiss on his girlfriend's lips, then wiped a blob of ketchup from her mouth, and licked it off his finger, before exiting again.

"But Purvis…" Patsy Einfalt called after him.

"Gotta go," he said from out in the hallway. "Don't worry. Everything works out. I'll see you before I leave for Blighty!"

Patsy picked a pickle from her hamburger and wondered. "Everything works out," she muttered, "get on with it yourself!" She looked down at the open binder. "I guess I have to."

- 5 -
The Sentimental Junkpile

Julius Rosen adjusted his reading glasses. Though he was already sitting up straight in his highbacked leather desk chair, he made a point of arching his back to reinforce the point.

Only then did he slide the desk drawer open, remove the portfolio and open it with the utmost solemnity.

"Cut the shit, will you, Julie," snarled Robert Valvano. "This ain't the Academy Awards."

Rosen looked over the top of his glasses at Robert sitting on the other side of his desk.

"We know what we're here for. We know what it says," continued Robert. "I don't know why you couldn't do this at the house instead of dragging me to your office." Robert looked around at the walls, bedecked with rows and rows of law books. "So this is what I'm paying for!"

"That's right," said Rosen, "you've never been to my office."

"Yeah, I've never been to the sausage factory, either," snapped Robert.

Meghan Valvano put her hand on her husband's arm. "He's only doing his job, Robert."

Robert jerked his arm free. "Shaddup! It's all for show. He just likes to make a big deal before he officially announces what we already know. Read the old lady's f**kin' will already!"

"Michael's not here yet," mewed Meghan.

"I informed him via registered letter…" began Rosen.

"He ain't showing," said Robert. "Nobody's heard from that *gavone* for weeks. He's got no respect for his own grandmother. The old bitch has been dead for a month. He didn't even show up to the ancient twat's funeral. He's got no respect."

"Maybe he…" started Meghan.

"You stickin' up for him?" snapped Robert raising his hand toward his wife. She gave him an icy stare, daring him to complete the gesture with the unspoken promise it would be his last. He folded his arms. "And he made off with a valuable employee of mine, too," Robert added. "No one's seen Alphonse since."

The room fell silent for thirty seconds.

Rosen smoothed out the document in front of him.

"You get it all," he said with abrupt resignation.

"I know that," growled Robert Valvano.

"He gets everything?" said Meghan. "She didn't leave anything to Michael? She gives everything to him?"

"What are you bitching about?" said Robert. "I'll take care of you."

"I didn't mean…"

Rosen pointed to the will. "It doesn't mention Michael or Robert or anyone by name. The late Mrs. Valvano stipulated that her entire estate would go to the oldest surviving Valvano. She did note that it was her wish that this person, as the new head of the family, would assume the responsibilities that came with that position."

"Don't worry, I'll take care of Michael," said Robert, "I'll take care of everyone."

"I don't doubt that you will," said a voice behind Robert.

He turned to see his brother, Michael standing in the doorway.

"Sorry I'm late," said Michael.

Meghan welcomed her brother-in-law. Robert merely sneered.

"I've informed Robert of the essentials of your grandmother's will," said Rosen.

"Yes, I heard," said Michael.

"Tough luck," said Robert without a trace of sympathy. "Just as well, you never wanted any part of the family's business. Besides, you wouldn't know what to do with it if you had it."

"I didn't come here because I was hoping to get something," said Michael. "I came out of respect. I missed her funeral, not knowing she had died."

"Yeah, well, that ain't my fault," said Robert.

Michael paused a moment to purposely ignore the remark. "So, this is my only way of saying goodbye."

"Where are you going?" asked Meghan.

"I meant saying goodbye to Nonnia," said Michael. "Robert might as well get the house and the business. He's cared for it, with your assistance, of course, Julius."

"So, that's that," said Robert, "thanks for dropping by."

"I suppose there's no mention of anyone else," said Michael. "By that, I mean Valerie Fierro. Of course, Nonnia only learned she had another grandchild a few hours before she died."

"True," said Rosen, "this will was last updated two years ago. Long before any of us knew of Miss Fierro."

"That's if she was related. He thinks so," said Robert pointing at Michael. "I don't. But it doesn't matter as it all goes to the oldest surviving Valvano. Even if she was one, she'd have to wait until I was taking a dirt nap."

"She's younger than I am, too," said Michael.

"Yeah, so, I get it all."

Michael nodded and said, "congratulations." Then turned to leave. He paused in the doorway. "What about her personal effects?"

Rosen glanced at the document in his hands. "It's part of the estate. It all goes to Robert."

"It's just a load of shit," said Robert. "I've been through it."

"I went through it," interjected Meghan.

Robert rolled his eyes. "Yeah, okay, she went through it. There was nothing valuable. No gold bars or diamond necklaces."

Meghan turned to Michael. "It was just her clothes."

Robert pointed his thumb in his wife's direction. "Two sizes too small to be of any use to… anyone."

Meghan sighed in exasperation. "And some photo albums and scrapbooks. Any jewelry was simple and not very valuable except for the sentiment."

"Like I said," reiterated Robert, "a real carload of crap."

"I'd like to have that," said Michael. "I mean the photos and scrapbooks."

Robert snorted. "I hoped you didn't mean the dresses. Not unless there's something you ain't telling me about. Of course, those long black dresses look like the ones you used to wear."

"Cassocks," said Michael.

"Watch your mouth around my wife," said Robert emitting a gravelly chuckle at his own joke. No one else appreciated his wit.

"Would you like the photos and the albums?" asked Meghan.

"I would," said Michael. "That is if you don't want them."

Robert shook his head in disbelief. "Sure, it saves me the trouble of throwing them out."

"Thank you," said Michael. "I'll appreciate the insight into the family's history."

"Yeah, you would," muttered Robert. "I got enough of Sicily and her shit while she was alive."

Meghan slapped his arm. "Have some respect."

"What?" said her husband, "she was my grandmother, but she's gone now. Life is for the living. I don't expect no one to cry over my picture when I'm gone."

"Don't worry, they won't," said Meghan.

– 6 –
The Copping of the Phony Feel

Verity Goodhue held her breath as she crouched over the body of Lorraine Innis in the back of the van as it sped down the highway. It had been a harrowing day.

First, there was the scene in the courtroom where her beloved, Chesney Potts, in the guise of Lorraine Innis, had made a valiant speech on the witness stand. Following this, as Lorraine received the praise of the judge, she fainted.

After that, events moved so quickly. It was only now, in the relative calm of the getaway van, that Verity had a moment to review it all. Emergency medical people came in to take Lorraine from the courtroom. Verity, accompanied by Li Gao, had tried to find out where they were treating Lorraine, but security prevented them from doing so. As strict as the security was, a momentary lapse afforded them their opportunity. They grasped it and literally ran with it. And they were still running.

With no news of Lorraine's condition and no hope of seeing her, they decided to leave. Li Gao and Verity were in Li's van, around the back of the courthouse, when they saw Lorraine Innis, still unconscious and strapped to a gurney, being wheeled to a waiting ambulance.

Without a word between them, but with unison of thought, Gao pulled next to the ambulance while Verity hopped out and ran around the far side to create a diversion. She fell to the ground and started screaming as if she was injured. The ambulance attendants, driver, and the two policemen on guard immediately rushed to the sounds of her screams.

As Verity rolled around on the ground, screaming and pleading for help, Li Gao hurried the gurney into the back of his van and sped away. Seeing his van depart, Verity made a remarkable recovery from her fit, dashed around the corner, and jumped into the van. They then drove off at a breakneck pace. Fortunately, Gao's familiarity with the winding, narrow streets of central London helped them escape. Before any alarm could be raised, they were miles away.

Verity laughed as her heart raced. "We did it. We didn't plan to do it, but we did it! You were magnificent, Gao!"

"Please save your appreciation for a successful heist - to use the argot of the criminal classes - until we have completed it. For now, prudence would dictate we take our passenger to a very discreet location," advised Gao. "Though my vehicle has no distinctive markings, I anticipate that the hue and cry has been raised for a white Ford van."

"Yes, you're right," said Verity catching her breath.

"And, if I may," added Gao with a tiny smile, "you were equally impressive in your role."

"I just did it. We just did it," said Verity. She glanced back at the still form of her beloved. "We can't go to a hospital, can we?"

"Most unwise," agreed Li Gao. "And I would caution against using your father's London home. My flat affords no privacy. I fear that trying to clandestinely convey our passenger up three flights of stairs on a stretcher would be difficult, not to mention indiscreet."

Verity thought a moment. "Then there's nothing for it but to go to Staffordshire. We can take him to grandfather's cottage. No one ever disturbs me there."

"I concur," said Gao, "though I suggest you make a cursory examination of our passenger to verify that his life is not in any danger."

Verity climbed over the seat into the back where Lorraine Innis lay strapped to the stretcher. She stared at the face, examining it for the first time at such a close range. Then she took Lorraine's hand in hers, pausing to stare at the perfectly manicured nails, and then proceeding to the wrist. There was a pulse, steady and strong. That was a good sign, at least. She nudged the body.

"Chesney, Chesney, my Beloved," she said in a whisper before pausing. What if he no longer responded to that name? She cleared her throat.

"Mrs. Innis, Lorraine, wake up."

Verity studied the face for a moment and then reached for her own purse. She took out a small bottle of moisturizer and started dabbing it on his face.

Li Gao noticed her actions in the rearview mirror. "What are you doing?" He asked.

"It's silly, but I, I just needed to take off this makeup," she explained. "So, he'd looked a little more..."

"Like himself," said Gao. "I understand. Also, if we were stopped, it would be best if Mrs. Innis looked a little less like Mrs. Innis and more like our Mr. Potts."

"Yes, that's another good point," said Verity.

Carefully she wiped the cosmetics from Chesney's face with tissues. She noticed that there was less makeup than she had anticipated. She ran her fingers across his chin and his upper lip. It seemed as if his facial hair had been permanently removed. No more mustache on my Beloved, she thought, though that didn't matter, not really.

She lifted his eyelid, expecting that might wake him up. It didn't.

"He's really out," she said.

"As are we," observed Gao, "at least we are out of the city and on the motorway. As for Chesney, it is quite possible that he was sedated after his initial collapse. He may sleep all the way to your home."

Verity nodded and glanced towards the front of the vehicle. Gao's eyes were on the road. She then leaned over and softly kissed the lips of her beloved, half expecting him to awake, like in some fairytale. Nothing, not even a stirring.

Then, driven by a curiosity that had been nagging at her from the moment she first saw Lorraine Innis, Verity lowered the blanket that covered Lorraine up to the neck. The body was still wearing the suit and blouse she had worn in the courtroom.

Looking up again to ensure Li Gao's eyes were on the road, she slowly unbuttoned the top buttons of Lorraine's blouse to expose her chest. There she saw a bra, as she expected.

Then, with conflicting emotions of foolishness, inquisitiveness, concern, and the feeling that she was somehow violating Lorraine Innis' privacy, Verity tentatively reached out to touch the garment. She ran her fingers slowly over the cup, then took a deep breath, closed her eyes, and reached underneath the fabric. She poked and prodded for a moment before opening her eyes. Suppressing a laugh, Verity pulled out a realistic-looking but obviously false breast. She stared at the item for a moment. It was warm from its owner's body heat. Verity felt her face redden, slid the faux boob back into its cradle, quickly buttoned up the blouse, and tucked the blanket back up around Lorraine's neck.

Only then did she breathe a sigh of relief. They weren't real.

– 7 –
The Failure to Foresee
the Unforseen

S he was on her way back to London. At least that's what Valerie Fierro thought when she agreed to accept a ride from the strange man in Wales. That was several days ago under the statue of the other strange man, the one wearing the peculiar hat.

"It's a fez," she was told.

"What?"

"You called it a nutty hat," said the man. "It's called a fez. It was his trademark."

"What? Whose trademark?"

In the light of a nearby streetlamp, Valerie could see the bewilderment on the man's face. Though from the look of him, he probably wore that expression more often than not.

"Why him," said the man pointing up at the statue. "Tommy Cooper. That's Tommy Cooper. I thought that's why everyone came to Caerphilly. That's why I'm here. I thought it was why you were here."

Valerie stared at the man. "Yeah, well, it's not."

"Oh," said the man, genuinely surprised. "I'm sorry, I just assumed. Why are you here?"

Valerie delivered another withering glare, but the odd man failed to dissolve under its strength. Finally, she sighed. "Everyone has to be someplace."

The man pondered that for a moment before brightening and nodding. "Yes, that's very true. Well, I'm glad that if you have to be someplace, that it's here."

"Yeah, sure…"

"And fancy that you don't know about Tommy Cooper."

"Nope, never heard of him," she said.

"I'd love to tell you all about him."

"Oh, no, I don't want to inconvenience you," said Valerie. She used those words but spoke them in a tone that really said: "Why don't you boil your head and then drop dead." Apparently, in addition to liking weird statues in weird hats, the man was also slow on the uptake.

"Inconvenience me? Not at all," he said brightening, "it would be my pleasure. We could go over there…"

Valerie was just about to scream in hopes of attracting a cop, when he said the magic words.

"…I haven't had dinner yet. I could tell you all about Tommy Cooper over a bite to eat, with you as my guest, of course."

Valerie eyed the man for a split second. He looked odd but otherwise seemed harmless. Normally, her head would not accept an invitation to what promised to be a boring meal. Still, her empty stomach rarely cared about the quality of the dinner conversation. Her head agreed that a free meal was exactly what she needed at the moment.

"Yeah, sure, I mean, yes, that would be very nice," she said.

"Splendid," said the man, "I noticed a nice little restaurant around the corner."

"It's not a pub, is it?" she asked recalling the petrified pork pies.

"No, a real restaurant," he assured her and started off. After a few steps, he stopped. "Oh, no, wait, I can't go in there with you."

Valerie looked down at herself. She may not have been at her sartorial peak, but even in the dark, she could tell she was more fashionably dressed than this guy. The only advantage he possessed was access to ready cash. She almost told him off, right there in the middle of Caerphilly, when he continued.

"I can't take you into a restaurant," he said, "that wouldn't be proper. We haven't been introduced. My name is Postlewaite," said the man, with a courtly bow. "Formerly, of London, now in the area of Norfolk."

"Okay, nice to meet you," she said with as much enthusiasm as she could muster, which was very little.

He just looked at her in the light of the streetlamp. Finally, he spoke: "Excellent, well, we're halfway home."

She almost said that there was no way she was going home with him, when she realized he was just waiting for Valerie to introduce herself. In the poor lighting, he obviously hadn't recognized her. Still, after she said her name, he would be visibly impressed.

"I am…" she said, pausing for effect.

"Have you forgotten?" asked Postlewaite, genuinely concerned.

"No, I haven't forgotten," she snapped. "Of course, I haven't forgotten. I am… Valerie Fierro!"

She waited for a gasp of delight; none was forthcoming. He obviously had never heard of her.

"That's fine," he said. "Now we can go eat."

What followed was a decent dinner and a boring conversation. The food probably tasted better than it was because Valerie was so hungry. Still, nothing could improve the prattling of Mr. Postlewaite. In the light of the restaurant, she could see he was probably in his mid-fifties, well-groomed after a fashion that she didn't find very fashionable and exceeding polite. He talked incessantly about the weird guy who was commemorated in the statue. Apparently, this Tommy Cooper was from Caerphilly originally and became some sort of comedian or magician. The only thing about Cooper that Valerie appreciated was that he had the good sense to leave Caerphilly.

"Speaking of leaving Caerphilly," interjected Valerie.

"What? Oh, yes, Tommy left Caerphilly when he was three," said Postlewaite, "with his parents of course."

Valerie sighed and had another forkful of her meal. Hopefully, she'd get out of there in less than three years, with or without the assistance of Mr. and Mrs. Cooper.

Postlewaite was describing some jokes or tricks or something about Tommy Cooper's act. She just stared at the non-stop lips of Mr. Postlewaite and was thankful that at least he didn't talk with his mouthful. For that matter, he hardly touched his meal, and Valerie wound up eating his dessert, while he jabbered away. He was so enthusiastic and excited, while at the same time being so horribly boring. There was only one other person she knew with those skills. Valerie almost interrupted Postlewaite to ask if he had ever met Chesney Potts. But, her facetiousness would have been lost on this earnest weirdo. Plus, she hoped he was reaching the end of his lecture. It was the most costly meal she'd ever endured, even worse than a dull dinner date that she knew would end in sex.

"Well, I could go on for hours," Postlewaite finally exclaimed after he had already done so.

Valerie almost slammed her forehead against the table, but there was still a bit of chocolate cake on her plate, and she didn't feel like washing her hair tonight.

"But, I've got to get an early start in the morning," he added.

Valerie perked up. "And you promised me a lift."

"What?" he said taking out some bills to pay the check. "Oh, yes, I'd be delighted for your company."

"Back to London?"

An odd look crossed his face for a moment, but it quickly blended in with the rest of his strange looks.

"London? Oh, yes, absolutely, I'm going to London."

The following morning he picked her up outside her hotel. Valerie was surprised to see an odd little trailer hitched to the back of his sedan. Its weirdness seemed perfect akin to the rest of Postlewaite.

"What's that?" said Valerie pointing at the trailer.

Postlewaite scurried around the trailer, examining the wheels and the lights and checking for dents. Finally, he looked at Valerie.

"What's what?"

"THAT!" she yelled. "That whole thing! That thing attached to the back of your car!"

He blinked several times, apparently pondering the matter. At last, he answered. "It's my teardrop."

"Your what?"

"My teardrop trailer," he said, opening the small door on the side of the trailer. "That's the shape. Like a teardrop."

"Well, what's it for?"

"It's where I sleep, see?"

Postlewaite waved his hand through the hatch and Valerie peered inside. Indeed, the interior was taken up with a mattress, over which were shelves containing a radio, some books, a light, and even a tiny stove.

Valerie shrugged. Like a bad fantasy film, she'd have to suspend her disbelief, at least for the few hours it took to get back to London.

"Okay, let's get going," she said. "The sooner I see the back of Wales, the more I'll like it."

"That's the Irish Sea," said Postlewaite as he held the car door for her.

"What?"

"The back of Wales, it butts up against the Irish Sea," he explained. "I wasn't going there, but if you really want..."

"I just meant I want to get out of here," she said. Valerie was trying hard to restrain her annoyance with everything, most recently with Mr. Postlewaite. She reminded herself that she needed him to drive her back to London. But once back there, she promised to inform him what an idiot he was if he hadn't figured it out on his own by then.

The ride was uneventful, at least at the beginning. Mr. Postlewaite kept rattling on about unfamiliar names as if Valerie would know who they were. She interrupted the first one or two times to ask: "who?" Postlewaite seemed genuinely surprised and vowed that the persons he spoke of were giants of British entertainment. As she didn't know any of the "stars," and even more, didn't care, Valerie just nodded as he continued his animated commentary. Finally, she decided it was easier just to pretend to fall asleep. This didn't help much, since her host continued talking, but at least she didn't have to respond.

After a few hours, they stopped at a roadside rest stop to use the bathrooms and get a cup of tea. As they started off again, Valerie noticed the highway sign marking the distance to London.

"190 kilometers," said Valerie, "how much is that in real distance?"

"Hmm?" said Postlewaite.

"It's 190 kilometers to London, how much is that in miles?"

Postlewaite gave her an odd look as if it were a strange question. "Oh, let's see, I'd say around 120 miles. Why do you ask?"

"So, about two hours or so," said Valerie.

"Two hours what?"

"Two hours driving time," she sighed.

He looked around in several directions and then shrugged. "Yes, I suppose so, depending on traffic."

"Well, let's go," said Valerie.

They set off again, and again Postlewaite began his lecture. Now he was going on about someone named Dodd, or more familiarly, "Doddy." Valerie feigned a yawn and quickly pretended to go to sleep.

An hour later, she opened her eyes to see a road sign and let out a piercing scream.

Mr. Postlewaite screamed, too, partially from fright, partially in some symbiotic response, as he jerked the car back and forth on the highway. The small trailer behind responded in a similar synergetic manner, causing them to sway wildly across several lanes. They barely missed being sideswiped by an articulated lorry carrying a shipment of pickled onions.

With Herculean effort, Postlewaite brought the car and trailer back under control and pulled over to the side of the busy highway.

"Are you all right," he panted, wiping his brow with a handkerchief.

"Why did you scream," snapped Valerie, "you could have killed me."

"You could die from a scream?" asked Postlewaite, "Is that some rare auditory condition?"

"Not from the scream," she screamed. "You could have killed me driving like a lunatic."

"Ah," he said, in a moment of sober reflection, "yes, I probably would have been killed as well."

"I know I should take some satisfaction in that, but I don't consider that a fair swap," said Valerie. "I have my whole life in front of me."

"I hate to be pedantic, noted Postlewaite, "but I doubt you'd get to go back and relive your childhood or anything else that you've already lived…"

"Knock it off," she said, "you screamed and started driving like a lunatic."

"You started it," he said. "You were sleeping and just screamed, and that frightened me, and I didn't know what to do, so I screamed. Then I scared myself and lost control of the car. So you started it."

Valerie thought a moment and then recalled why she had screamed. "No, no, you can't blame me. I screamed because I woke up and saw you were going the wrong way."

Postlewaite looked around and then nodded his head knowingly. "We're definitely going the right way. You're just confused. We English drive on the opposite side of the road than what you're used to."

"No…"

"Yes, we do," he said confidently.

"Okay, I'll give you that, but that last road sign we passed said it was 230 kilometers to London."

"Oh? I suppose that's right."

"But that other sign said it was 190 kilometers," she said. "So, that's 40 kilometers further away."

Postlewaite squinted one eye as he ran the mental calculation. "Yes, that's right."

"So we're going the wrong way!"

Postlewaite looked around in each direction, north, south, east, and west. Then he pulled a map from between the seats and made a similar analysis of that. Finally, he folded up the map and smiled.

"Not to worry, my dear," he said in a soothing, almost condescending tone, "we're right on track. We should be in Liverpool in a few hours."

"Liverpool!" wailed Valerie.

"Yes, in a few hours," said Postlewaite, cautioning: "without any unforeseen incidents."

Valerie stared at the driver and could foresee multiple incidents. All of them involved tire irons and Postlewaite's head and would be perpetrated by her.

She took a deep breath. "I thought you said you would take me to London. You promised."

Postlewaite seemed genuinely surprised. "And I will! A Postlewaite is true to his word. It is his bond. We'll get to London…" he picked up a small notebook with "British Comedy Legends Tour" written on the front. He licked his finger and flipped the pages. "Let's me see… oh, yes, I anticipate we'll arrive in London in a fortnight, or a fortnight and a half. Two weeks, three weeks at the top, without any unforeseen incidents."

– 8 –
The Cryptic Family Crypt

Package for you, Mr. V.," said Alphonse carrying a large parcel into Michael Valvano's apartment.

"Al, I told you, call me Michael or Mike," he said. "You're not working for my brother. You're not even working for me."

"Sorry, it was a habitual habit," said Al. "I'm not working for you, but you are letting me use your place as an abode. Like that one? Abode, it means like a house."

"Very nice, Al," said Michael, then nodded at the box. "You can put that down on the table. It looks heavy."

"Nah," said Al. "Well, yeah, okay, a little heavy, but I'm glad to hold if you wants me to. I'm what you call appreciative. I don't want to go back to my old place over your family's garage. I was appreciative of that, too. It was a nice apartment, only now, I don't think your brother would be too appreciative of me aboding there after our professional relationship was, uh, um… unconsummated."

Michael laughed. "Yeah, well, don't feel too badly, Al. My brother Robert has a way of unconsummating a lot of his relationships. I wouldn't be welcome there either."

Michael examined the carton. The address label was written in his sister-in-law's handwriting. He took out his penknife, cut the string and packing tape, and opened the box. The musty smell of old paper rose from the parcel like a genie released from its lamp. There was a note on top.

"Dear Michael," it began. *"Here are your grandmother's personal photo albums and other papers. I hope you will find them interesting, some more interesting than others. I've looked through all of it, and while I tried to share some of it with Robert, but he couldn't be bothered. Mainly, he wanted to*

know if there were any stocks, bonds, or other items of value. Once I assured him there weren't, he told me to throw it all away. So, it's up to you to handle all this. I trust you will know how to make the best use of it all. Yours, truly, Meghan."

Michael reread the note and scratched his head. "That's rather cryptic."

Alphonse looked up. "I can't do those either."

"Excuse me?"

The gentle henchman held up a puzzle magazine he was reading. "I do the crosswords, the hidden words, and them types. But the first time I saw them cryptic things, I nearly went crazy trying to find those words in the dictionary. Turns out they're like code."

"I mean," said Michael, "that Meghan's letter is mysterious."

"I can loan you my pocket dictionary," said Al.

"Thanks, but I think I'll try to figure this out by myself."

Alphonse nodded and went back to his puzzle book. "I always like to do them myself, too. It provides a greater sense of accomplishment."

Michael smiled and started to unpack the carton. It was like going through the Valvano family crypt. On top were several photo albums. The first one was the most recent and contained pictures of people and places familiar to Michael. There were several pages of photos of Robert's family.

Next, there were pictures of Robert and Michael's childhood. Michael grimaced as he reflected on the different paths he and his brother had taken.

The last albums were filled with faces from Michael's earliest years; the generation before his, most of them born in Sicily. His parents, and several aunts and uncles, all of whom had died before their ancient mother.

"You were one tough lady, Nonnia," Michael muttered as he scanned the photos. "You single-handedly carried a family to America."

The earliest photos were fuzzy and yellowed. They had been taken back in Sicily. The people were unremarkable, except for the vague family resemblances. But as he turned back through the years, Michael had the oddest sense that one face was standing out. Finally, as he reached one early portrait, it hit him like a slap across the face.

"Valerie," he whispered. He stared at the professional photograph. It was obviously Nonnia, but aside from the different hairstyle, it could have been Valerie.

No wonder Nonnia reacted the way she did when she got a good look at Valerie. He turned over the photograph. There was no date, no inscription. Nonnia must have been around the same age as Valerie was now. He saw other pictures. Nonnia in some small Sicilian village. Nonnia with a small boy. Michael guessed that it was Valerie's father. He recalled family stories about the boy who disappeared during the war, presumed dead. In the final picture with the boy, Nonnia was pregnant. Not terribly pregnant, maybe just showing, but at the same time, she seemed to be trying to shelter that fact from the camera. Oh, well, he thought, that was the way back then; not like today when women displayed their bare baby bumps for all to see.

The next picture was of Nonnia seated, holding a baby. There was a fat woman beside her, but no picture of the father. Michael flipped over the photo. All that was written on the back was "1943." The baby must have been Michael and Robert's father. The expressions on the faces were interesting. Nonnia had an odd mixture of pride and embarrassment. The fat woman looked annoyed.

In the back of the album was a bundle of yellowed papers tied up in a red piece of string. Michael carefully untied them and started sorting through them. They seemed official. First was a marriage license from 1939 for Dante Valvano and Josephina DiRenzo.

Josephina was Nonnia's Christian name, but he rarely heard it. Next was a birth certificate dated approximately seven months after the wedding license. Michael recalled Nonnia's outrage that Robert had to marry Meghan after getting her pregnant.

"The Valvanos don't fall far from the tree," observed Michael.

Next, there was a baptism record and then a document that had Dante Valvano's name and was dated 1940. At first, he couldn't make out the writing. Most of the Italian he'd picked up at home was slang or profanities. He guessed that official documents had very little of that. Then it dawned on him. These were enlistment papers into the Italian army. Michael flipped back to the photo album. There was a picture of Dante in a uniform, standing next to an older man. The older man looked proud. Dante looked miserable.

An official-looking letter followed from the Red Cross. He deciphered enough of the Italian to realize this was the notification that Dante had been taken as a prisoner of war. Michael looked at the date of the capture. It was several months earlier than the date at the top of the letter. Then came a birth certificate for Corrado Valvano, the father of Robert and Michael. He looked at the different dates and did the math in his head. Something didn't seem right. They didn't fit. There must be an explanation.

The possible explanation came in a separate bundle of letters tied up with a ribbon. The letters were in German, but above the writing, someone had translated them into Italian. The final letter in the stack was addressed to someone named "Kurt Zimmer," but it was unopened, and "Verstorbene" was stamped across it.

Michael opened the envelope. It contained a letter in Italian, signed "Josephina." It also included a photograph of Nonnia holding a baby. On the back was written: "Corrado."

- 9 -
The Gong with the Mink-Covered Desk

L ord Bagnold sat in his high-rise offices in Paper House, the headquarters of his toilet tissue empire, pondering the disappearance of Lorraine Innis. He checked his pocket watch and then waited.

"I didn't not become a corporate maggot," he muttered to himself, "not without knowing wot the next move of the h'enemy was going to be. Ha! Not no how."

His desk intercom buzzed.

"Mrs. Innis' lawyers, Ms. Friseur and Ms. Madison are here," his secretary announced.

Bagnold laughed sardonically.

"As they does not have an h'appointment, make them wait. Hee, hee."

There was a pause.

"Do you want them to make an appointment and come back when you're not busy?"

Bagnold snorted. "I h'ain't busy now. I was waiting for them to show up because I knows they was going to. That's what comes out of being a business genius with a military background. H'anticipate your h'enemies' moves, but don't let them know you knows what they're doing."

The secretary paused again. "Um, your Lordship, you're on speaker, and Ms. Friseur and Ms. Madison are standing right here."

Lord Bagnold felt his face glow red. He clicked off the intercom, counted to five, and the clicked it back on.

"Is my next h'appointment here?" he snapped officiously. "I means them two Yank lawyers."

"Uh, yes, Your Lordship," replied his secretary.

"Well," he said, "if they is 'ere, show them in."

Lord Bagnold snapped off the intercom. He grabbed an unimportant pile of papers and began studying them as if they were the formula for eternal youth.

The doors opened, and the loud lawyer, Lindsay Friseur, blew into the room like a small tornado but kept her eyes focused on Bagnold. Behind her, much more discreetly, was Hilda Madison. Though his head was tilted downward, His Lordship's right eye scrutinized Friseur. Had they not been adversaries, he would have called her a "handsome" specimen of womanhood. She was just the type of woman who would give him a good tussle, both intellectually and physically. That would have been an enjoyable workout in both realms, though he was confident he would have come out on top.

Bagnold was surprised when Hilda Madison spoke first.

"Thank you for seeing us, your Lordship," she said. Again, her tone was respectful, without being condescending, "especially, as we didn't have an appointment."

His Lordship merely hummed, as if the visitors were no more important than the cleaning woman. He kept pouring over the third-quarter pulp paper figures.

Hilda Madison cleared her throat. "We know you're quite busy, your Lordship..."

Her speech was cut short as a thick blanket of fur suddenly covered most of Bagnold's expansive desk.

"Wot! Wot the..." he spluttered. Lord Bagnold looked up. Lindsay Friseur was standing in front of him, her arms folded and wearing a smug smile. "'Ooh threw this overgrown rat on me desk?"

Ms. Friseur picked up the closest sleeve of the fur coat, stroked it with the grain, and then blew carefully into the nap.

"I said..." began his Lordship.

"This was always one of my favorite sables, Hildy," said Lindsay Friseur. "That's natural, not dyed, full pelts, and not at all stagy."

Then, with one sweeping movement, Lindsay Friseur whisked the coat from the desktop, sending papers flying. She sat down directly across from Lord Bagnold, smiled broadly at him with closed lips, then gestured for Hilda to take the seat next to her. For his part, Bagnold was puffing like a prototype of Watt's steam engine.

Hilda opened her mouth, apparently groping for the right words to soothe these two opposing forces of nature. While she did so, Lindsay calmly draped her fur over the chair on her left. Then she opened her purse, pulled out a compact mirror, rubbed the corner of her deep red lips, serenely closed the mirror, and returned it to her bag. Only then, as if she had patiently awaited his arrival, she reached up and extended her hand toward the desk.

"Lord Bagnold," she said, "My name is Lindsay Friseur, that's F-r-i-s-e-u-r. I believe we saw each other in court." Reflexively, Bagnold reached for her hand, which was at least three feet beyond his grasp, and he started to stand. As if he weren't there, Lindsay retrieved her hand. "It was Lord Bagnold," she said, "wasn't it, Hildy? Oh, excuse me, this is my partner at law, Hilda Madison."

Hilda Madison emitted a slight sigh.

"A pleasure to meet YOU, Ms. Madison," said Lord Bagnold. He then glowered at Lindsay Friseur. She returned the look, dagger for dagger. Lord Bagnold then raised his right hand and made a checkmark in the air. Then repeated the exercise with his left hand as if to indicate the score was now tied.

Lindsay Friseur's mouth relaxed into a more genuine smile. "Now that we understand each other…"

"We does, madam," said Bagnold with a grimace.

They stared at each other for a moment, each waiting for the other to play the next card, each confident that they would trump it. Hilda Madison's eyes darted back and forth between them.

Finally, as if they were opposite ends of transatlantic bookends, they spoke in unison:

"What have you done with Lorraine Innis?"

The effect was almost perfect stereo. The only difference being the timbre of their voices and the fact that Lord Bagnold dropped the "h" from "have."

Both looked at each other, stunned that the other had the affrontery to level the same accusation they had hurled. There was a pause of two-and-a-half seconds.

"Me?" both Lindsay Friseur and Lord Bagnold cried. "It was you!"

"Excuse me," Hilda began, "but you're both behaving like a double-act in show business or an old married couple completing each other's sentences simultaneously."

"Old couple," said Lindsay.

"Show business," snorted Lord Bagnold.

Hilda looked at both of them and smiled. "Well, at least you've been broken of that habit. Both of you seem to be working under the sincere belief that the other has sprited away Mrs. Innis."

Both of the accused started to speak until Hilda waved them to be silent. "I doubt either of you is responsible. Lord Bagnold, I've never known a lawyer who had their client abducted, even when that client rejected their counsel in open court as Mrs. Innis did. And Lindsay, there is little to be gained from Lord Bagnold or the ladies he's leading in the suit to do away with an adversary offering generous settlement terms. So, I would suggest that you both would achieve your goals more quickly if you worked together. It's nothing less than Mrs. Innis suggested all along. And, I believe it is what we owe Mrs. Innis if we have any concern for her."

Lord Bagnold's brow lowered. "That does put a slightly different complexion on it; it does. I was thinking you twos 'ad 'er. But if yous twos don't, and I h'ain't debating that point, then what all 'appened to the woman? The news reports just say she's been taken to a private location. If she h'ain't in my private location, and she h'aint in your private location, then in oo's privates is she being located?"

The three of them fell silent in thought.

Finally, Lindsay Friseur spoke. "Well, your Lordship... look, if we're going to be in this together, I can't keep calling you 'your Lordship.' What's your given name?"

"Goodhue," he said, dropping his head bashfully. "Claude Goodhue."

"Okay, Claude..." she gave him a funny look, "Claude? Okay, sorry, I just assumed you had some sort of arrangement with the court or with some private hospital. But I can assure you that we don't."

"Ms. Friseur...Lindsay," he said, "I 'ave known enough low-lifes and disputable characters in me time, I'm afraid that someone, unknown to the three of us, has made off with our bird!"

"Kidnapped," said Hilda.

"It was a possibility in the back of my mind," said Lindsay, "though you know me, Hilda, I don't jump to conclusions without evidence. I would think if someone kidnapped Mrs. Innis, we, as her legal representatives, would have been approached with a demand for her release."

"That is," said Lord Claude, "if oo ever snatched 'er wanted money."

"What else would they want?" said Hilda.

Lord Bagnold's eyes rolled up in his head, and his eyelids fluttered. "Oooh, it don't pay thinking of what grubby little types would do with an 'andsome woman like Mrs. Innis. Ooh, no, 'ave either of youse ever been in the H'army? No, I don't expect so, but there's a lot of nasty types out there."

Both women stared at him, their mouths agape.

"Not me!" he said. "Don't look at me that way. I was a sergeant major. I was the cream of 'er Majesty's forces. I wouldn't not do nothing to a fine woman like Mrs. Innis, not no 'ow!"

"No, you'd just sue her," said Lindsay Friseur.

"Only cause I wanted 'er to do me adverts," he demurred.

Lindsay stared at him. "You sure have a way with women. You're either suing them or growing beards on them."

Lord Bagnold snarled.

"Please," interrupted Hilda, "this is doing none of us any good, especially Mrs. Innis. We've got to call the police."

"Yes, Hilda's right," said Lindsay, "forgive my petty sniping."

"T'was not nothing, no 'ow," said Bagnold magnanimously. "But I wouldn't not call the police. Oh, if your pocketbook was pinched..." he shrugged. "But, this case is 'igher profile. Probably we's dealing with international criminals, masterminds, and that sort."

"Well, then..." said Lindsay.

"Well, then," said Lord Bagnold, "we goes to the top! To the tippy top. Fortunately, when you've got a gong, doors which wouldn't not 'ave been open to you otherwise... is." He picked up the phone and dialed.

"Gong?" said Lindsay to Hilda.

"I believe that's a reference to his knighthood," said Hilda to Lindsay.

Lord Bagnold winked and nodded at Hilda.

"Hullo, Bagnold here," he said into the receiver. "Is 'e in? Good. Yes, I'll 'old." He put his hand over the mouthpiece. "You've 'eard of MI-5, MI-6?" The ladies nodded. "This goes up so far they's run out of numbers. Top of the services..." He took his hand from the receiver. "Hullo, your Lordship, this is another Lordship, Ha! That you, Stinky? Yes, well, not so good... Oh, you 'eard what 'appened in court, well, it's relatives of that! I need your best man, pronto! You knows the one!"

– 10 –
The Heavenly Kiss

Chesney Potts felt a soft pair of lips caress his cheek.

His eyes were closed. Had that encounter with Aunt Elinor been a dream? He lay still, not wanting to open his eyes, bracing himself for what he might see.

He felt a gentle hand brush across his forehead.

Wherever he was, whether alive or dead, at least the surroundings seemed caring. His eyes twitched, though still closed.

"Chesney, Chesney, can you hear me?" said a soft, familiar voice. It was a woman's voice with a lovely British accent. Though he hadn't heard it for years, it could only belong to one person: his beloved Verity Goodhue.

It meant that he was dead, or as his Aunt had told him, that he was "out of time," finally.

A smile crossed his lips.

"Chesney, my Beloved," said Verity's voice. "You're waking up."

Pausing a moment, savoring the anticipated reunion, Chesney's eyes remained closed, though his lips parted in a broadening grin.

"Verity," he whispered. "Is it really you?"

Verity laughed, "Yes, yes, it is, dearest. Can't you open your eyes?"

Chesney laughed. "I can, but I wanted to enjoy the moment for just a moment more.

He felt her hands clasp his. It surprised him that neither her form nor his hadn't changed. It was just like they had earthly bodies.

"You feel just like before," said Chesney.

She laughed again. "Why wouldn't I?"

Chesney screwed his eye tightly for a moment and then slowly opened them. There was Verity sitting on a bed beside him, smiling.

"You're as lovely as ever," he said, "this agrees with you."

A puzzled smile crossed her lips. "What agrees with me?"

How had Aunt Elinor termed it? Oh, yes. "You know," he said, "being out of time."

Verity knitted her brow. "Out of time? I'm sorry, dear, I don't understand."

"Out of time," he repeated. "We're all out of time now. Though it all feels much the same, at least it does to me. Maybe I've got some sort of probationary period, like freshman orientation, to get used to it all."

Verity felt his forehead. Her touch certainly felt real.

"You collapsed, but I didn't think you had fallen on your head," she said, mainly to herself.

Chesney reached up, touched his head, then looked at her and laughed.

"No, I'm fine, though that doesn't matter anymore, does it," he said. "You can't get hurt here, can you?"

"In Staffordshire?" asked Verity.

"Staffordshire? I've never heard it called that before," he said.

"That's all we've ever called it," said Verity. She studied him for a moment. "Where do you think you are?"

He searched his mind for the correct answer. He didn't want to get it wrong, not on the first day. "Um, heaven?"

"Heaven?"

"The netherworld? The afterlife? Paradise? Nirvana?"

She opened her mouth to speak and paused.

The door opened, and Li Gao entered the room.

"Ah, he's back with us," said Gao.

"Sort of," said Verity, with deepening concern.

"Gao!" cried Chesney. "Then you're here, too. How wonderful. I didn't know you'd passed on, too. That's too bad, but then it isn't, is it? You must have seen Aunt Elinor."

Li Gao's mouth dropped open.

"He thinks this is heaven," said Verity in a whisper, though in the small room, it was clearly audible.

"Quite understandable," said Gao. "Let us tread carefully."

Verity stroked his hand and looked into his eyes. "Chesney, darling, this isn't heaven."

Chesney knitted his brow. "No? Well, that would explain one thing."

"And what is that, my Beloved?"

"Why Martina isn't here," he said, though he immediately regretted the comment.

Now it was her turn for concerned looks. Verity's countenance darkened. "Who is Martina?"

Chesney's mouth hung open as he searched his mind for a reply that would keep this heaven from turning into hell.

– 11 –
The Lone Commando
and the Erroneous Rescue

Clodagh Clott had finally fallen into a fitful sleep. It was no small feat given that she was in a cold, dark, concrete bunker, tied to a Russian President. Her eyes were uncovered, though there wasn't much to look at in the dim light. Her mouth was gagged and taped. Kropotkin had his eyes blindfolded, but his mouth was free. She wished their situation was reversed, if for no other reason than he would know she wasn't Lorraine Innis and would stop talking to her as if she were.

When he wasn't reassuring her that he would save them from their dire predicament, Kropotkin was pledging his undying love for Lorraine. Then there were the occasional kisses. These were blessedly few. Even amorous Russian presidents didn't enjoy smooching duct-taped mouths.

Despite all this, and being hungry, and having to go to the bathroom, Clodagh had fallen asleep. She dreamt of standing at equal distances between a hot dog stand and a public restroom, not knowing which urge to satisfy first. Then the choice was taken from her when they both exploded, blasting her out of dreamland.

Clodagh opened her eyes. It was still dark, and cold, but now it was also noisy. She heard muffled gunfire, like a machine gun. Then the gunfire stopped, and it was almost silent. Now the only noise came from Nikolai Kropotkin. He was snoring.

Clodagh tried to speak, but if a small battle going on outside didn't wake him, her muffled pleas wouldn't rouse him. She tried kicking him, but with her legs tied together, this, too, proved ineffective.

Then she heard a clattering of keys in the door lock, and a gust of air swept into the room. The fresh air would have been welcome if it weren't so cold, and Clodagh was wearing a skirt. It must have been night because no daylight accompanied the air. Instead, a flashlight beam pierced the darkness.

"Don't worry," said a voice that was distinctly American. "I'll get you out of here."

Clodagh replied as best she could.

The figure approached. Though most of his details were obscured by the light, Clodagh could make out that he seemed to be wearing military gear. The light was attached to his head, and he was carrying some sort of rifle. Even from her position on the floor, Clodagh could tell he wasn't massively tall. Heck, if she were standing, she guessed he wouldn't be much taller than she was.

"I had to kill the guard," the American said.

"That's okay. I didn't think you were shooting Nerf bullets," mumbled Clodagh, though the observation was only apparent to her.

After being kidnapped in Delaware, bundled in a sack, and lugged halfway across the world, Clodagh was okay with her captors meeting a violent end.

"Hold on," he said, grabbing the end of the tape across her mouth. "This will hurt for a second."

He gave it one quick yank, freeing her mouth.

"Oh, thank you," said Clodagh, "you have no idea how glad…"

She stopped talking as she saw his eyes widen and his mouth drop open.

"You're not her," he whispered.

Clodagh rolled her eyes while she flexed her mouth.

Her rescuer looked around, scanning the entire room with his lamp. He then looked back at Clodagh. "Where is she?"

Clodagh didn't have to ask who. This was at least the fourth person who had mistaken her for Lorraine.

"The last time I saw her," sighed Clodagh, "she was in Delaware, safe and sound."

The man looked at Kropotkin, still snoring.

"Yes," said Clodagh, anticipating the man's next question, "that's Kropotkin. I'm sorry I disappointed you, but I'm grateful that you rescued us."

The man looked around. His expression betrayed a furious series of computations going on in his mind. Then, without another word, he sprang up and started for the door.

"Hey, wait," said Clodagh. "What about us?"

The disappointed rescuer stopped, rushed back, and unsheathed a knife from around his leg. In one rapid motion, he cut the bonds around Clodagh's wrists and legs. He made a short parry towards Kropotkin but stopped.

"No, you can take care of him," he said as he jumped up.

"Wait, you can't leave us here. Where are you going? Where are we?"

The lone commando stopped halfway to the door. "Look, lady, I'm no superhero, and I ain't no travel agent. Take it as a favor that I neutralized your guards and cut you loose. The rest," he nodded towards Kropotkin, "is up to you two. I'm at least a thousand miles off course. I got to make up time."

"But..."

"Oh, and here's another piece of advice," he said, raising a cautionary finger, "you don't know me. You didn't see me. Understand?"

Before Clodagh could reply, her rescuer was out the door, no doubt hurrying to make up that thousand-mile deficit. She slowly climbed to her feet, rubbing and stretching her aching legs. She flipped the light switch by the door several times. Nothing happened. Her rescuer must have knocked out the power before making his assault. Either that or her abductors hadn't paid the electric bill. Walking to the door, she craned her neck around the corner. The first light of dawn provided just enough illumination to continue. There was a small anteroom, beyond which was another open door leading to the outside. In that doorway was the body of a dead guard. Gingerly, she inched towards the body. In the anteroom, on a desk, was a flashlight. She turned it on and directed the beam to the body in the doorway. It wasn't the man who had interrogated her yesterday. Too bad, she thought. It meant that lunatic was probably out there somewhere.

"Great," muttered Clodagh. She was stranded in the middle of Russia with a Russian President who thought she was Lorraine Innis. Soon she would be hunted by another Russian who had thought she was Lorraine but no longer labored under that misconception.

She wondered with which idiot foreigner she stood the best chance. After weighing her options, Clodagh sighed and went to wake up Nikolai Kropotkin.

– 12 –
Filling in the
Empty Family Plot

Uh, w-who is…" Chesney stammered.

"…Martina," said Verity Goodhue. She didn't seem angry, like a woman asking about a strange shade of lipstick on her husband's collar. Rather, her tone was straightforward. She wasn't jumping to any conclusions. In some ways, that was worse. She wasn't giving him any reason to be defensive.

"It's… it's a long story," said Chesney.

"We have time," she said.

Li Gao studied their expressions and announced: "I'm going to put the kettle on."

"Oh, yes, just what I need," said Chesney. "A cup of tea, yes, please." He could use a cup of tea, but the break in the confrontation was even more welcome.

After Gao excused himself, Verity sat on the edge of the bed and gently stroked her fiancee's shoulder-length tresses.

"You have beautiful hair," she noted. "Very much like your aunt. In fact, you're almost the exact image of Elinor."

"It's all a long story," repeated Chesney, "a very long story. I'm sorry."

"Sorry for what?" said Verity. "I can't judge you for anything that's happened."

"Thank you," said Chesney with a sigh.

"At least not until I hear what you have to say," she added.

Chesney swallowed hard. "I suppose you'd like to know what happened."

"Very much," she said, "I've been wondering since I first saw Lorraine Innis on the news last October."

"You've known that long?" he said.

"I knew you the second I saw you," said Verity. "You are my Beloved. I lost you, I thought forever. And then I saw you on television. Then, there were only two possibilities; both involved a bodily resurrection: either of you or Aunt Elinor. The second would not only involve a return to life but a rejuvenation of about 25 years. I strongly suspected the former, but the only way I could prove it would be to dig up your grave."

"My grave? But you were the one who was buried."

She squeezed his hand. "We were both buried in a sham burial. We shared the same grave. We even shared the same headstone. That's how I twigged to the whole scheme. It seems for all his intricate machinations, someone couldn't resist using opposite sides of the same tombstone."

"Your father!" cried Chesney.

"Yes, the very same. Apparently, Father had three identical sports cars. He burned one and put it down that ravine, then faked our deaths to each other. He would have gotten away with it if it wasn't for…"

"Being too cheap to buy two headstones!"

"No, that just confirmed it," said Verity. "Actually, I'd never have known if a certain lady hadn't ruined his whole plot."

"Who was that?" asked Chesney. "I'd like to thank her. Was it your father's housekeeper or the cook?"

Verity laughed. "No, silly, it was a lady named 'Lorraine Innis.'"

Chesney reached up and touched his long hair and felt his smooth face. "Oh, right. Sitting here with you, it's almost like Lorraine never existed. It's like all the years in between never happened."

They looked into each other's eyes, lost for a moment in the contentment of their reunion. Finally, Chesney let out a deep sigh.

"And you want to know what it's all about," he said.

"Yes, very much so," said Verity. "I've been waiting and wondering since last October. But I don't want to rush you. You can tell me when you're ready. We have time."

He grimaced. "I've learned not to take time for granted. Once we thought we had all the time in the world. Besides, you've been waiting. But it's a long story."

"Whenever you're ready, my Beloved."

Chesney looked around. "Is there anyone else home? I mean, aside from you and Gao?"

She assured him they were alone.

"What about your father?"

Verity laughed. "Not likely! We brought you up here to keep you hidden from prying eyes… especially Father's."

"He doesn't suspect my true identity?"

"Far from it," said Verity. "After the Queen, Lorraine Innis is his favorite woman in the world."

"Another reason to get rid of Lorraine Innis as quickly as possible," said Chesney. He lifted up the comforter and peered beneath.

"They're grandfather's pajamas," said Verity. "Li Gao changed your clothes. Your… that is, Lorraine's clothes are in the wardrobe…"

"What about my, uh, her…" he gestured toward his chest.

"Yes, all your supplemental items are there, too," she said. "And I'm grateful that they're only supplemental."

"I am, too," Chesney nodded. "Well, if you don't mind, as comfortable as your grandfather's bed is, I'd like to get up and find a better spot to explain this all. Does the cottage still have that wonderful fireplace?"

"No, we had it removed and put in a snooker table," she said.

"Huh?"

"Of course, we still have the fireplace, silly!" She kissed him on the nose.

"And those wonderful big easy chairs?" he asked.

"I haven't changed a thing." Verity stood and retrieved a man's robe from the back of the door. "Here's grandfather's robe, and there are his slippers unless you want to change into something else."

"The only clothes I have are mine, I mean hers, that is, Lorraine's," he said. "And I think I'd like to try and tell my story from the masculine side."

"I'd like that, too," said Verity with a smile.

After fifteen minutes to build a cozy fire and steep some strong tea, they sat opposite each other in overstuffed chairs in front of the stone hearth.

"There, that should warm you," said Li Gao, poking the embers and placing another log on the fire. "If you'll excuse me."

"Don't you want to hear my story," asked Chesney.

Gao bowed slightly. "There is sufficient opportunity for that another time. I was glad to provide humble support to Miss Goodhue. At this moment, however, prudence dictates that this is a conversation best reserved for two."

"Thank you, Gao," said Verity. "For everything."

Chesney added his gratitude, and Gao excused himself.

"It all started that horrible day," Chesney began, "three weeks before what was to have been our wedding day."

– 13 –
Clott Clodagh and the Rude Slap of Reality

Clodagh Clott watched as the dawn broke over the remote Russian forest. In the light of the new day, she surveyed the landscape surrounding the bunker where her abductors had deposited her. With the toe of her shoe, she gingerly poked the bullet-riddled body of one of them. He was dead. She hadn't doubted that. The strange American who had left ten minutes earlier had completed his mission thoroughly. Whatever mission that had been. All she knew was the source of her current predicament came from everyone mistaking her for Lorraine Innis.

"You poor sap," remarked Clodagh to the dead guard, "you all got it wrong. If you only knew the real woman you want isn't even a real woman!" She sighed and clenched her fist, then muttered: "Chesney, when I see you again, if I ever see you again, I'm going to give you a sock right up the nozzle!"

She walked up the dirt path a few feet away from the bunker and looked around.

"Nothing! I'm in the middle of nowhere. Well, the sun rises in the east, so that's east. Not that it does me any good. I could be a hundred miles from anything in every direction, or there could be a town a few miles away. But how would I know…"

Clodagh's musings were interrupted by a bellow from inside the concrete bunker.

"Lorruska! LORRUSKA!"

"Oh, great, President Charming is finally awake," snorted Clodagh. "Well, at least it will be fun giving him a rude slap of reality."

She stepped over the dead gunman and walked into the blockhouse room. Clodagh tried the switch again. This time the lights flickered on.

"LORRUSKA! Where are you?!"

Nikolai Kropotkin was writhing on the floor, still blindfolded, feeling for the body that had been lying next to him.

"Okay, okay, keep your shirt on," said Clodagh.

Kropotkin struggled to sit up and turned his head, though he was still sightless. "Who is that?"

"I'm your Lorruska," said Clodagh. "Or at least you thought I was."

"What? Who are you?"

"My name is Clott, Clodagh Clott. Lorruska couldn't make it, so she sent me."

"Where is she? What did you do with her? Why are you keeping us here? Where is Teplov?"

"Whoa, buster," said Clodagh, "hold on, take it easy."

"I shall not take it easy," barked Kropotkin. "I am the president of Russia, and I demand you untie me so I can strangle the truth out of you."

"Yeah? Well, that's the best offer I've had since your pals grabbed me in Delaware and shoved me in a sack for this lovely holiday excursion."

"Untie me!"

Clodagh shook her head and removed Kropotkin's blindfold. "Let's start with this. Now, I hope you can see that I'm not as dumb as I look. I'm certainly not stupid enough to untie your arms and legs just so you can beat me up."

With his sight restored, Kropotkin blinked several times, looked around the room, and then back to Clodagh.

"You are a woman," he said.

"Thanks for noticing," she smirked. "I hope you didn't think you'd been tied up with a boy soprano!"

Kropotkin studied her for a moment. "But you are not Lorruska."

Clodagh rolled her eyes. "And the hits keep coming!"

"I am not going to hit you," said Kropotkin.

"That's not… it's an expression," she said. "Never mind. Look, can you stop being a pushy politician for a minute and listen? You might learn something."

A snarl spread across Kropotkin's face, but after a moment, realizing he had no other options, he relaxed. "Proceed."

"Thanks a bunch," said Clodagh, as she pulled up a chair in front of him. "Okay, I told you, my name is Clott, Clodagh Clott. I'm a friend of Lorraine… Lorruska…"

"Where is she?" snapped Kropotkin.

Clodagh shook her head. "Listen, big boy, the more you keep interrupting me, the longer this is going to take. They left some duct tape over there. If you don't be quiet, I'll gag you until I'm done."

"I apologize," said Kropotkin.

Clodagh eyed him suspiciously, wondering how contrite he really was. After he was silent for another ten seconds, she began. Clodagh explained everything that had happened to her from the time she was abducted until she was untied by the strange American. Kropotkin listened intently. At times, he seemed ready to interrupt but managed to control his imperious impulses. When she reached the end, Clodagh just looked at him and nodded.

"Okay, that's it," said Clodagh. "You may ask questions, though I probably don't know the answers."

"Lorruska is safe?" said Kropotkin.

Clodagh shrugged. "She was fine when I left her."

"And you don't know who abducted you?"

"Well, it wasn't one of your friends," said Clodagh. "He was pretty upset when he realized I wasn't Lorraine."

Kropotkin frowned. "I, too, am sorely disappointed."

She stared at him. "You sure know how to sweet talk a girl! And you still want to be untied?"

"Of course I do! And I am not sweet talking you, Clott Clodagh!"

"It's called sarcasm, Ivan!"

"Nikolai…"

"I know your name. That was sarcasm, too," she explained. "Sorry you're not used to American women."

"Lorruska is not like that!"

Clodagh snorted. "Yeah, well, there's a lot about 'Lorruska' that you won't find on the average American woman."

"More sarcasm," said Kropotkin.

"Nope, that was pure honesty," she said, "but we won't go into that now."

"Hmm," nodded Kropotkin. Fortunately, he didn't press for clarification on Lorraine's extra assets, not that Clodagh would have volunteered the information. He thought for a moment, then spoke. "I suspect Teplov."

"Well, the guy who was here seemed to be in charge. He sort of looked like a ferret with a close haircut."

"Yes," agreed Kropotkin, "that is Gregor Teplov. He is my lifelong rival. He is ex-KGB."

"Well, by his tactics of grabbing women off the street in Delaware, it looks like you can take the boy out of the KGB, but you can't take the KGB out of the boy." Kropotkin stared at her. "Not sarcasm," Clodagh clarified, "just an old American proverb."

Kropotkin nodded, then raised his bound feet. "If you would…"

"Oh, sure," said Clodagh. "I think you understand that I'm a victim of circumstances, and I'm not involved in this whole thing."

"Da, you are on my side."

"Let's just say I'm on Lorraine's side and my own side." Clodagh found a knife and started cutting through Kropotkin's bounds. "I don't know anything about Russian politics, and I don't care. I just want to get out of here and avoid getting shoved into any more sacks."

"Do not worry," said Kropotkin, "I will guarantee your safety."

"Turn around," she said, "I'll free your hands. Guarantee my safety? Thanks, it makes a girl feel so secure being taken care of by a guy who walked into a trap."

"You're welcome," said Kropotkin, who either wasn't listening or missed her sarcasm once more. "And you're sure you didn't recognize the man who rescued us?"

"I told you I didn't. I'd have remembered if it was an ex-boyfriend. He was just the way I described him, a non-descript American."

"That is odd," mused Kropotkin.

"Yeah, like everything else around here is perfectly normal. Okay, there you are," said Clodagh. "You're free."

"Thank you, friend of Lorruska."

"I do have a name, you know!"

"Oh, yes, how rude. Please forgive me. I have forgotten your name, Miss…"

"Clott, Clodagh Clott."

Kropotkin stared at her for a moment and then nodded. "Yes, well, Clott Clodagh, I will scout out the situation and devise a strategy for our escape, Friend of Lorruska."

Kropotkin walked out the door. Clodagh threw up her arms.

"Great! Thanks!" she muttered.

– 14 –
The Adonis with the Unlisted Number

The intercom on Lord Bagnold's desk buzzed. He cast a confident nod to Lindsay Friseur and Hilda Madison and pressed the button.

"Your visitor is here," said his secretary.

"Send 'im in," said Bagnold. "There, I told you, 'e's the best, and…" he glanced at his watch, "and in record time. The best comes to the best, and damned sharpishly, too!"

The door opened. Hilda Madison glanced toward the person who entered and then took a protracted look. The man was the most striking figure she had ever seen. He was perfect. He was dressed impeccably. His suit, while expensively tailored, was only enhanced by the body that it had the privilege to enrobe. Beneath the suit was a physique toned to perfection. His face was as if it had been chiseled by a Michelangelo. His dark hair was perfectly groomed, though casually as if it was the way all hair was meant to be. The only flaw, and on him it was an asset, was a scar along his cheek. He was the most perfect man she had ever seen, and while he exuded a raw, dangerous sexuality, Hilda did not feel attracted, only grateful that she was allowed to witness this Adonis, if only for a moment.

"Come in," said Lord Bagnold, "I want you to meet two people."

Hilda couldn't help but notice that the usual sloppy speaking patterns of His Lordship either consciously or unconsciously reformed in the presence of this man.

The man turned and smiled. It was a genuine smile but still contained an undercurrent of warning, even danger.

"How do you do," said the man. His voice was as smooth as the rest of him. "My name is Verve, Nigel Verve."

He shook Hilda's hand and then turned to Lindsay Friseur. For the first time in the years that Hilda had known her, her law partner was nearly speechless.

"I... I'm..." Lindsay's mouth started moving, though nothing more came out.

"Lindsay Friseur," said Hilda, "my partner in law, Lindsay Friseur, I'm Hilda Madison."

"You're American," said Nigel Verve.

"M-me t-too," babbled Lindsay, "me... American."

"How very charming," said Verve. He sat on the edge of the desk as if it were a throne, yet without the slightest bit of pretense. Then he pulled a silver cigarette case from his pocket and, in one fluid motion, lit a cigarette without excuse or apology. Only after the first smooth drag did he speak.

"How rude of me," he said, indicating the cigarette case. "Would you like one? I have them personally rolled for me by a little shop in Cairo."

Lindsay started to reach for the case, until Hilda tugged her arm. "You don't smoke," she whispered. "You've never smoked."

Lindsay looked crossly at her partner. "Maybe I was thinking of taking it up, Hildegarde!" She looked back at Nigel Verve with a sweet expression. "No, thank you. Perhaps some other time."

"Of course," said Verve with a nonchalant air. He offered the silver case to Lord Bagnold, who shook his head.

"Ciggies? Not since I was a squaddie, thank you," said Lord Bagnold. He turned to the Americans. "I've called in a few favors and pulled on the strings of a few old oppos to get the best. And here he is, ladies, Nigel Verve, CBE."

"CBE?" asked Lindsay Friseur.

"Commander of the Most Excellent Order of the British Empire, my dear lady," said Verve. He lowered his gaze slightly. Hilda couldn't tell if he was being genuinely modest or only acting so. Either way, it was quite convincing.

Lindsay tittered. Hilda wanted to kick her ankle.

"Services rendered, that sort of thing," said Nigel, examining his fingernails.

"Don't buy that," said Bagnold to the women. "That's only a gong lower than meself, uh, I mean, than what I am." He cleared his throat. "This man is probably Her Majesty's top man in..." he stopped and gave a confidential wink. "...the field."

Lindsay's mouth dropped open. "You mean like a spy? How exciting!"

Nigel Verve shrugged as if to downplay the assertion while actually raising it.

"Oh, like in the movies," said Lindsay. "Double-O, and all that?"

Nigel smiled slightly.

"Do you have a number and everything?" she asked.

"Number? Haw!" said Lord Bagnold clapping his hand on Verve's shoulder. Nigel Verve darted a glance in his direction, and His Lordship quickly removed his hand.

"That's all for cheap novels," said Verve. "I had a number, but now it's unlisted."

"And do you have a license to kill?" whispered Lindsay.

"It's more of a permit," said Verve. "Some of the lads can't be trusted, and it was getting untidy in foreign capitals. Now, it's on a need-to basis."

They sat frozen for a moment: Lindsay staring at Nigel Verve with a school-girl expression; Lord Bagnold smiling with pride that he'd finally topped this American lawyer; and, Verve acting as if this was just the normal amount of adoration due to him. The only level head sat upon Hilda Madison's shoulders.

"Well, you certainly come highly recommended, Nigel," said Hilda, but in a tone one might deliver to a clerk applying for an office job. "But, what exactly are you going to do?"

Nigel Verve remained calmly self-assured. "Do? My dear lady? I do whatever is required to get it done." He paused for a moment and then glanced over his shoulder. "What seems to be the trouble, Lord B?"

Lord Bagnold coughed. "Nothing what you can't not handle."

"Though something others are finding a sticky wicket, no doubt."

"It's Lorraine Innis," said Hilda.

Verve lifted his right eyebrow slightly, then glanced over Lord Bagnold's desk. He picked up a photograph of Lorraine.

"Yes," said Verve studying the photograph with an enigmatic smile. "She shouldn't be too much trouble."

"We want you to find her," said Lord Bagnold.

The smile grew into the hint of a leer. "Yes, well, I always have to find them before..."

Lindsay Friseur's mouth dropped open. "Before what?"

"Before..." said Nigel Verve, his grin maturing, "...before anything else, of course."

After glancing at the picture again and placing it in his breast pocket, Nigel Verve stood.

"I'm apprised of the situation..." he began.

"But she disappeared over 24 hours ago," said Hilda.

He gave her a patronizing look. "I'm apprised of the situation," he repeated as if omniscience were standard issue at his agency.

"So, you'll find Mrs. Innis," said Hilda, "and return her safely?"

Nigel Verve was already at the door. He turned and smiled. "Oh, I'll return her safely... and better than new!"

– 15 –
Fully and Forever Forestalled

W ell, that's the story," explained Chesney. His head was bowed, afraid to look at Verity, fearing her reaction to his romance with Martina and the circumstances that led to the creation of Lorraine Innis.

He sat in silence, the only sound, indeed the only light, coming from the fire crackling in the large stone fireplace. Evening had fallen. He had been speaking without interruption for almost four hours.

Chesney sighed. He wouldn't blame Verity for being angry, or at least disappointed, at his unintentional unfaithfulness. Finally, he looked up. Verity was curled up in the overstuffed easy chair opposite him. Her cheeks glistened in the firelight, wet with tears. She daubed at her eyes with a linen handkerchief.

"I'm sorry," he said.

"Sorry? For what?"

Chesney looked down at his painted fingernails before tucking them in the pockets of his robe. At the moment, he wished Lorraine Innis were a million miles away while at the same time wishing for a little of her wisdom.

"I'm sorry for... everything," he said. "I'm sorry I.. well, that I cheated on you."

"You can't cheat on a corpse," said Verity. "Till death us do part is the expression, and as far as you knew, I was dead."

"Yes, that's true, but you weren't unfaithful to me, or at least my memory." He paused. "Were you?"

Verity rose from the chair. For a second, he was unsure of what she was doing or where she was going. Perhaps she was getting ready to throw him out. She stood still for a moment before gently shoving him over and climbing in the chair beside him. Fortunately, the chair was oversized, and Chesney was half the size he once had been. She kissed him on the nose and ran her fingers through his shoulder-length tresses.

"I wasn't unfaithful to you or your memory."

"Then, I'm still your Beloved?"

She smiled. "You will always be my Beloved till death and beyond."

Chesney returned the smile before frowning. "But you didn't almost get married like I almost did, and you were much more upset than I was."

"I don't think mourning is a contest," said Verity. "I didn't almost get married, but then I wasn't likely to have many romances mourning in this cottage. Let's just say for grief, it's probably a draw."

Chesney nodded. "A draw," he said. Simultaneously they leaned in for a passionate kiss.

"It's reassuring that beneath that beautiful coiffure and smooth face, you're still the boy I fell in love with," said Verity.

"With whom I fell in love," he said.

"Glad that hasn't changed either," she added.

"Well, I can't grow a mustache," said Chesney, "but as soon as I'm able, I'll get my hair cut and look much more like myself."

Verity smiled, but then a concerned look darkened her expression.

"What?" said Chesney.

"Beloved, I don't think our situation just needs a visit to the barber. It's a little more complicated than that. As much as I'd like to turn the page and resume our lives where we left off several years ago, there are other issues to consider. What about Lorraine?"

"What about her?" said Chesney. "She wasn't going to be around forever. Initially, the plan was to have her exist for a few weeks. I think I've given enough of my life to the inspirational Mrs. Innis. I don't owe her anything."

Verity looked down in thought. "No, you don't owe Lorraine anything, my Beloved. But, you're forgetting someone."

"Who? Valerie? Patsy? Purvis Twankey? Nikolai Kropotkin? Am I leaving someone out?"

Verity looked in his eyes. Hers were moist with the beginning of tears. She caressed his cheek and then nodded. "You're forgetting Martina."

Chesney swallowed hard.

"Yes, well…"

"More than anything, I want you, Chesney Potts, back, fully and forever. But, I also know that you must finish what you set out to do. For Martina."

He looked deep into her eyes. They were filled with emotion but also resolve.

"I… I just thought, you rather forget all about her. That maybe…"

"Maybe I was jealous of her?"

He nodded.

"I won't lie," said Verity. "When you first mentioned her name, I wanted to be jealous. And perhaps I was for a moment. But then you explained everything. She sounds like a remarkable young woman."

Chesney bowed his head and nodded.

"And I will be eternally grateful for all she did," said Verity.

"For me?" he said.

"For the both of us," continued Verity. "I still had my home and my memories of the dear grandfather with whom I shared that home. You had nothing. You had given up everything when you came here. You placed all your eggs in my basket, and then it was cruelly taken from you. Martina put you back together. She was like an angel sent to you. I've come to realize so many things through all this, but most of all, I've realized that there is a God who is good and who is also in control. There are no accidents, and while there is so much that we don't understand and may never understand in this life, there is grace and purpose in all He does."

"You sound like Aunt Elinor," said Chesney.

Verity reached up and gently tugged his long hair. "And you look like her," she laughed.

He smiled, then his smile faded. "When I lost you, Gao tried to console me by saying the tragedies in life would make me more like Aunt El. I suppose I took that too literally."

She kissed him on the nose. "You could pick worse role models."

He fingered the lapel of the robe. "And now I'm wearing your grandfather's clothes; another good choice."

"That'll do ye good," said Verity, imitating her grandfather and his famous catchphrase.

"So, I suppose I need to be Lorraine a little while longer," he said. "for Martina."

"For Martina," she agreed.

There was a knock on the parlor door, and Li Gao stuck in his head.

"Please, forgive the interruption," he said. "According to the news reports, there is precious little time to act."

"What do you mean?" asked Chesney.

"It would seem that our daring rescue of our friend here has generated much attention," Gao explained. "While the deed itself was not witnessed. Security camera footage captured my van driving away around the corner from the locale."

Verity jumped to her feet. "Then we'd better get moving."

"No," said Chesney, "I can't implicate you. You stay here. It's better that way. I'll get dressed and drive back alone as soon as it's light."

"If you're going alone," said Li Gao, "I shall go with you."

– 16 –
The Tit for Tat Tat

"You keep looking at your watch," said Mr. Postlewaite.

"How foolish of me," muttered Valerie Fierro, "I should have been staring at a calendar."

Valerie had spent the last week traipsing around England on Postlewaite's tour of British comedians she'd never heard of before and never wanted to hear of again. When he promised to take her to London, she didn't realize it was the last leg on the voyage of the damned comics. She tried to remind herself that Postlewaite had been the perfect host. He had given her the bed in his weird little dewdrop trailer while he slept in the car. He had insisted on buying her meals. He had even offered to buy her books and souvenirs at the various stops on their pilgrimage, though she never took him up on that offer. It was bad enough visiting Arthur Askey's birthplace once without forever having a reminder of it.

Where did he find these people, she wondered. But then realized she didn't care to know the answer.

Today they were somewhere up in the north of England. She guessed it was north because it was cold, dreary, and further away from London. She thought of London and sighed. Cozy luxury hotel suites with comfortable beds, linen sheets and down comforters. Suites with marble bathrooms, heated towel racks and oversized tubs. Hotels with bars where you didn't have to ask twice for civilized cocktails, then explain the recipe, and they'd have all the ingredients. Valerie hadn't had a Cosmo in weeks. She was trapped in a brown ale purgatory.

Now, for a change, they weren't visiting a museum, not that any place they'd been to on this idiot's tour could really be called a museum. Most were pokey little affairs in some cheap storefront or shabby row house. They were filled with pictures and artifacts that were only interesting to

Postlewaite and other boring geeks. She had often tried to stay in the car, but Postlewaite always insisted that she come inside. Perhaps he thought Valerie would be infected by the geek virus that made him enjoy wandering around this loser country visiting stupid sites.

Today, they were at an auction house. It wasn't very large. Maybe it was a house with an auction in it. The place was full of tatty old stuff, books, furniture, and other crap. Postlewaite was looking at the photocopied list of items for bid.

"I'm pretending to be interested," he muttered to Valerie out of the side of his mouth.

"Welcome to my world," said Valerie at full volume.

"Shhh," cautioned Mr. Postlewaite, "not too loud." Then in a booming voice, he announced, "My, my, aren't these candlesticks exquisite."

"That one's broken," said Valerie, "and the other has a big dent. And they're not even brass or pewter."

"Keep your voice down," he said.

Valerie picked up a hand mirror, partially to see if the frame was genuine silver and partially to look at herself.

"These are the last effects of a chap I knew."

Valerie dropped the mirror. "Ewww, this is dead people stuff?"

The other patrons around the room stopped and stared at her.

Postlewaite picked up the mirror and placed it back on the table. "Lucky for you, it wasn't cracked," he said. "That would be seven years of bad luck."

"Yeah, I'd hate to ruin my current streak," she said. "So, why are we poking around some dead guy's stuff. This guy wasn't one of your famous comedians, was he?"

"No," said Mr. Postlewaite out of the corner of his mouth, "he was a fellow aficionado of humour."

Valerie looked around at the assortment of items on display. She would have guessed he was a fellow aficionado of old man junk and bad taste.

"Not, this stuff," said Postlewaite, following her eyes. "He's got a few items of great interest." He held up the photocopied sheet and pointed to the bottom while looking away.

"Vintage tie and braces?" said Valerie, evidently a bit too loudly for Postlewaite's comfort. He quickly shushed her.

"Pretend not to be overly interested," he said, guiding her to another table.

"That's a cinch," she promised.

"Good," he said, missing her dig. Postlewaite nodded at the next table. "Look at them, but don't look, you know?"

"All I see," she said, looking but not looking, "is an old bow tie and some suspenders."

Postlewaite looked down at the item. "They're called braces over here, suspenders, well, that what ladies use to hold up their stockings.

"Okay, have it your way," she said.

"The fellow who owned them was a fellow memorabilia collector,"explained Postlewaite. "I happen to know they once belonged to Stan Laurel."

"It's an old tie and braces. Ewww, and they look dirty."

"That's from the potato salad," he said. "Stan Laurel actually wore this tie in the film *Tit for Tat*. That's his *Tit for Tat* tie."

"Looks more like his *Tit for Tat* tat," she said. "I suppose he wore the suspenders, sorry, the braces then, too."

Postlewaite looked at Valerie as if she were a simpleton. "No, he wore overalls in that film. Everyone knows that."

Valerie rolled her eyes. If she had more than a few pounds in her pocket, she'd tell her host what she really thought. That included what a dull loser he was. As she didn't have any more money, she just sighed.

"So the plan is," continued Postlewaite, "that we just play it nonchalantly."

"That's the plan, huh?"

"I just said it was."

"Yeah, that's where I heard it," she muttered.

"They only have them listed on the sheet as 'vintage tie and braces,'" he explained. "I doubt his heirs know what they are."

"Or care," said Valerie.

Mr. Postlewaite gave her a blank expression. "That goes without saying. If they don't know, how could they care? But that's to our advantage."

"Ours?"

"I can get these at a very reasonable price," he continued. "They will go very nicely with some of the other priceless artifacts I've picked up on the tour. You remember that pair of Eric Morecambe's socks."

"How can I forget?" she said. "There's only so much excitement a girl can stand." Valerie still didn't know who that was, and she didn't care if he wore socks or if he'd gone through his entire life barefoot.

Thirty minutes later, which Valerie equated to seven years in real people's time, the auctioneer took his place at a small desk and banged his little wooden gavel. The first ten items, old furniture and books, went cheaply and with little fanfare. Valerie glanced at Postlewaite. He seemed like a mainspring that was wound a little bit tighter with each successive item. They were only three items from the prize when suddenly he went pale and grabbed Valerie's forearm.

"Hey!" shouted Valerie.

"Three pounds fifty," said the auctioneer pointing his gavel at Valerie. "Any advance on three pounds fifty? Going once, twice, thrice. Sold to the lady with the brown hair and gritted teeth."

"What?" Valerie looked back to the auctioneer and then to Postlewaite again. "What did I just buy?"

"He's here," said Postlewaite out of the side of his mouth.

"Who's here, and what did I just buy?"

"Him, he's here, that man who just came in, it's Rathman."

"Who's Rathman, and what did I just buy?"

"He's a rival for the tie and braces."

"Big deal, what did I just buy?"

"Don't worry, you got a bargain," said Postlewaite.

"Young lady," said the auctioneer, "please step into the next room and pay for your item."

Valerie made her way to the desk in the adjoining room.

"Three pounds fifty, dearie," said a middle-aged woman sitting behind the desk. She wrote the amount in her ledger. "My, you did get a bargain."

Valerie opened her handbag. With only a five-pound note in her purse, three pounds fifty was potentially a fiscal disaster. She handed her last fiver to the woman. "What did I just buy?"

The woman took the note and gave her back a pound-and-a-half in change. Then she nodded to a box on the desk. "You got the departed's Victoriana collection."

"Collection of what?" said Valerie, opening the box.

"Oh, he was very proud of it," said the woman.

Valerie reached inside the box and pulled out the top item. It was some kind of metal contraption with straps.

"Some of those are very rare," continued the woman. "It's probably the finest collection of Victorian medical devices in all of Cumbria. Oh, that's one of the rarer pieces."

Valerie held it up. "What is it?"

The woman looked at her as if it was obvious. "Why, that's a Victorian Nasal Corrector."

"A what?"

"Nose straightener."

"EWWW!" screeched Valerie. She dropped the item back into the box and closed the lid. "Is everything in this box as disgusting?"

The woman shrugged. "Aye, or more so."

"Well, I don't want icky stuff like that," said Valerie.

"I suppose you can throw it out," said the woman. "But not here, so take your winnings and congratulations."

Valerie cast her most evil eye on the woman, though it didn't seem to penetrate her Cumbrian shell. No wonder the Romans didn't get much further than here in England. She picked up the box, carrying it at arm's length and vowing to deposit it in the first rubbish skip she encountered. Valerie returned to the main room, where the auction was still going on. She was stunned to hear Mr. Postlewaite speaking more loudly and animatedly than she'd ever witnessed before. He was standing, waving his arms in response to the one he called "Rathman." Rathman was behaving in a similar manner.

"Two hundred pounds," shouted Rathman.

"Two hundred ten," countered Postlewaite.

Valerie watched in astonishment as the two men leapfrogged over each other's bids. She had no idea Postlewaite was carrying that much cash. If she had, she would have asked him for a loan days ago.

The bidding war escalated as the auctioneer struggled to keep the proceedings orderly. It was no use. Mr. Postlewait and Mr. Rathman ignored any semblance of auction rules, holding what amounted to a private argument spoken only in monetary amounts.

"Three hundred pounds," cried Rathman.

"Three-ten," demanded Postlewaite.

"Three twenty!"

Postlewaite gritted his teeth. "Four Hundred!"

The others in the room gasped, having no understanding of the significance of the old tie and braces.

Rathman clenched his fists as he squinted at Postlewaite across the room. "Four Hundred and Five!"

Postlewaite was practically frothing at the mouth with a passion that Valerie had never seen before. He took a deep breath, like a man rearing back to deliver a mighty blow.

"Five Hundred Pounds!" shouted Postlewaite.

Rathman staggered back as if a physical kick had been delivered. He regained his footing, reached into his pocket, pulled out his wallet, and peered into it. His eyes were filled with worry.

"Sir," said Rathman waving to the auctioneer, "point of order."

"Yes?" said the auctioneer, grateful to be put back in charge, even for a moment.

"I can pay with cheque, can't I?" asked Rathman plaintively. "That is, mostly cash, supplemented by a cheque."

The auctioneer shook his head and pointed to the sign he'd brought for just such an occasion. "All winning bids must be claimed immediately and for cash only."

"Damn," spat Rathman.

"The bid is five hundred pounds," said the auctioneer.

Rathman rifled through his wallet, reached into his pockets, and quickly counted the change.

"Five hundred pounds, once," said the auctioneer, raising his gavel, "five hundred pounds twice..."

A triumphant smile began spreading across Postlewaite's lips.

"Five hundred eight pounds, 82 pence!" Shouted Rathman.

"Five hundred nine pounds," spat Postlewaite, with the finality of a fatal dagger plunge.

Rathman collapsed in his seat and threw up his hands.

"Sold for five hundred nine pounds," said the auctioneer, banging his gavel. "Pay the cashier in the next room."

- 17 -
The Single Digit Sincerity

"Come, let us go," said Nikolai Kropotkin pulling on Clodagh Clott's arm.

"Ow, okay, okay," she cried, "give me a second. It's not so easy in these shoes."

Kropotkin paused and looked down at her open-vamp pumps.

"You should have worn more suitable footwear," he noted. "Something athletic, or combat boots. Yes, sturdy boots would have been the best choice." He clambered over the dead body just outside the doorway.

"Yeah, it's entirely my fault," said Clodagh. "When I got ready for work that morning, whenever that was, I should have guessed I was going to be kidnapped and then make my escape hiking across Russia."

"No use to dwell on mistakes," he said, taking her hand. "You will know next time. Always be prepared. That is how I got where I am today."

Clodagh stopped and put her hands on her hips. "Okay, a few points; first, that was sarcasm."

Kropotkin rolled his eyes. "Again, with your ironic American mockery. I cannot tell when you're dealing with me honestly."

"Tell you what," she said, "I'll put up two fingers when I'm using sarcasm."

"What if you only put up one finger?"

"I promise you," she said, "that will be totally sincere. And as for where you are today, pal, you're exactly where I am despite your meticulous planning."

His eyes narrowed. "Yes, but I have on insulated overalls and strong boots."

She raised one centrally placed finger at him.

"Ha," snorted Kropotkin, "you cannot argue with that. You are completely sincere."

"Right you are, sport."

Clodagh followed him to a small rise by a thicket of trees. He crouched down and pulled her to the ground.

"Hey, easy," she said, "I'm wearing a skirt. Yeah, I know; I'll plan better next time I'm abducted."

"Good, you are learning," said Kropotkin. "Stay low. Just over there, beyond the next hill, about two kilometers distance, is a small village."

She started to stand. "Well, what are we waiting for?" He yanked her back to the ground.

"HEY! I TOLD YOU…"

Kropotkin clamped his hand over her mouth. "Get down and keep your voice down. We cannot go that way." He slowly removed his hand while putting his other finger to his lips.

"Why not?" Clodagh whispered.

"Because Teplov, the man who had you abducted, may be waiting there. He is a ruthless man who will stop at nothing to secure his goals. I still do not understand what he hoped to gain by kidnapping you."

Clodagh stared at him and shook her head. "Look, I don't have a pad and pencil, or I'd draw you a diagram, so I'll explain this slowly. Who did you think you were rescuing?"

"Why, Lorruska, that is, Mrs. Innis, of course!"

"Yeah, well, your friend Teplov made the same mistake," said Clodagh. What does Teplov want anyway?"

"To rule Russia, of course," said Kropotkin.

"And he figured out what you want, too," she said, "even if you can't see it."

Kropotkin nodded. "Lorruska. I would do anything for Lorruska."

"Even resign as president?"

Kropotkin thought a moment. "Yes, I would; in fact, I said as much to…"

He stopped in mid-sentence, and his mouth dropped open.

"This moment of enlightenment," said Clodagh, "is coming to you courtesy of…"

"Enough sarcasm," he snapped. "Teplov must have had me bugged. I only shared that with my daughter. She would not betray me. So, he must have had an electronic device. He is ex-KGB. How could I have been so stupid? He thought I would trade my office, my place of trust, for Lorruska's safety."

"Wouldn't you?"

"Yes, no," said Kropotkin. "I would give up my office for her, but not to a scoundrel who would use an innocent woman as a pawn."

"Great," said Clodagh, "now that that's settled, what are we going to do?"

Kropotkin looked around, then nodded his head. "We are going to beat Teplov at his own game. I know how he thinks. Now that I know what he wanted to do and how, I can out-think him. In our army days, I could outfight him on the training ground, but more importantly, in the barracks at night, I could out-think him, playing chess. He only beat me once, and that was because he cheated. He is cheating again in a much bigger game, but I'm ready for him."

He rose to a crouch and pointed away from the village toward the forest. "Come with me."

Clodagh sat on the ground and sighed. "Still a pawn, I suppose."

Nikolai Kropotkin held out his hand to her. "No, I will never treat you as a pawn. I promise to bring you to safety, on my honor. That is my first goal, even above dealing with Teplov. Come... please."

Clodagh took his hand and was pulled up from the ground. "Well, that's the best offer I've had since being shoved in a sack."

He looked back at her. "More American humor?"

"No, sorry," she said. "That was on the level. Let's go."

– 18 –
Mrs. Postlewaite's Birthday Commode

Magnificent, simply magnificent," beamed Mr. Postlewaite admiring his prize. "Stan Laurel's bow tie and braces! I spent nearly every penny in the budget, but I got them. Thankfully, Rathman didn't come as well armed, financially speaking."

Valerie looked at him across the table in the pub and smirked.

"Yeah, great," she said. "And I got a box of Victorian nose straighteners."

Postlewaite looked up. "I'm sorry, I've been terribly selfish. Had I known of your fascination with that sort of thing, we could have visited some sites dedicated to your hobby."

"My hobby," screeched Valerie. "Do you think I'm into this crap?"

"Well, you did win a whole box of them," said Postlewaite.

"By accident!"

"So, you don't like them?" asked Postlewaite, reaching into the box and picking up one of the devices.

"As if!" said Valerie. "It's just a box of weird junk."

Postlewaite sorted through the various pieces. "It's not my line, so I couldn't give you a firm evaluation, but I'd say the collection is worth quite a lot."

"Yeah? How much?" she asked.

He shrugged his shoulders. "I'd say one or two hundred pounds, maybe, to the right dealer. Not around here, of course, but I used to have a shop in London. I carried entertainment memorabilia, but I knew other purveyors of antiquities."

"Old junk dealers," muttered Valerie.

"And some of those would be interested in your little collection. They're in London, of course. So, cheer up, you've made a wise investment, and you didn't even know it."

"Yeah, I wasn't exactly sure," she said sardonically. "So let's go to London."

"All in good time," said Postlewaite. "I promised to take you to London, and a Postlewaite always keeps his word. We have several more stops on our tour, and then we'll be straight back to London. Don't worry; it will only be a few more weeks."

Valerie rolled her eyes. If she had to spend one more night in Postlewaite's little teardrop caravan, she'd lose her mind. Nights in a tin trailer, washing up in truck stops, pub food, and the highlight: traipsing around the haunts of long-dead British comedians.

"And there's one more stop I must now make," he announced, rising. "I have to visit the gents!"

"Yeah, well, don't fall in," she said, wishing for the opposite.

Postlewaite tipped his hat and excused himself.

Valerie sat staring at the half-finished pints of beer, the box of Victorian personal improvement items, and Postlewaite's prized wins. If there was any way to get to London now and figure out her next...

"I thought I recognized you from the auction," said a voice behind her.

Valerie turned around. It was the man Postlewaite had been bidding against.

"We haven't been properly introduced," he said. "My name's Rathman."

"Yeah, hi," said Valerie.

He sat beside her, then asked for permission to do so.

"No hard feelings," he said, nodding towards the bowtie and braces. "It can get pretty heated between collectors. I didn't count on there being such passionate opposition. I just don't want there to be any bad feelings between me and your husband."

Valerie turned toward the man. It was insulting enough to travel with Postlewaite without being mistaken for his wife.

"He's not..." she stopped. An idea flashed into her mind. "That is, he's not upset. Actually, he really didn't want it that much."

"He didn't?" said Rathman. "Then why..."

"Why was he such a tiger in the bidding," said Valerie with a smile. "He thought I wanted it. It's... it's my birthday."

"Oh, happy birthday, Mrs..."

"Postlewaite. Valerie Postlewaite," she said. "No, he thought I wanted it, but I actually wanted the item after it."

Rathman pulled out the auction list. "The po?"

"Po?"

"The commode, po is the slang term."

"What?" Valerie recoiled in revulsion. "Oh, I mean, yes, the commode. I collect them. I'm simply passionate about them."

"Potty about commodes, eh?" laughed Rathman.

"What? Oh, yes, ha, you Englishmen are so witty." She looked toward the rear of the pub. Still no sign of Postlewaite. This would have to be done quickly. "Anyway, Postlewaite, that is, my husband, when he found out I really wanted the commode, tried to return the tie and braces, but they don't do that at auctions. He wanted to buy me something nice for my birthday, but he spent all his money on something I didn't even want. I guess we're stuck with it."

Rathman nodded sympathetically. Come on, thought Valerie, bite, bite.

After five interminable seconds, Rathman's face brightened. "Hey, I could buy them from you, that is, if you really don't want them."

"Really?" said Valerie, trying to sound surprised. "What a wonderful, clever suggestion. I should have thought of that."

Rathman's face lit up. "Wow, that would be great." Then his smile faded. "I couldn't pay what you paid for them."

"Of course not," said Valerie. "Otherwise, you would have kept bidding. How about the last bid you were willing to pay? Whatever that was."

"That was five hundred pounds," said Rathman.

"Actually, five hundred, eight pounds and 82 pence," said Valerie. His eyes narrowed slightly. She realized she might be wising up a sucker and quickly added. "But five hundred would be fine. Do you have it on you?"

Rathman reached into his pocket and pulled out a wad of cash. "Sure do, right here."

He started to count the bills, most in 20-pound notes. Valerie glanced nervously toward the restrooms.

"Oh, no need to count it," she said, grabbing the cash from his hands and handing him the tie and braces. "This is exciting! Thank you so much. I need to phone an antique commode dealer we chatted with yesterday."

Valerie got up and dashed for the door of the pub.

"Hope you get a nice po," Rathman called after her.

Once outside the door, Valerie hailed a passing cab.

"Take me to the nearest train station," she said. "And step on it!"

– 19 –
My Well–Accessorized Fiancé

"Kiss me before I put on my lipstick."

Verity Goodhue smiled half-heartedly. "I never thought I'd hear my Beloved say those words."

Chesney Potts shrugged his shoulders. "Neither did I."

He looked down. He was in his full Lorraine regalia, including all the padding that gave Lorraine her feminine allure.

"I feel stupid," he said.

"You look, well, lovely," said Verity.

"Thank you, I think," he said.

"Did you feel stupid before?"

"No, even when I was in my right mind, that is, not in a trance or under a delusion, I felt confident. I created the character of Lorraine. I rehearsed Lorraine. I was Lorraine. Only now, it's different. Before, I didn't think you were there, seeing me as Lorraine. Now, I feel like a guy in a dress, that is a suit, a woman's suit."

"It's just a little while longer," she said as she squeezed his hand. "And then we can retire Mrs. Innis."

"For good," he interjected.

"For good," she agreed. "But for now, we need Lorraine. And remember, I'm very grateful to you, Lorraine." Verity hugged him tightly and then pulled back. "Excuse me. I never had to come up against those before... My Beloved."

Chesney looked down at his breasts. "They do get in the way at times."

"Sometimes," said Verity. She reached up and gently poked one.

"OW!" cried Chesney.

Verity's eyes grew wide, and her mouth dropped open until she saw the glint in his eyes. "Very funny."

"Sorry, I couldn't resist," he said. "Besides, I have to react as I would in character, don't I?"

"I suppose," she said, pulling him towards her, "after this."

For a moment, locked in a loving embrace, Chesney forgot Lorraine, forgot everything but Verity. They would have remained attached at the lips had not a cough been heard behind them. They turned to see Li Gao, standing in the doorway, trying not to intrude, but failing at that.

"Pardon me," said Gao, "but I must return our Mrs. Innis to London before she is discovered here."

"Yes, you're right, thank you, Gao," said Lorraine. "The last thing we want to do is establish a connection between you and Lorraine, at least right now. It would be very difficult to explain."

Verity reluctantly agreed and escorted them to the cottage door. Li Gao climbed into the van and started the engine.

"Be careful, Beloved," said Verity. "I love you."

"I love you, too. Don't worry. I'll be back," said Lorraine. "It will all work out now that I know you're alive."

Lorraine looked back longingly at Verity and started to get in the passenger seat. Suddenly, she stopped, turned, and rushed back towards the cottage.

"I forgot…" said Lorraine.

Verity smiled and held out her arms, expecting one final embrace, but was surprised when her Beloved dashed past her into the house.

A moment later, Lorraine jogged out, holding up something.

"Forgot my handbag," she said, waving her black leather purse. Lorraine climbed in the van, shut the door, and they were off.

Verity Goodhue watched as they drove through the front gate of the estate.

"I wouldn't mind so much," she sighed, "but he's got a nicer purse than mine."

– 20 –
The Bellboy Who Tipped the Guest

Paul Rocher knocked on the door of the hotel suite. A moment later, he was greeted by Margaret Mackay.

"Mr. Rocher," said Margie, "I'm so relieved to see you. Please, come in."

Rocher entered the suite's sitting room and whistled. "Wow, this is some spread, Agent Mackay. Glad you're not doing this on the taxpayer's dime."

Margie rolled her eyes. "Yes, well, this obviously isn't my suite. I'm just here as a guest of Lorraine, this is, Mrs. Innis."

Rocher walked to the drapes and fingered them, admiring the quality of the material. "She always struck me as having simpler tastes."

"It's her legal team," explained Mackay, "or rather Ms. Friseur. This is their base of operations. Ms. Friseur insists on always going first-class."

Rocher examined a bit of porcelain on the mantelpiece. "I think you'd have to tone down the place to get back to first-class. But then, I didn't come here to see how the upper-class lives. Even though you're officially on leave while you're assisting Mrs. Innis, I'm glad you're here. A lot of people in Washington are concerned about her, or at least what happened to such a prominent American."

"I can appreciate that, Sir," said Margie.

"So what happened?" he said. "You were there in the courtroom when she collapsed."

"Yes, Sir," said Mackay nervously. "After Mrs. Innis collapsed in court, the bailiffs, if that's what they're called over here, took her out to an anteroom. The security was pretty tight. They even kept me out."

"Obviously, the security wasn't that tight," said Rocher. "Someone managed to snatch the most famous woman in the world right from under their noses."

"I feel terrible about it, Sir," said Margie. "I should have done more. I shouldn't have left her side."

Rocher shook his head. "Don't blame yourself, Agent MacKay. You're out of your jurisdiction. You have no authority. No weapons. Even if you had been there during the abduction, there would have been little you could do to prevent it. You're a good agent. You'd take a bullet for someone you're guarding. The consensus in Washington is that this had to be a well thought out, perfectly executed operation, meticulously planned and carried out by a team of professionals."

Agent Mackay nodded, though her face was still clouded with regret.

"So," Rocher said, looking around, "where's Mrs. Innis' legal team? I'd like to confer with them for my official report."

"They're at a meeting with Lord Bagnold's people," she said. "It was Lorraine's wishes that they work out a settlement. I'm manning the base in case..."

There was a knock at the suite's door. Agent Mackay excused herself and walked down the entry hall.

"Room service," said a man's voice.

Rocher studied a painting over the mantelpiece as he heard Mackay open the door.

"I didn't order room service," said Margie.

"Penthouse suite," said the waiter, "I was told to bring tea every morning at this time."

"Oh," said Mackay, "that must have been Ms. Friseur's order. She's not here, but please, bring it in."

"Very good, ma'am," said the waiter.

Rocher heard the door close, the rattle of the tea trolly, and then the sound of a grunt, followed by the sound of a body landing on the floor, muffled by the hotel's plush carpeting.

Rocher wheeled around and reflexively reached for his gun before remembering he wasn't carrying one in England. He grabbed a candlestick from the mantel and assumed a defensive stance.

The waiter entered the sitting room in what could only be described as a saunter. He looked at Rocher and laughed.

"Okay, pal," growled Paul Rocher, "I may be older, but I can still wipe that smile off your face. I still pass the agency's annual qualifying course."

The waiter nodded at the candlestick. "Come on, baby, light my fire." Then he peeled off his mustache and removed his eyeglasses.

Rocher relaxed as he recognized the intruder and then tensed up again at the realization of who it was: Vyvan Lily, the most dangerous ex-CIA agent he had ever met.

"What are you doing here?" said Rocher. "And what did you do to Agent Mackay?"

Lily glanced back over his shoulder. "Nothing permanent. She'll be out for about a half-an-hour. No long-term effects. It's my own formula. It avoids the headaches of some of the common knock-out drugs."

"For use when you're feeling particularly benevolent towards your marks," said Rocher disdainfully.

Lily just smiled and sat on the settee.

"Mackay, huh?" said Lily. "She can just chalk it up to extra on-the-job training. Bet she won't trust a room service clerk again. Good thing I wasn't an enemy."

"Just a lethal pal," said Rocher.

"Lorraine Innis," said Lily.

"What about her?"

"Where is she?"

"Don't you know," asked Rocher, sitting down across from him. "I thought it was your business to know everything."

Lily leaned forward. The smile disappeared. "Cut the shit. This is a friendly visit, or else your pretty little agent chick would be dead. Where is Lorraine Innis?"

"I don't know," said Rocher. "Haven't you seen the reports on her abduction?"

"Yeah, a little too late," he said. "I was already in Russia."

Rocher knitted his brows. "What were you doing there?"

"Rescuing someone who wasn't Lorraine Innis," said the rouge agent. "I don't know who she was. She looked like Lorraine, at least enough to fool whoever snatched her and Kropotkin."

"Kropotkin, the Russian President?"

"No, Kropotkin, the plumber from Jersey City," snapped Lily.

"There's no news of Kropotkin being abducted."

"And don't go telling your pals in Washington," warned Lily. "Or at least don't tell them who told you. When that whole Innis for vice-president deal went south, I told you unknown powers were in the game. I don't like someone knowing more than me."

"But who…"

"Ever hear of a Russian snot rag named 'Teplov?' He's Kropotkin's rival."

"I heard of him," said Rocher.

"Yeah, well, I think he had something to do with that snatching of my birdie. Only he got the wrong girl. I followed the trail from Delaware to Bulgaria and then to Russia."

"Not the nicest holiday tour," said Rocher.

"Yeah, usually any trip that starts by leaving Delaware is a pleasure," snorted Lily. "Still, when I got there, they had Kropotkin and this other broad. She looked like my girl, close, but this ain't horseshoes."

Rocher looked at him sideways. "You keep referring to Lorraine Innis as 'yours.'"

"Well, she is mine," he paused, "okay, okay, I know she reminds you of your old girlfriend. Let's say she's ours. I just don't want anyone to be playing with our..."

"Toy?"

"Property," said Lily. "Look, we created her, at least from last October. She wouldn't be where she is now without us."

"Wherever that is," snorted Rocher.

"Exactly," Lily snapped his finger. "I owe it to her. I wouldn't want anything to happen to her... for a variety of reasons."

Rocher studied Lily's face for a hint at any of those reasons, but his stoic expression didn't slip an inch. There were any number of reasons why Lily was going to such lengths. Rocher wondered what he would do if he found Lorraine. He doubted he would set her free to live a happy, productive private life. At that moment, Rocher decided he would have to sidetrack Lily's mission. But how?

"You said you rescued Nikolai Kropotkin," said Rocher, diverting the conversation, to buy himself time to think.

"Yeah," said Lily, "so?"

"Well, there hasn't been anything in the news about Kropotkin being missing."

Lily flashed a disbelieving look. "Would you call up the Moscow Gazette and say: 'By the way, have you seen the leader of the country? We seem to have mislaid him.' You've been around enough esteemed leaders to know they're not always where they seem to be. His staff probably think he's shacked up for a few days with a hot bit of borsht."

"You released him," said Rocher, "right?"

Lily, who had been examining a painting, turned around. "No. Why would I? Look, I went there for my prop... uh, my friend. I don't care what one Russian does to any other Red bastard."

"What about the girl?"

Lily's expression softened. "Ah, well, I was nice. I untied her."

"Is that all?"

"Hey, she'd just been kidnapped. I wouldn't take advantage of a woman in that situation. I do have morals... well, sexual morals."

"I meant," said Rocher, "you only untied her?"

"What else do you want me to do?" cried Lily. "I took out two Bulgarians, I think they were Bulgarians, guarding the place. Besides, Kropotkin was blindfolded and tied up. He looked like he was drugged or sleeping. I didn't want to wake him up to find out. Once I got out of there, and back to civilization, I found out my bird was last in London. Don't worry, I'll find her."

Rocher wracked his brain for a way to throw him off the trail.

"I must be slipping," muttered Lily. "I go halfway around the world, and it turns out she was in England on that cockamamie lawsuit. Beards on broads! And just like her to bend over backward to settle it. But what can you expect with all that charity stuff she does?"

"Of course," Paul Rocher thought aloud, "the money."

"What? What did you say?" said Lily facing him.

From his years in Washington, D.C., surrounded by politicians, Rocher had learned a few things about dealing with paranoid minds. Lily had a wild look deep in his eyes. The ex-agent had spent so many years dodging threats and enemies that his phobias were now on a hair trigger. He had begun the Lorraine Innis case as if he were playing a game. But now, instead of making the moves, he was reacting to those of an unseen adversary. Why else would he have first gone to ground, then chased her ghost halfway around the world. Rocher needed to divert his attention, throw him out of Lorraine's path – wherever that was – lest Vyvan Lily do her permanent harm.

Rocher paused, pretending not to hear Lily's question. He would have to play this carefully, or it would arouse his suspicion. "Hmm? Pardon?"

"You said something about money," said Lily.

"Money?" Rocher looked up. "Did I? I must have been thinking aloud. What did you say?"

"I mentioned her charity."

Rocher sat down and put his hand on his chin. "Charity... money..." he shrugged. "It's just when we were doing any sort of investigation, not that it applied here..."

Lily studied Rocher's face. "The money," he said, "you follow the money."

Rocher smiled and waved his hand dismissively. "Yes, well, that's standard investigation procedure, but I don't think it applies here."

"No? Why not?" The manic look in Lily's eyes intensified, building like a thundercloud.

"Well," said Rocher, leaning back and looking as relaxed as he could, "it's different, isn't it? Lorraine Innis isn't interested in money. She'd give away her fortune, well, her charity's fortune, just to give justice to a bunch of women who happened to grow beards. That doesn't sound like a girl interested in money. No, following the money wouldn't..."

Lily sat next to Rocher. His face lit up. "She's not interested in money."

"Yes, that's what I said. Glad you see my point."

"She's not interested in money," said Lily, "but she's not the only one in that organization. She's just the... what would you call her?"

Rocher shrugged. "The president, the head?" He laughed. "You certainly wouldn't call her the figurehead..."

Lily snapped his fingers. "Figurehead! That's it, exactly. She's the figurehead. And for whatever reason, someone in her organization is trying to torpedo me."

"You?"

"Her, her," said Lily jumping to his feet. "I meant her, and they're trying to subvert all my work. Follow the money. That will lead to whoever is trying to get us."

"Us?"

"Lorraine Innis and me," said Lily.

A groan came from the hallway. Lily looked toward the hall and then back at Rocher.

"Agent Mackay is coming to," said Rocher standing.

"Don't worry, she'll be fine," said Lily hurriedly. He started for the door, stopped, and pointed at Rocher. "Not a word. You didn't see me here."

"Of course not. Where are you going?"

"Back to the States, obviously," said Lily, then he shook his head. "You really are getting slow, old friend."

Rocher smiled. "Yeah, I really should retire."

"And not before time. Be careful out there."

"And you, too," said Rocher, "whoever you are."

Vyvan Lily winked and dashed out the door over the recumbent form of Margaret Mackay.

– 21 –
The Rescuer with
the Debonaire Smile

I feel better with every mile we place between ourselves and Verity," said Lorraine as she rode down the highway toward London. "It wouldn't do for me to be found with her. If her father knew she was complicit in all this, he might start figuring out things; things I'd rather wish he didn't know."

"We are miles away," said Li Gao from behind the wheel of his white panel van. "I doubt anyone would suspect Miss Goodhue, now. You can put your mind to rest, Elin..." He caught himself.

Lorraine looked at him.

"Please, forgive me," said Gao, a blush rising to his cheeks. "It is just that you look so much like your dear Aunt. The further we travel, the more you seem as she did."

Lorraine nodded. "I'm feeling more like myself; that is herself, that is Lorraine. I just couldn't get into the character in Verity's presence, nor did I want to, but now, I'm back to my other mindset. I have a job to do, and these are just my working clothes."

Li Gao nodded. "An exemplary attitude towards a difficult task."

They fell silent for a moment.

"Do I..." began Lorraine haltingly, "I mean, I am very much like Aunt El?"

Gao smiled. "I imagine this entire adventure has been quite taxing upon you, my boy... uh, girl... But I confess a strange pleasure feeling that, for a short time, Elinor walks among us once more. You do your dear aunt proud."

"Thank you," whispered Lorraine.

"I cannot help but recall the first time we traveled this road together," said Gao, "albeit going towards Staffordshire rather than away from it."

Lorraine sighed. "Yes, that was several years and a few lifetimes ago. I had just come to England to write Lord Bagnold's biography. Little did I know when you drove me there all that would happen."

"The book of Proverbs tells us: 'The mind of man plans his way, but the Lord directs his steps,'" noted Gao.

They drove several more miles before Gao spoke again. "On that subject, have you formulated your plans?"

"Well," said Lorraine, "I need to figure out who is responsible for Martina's death. Then I have to decide how to get rid of Lorraine Innis. I could just disappear, say she was going to retire and become a recluse, or I could reveal my true identity."

Li Gao nodded. "Actually, I was inquiring as to your immediate plans when we arrive in London."

Lorraine shrugged. "I suppose you can just drop me off on some corner and then drive away."

"That describes my part," he said, "but I meant, how will you explain what happened and where you've been?"

"I wouldn't implicate you," said Lorraine.

"Nor did I expect that you ever would, dear boy…, I mean, Mrs. Innis."

"You saved my life," she said. "Apart from the fact that you helped reunite me with Verity. When I think of what her father did to her, to both of us." Lorraine clenched her fists. "I could strangle him with my bare hands."

Gao drove on for half a mile until Lorraine felt the conviction of his silence.

"I suppose that's not a very good plan," said Lorraine relaxing her fists. "Is it?"

Li Gao kept his eyes on the road. "It is wise not to act upon that urge, understandable as it may be. Given the conditions to which you will return, it would not be surprising to find yourself meeting with that gentleman. He was, after all, the lead plaintiff in the suit against you."

"Yes," said Lorraine, "and I agreed to make restitution."

"An admirable gesture," said Gao.

"I had to do it," said Lorraine, "that perfume base on my genetics was responsible for those women growing beards."

"I agree," he said.

"And Lord Bagnold will probably see that as a mark of weakness," said Lorraine.

"It is never weak to act justly," assured Gao. "Quite the opposite; it takes considerable strength."

"Ms. Friseur, my lawyer, probably thought I'd lost my mind."

"In a world of lunatics, the sane man, pardon me, lady, would appear most insane. But that aside," he continued, "you will probably have to have a defense ready, a reasoned explanation for all persons concerned: His Lordship, your attorney, and no doubt, the press."

"I hate to lie," said Lorraine.

"Little good ever comes from falsehood," said Li Gao. "Lies are fertile creatures, reproducing until the one who created them is overrun and swallowed whole by those fabrications. Though you could easily avoid deception with a careful rationing of the truth."

Lorraine thought a moment. "Say I was abducted."

"It did happen."

"By... by admirers..."

"You have no greater admirer than Miss Goodhue," said Gao, "and my fondness for you is boundless."

"But I know where you took me," said Lorraine pausing. "But, at first, thought I was dead. Yes, I feared for my life. I woke up in a strange bed, and after some initial confusion, I realized that my abductors meant me no harm. In fact, they offered to take me back to London."

Lorraine smiled and nodded. "That was easy."

Li Gao returned the nod, then focused his attention on the highway. After thirty seconds, he spoke.

"Who were your abductors?" he asked. "Did you recognize them? Can you describe them?"

The triumphant smile faded from Lorraine's lips. "Oh..."

Gao gave her an understanding smile.

"I suppose I need to think this through a little more," said Lorraine. "But I could say..."

Before Lorraine could complete her thought, her words were drowned out by a loud noise overhead. She shouted something to Li Gao. He yelled something in return, but it did no good against the roar above them. The source of the din was quickly revealed as a helicopter's landing skids dropped into view ten feet in front of the van. Gao slowed the van, not wanting to stop abruptly on a busy motorway. Lorraine looked in the side view mirror. There was no traffic directly behind them, probably because another helicopter had landed there. Behind that helicopter, a phalanx of cars with flashing lights had stopped the flow of southbound travel.

Gao brought the van to a stop, shut off the motor, and placed his hands on top of the steering wheel in full view. The front helicopter still hovered about five feet over the pavement. A man in the front passenger seat was looking through a pair of binoculars into the van, though he was scarcely ten yards away at this point. Apparently satisfied with what he saw, the passenger motioned to the pilot to put the craft down. Once on the ground, he emerged from the helicopter. He started toward the van, speaking into some sort of radio with one hand and executing signals with the other.

He was perhaps the most confident individual Lorraine had ever seen, strikingly handsome with a rugged look that was at the same time terribly refined. Similarly, his thick black hair was tousled but in a way that seemed purposeful and as unmovable as if it had been chiseled by a sculptor. Had she actually been a full-blooded female, Lorraine would have had palpitations over the man. Even as it was, she momentarily forgot her connection to either sex. She just watched him with an awe that overrode being stopped on the M-40 motorway by a brace of helicopters.

Lorraine's lapse into wonderment was only shattered by the simultaneous rapping on the doors on either side of the van. The doors were opened by men in authority. They weren't exactly police nor military, but obviously from some government entity in that general category. Gao's door opened first as a man in a dark jumpsuit holding a gun reached in, turned off the ignition, grabbed the key, and pulled Li Gao from his seat. It was done so efficiently that neither Gao or Lorraine had a moment to utter a word of protest, not that either would have been heard over the helicopter rotors.

Li Gao looked back at Lorraine. His expression, as always, was placid and untroubled. It was as if he was telling her not to worry, least of all for him. The look was brief as he quickly disappeared from her view, probably up against the side of the van.

"Don't hurt him," Lorraine cried as loud as she could, but her words were muffled, even to her.

Lorraine's door was opened, though less aggressively; instead, with the deference a valet might display at a posh hotel. The man opening it was similarly armed, though his weapon was holstered. He held the door open and stepped aside while the striking man from the helicopter approached. He paused to take off his dark glasses with a gesture that could only be described as "panache." His eyes were a deep and piercing blue. Then he extended his hand to Lorraine.

Under the roar of the helicopters, Lorraine had no other alternative than to take his hand and be helped from the van. She tried to see what was happening to Li Gao but could not. Before she knew it, she was escorted aboard the waiting helicopter by irresistible but courteous force.

Her guide led her to the rear seat of the chopper. She was seated next to a woman, also in special operations gear, who had remained in the helicopter throughout the operation. Lorraine imagined her role was something akin to a chaperone. The woman helped Lorraine with the safety harness and then motioned to the man in the front, who, now wearing a headset, gave a command to the pilot. The helicopter rose into the air. The whole action had taken less than three minutes.

As they rose from the pavement, Lorraine looked down at the van. Li Gao was handcuffed and was being escorted into one of the security vehicles. One of the team was climbing into the driver's seat of Gao's van.

"What are they doing? Where are they taking him?" Lorraine shouted.

Her chaperone handed a headset to Lorraine. She put it on and repeated her questions.

Rather than receive an answer, Lorraine was questioned.

"Are you all right, Mrs. Innis?" the woman asked.

"What? Yes, yes, I'm fine," said Lorraine. "Where are they taking…"

"We're going to a secure location," said the woman. "You're safe now."

Lorraine almost insisted that she had been perfectly safe before and started to ask what they were going to do to Li Gao. She stopped herself and thought of the Scripture Gao had just shared. She also thought that asking too many questions about her supposed captor would not bode well either for him or Verity. Instead, she just looked at the woman, smiled, and said: "thank you."

"Don't thank me," said the woman and gestured to the man in the front passenger seat.

He turned around and, for the first time since he came into view, flashed a debonaire smile.

"I haven't had the pleasure... yet, Mrs. Innis," he said. "The name's Verve, Nigel Verve."

– 22 –
Mr. Stevenson's House of Antique Secretions

Valerie Fierro felt guilty, well, just a little guilty. She had taken Mr. Postlewaite's prized possession and sold it. As she sat in the first-class compartment of the train to London, Valerie tried rationalizing it in her mind.

No one actually needs a bow tie that once belonged to a dead guy, did they? No, of course not.

Valerie really needed money to get back to London, didn't she? Of course, she did.

And if she ever saw the strange Mr. Postlewaite again, she'd make it up to him. Probably. Valerie thought about the days she'd spent wandering around the backwaters of England with the odd man. He had treated her to three meals a day, plus snacks, and he had gallantly given her the use of his trailer while he slept in the car. Still, she had given him the benefit of her company. His reputation was probably boosted by being seen with her. Even Rathman, the guy from the auction, was impressed when he thought Valerie was Postlewaite's wife. No, Valerie concluded, 500 pounds was a bargain for Postlewaite. Maybe someday she'd buy him another tie, a nice new tie.

When she wasn't rationalizing away her theft, Valerie was thinking about where she could sell the other items, the Victorian nose straighteners. Postlewaite said they were collectible, at least to the right person, and there were shops in London that catered to that sort of thing. According to him, they could fetch up to two hundred pounds. She'd need to sell them for some much-needed cash and also so she wouldn't have to carry around the creepy things.

She arrived at Kings Cross Station and hailed a cab.

"Where to Miss?" asked the cabbie.

"Antique shops," said Valerie, standing aside the driver's door. "Where do they have antique shops?"

"Depends on what you want to buy, Miss."

Valerie snorted. "I'm not buying that old crap. I want to sell a valuable collection."

"What kind of collection?" the cabbie's eyes filled with interest.

"This kind," said Valerie taking the lid off the box and holding it out for the cab driver to see.

His lips curled in disgust, and the interest flickered out of his eyes. "Dead kinky, that is! What are they?"

"Victorian nose straighteners," she said.

He nodded and gestured for her to return the lid to the box. "Very nice," he said. He thought a moment. "Yeah, I think I know a place that might go in for that. Dead kinky stuff. But I suppose there's a market for just about every taste. They didn't work for you, then."

Valerie gritted her teeth. "They were... given me... as an inheritance. Do you think I need a nose straightener?"

The cabbie stared at the kink in her nose for several seconds and said: "No, of course not. Like you say, an inheritance. Hop in. I can take you to a shop that may be interested. They sell lots of old items like that."

Valerie climbed into the back of the cab. "Listen, go straight there," she warned. "I'm not a tourist. I know when I'm being taken for a ride."

As far as she could tell, the cabbie kept to a direct route, and fifteen minutes later, he had pulled up to a mews lane.

"Up there," he said, "see the sign?"

Valerie noticed the lane had many signs hanging on either side of the narrow street. "Which one?"

"That one, the third one along on the left," he said.

Valerie looked at the sign. "That couldn't be it; that's a lingerie store. Victoria's..." She stopped and reread the sign. "EWWWW! *Victorian Secretes*, that's like a secretion. EWWW! What a yucky store!"

"I didn't make the shop," said the cabbie, "I just drove you here. That's the kind of place you wanted or at least one that would be interested in a box full of those thingummybobs."

Valerie sighed. He was right. Still, it didn't make entering such a place any easier. She pulled out her purse and reluctantly handed the cabbie his fare. The cabbie thanked her, wished her luck, and drove off. For a moment, Valerie stood at the end of the narrow street, wondering if she should just throw the box in the trash and run as fast and as far as she could from such an icky place.

Still, she needed the money. There was no telling how long Lorraine would be missing or if she'd hold Valerie accountable for the perfume debacle. No, she'd have to grit her teeth and make a quick sale of the nose straighteners.

Valerie crept up the lane and stopped under the sign. She peered in the window. It looked like a typical antique shop, which meant cluttered and musty. She didn't see anything terribly creepy. Valerie touched the charm on her necklace.

"Okay, Daddy," she whispered, "here goes." She turned the knob. A bell attached to the top of the door tinkled. She wondered if it was an antique bell.

A rather ordinary man emerged from behind a velvet curtain at the back of the shop. He took his place behind the counter and smiled.

"Yes, madam, may I help you?"

Valerie smiled back and placed the box on the counter. "Yes, please, I'd like these appraised. I suspect they're quite valuable. Cherished family heirlooms."

"Of course, madam," said the man and asked permission to open the box. Valerie pulled back the flaps, and the shopkeeper pulled out the first item. He handled it gently, almost reverently. That was a good sign; he must have an affinity for old crap, she thought.

"Oh, I see you have several," he said, looking back in the box.

He gently placed the first nose straightener back in the box and reached under the counter for a piece of black velvet. He spread it out and then, as if he were a jeweler displaying precious gems, placed the disgusting nose straighteners on the material. When the last one was arranged on the velvet, he stepped back to take in the entire collection. Then he extracted a small magnifying glass from his waistcoat pocket and began an individual examination of each.

Valerie almost wanted to tell him to hurry up or ask what he thought of them. But the shopkeeper was so engrossed by these gross items she didn't want to lower the price by breaking his trance.

Finally, after several minutes, he looked up.

"You say these are family heirlooms," he said.

"What? Oh, yes," said Valerie, thinking that would make them more valuable. "Yes, my, um, great, great, great, grandmother used them." She wasn't sure if she'd added too many greats.

"I see," said the shopkeeper with a non-committal air.

"Yes, she was Victorian," said Valerie, "that is, that's when she lived."

"Umm," nodded the man and examined one or two of the items more closely.

Valerie could feel tiny beads of perspiration on the back of her neck. She felt the need to say something. "Oh, yes, great great grandmother had a crooked, I mean, well, she felt the need for... that is, well, she must have been very vain."

The shopkeeper raised his head, the magnifying glass still over his eye. He squinted at Valerie's own nose. "Um, yes, the Victorian's could be quite vain. Evidently, a trait eradicated in subsequent generations."

Valerie bit her lip and suppressed the urge to make this musty antique dealer a candidate for his own nose straightening.

The man rubbed his chin. "They're an interesting collection; rather eclectic in nature. So, you say your ancestor acquired them."

"Yes," said Valerie, "why?"

The shopkeeper shrugged. "It's just such a diverse group. This one, for example, is an early model that predates the others by at least a decade. While the most recent article is rather late in the period."

"Well, my great-grandmother probably kept trying," said Valerie. "I mean, these things don't look like they'd actually straighten a nose, do they?"

"No," laughed the man, "that would be highly doubtful. So, did you want to sell them?"

Valerie adopted a diffident air. "Oh, I don't know. They've been in the family for over a hundred years. Still, no one needs them for their designed use. Uh, what are they worth?"

"It's a nice assortment," said the shopkeeper. "It's such a representative sampling of the items. That's why I asked if they were a collection. I suppose they'd be worth several hundred pounds to the right buyer."

"Are there buyers for these sorts of things?"

The man smiled. "In my business, you'll find there's a buyer for just about anything. Still, I could only give you about forty pounds."

"Forty?"

He smiled a little more broadly. "You're a nice lady; let's make it forty-five... no, fifty."

Valerie eyed him suspiciously. She had negotiated with enough car salesmen in her day to know he was lowballing her. She carefully picked up the items and returned them to the box. "Oh, that's okay, you know, they are kind of cute. Maybe I'll just put them on display. They'd make wonderful conversation pieces."

A look of urgency filled the shopkeeper's eyes as she headed toward the door. Valerie put her hand on the knob and paused. Would he bite?

"Oh, wait, just a minute," said the man.

With her back to him, she smiled. He bit. She dropped the smile and turned. "Yes?"

The shopkeeper licked his lips. "Uh, I just thought of a customer who might be interested. I don't know why I didn't think of him before. He collects items similar to this. He never asked about nose straighteners, but this may pique his curiosity. You never know. He was in just the other day. In fact, I'm delivering an order to him this afternoon. I could take your collection along, on consignment, of course, and if he's interested..."

Valerie smirked. "Look, Mr..."

"Stevenson..."

"Look, Steve," she said, leaning across the counter, "I didn't just fall off the boat, and my father didn't raise the village idiot. You take my family heirlooms to this guy who obviously would be interested, and you keep most of the profits, and I get next to squat."

"I can assure you I don't do business that way," Stevenson blustered.

"Good," said Valerie, "neither do I. So, call your buyer and tell him we're both coming over, and if he's interested, he can agree on a price with both of us. And you'll get a nice ten percent for the introduction."

"Sixty…" countered Stevenson.

"Fifteen," said Valerie.

"Fifty…"

"Look, let's just say thirty," she said. "That will ensure you have plenty of incentive to get the highest possible price."

Stevenson nodded. "I'll call my client now and see if he's interested."

"You do that."

Stevenson fished a card from his pocket and dialed the number.

"Hello, yes, It's Mr. Stevenson of Victorian Secretions," he said into the receiver. "Yes, I'm bringing your items along this afternoon, just as we arranged. I've come into another collection that may interest you, as well. May I bring them along? …. they're Victorian devices…. It's a fine collection, a family heirloom held in a private estate… the owner is in my shop now. She would be coming along to assure their provenance. As I said, they're from an old established family collection, the…." The shopkeeper looked up and winked. "It's from a very prominent family collection; you've probably heard of it. The…"

"Fierro," said Valerie, winking back. Valerie appreciated this guy now that they were working the same side of the con.

"They're from the Fierro family collection," said Stevenson with a conspiratorial nod. "Perhaps you've heard of it…. You have? Excellent. We'll see you in about an hour."

Stevenson hung up and rubbed his hands together.

Valerie laughed. "That was pretty slick. He really said he'd heard of the Fierro Family collection!"

Mr. Stevenson waved his head modestly. "It's all for show, Miss Fierro. The punters, that is, the customers, would rather die than admit they didn't know something, even when it's a complete fabrication. In any event, he's quite eager to see the Fierro family heirlooms. Let me put them in a fancier case, all part of the presentation. I only hope he doesn't see through our little act."

"Well," said Valerie, picking up one of the implements, "if his nose gets out of joint, he can always use one of these to set it straight!"

– 23 –
Boris and Natasha Go Visiting

"This is ironic," said Clodagh Clott as she crouched behind a cottage on the outskirts of a Russian village. "You, the President of Russia, sworn to uphold the laws of the land, stealing clothes off a washline."

"The situation dictated my actions," snapped Kropotkin as he threw a simple dress at Clodagh. "Your present clothes would give us away."

"Turn around," said Clodagh as she began to unbutton her blouse.

"We are married," said Kropotkin.

"Yeah, well, that's your cover story," she said, "but it's just a story. Being a phony husband doesn't give you the right to see my genuine body." Clodagh reflected on what she had just said. Kropotkin was in love with Lorraine, and she didn't have a genuine body, at least not a genuine female one.

"What if someone saw us," said Kropotkin. "Why would I say I'm not looking at my wife?"

"You could say: 'been there, seen that,'" she replied.

"Been where?"

"It's an American expression," said Clodagh, "now turn around."

Clodagh took off her American business suit and slid into the plain Russian dress. She carefully folded the skirt, blouse, and jacket. "Okay, turn around."

"Much better," said Kropotkin with a nod of approval. "Now you look like a plain Russian worker's wife."

"You know how to sweet talk a girl," muttered Clodagh.

"Not at all," said Kropotkin. He held out his hands and nodded at her suit. She handed the ensemble to him, thinking he was offering to carry it for his "wife."

"Hey," she cried when he threw the clothes into a nearby pond. "That's a new suit. Do you know how much it cost?"

"Quiet," he said, "it would be very suspicious for a country wife to be carrying a stylish American suit."

Clodagh grimaced. At least he called her taste: "stylish."

Kropotkin started toward the village and nodded for her to follow. He stopped and looked at her shoes.

"Oh, no," said Clodagh, "I'm not going barefoot."

"You are right," he agreed, "that would look suspicious. Sit down."

Clodagh sat on a tree stump and cried out when he snatched the shoes from her feet. He examined the three-inch heels and then nodded. Before she could protest, Kropotkin snapped the heels from her shoes, converting the designer pumps into a ragged pair of flats. Then, he looked around and, noticing a puddle, scooped up a handful of mud and smeared it all over her shoes. He handed them back to her.

"Oh, perfect," muttered Clodagh surveying the damage. "Before I met Lorraine, I never wore designer clothes. I was strictly a knockoff kind of a girl."

"You should feel right at home," said Kropotkin. "I knocked the heels off those shoes."

She smirked. "Your first joke. Can it get any better?"

He studied her face. "Yes," he said and took out a handkerchief. Dipping the cloth in the puddle, he began scrubbing her face.

"Hey, come on," she cried.

"Quiet," he said. "Someone will hear you."

"If I knew the Russian word for 'rape,' I'd yell it now," she said.

"I would teach it to you," he said, "but I'm afraid you'd use it. There!" Kropotkin stepped back. "Now you look like an average Russian countrywoman: plain, not unattractive, and without all that American muck on your face."

"No," said Clodagh, feeling her cheek and examining a bit of dirt on her fingers, "I've got that good old Russian muck now."

Kropotkin nodded. "Da, is much better!"

"I was being sarcastic," she smirked.

He stared at her for a moment and then smiled. "And so was I." Kropotkin offered Clodagh his hand and helped her to her feet. "Come, we will see about getting something to eat. I'm sure you are hungry."

They walked toward the village. Kropotkin took her hand.

"For appearances," he said. "We must blend in. Teplov will be looking for me, for us, once he returns and finds his bunker is empty and his hired stooges are dead. I've never been to this place, but I think it will be safe."

"You said you knew where we were," said Clodagh.

"I did," said Kropotkin, "but we must not go back the way I came. Again, that is what Teplov would expect. Before I could get us to safety, we would be ambushed. Unfortunately, since he now knows you are not Lorruska, he may not be as gentle as before."

"Gentle," snorted Clodagh, "I was tied up and stuck in a sack."

"And that was when he thought you were of value to him," said Kropotkin. "He will not be so mannered if you meet him again. Trust me, Clott Clodagh."

"I told you, my name… oh, forget it, it doesn't matter."

"The only thing that matters now is my safe return," he said. "With you, of course. That is why we must take a circuitous route."

"What happens when you're recognized?"

Kropotkin rubbed his chin. "Fortunately, my family has always enjoyed lush, quick-growing beards."

"Too bad for your sister," said Clodagh.

"I have no sister," he said. "Oh, another American joke. Quite amusing, you are quite the wit. But as I said, I have not shaved since I left Moscow, and my beard, and these plain clothes, will be disguise enough. I spent my youth among simple folk. I can speak as roughly as them."

"I had three older sisters," said Clodagh, "so I can talk rough, too."

Kropotkin stopped and looked at her. "No, you must not speak. It would give you away. You will be my dumb wife."

"Hey!"

"Meaning you cannot speak," he explained.

"Can't I be your mute sister?"

"I can more easily protect your virtue if you are my wife," said Kropotkin. "Can you say 'da,' and 'nyet?'"

Clodagh repeated the words. Kropotkin nodded. "It is good enough. I will say you are my shy little bride. If I need you to say 'da,' I will squeeze your hand. If I give you a little pinch, say 'nyet.'"

She rolled her eyes. "Yeah, okay. I suppose that's as good a plan as any."

"Very good, come, let us go, Natasha."

Clodagh stopped in her tracks. "Natasha?"

"You need a good Russian name, and Clott Clodagh is not a Russian name," he said.

"Look, my name isn't Clott Clodagh…"

"Yes, you are learning; it is Natasha," said Kropotkin. "And, let me see, I shall be…"

"If I'm Natasha, you're Boris," said Clodagh.

"Yes, that is good," he said.

The newly christened Natasha shook her head. "Only hope we don't meet a moose and squirrel."

"What?"

"Never mind," she said, "I'm going to be shy now. I may be shy the rest of my life!"

- 24 -
The Exasperating Rescuee

Lorraine was sitting alone in a windowless room somewhere in London. The fixtures were austere. Just a table, some plain chairs, and a microphone. Across from her was a large mirror. At first, she made a face toward the mirror until she realized that it was probably one-way glass and she was being observed.

The helicopter had brought her directly there, landing on the roof of a large building beside the Thames. Before she had a chance to speak, she was ushered to the room where she now sat. Lorraine looked at her watch. The "rescue," the ride to London, and the installation in this room had taken just thirty-five minutes.

The door opened. The man from the helicopter, the apparent leader of the operation, entered. Now, instead of a black ops jumpsuit, he was dressed in a stylish Saville Row suit.

"Ah, Mrs. Innis," he said nonchalantly as if he hadn't expected to meet her there. "Can I get you some tea? Or perhaps something stronger?"

"No, thank you," said Lorraine. "I don't drink."

"Except for the occasional glass of white wine," he said with a smile, "which you sip but never finish."

"How did you…"

"It's my duty to know," he said.

"When do you go off duty?" said Lorraine. She had meant to be flippant with this ultra-professional agent. But as soon as she said it, his eyebrow shot up, and a slight grin appeared around the corner of his lips. He obviously had interpreted that as an invitation, or at the very least, flirting.

"There will be time enough for that," he said self-assuredly.

"I meant…"

"But there's debriefing…first," he said with a subtle glint.

"Look, Mr. Nerve…"

For the first time, Lorraine saw his assurance punctured, ever so slightly.

"Verve," he said, quickly repairing the lesion in his ego. "Nigel Verve."

"Sorry, Mr. Verve," said Lorraine, "it was hard to hear clearly in the helicopter.

"You may call me Nigel, Lorraine."

She almost told him he could call her 'Mrs. Innis.' But she was afraid he'd only take that as some sort of verbal foreplay.

"What do I need to be debriefed concerning?" she asked.

"Your abduction," said Verve, sitting on the edge of the table directly in front of her.

"But you were there," said Lorraine.

"That was your rescue," he said.

"Oh, pardon me," said Lorraine. "An abduction is the illegal carrying away of a person, especially interfering with a relationship. Technically, that applies more to you in this situation. I didn't ask for your interference."

"So, you wanted to be in that van?"

"As much as I wanted to be in your helicopter," she said, "in fact, more so. I asked for that ride."

"It's well documented that a victim will start to treat their kidnappers sympathetically."

"I believe you're referring to the Stockholm Syndrome," said Lorraine.

Nigel Verve nodded. "And has that occurred in your case, Mrs. Innis?"

"I can assure you, Mr. Verve, I will resist any urge to treat you sympathetically."

"That proves my point," he said, standing, "you see me as the villain in this. Can't you see I rescued you?"

Lorraine shrugged. "I wasn't being held captive. The driver of that van kindly agreed to give me a ride to London."

"Did he tell you his name?"

Lorraine shook her head. She wasn't lying. She knew Li Gao's name when she got in the van.

Verve picked up a folder. "He was driving a white van."

"I'm not familiar with English laws, but that's not a crime in America."

He shook his head. "When you disappeared from the Old Bailey, it was believed that you were taken away in a white panel truck, similar to the one you were just riding in."

"In which you were riding," corrected Lorraine. "We'll get on much better if you don't end your sentences with prepositions."

"Fine," he said, "the white truck in which you were riding."

Lorraine shrugged. "I was unconscious when I was removed from the court, so I can't attest to how I was taken away. But if you say you have proof of that…"

"Not exactly proof," he said, "a white van was seen at that approximate time, in that general vicinity."

"Well, then," she said, "It doesn't seem as if either of us can affirm that it was the same van or if that driver was there."

"What can you tell us about the driver?

Lorraine thought a moment. She would have to be careful not to divulge too much knowledge of Li Gao while remaining truthful. "He was Asian," she said.

"That's rather obvious."

"I'm just telling you what I observed," said Lorraine. "He seemed very nice. He didn't speak much, but he did have an English accent. He was very mannerly and kind."

"What about before that?" said Verve. "Tell me what you can remember from the beginning."

Lorraine tried to be truthful but exasperating in the hope that Verve would tire of the interview. He seemed more a man of action rather than an interrogator. "Well, I was standing in the courtroom, in the dock," she began. "That's what you call it, correct? Back in America, we usually call it the witness stand."

"What you call it, or we call it isn't important, Mrs. Innis."

She smiled sweetly. "I just want to get it right for you. So, I was standing there in the courtroom, and I felt lightheaded."

"As if you were drugged?"

"I'm not sure," said Lorraine, "I don't recall being drugged, at least not to my knowledge, so I don't have much with which to compare this experience. But I felt faint, and then…"

Nigel Verve leaned forward. "Yes? Then what?"

She raised her hands. "Then, I don't know because I must have fainted. Anything else about being kidnapped, or taken away in a van, is beyond my field of comment. I assume I had passed out."

Verve ran his hands through his hair in frustration but then turned and rearranged it again in the large mirror. "Yes, of course," he said, looking in the file folder, "you passed out. You were taken from the courtroom to the judge's chambers. When they couldn't revive you, a doctor administered a sedative."

"Really? A sedative?" said Lorraine. "Isn't that a kin to giving a sleeping person a sleeping pill?"

"I believe it was precautionary before transporting you to hospital."

Lorraine nodded. "I always thought that was interesting in England."

"What? That we're an overly cautious people?"

Lorraine laughed. "Oh, no, not that, I was referring to the use of the definite article. You said 'to hospital.' In America, we'd say 'to the hospital.' Don't you find language usage fascinating?"

"Riveting," he said, though she could see the muscles tightening in his jaw. "Language usage aside, they placed you on a gurney to take you to *the* hospital. Then when they were behind the Old Bailey, loading you into the ambulance, a young lady appeared and seemed to be in distress."

Lorraine smiled. She could imagine Verity springing into action on behalf of her Beloved.

"Why are you smiling?" asked Verve.

"What? Oh, sorry, I was miles away," said Lorraine. "Please continue."

"Well, that's it," he said, closing the file folder. "You were miles away by the time they realized what was happening."

"Didn't the ambulance or the police or whoever give chase?"

Verve looked at her severely. "Have you ever been through the small, winding streets of that part of London?"

"Apparently, it would seem," said Lorraine, "but not consciously."

"Yes, of course," he said. "Tell me about when you woke up."

Lorraine bit her lip. She would have to be extra careful here. "Um, well, my mind was a bit fuzzy. You said I was given a sedative."

"That's correct."

"That would account for it," said Lorraine. "I confess that I had trouble distinguishing reality from a sense of twilight or dreaming. It may seem silly, but I thought I was dead."

"You were afraid of losing your life at the hands of your captors?"

"No," she said, "I imagined that I had actually died. I thought I was in heaven."

"Really?" said Verve. He seemed to be restraining himself from laughing.

"Yes, I do believe in heaven," she asserted.

"And what made you think you had attained that higher plain of existence?"

"When I opened my eyes, I saw someone who reminded me of a deceased love."

Verve nodded. "Despite the fanciful nature of your misconception, this may be useful."

"Oh?"

"Yes, we know your abductor, or at least your captor was a man."

Lorraine smiled. She was hoping he would leap to that misconception. "My, you certainly are clever, Mr. Verve."

He gave her a patronizing smirk. She almost expected he would pat her on the head. "Thank you. It's gratifying to know that my skills are well-honed to serve Her Majesty."

"Please, just call me 'Lorraine.'"

"I meant the Queen," he said. "Did you recognize the man who awoke you?"

"I can honestly say I did not," said Lorraine.

"Were you awakened by the Asian man, the one who drove the van?"

"No, I was not."

"Could you describe the man who awoke you?"

Lorraine shook her head. "Unfortunately, I can say that would be almost impossible." Especially, she thought, since they weren't a man.

101

"Yes," said Verve, "due to the drugs, no doubt."

Lorraine smiled and hoped he would interpret her expression as bowing to his expertise on such matters. He did. She wondered how long she could dodge his questions when suddenly the door flew open in a gust of mink.

"There she is," bellowed the unmistakable voice of Lindsay Friseur. "You found her."

"Of course," said Nigel Verve nonchalantly.

Lindsay sidled up to Verve, much as a cat might stroke against a person's leg. Nigel seemed grateful for the adulation, though not overly so. Lorraine had never imagined fawning was in the lawyer's repertoire, but there it was.

"Hello, Lorraine," said Hilda Madison. Against such overpowering egos as Lindsay and Verve, she was almost transparent.

"Ms. Madison," said Lorraine. "It's good to see a friendly face."

Lindsay Friseur ratcheted her attention away from the chiseled features of Nigel Verve. "I suppose I'm not a friendly face, Mrs. Innis."

"I only meant…"

"I can assure you that we were equally concerned for your safety," said Lindsay. "Even though the last time I saw you, you were fricasseeing me in open court."

"I didn't mean to."

"Still, I'm not one to harbor a grudge against a client who not only ignores my advice publicly but actually works in opposition to it. But as I said, I don't harbor grudges."

"No," muttered Hilda, "you don't harbor grudges, but you do take them sailing, Lindsay."

Lindsay flashed a patronizing smile at her law partner. "How droll, Hildegarde."

"Lindsay," said Hilda, "Lorraine made it clear from the start how she felt about the case and her feeling of obligation to make restitution."

"That's true," said Lorraine. "I didn't mislead you, Ms. Friseur."

"Dear sweet, Mrs. Innis," said Lindsay, stroking Lorraine's hair. "When you've had as many suits as this it's just natural to assume the client is putting up a front to look good while their attorney does the dirty work. If I naively mistook your sincere desires as an act, that's my fault, I can assure you."

"I forgive you," said Lorraine.

Hilda laughed while Lindsay forced a smile. "Thank you."

"I suppose you also want me to thank you," said Lorraine, "for sending Mr. Verve to rescue me."

"She didn't send 'im," said a voice. "I did!"

Lorraine looked up. In the doorway, plucking the ends of his mustache, stood Lord Bagnold.

– 25 –
Who Put the Con in Consternation?

As they waited for the hotel elevator, Stevenson was coaching Valerie on their strategy with the prospective buyer for the nose straighteners.

"I'll let you in on a few trade secrets," Stevenson began, "when we meet the client…"

He was interrupted by a ding, and the elevator door opened. It was too full to continue confidential business discussions. Mr. Stevenson excused himself as he squeezed in with the rolling merchandise case that contained the client's order. Valerie followed him, carrying a heavy wooden display case. It weighed a ton, but it was more impressive than the cardboard carton that initially held the nose straighteners. The weight would be worth it, she hoped.

"Five, please," said Stevenson, and one of the other patrons pushed the appropriate button.

The car stopped on every floor. Valerie still wasn't used to the fact that the British called the first floor the ground floor, and what she regarded as the second floor, they called the first floor. So they were actually going up to the sixth story. One extra floor, along with the frequent stops, made the case feel that much heavier.

Finally, they reached their floor and got out. Stevenson opened his mouth to continue his confidential advice, but another couple followed them out. They walked down the corridor in the same direction, stopping at the door across the hall.

Stevenson rolled his eyes in the couple's direction as he knocked on the door. "Never mind," he said under his breath. "You're a clever woman. Just follow my lead."

The door opened to a dark, narrow hallway, the kind often seen in hotel rooms, with doors on either side apparently leading to a closet on one side and the bathroom on the other.

A man cloaked in the darkness, muttered words of welcome. Stevenson led the way into the room proper. He nodded to Valerie.

"You can just place the case on the table," said Stevenson. "Carefully, but then, I don't have to tell you to be gentle with your family's heirloom, do I, Miss Fierro."

Valerie placed the case on the table as if it contained the crown jewels. It was fun to be in on a con. She was enjoying this.

"This is the lady I was telling you about," said Stevenson. "Miss Fierro. Her family was one of the oldest in Europe. They came from Italy in the mid-nineteenth century, isn't that right, Miss Fierro."

"Really?" said the client as he closed the door and turned. "I knew a Fierro years ago, but that was over in the States. I'm sure they're no relation."

Valerie's mouth dropped open. The con was on her.

"Albrecht Eckner," she gasped.

– 26 –
Recollections of an Einfalt

H ow do, love?"
     The toothy grin of Purvis Twankey popped around the door of Patsy Einfalt's office. Patsy looked up a gave a weak smile from the pile of paperwork atop her desk.

"Hello, Purvis," she said, trying to return his cheery grin, but her full smile was lost somewhere under a blizzard of memos, contracts, and forms. "All ready to go?"

Purvis stepped into her office and placed his suitcase down. "Aye, I was, but I don't feel right leaving you with all this mess. I should stay and help."

Patsy picked up one binder. "Know anything about endorsement contracts?"

"Uh, no, but..."

"Regulatory filings? Qualifications for 501c-3s? Insurance forms?"

Purvis brightened. "Aye, that! I had insurance once, then they took it away because I couldn't pay the premium. That was just a'fore I hit Miss Valerie's car. So you could say I had some experience with insurance."

"Thank you, dear," sighed Patsy. "I appreciate the offer, but I think it would be easier if I did all this alone. You go visit your mother."

"I wish you were coming," he said. "You've never met Mum. And she's never met you, either. You'd like our Mum. She's the second most wonderful mum in the world... after you."

"Thank you," said Patsy. "It hasn't been easy. And that's something I wanted to fully explain."

Purvis blushed. "No need. I learned all about that sort of thing years ago."

"I didn't mean in general," she said, "I mean I've never shared the full details about, well, where Rachel came from."

"She came from you," said Purvis, "I'm not so daft that I think you found her under the cabbage leaves." He stopped. "You are Rachel's mum, aren't you? I mean, she favors you. She's got your nose and eyes and smile."

"Of course, she's my daughter," said Patsy. "Please, Purvis, sit down. I need to explain, in case, well, in case you wouldn't want to marry me."

Purvis pulled up a chair. "There's nothing would change me mind about.... Whoops." He started to sit and rose again, pulling some paper from his bottom. "Need this?"

Patsy looked at the form. "Oh, that's the receipt from the alarm company. They said our smoke detectors weren't right. Something about the old system not being up to code. They fixed it, so I can file that." She opened up a cabinet and tucked the form in its proper place. Then Patsy sat down, took Purvis by the hand, and sighed.

"That warn't a gooey sigh," he said. "I'm a right puddin', but I know a bad sigh when I hears it. What did I do? Are you upset about me going to see me mum?"

"No, I told you I wasn't," she said. "This isn't about you, Purvis, this is about, well, I think I need to tell you the full truth about... Mr. Einfalt."

Purvis nodded. "I wondered about that. It don't make a difference to me. I mean, you must have done something terrible to make them change their name."

"Who?"

"Your dad and your mum," said Purvis. "I mean, I think they're proper champion, but I always wondered why they changed their name, and you didn't."

"My parents didn't change their name," said Patsy, "I did."

"You mean you weren't always Patsy?"

She squeezed his hand, mainly to keep her from using her own to sock him on the nose.

"I've always been Patsy," she said, "I wasn't always Einfalt."

"No? What were you?"

"Zyobidinski."

"Like your folks."

"Of course," she said, "your parents were Twankeys, weren't they."

Purvis nodded. "Oh, yes, I come from a long line of Twankeys. We've been Twankeys as long as, well, as long as we've been Twankeys."

"It's the same with me."

"You're not a Twankey, not yet," said Purvis.

"I mean, I had the same name as my parents," explained Patsy. "I only changed it after Rachel was born so she'd have the same name as her father."

"Who's he when he's at home?"

Patsy's shoulders drooped. "That's the problem. I only know his name and his last name at that. I was very foolish. There was a Christmas party, and I got very tipsy, and well, a man was there, and we..."

She waved her head and rolled her eyes. Purvis did the same and then shook his head.

"Ya what?"

Patsy sighed. Most times, it was cute having a boyfriend slower on the uptake than herself. This wasn't one of those times.

"We had sex," said Patsy with clenched teeth.

Purvis' brow furrowed for a good thirty seconds, then he nodded. "That would explain your daughter."

"Yes, it would," said Patsy. "As I said, I was drunk. And he had his way with me, and I got pregnant. But I was careful to ask him his name. I thought he would be my husband, or at least my boyfriend. He said his name was 'Einfalt.' No first name, just Einfalt. And then he left. I was sure he'd come back, but he never did. And when I got pregnant, I was even more sure that somehow he'd find out and come back and fulfill his responsibilities to his child. I was so positive that I changed my name to his so that when Rachel was born, she'd have her father's name. Then, when he came back, we'd be a proper family."

Patsy exhaled a deep breath and then collapsed into tears. Purvis took her in his arms and hugged her tight.

"It's okay, pet, it's okay," he kept repeating while he stroked her spiral perm. "Your Purvis is here. We'll be a proper family."

"I guess I was a dope," said Patsy. "Thinking he'd ever come back. I asked everyone at the party, and no one knew who he was. He was hired to be the Santa Claus, but Mr. Eckner, he was the one who hired him, called the place where they got him, and they didn't know either. I wish Rachel could have known her father, but if that's the kind of person he was, maybe it's better she doesn't know him."

Purvis hugged her tight. "It's nowt a crime to be a dope. If it t'were I'd be serving a life term in the Scrubs."

"Where?"

"It's a big prison back home," he said. "As for Rachel having a daddy, well, maybe she could think of me as her dad, maybe? Our mum says I'd be a grand father. Not a grandfather, but a great... oh, 'eck, now I'm a great grandfather."

Patsy smiled and pushed the tears from her eyes. "I understand. And yes, we'll make a wonderful family."

Purvis held her at arm's length and flashed his toothy grin. She smiled back.

"All better now?" he said. "Only, I wouldn't want to go off to England with you in a right tizzy."

"I'm fine," said Patsy, "more than fine now that you know the truth about everything." She looked down at the pile of papers on her desk. "I just have to sort out the Foundation's mess."

"Do you want me..."

Patsy laughed. "You're a wonderful man, Purvis. Generous, tenderhearted, sweet, funny, creative, inventive, but I don't think you're a financial genius."

He nodded. "You're right there, pet. I can earn it all right, but I don't know what to do with it when it's just lying around. You need a real financial genie, you do."

◆

A few blocks away sat a panel truck emblazoned with the name: "Superior Alarms." Inside, Vivyan Lily took off his headphones and smiled.

"This is going to be easier than I thought," he said.

Lily spun around to a laptop computer and opened a print shop program.

"Let's see..." he closed his eyes and leaned back. "Joe? No, too plain. Henry? No. Alliteration is always nice... Edward? Edgar? I know... Egmont. Yes, Egmont Einfalt."

– 27 –
His Lordship's Shin Shiner

Seeing Lord Bagnold again was like being whacked across the face with a 20-pound mackerel, though not quite as enjoyable. Despite trying to control herself, her antipathy must have been evident on Lorraine's face. The smile he wore upon entering the room quickly dropped from the life peer's mug.

"Uh, ahem, yes," said Bagnold. He had offered his hand. But after hanging for several seconds, he waved it loosely, finally deciding to rub his nose, then smooth his hair. "Mrs., ahem, Innis, I believe... uh, wot I means to say is, I believe I h'ain't 'ad the pleasure...."

"We saw enough of each other..." Lorraine started, then stopped. She had almost forgotten herself and responded as Chesney Potts would. "That is, I saw you in court, and of course, through your attorneys. But you're correct. Neither of those previous encounters could be termed pleasurable."

Bagnold attempted to chuckle dismissively. Instead, it sounded like he had a gobstopper stopping up his gob. "Yes, well, I wish to h'explain..."

"Any explanation can be delivered directly to my attorneys," said Lorraine. She turned to Lindsay Friseur. "Ms. Friseur..." She almost said, "sic 'em," but just nodded at him.

Lindsay Friseur was uncharacteristically silent. Lorraine felt Hilda Madison's hand gently touch her arm.

"Lorraine," said Hilda softly, "we have been in consultation with His Lordship, entirely on your behalf and with your best interests in view."

Lorraine sneered. "Really? He's still breathing."

Some of the starch returned to Bagnold's spine. "That's gratitude for me," he blustered. "Go ahead, tell 'er, tell 'er 'oo rescued 'er!"

"I did," said Nigel Verve.

"Wot? Oh, yes, you did that," said Bagnold, "but oo put you on the case? Me! That's oo! Look, Missy, don't come all high and snotty with me. I knows 'ow to deal with spoiled girls. I've been doin' it all me life! I h'am a father!"

Lorraine felt the blood rushing to her face. Now, Lord Bagnold was calling Verity a spoiled girl. If she hadn't been in lady mode, she would have socked him. Still, she had some weapons. Lorraine feigned to slap him, and when he bobbed his head back, she delivered a bruising blow to his honorable shin with the point of her shoe. Lord Bagnold started hopping around on his good leg, massaging his other limb, while using military epitaphs that probably translated into swear words.

"I am not a girl," said Lorraine, "I mean a spoiled girl. That is, I'm a grown woman."

"Of course you are, Doll," said Lindsay Friseur, putting her arm around Lorraine. "Why don't we all calm down, and we can explain everything."

"Yes, I'd like you to try," said Lorraine, regaining her composure. "Here I was, minding my own business, making my own way back to London when we were practically assaulted on the highway and forced against our wills..."

"Our wills," said Verve. "So you did know the man driving the van?"

"I said 'our wills,'" she explained, "because two people were forced to stop."

"We were rescuing you," said Lindsay.

"I didn't ask for rescuing," said Lorraine

"Next time, I won't bother," said Lord Bagnold, sitting down and massaging his shin.

"Promise?" snapped Lorraine. "I didn't need rescuing."

"How do you know?" asked Verve. "I've had more experience in this sort of thing than you or anyone in this room."

Lord Bagnold pointed. "Verve is right. You don't knows wot you were being taken to. You thinks you were going to London, but what part?"

"He said he was going to take me to my hotel," said Lorraine. "He seemed a very honorable gentleman."

"Appearances can be deceiving, Mrs. Innis," said Verve.

Lorraine scrutinized the people in the room. "You're right."

Lord Bagnold shook his head. "You don't knows you're born, young woman! Of course, 'e seemed like a decent bloke; they all seems like decent blokes. That's to get you in their cars. And certainly, 'e promised to drop you off wheres you wants to go. Wot did this fellow look like?"

"Fifty to sixty years of age," said Verve, "average height, Asian..."

"An H'oriental?" Bagnold laughed derisively, "Mrs. Innis, you no doubt was h'ours, maybe minutes away from becoming white cargo."

"What?"

"A bit of good old European stuff to entertain them h'orientals in their opium dens," said Bagnold. "I saved you from spending out your days in some Singapore 'ouse of ill dispute. You were about to be Mr. Wu's favorite bit of the other! And the thanks I get is a bust in the shin." He rolled up his trouser leg. "Coo, that's going to be some mouse! Look at that shin shiner!"

Lorraine rolled her eyes. "He wasn't dangerous. He was a very nice gentleman."

"All men is nice gentlemen," said Lord Bagnold, "before they h'ain't not so nice."

"Including you and Mr. Verve?" said Lorraine.

"Naturally," said Bagnold before catching himself. "Wot? No, no, not no way, no 'ow. I'm a peer of the realm, and Verve 'ere is one of 'Er Majesty's finest. Your own lawyers can vouch for me, can't you?"

"Yes, well…" began Hilda Madison.

"What my partner means," interrupted Lindsay Friseur, "is that we can vouch for His Lordship." She patted Lorraine's shoulder. "Lorraine, you have to view the situation through my eyes, from an attorney's viewpoint. You're taking this all too personally."

"Yes, you're right," said Lorraine, "I shouldn't take someone suing my person personally."

Lindsay laughed patronizingly. "Oh, my wonderfully idealistic Lorraine. That's why the world loves you. You still see things through the prism of an ordinary person. If I harbored a grudge against every one of my legal adversaries…"

"New York harbor wouldn't hold the ships." muttered Hilda.

"My learned partner is right," continued Lindsay. "But a good attorney must not take things personally."

"Especially since it's not you being sued," said Lorraine.

"Lorraine, Lorraine, dear Lorraine," said Lindsay, "I hesitate to remind you that I was fighting for your side even when you had thrown in the towel. It was you, not I, who conceded to the demands of the claimants in the suit. If you'd left it to me, I would have sliced up this monkey," she pointed at Lord Bagnold, "into more pieces than a jigsaw puzzle. No offense, Your Lordship."

"Wot?!" blustered Bagnold, "oh, yes, 'aw 'aw, of course, none took. Yes, monkey, quite good. No offense taken at 'all. See, Mrs. Innis? Fighters in the court ring, but good pals where it really counts, still able to do business."

Lorraine did a double-take. "Business? Do business with whom?"

"Why with me, of course," said Bagnold.

"You mean compensating the victims of the perfume," said Lorraine.

Bagnold shrugged. "Yes, well, they'll get something. I was referring to…"

Lindsay Friseur stepped in between Lorraine and the peer. "Lorraine, we've worked things out, on your behalf, and in your best interests, of course."

"Oh? And what have you worked out on my behalf?" asked Lorraine.

"Lord Bagnold is willing to drop the suit," said Lindsay.

"What about the women in the suit? With their facial hair?"

Bagnold coughed into the back of his hand. "Yas, well, I've decided to pay them off, to provide full compensation and resuscitation."

Lorraine squinted at him. Bagnold squirmed under her scrutiny.

111

"Yas, well," he said, "I thought it was the least I could do under the circumvention. Don't worry; I'll foot the bill for their hair removal."

"Permanent hair removal?" asked Lorraine. "I don't want you fobbing off those poor women with a razor and a can of shaving cream. They'll all be entitled to professional laser and or electrolysis."

Bagnold looked at Lorraine sideways. "Something of an h'expert of the topic, is you? A little fuzzy wuzzy, was you?"

"None of your business," said Lorraine. She turned to Hilda Madison. "The victims need to have their faces restored to their original states, plus compensation for their trauma."

"We've reached that agreement in principle," assured Hilda.

"But not in practicality," muttered Bagnold.

Lorraine stood and went toe to toe with the life peer. "You will not weasel out of this. I've seen how you work. I haven't forgotten..." She caught herself.

Bagnold raised his eyebrows in surprise. "You 'aven't forgot wot?" He turned to Verve. "Did you 'it 'er on the 'ead during the rescue, Verve? I've dealt with frantic females all me life, but this one's definitely doolally!"

Lorraine gritted her teeth. She could relate how Bagnold had treated his father, Hugh Goode, how he'd bullied his staff, and how he'd cheated Chesney when he was writing Bagnold's biography. All those paled when compared to faking the death of his own daughter just before her wedding. She closed her eyes and counted to ten in her mind.

"Let's just say," said Lorraine, "that I wouldn't be here today in this predicament if it wasn't for you!"

Bagnold's jaw tensed, and Lorraine braced for a fight. Just then, his face relaxed into a smile. "Now, now, let's not get all 'asty 'ere. You is a fine lady, Mrs. Innis. You have the privilege of being a lady. Just like our dear Queen, when the demands on you h'ain't not so demanding, it's easy to be a lady."

"You have no idea," muttered Lorraine, her fists clenched.

"Whereas I gots to be a businessman," continued Bagnold, "ruthless always, devious and despicable quite often. I suppose our worlds is apt to have a bit of fraction when they collide. That's why you're so lucky to have Ms. Friseur 'ere, and Ms. Madison, looking out for you. They're used to dealing with rotters and bounders the likes of wot I am. Perhaps it will go down better if I lets them explain."

Hilda guided Lorraine back to her seat while Lindsay sat across from her and smiled.

"Go ahead," Lorraine said cautiously, keeping one eye on Lord Bagnold.

"It's very simple," said Lindsay. "We came to a very amicable settlement with His Lordship. He agreed to drop the suit and make restitution to the women."

"On the terms I described." said Lorraine.

112

"We haven't worked out the particulars, Lorraine," continued Lindsay, "but I assure you that any agreement is contingent on your accepting it. Basically, you will dictate the terms."

Lorraine looked at Lindsay Friseur. She was smiling, but it wasn't entirely a sincere expression, even for a lawyer. Lorraine turned to Hilda Madison and received a more authentic, reassuring look. Finally, she looked at Lord Bagnold. His expression drooped slightly. He shrugged and nodded.

"So, I get what I want for the ladies?" said Lorraine.

"Yes, you do," said Lindsay. Hilda nodded.

Lorraine sat back in her chair and relaxed until a thought crossed her mind. She had gotten everything? The ladies would get hair removal and some compensation to be negotiated. But what did Lord Bagnold get? She recalled the first and last time she had seen him conciliatory. It was when he conceded to Verity and Chesney's marriage. And she remembered how that had ended.

"Just one thing," said Lorraine. "If the bearded women are cared for, and the lawsuit is dropped. What does he get?" She pointed at Lord Bagnold.

His Lordship smiled a genuinely happy smile. It looked so out of place on his face; it had to be real. He reached into his breast pocket and pulled out a folded sheath of papers.

"Oh, not much," said Bagnold. "I gets the most wonderful, most charming, most beautiful spokesman, uh, spokeswoman, for all my worldwide advertising."

"Who?" asked Lorraine.

"Why, you, of course, my dear," he said. He bowed toward Lorraine. She almost thought he was going to kiss her. In which case, she would definitely vomit. Instead, he handed Lorraine the papers. "Just sign 'ere, and we's in business."

Lorraine looked at the contract. Then looked up at Lindsay.

"It will not only settle the suit and compensate the victims," said Lindsay, "but it will make you a very wealthy woman."

"Wealthy woman?" said Lorraine.

Lindsay nodded.

"A very, very wealthy woman," agreed Lord Bagnold. He was positively beaming. It wasn't a pretty sight on a face accustomed to more sour expressions.

Lorraine looked at the contract and then back at Bagnold. Then she tore it in half and shouted: "NEVER!"

– 28 –
The Repentance of Albrecht Eckner

lbrecht Eckener," cried Valerie. "Albrecht F—kin' Eckner."
Mr. Stevenson looked confused. "You know each other?" said the antique dealer.

Albrecht smiled his prissy little grin. "We do, but apparently not that well. If we had, she would have known my middle name is Hans."

"Albrecht Eckner," Valerie snarled from behind gritted teeth. "You knew…"

Albrecht just shrugged like a kid caught stealing from the cookie jar.

"You're not interested in these f—kin' nose benders," said Valerie. "It was all a big joke."

Mr. Stevenson's face dropped. "You don't want my…"

Albrecht walked over to Stevenson's carry case. "Yes, yes, of course, I do, very much," he said, unzipping the box. He held up a cumbersome Victorian corset. "Oh, yes, marvelous! Absolutely marrrrrvelous!"

"I should have known!" Valerie slapped herself on the forehead. "Who else would come halfway around the world to itch his twisted fetish."

Albrecht looked up from his examination of a 19th Century truss. "First of all, this is not a fetish. This is… research. You knew my family's business."

"It's their business. It's you're sick, icky hobby," she said.

"Second," he said, ignoring her comment, "I regularly come to London from Gibraltar, which is not halfway around the world. Mr. Stevenson has long been looking out for items that interest me. And this time, he's far exceeded my expectations." Albrecht smiled at Valerie, then nodded to Stevenson.

"Oh… oh!" said Stevenson, returning the nod. "Then you're happy with my delivery."

"More than happy, Mr. Stevenson," said Albrecht. "Absolutely delighted." He drew an envelope from his breast pocket. "I believe we agreed on five hundred pounds, and," he reached into his trouser pocket. "And let's say a bonus of two, no, three hundred, for the added service."

"For my nose straighteners?" said Valerie.

Albrecht made a sour face. "Good heavens, no. Those look repulsive!"

"But…" Valerie started to protest.

"I think we can come to an arrangement on what you have to sell," said Albrecht. "And I think we've taken up enough of good Mr. Stevenson's time. Thank you, Mr. Stevenson. Again, service beyond mere satisfaction."

"Thank you, Mr. Eckner," said Stevenson, heading toward the door. "Always a pleasure to serve a discriminating client."

"You're too kind," said Albrecht, holding the door for him. When Valerie tried to follow, Albrecht put his arm across the narrow hallway. "Valerie, I thought you wanted to sell your little implements."

"You hold on to them," she said through clenched teeth. "Look them over. I… trust you."

Albrecht smiled. "Of course you do." He turned to Mr. Stevenson, who was now in the corridor. "Thank you again, Mr. Stevenson, for everything."

"Happy to be of service," said Stevenson. "And if I find any other items of interest…"

"You be sure to call," said Albrecht, closing the door. He turned to Valerie. "Though he couldn't find me a more interesting artifact than the one he delivered today."

Valerie considered her next move. She could knee him in the groin and make a run for it. But Albrecht would probably tell Robert Valvano where she was. She wouldn't put anything past him, not after all he'd done in the past.

"Please, Valerie," said Albrecht taking on a kindly tone. "You look absolutely beat."

"No one is going to beat me," snapped Valerie.

"I meant you looked exhausted," he said. "Tired. Hungry too?"

Valerie bit her lip. She hadn't had a really good meal for days. The reminder made her stomach growl involuntarily.

"Oh, you must be starving," said Albrecht walking toward the phone.

Valerie gave a start. "Who are you calling?"

"Room service," he said. "Who else would I be calling?"

"Your boss," she said.

"I'm the president of the bank in Gibraltar," he said.

"I meant your real boss: Robert Valvano."

Albrecht blew out his lips derisively. "Him? Yes, technically, he is at the top of the ladder. But his rungs are an ocean away. He's never been over here, and as long as I'm not too extravagant in my business dealing, he is the most silent of partners. I have no desire to see him. Fortunately, we share a mutual antipathy. Sandwiches?"

"What?"

"Or something hot to eat?" asked Albrecht.

"Oh, yes, thank you," said Valerie. "Sandwiches would be fine."

He nodded. "Fine it shall be." He placed the order and sat down on the suite's sofa. Valerie slowly sat in the easy chair opposite him. They looked at each other for several minutes in silence. Valerie tried to guess the ponderings of his perverted little mind. But he sat there placidly as if he had never entertained a twisted thought.

"Still collecting weird shit, huh?" she finally said, nodding toward the newly purchased items.

He shrugged. "It's more for the family," he said. "You remember my family's store, the surgical supplies."

"I'm not likely to forget," she said.

Albrecht laughed. "Yes, of course; please forgive me."

"Forgive you?" she was stunned. Was he apologizing?

"Well, okay, forgive my family," said Albrecht. "When you grow up around those things, they become almost, well, normal. But moving away from the family business, well, it provides perspective. First, going into financial services…"

"I always wondered about that," said Valerie. "I would have thought you'd go into the family's business."

Again, he shrugged. "Totally selfish on my part, I confess. I mean, really, what kind of a life can you build around walkers, trusses, and home health care implements? It was fine for my parents. They sort of stumbled into it. But…" Albrecht paused. "Can I be honest with you?"

Valerie snorted. "I don't know, can you?"

"I deserved that," he said. "I've behaved terribly, especially in school, especially toward you."

She almost reminded him of fathering Patsy's daughter and then not telling her. But if any apologies were coming, Valerie wanted them all for herself.

"Perspective," he said again, almost wistfully. "It's a wonderful thing. Time and distance are marvelous for providing an accurate assessment of oneself."

"Really," she said, though her skepticism had lost a few degrees of harshness.

Albrecht stood, walked to the window, and gazed at the city below. He was silent for several minutes, then let out a deep sigh. "I've been a terrible person," he said quietly, almost as if he were confessing to himself. "And what for? How pointless. What a waste of human potential, that is if I ever had any. Or was mine a life constructed of nothing but scheming and conniving. No goal but to satisfy my own selfish desires. What a waste."

Valerie sat with her mouth open, partially from the shock, partially wondering if she should say something. But he didn't seem to be speaking to her.

"Carrying out the orders of scoundrels like Peter Liverot and his disgusting overlords, the Valvanos. Helping the likes of those vermin while denigrating decent people like Patsy Zyobidinski, Martina Fergus, and poor old Chesney Potts."

Valerie's jaw hung slack. She had never heard Albrecht utter a kind word for those people, especially not Chesney. Valerie shut her mouth quickly when he turned around.

"...and you most of all, Valerie."

"m-me?"

He sighed again, then turned away and bowed his head. She thought she had seen the glimmer of wetness in his eyes. Albrecht Eckner crying? This was unbelievable but true. Valerie thought she had seen everything when Chesney turned himself into the most famous woman in the world. But even that was more plausible than Albrecht Eckner growing a conscience.

He stood by the window with his back to her, shielding his eyes, undoubtedly weeping. Had it been anyone else, Valerie would have gone over and comforted them. As it was, she just sat there.

After another few minutes, there was a knock at the door.

"I'll get it," said Valerie. Albrecht, still facing the window, just nodded. His shoulders shook.

She opened the door. It was a bellhop with a room service cart. She told him to enter. While she was still in the hallway, she heard the bedroom door shut.

"Just put it over there, please," said Valerie, signing for it and adding a tip. The bellhop thanked her and left.

The cart was filled with a generous assortment of sandwiches, a pot of tea, and even an array of desserts. It was the best spread she'd seen in weeks. Valerie's mouth began to water.

She crossed to the bedroom door and tapped softly. "Albrecht," she said in a gentle voice, "the food is here."

His voice, quavering with tears, replied. "P-please, go ahead, don't worry about me. I-I've eaten. Please, enjoy yourself. I'll be out...soon."

Valerie nodded and made up a plate for herself. Then she poured a cup of tea and sat down on the sofa. Valerie was about to take a bite of the first sandwich when she paused and looked toward the bedroom door. She almost expected Albrecht to jump out naked, or more likely, wearing one of his Victorian supports, and laugh at her. Valerie waited a few minutes, then shrugged and started on the sandwich.

After weeks of cheap food with Mr. Postlewaite, posh sandwiches at one of London's finest hotels were an unexpected pleasure. But not nearly as surprising as the possibility of a repentant Albrecht Eckner.

– 29 –
The Relenting of Lorraine

The world may love you," muttered Lindsay Friseur after Lord Bagnold stormed out of the room, "but I doubt many lawyers would. At least not any who have to represent you."

Lorraine shot a glance at Lindsay, and for the first time she'd known the self-assured attorney, she saw her flinch. As usual, Hilda Madison intervened.

"Now, please, both of you," said Hilda, "let's not get carried away. Lorraine, Lindsay is just frustrated on your behalf. She worked hard negotiating that agreement with Lord Bagnold. If it isn't exactly to your liking, then we can amend it, I'm sure."

"I poured my blood into wrestling with that baboon," said Lindsay, "and my client, the girl I'm fighting for, rips it up and tosses it back in his face. What am I to conclude?"

"Not to wrestle with baboons," said Lorraine.

"Look, honey…" said Lindsay, rising to her feet.

"Please, Lindsay," cautioned Hilda, guiding her back into her chair. "Lorraine, I know you feel abused by Lord Bagnold after he profited from your perfume and then sued you over it."

"That's not it," said Lorraine. "Well, not all of it…."

"What else is there?" said Lindsay.

Lorraine opened her mouth, then closed it again. She couldn't very well mention Chesney's history with the life peer, not without dragging Verity into it all. "I'd… I'd rather not say. All I can say is that I don't trust him, and I never will."

Hilda patted Lorraine's arm. "That's why there are lawyers, Lorraine. We negotiate and then draft contracts to contain people and keep them honest."

"The only container that would keep His Lordship honest is a pine box buried six feet underground." The remark made her think of Verity explaining how she'd dug up Chesney's empty grave. Lorraine started to cry.

"There, there," said Hilda, "we're just trying to do what's best for you."

"I appreciate that," said Lorraine daubing her eyes. "I just wouldn't want to be the face of toilet paper, especially not for a person like him. I'd rather pay the damages to those women myself, not that I have very much money. I'd hate to take it away from the charity. But it would be right for Bagnold to pay most of it, seeing as he got all the profits."

Lindsay Friseur looked up from some spreadsheets. "That's not entirely true."

"Yes, well," said Lorraine, "technically, I own all the rights to the perfume now, but when it was making money, he was getting the profits."

"Not all of them," said the lawyer, "in fact, not even the majority of them. Those went to your cousin."

"Valerie?"

Lindsay Friseur placed the spreadsheet in front of Lorraine.

"Valerie made all that?" said Lorraine incredulously. "But she transferred it back to me, didn't she?"

"She transferred the rights," said Hilda, "and the liability to you."

"So, she has all the money?" asked Lorraine.

"Yes, and no," said Lindsay. "It's sitting in escrow because of the lawsuit. Lord Bagnold is holding it."

"But it's not his," said Lorraine. "It belongs to those women who were damaged by the perfume."

"Technically, it belongs to your cousin," said Hilda.

"But I'm sure Valerie would do the right thing," said Lorraine.

Both attorneys just stared at her. Lorraine could only guess what they were thinking. If Valerie was bound to do the right thing, where was she now? Lorraine shook her head. They didn't know Valerie. Valerie must be in trouble to have disappeared.

"That's why," said Lindsay breaking the uncomfortable silence, "we had to forge that agreement. He doesn't care about the perfume or those hairy girls. He just wants you."

"But why?"

Lindsay gave Lorraine another patronizing look. It was depressing when your own attorney thought you were a sap. "You are the most popular person in the world. His Lordship is only motivated by business, pure and simple. He wants you to be the face of his paper products so he can expand past England and go global."

Lorraine grimaced. "That's what I was afraid of," she said, "and the one thing I'd want to avoid. He's not a nice man."

"Not nice men have a way of getting what they want," said Hilda.

"Perhaps," said Lorraine, "but all it takes for men like him to succeed is for honest people to do nothing to stop them. I appreciate all you've done for me, and I apologize for being such a difficult client. But there has to be another way. I am adamant. I will not be the spokesperson for anything connected with Lord Bagnold."

Lorraine folded her arms across her chest.

"'IM? 'IM?" Lord Bagnold's distinct, h-dropping voice could be heard several rooms away, despite the soundproofing of the interview rooms.

"I SMELLS A RAT," Bagnold could be heard shouting. "A RAT NAMED 'DAUGHTER!' I 'AVE BEEN 'ARBORIN' A SNIPER IN ME BOSOM!"

"Now what?" said Lindsay rushing to the door. She flung it open, and Bagnold's ranting grew louder. "I'll be right back."

Lorraine just looked at Hilda, who merely shrugged her shoulders. Apparently, Verity had done something to upset her father. That wasn't too surprising. Something was always irritating His Lordship. Lorraine hoped that Verity hadn't shown up. Lorraine would have difficulty maintaining her feminine alter-ego with Verity there.

After a few minutes, Lindsay Friseur returned.

"Well, we might as well get going," she said, "Lord Blowhard is erupting again."

"I'm free to go then?" said Lorraine.

Her attorneys gave her a puzzled look.

"Free to go?" asked Hilda.

"You mean they're not holding me?" said Lorraine.

"You're not being detained," said Lindsay. "You're the victim, remember? You were just being debriefed so they could get information on your abductors."

Lorraine thought of Li Gao. "Certainly, they're not holding that poor man who gave me a ride."

Lindsay Friseur laughed. "Ah, that's where it gets interesting. That's what made Lord Bigbags lose his marbles just now. It turns out he knows the man."

"W-what man? Who?" asked Lorraine, her anxiety level rising.

"The guy who gave you a ride," said Lindsay.

"You mean they're friends?"

"Hardly, dear," said Lindsay, gathering up her mink coat and handbag. "Turns out he's a friend of Bagnold's daughter."

"Oh, no," said Lorraine. "I-I mean, Lord Bagnold has a daughter?"

Lindsay nodded. "Yeah, could you imagine that monstrosity spawning? The poor girl probably looks like the bride of Frankenstein."

Lorraine clenched her fists, then recalled you couldn't really insult a person about whom you knew nothing. "Ha, yes, maybe, but then I'm sure she's probably very nice, even lovely."

Lindsay Friseur shook her head. "No wonder you're so nice. You even stick up for the kid of the guy you hate."

"Oh, hate's a strong word," said Lorraine, "I don't hate Lord Bagnold. I just can't stand the sight of him. It's more the things he does."

"Sure, like breathing," said Lindsay.

"I'm sure his daughter is a sweet girl," said Lorraine, "though, of course, I don't know, never having met her."

"Okay, if you say so," said Lindsay.

Lorraine wracked her brain. If Lord Bagnold made a connection between Li Gao and Verity, Verity would easily be dragged into the whole mess. She had to shield Verity. There was only one way. She rose to leave and then stopped.

"Oh," said Lorraine to Lindsay, "I'm terribly sorry for putting you and Ms. Madison through all this."

Lindsay shrugged. "It's what we get paid for, Doll."

"Yes, but after all you've done on my behalf," continued Lorraine. "All that negotiating and all your efforts to have me rescued."

"You said you were on your way back anyway," said Hilda.

"Yes, if indeed that man was bringing me back," said Lorraine.

The two lawyers looked at her sideways.

"You said he was such a nice man," said Lindsay.

"Yes, well," Lorraine threw up her hands, "who can tell, right? I'm not worried about him right now. I feel terrible tearing up all your hard work." She picked up the pieces of the contract. "Could you ask His Lordship to come back in here? Please?"

– 30 –
The Striking of the Bad Tooth

Corrado
Michael Valvano cradled the photo of Nonnia and the baby that grew up to be Michael's father. On the back was the simple inscription "Corrado." He had found it in a letter returned to Nonnia from some German named Zimmer. Now, he was trying to confirm his suspicions.

"You know, Mikey, they make Italian food here almost as good as at home!" Alphonse took another forkful of pasta as they sat at the small café.

Michael smiled. "Yeah, imagine that, Al. We stopped so I could use the restroom. I didn't expect you to order a second lunch." He glanced at his watch. "It's three o'clock."

"What time does that make it at home?"

"I don't know about nine or ten," said Michael. "Why?"

"My stomach is still on American time," said Alphonse breaking off a piece of crusty bread. "So, it's like a late breakfast or an early lunch there."

"And a late lunch and an early dinner here," laughed Michael.

"Going all over Sicily works up an appetite. These winding roads and mountains really give me a workout."

"Next time, we'll get a car."

A confused look crossed Alphonse's face, and he looked over his shoulder at their rented Fiat.

"We got a car…" he said before a knowing smile broke out on his lips. "Oh, I get it. It's a joke."

"Yeah," said Michael, "and I'm only kidding. *Manage*, Alphonse, *manage!* I don't mind, besides your company makes…" He stopped in mid-sentence.

Alphonse stopped in mid-chew. "What's the matter, Mikey?" He asked, his mouth full of vermicelli.

Michael stared across the plaza of the small Sicilian town. "That woman, over there, the old one..."

Alphonse turned. "You mean the ten pounds of sausage in the five-pound casing?"

Michael reached for his briefcase, opened it, and pulled out the pile of photographs. He rifled through them before he found the one that he wanted. "Here it is," he said, placing it in front of Alphonse. "See?"

Alphonse studied the picture. "Yeah? It's your grandmother holding the baby, standing next to some crab."

Michael tapped the photograph and then pointed across the square. "That's her, that's the woman. The one that just went into that shop."

"Yeah?" Alphonse looked at the shop, though the woman was no longer in view. He looked back at the photograph, then back across the street, and then shook his head. "Nah!"

"Come on, let's go," said Michael rising from the table.

"Hold on, I didn't finish!"

"Okay, you finish. I'll be right back."

Michael hurried across the square into the shop. It was a small grocery store. Aside from Michael and the clerk, the store was empty.

He looked around. "That woman that just came in here..."

"*Che cosa?*" said the clerk.

"Oh, right," said Michael. He scratched his head. He'd never asked anyone where they were hiding a fat old lady in any language. Finally, Michael decided to act out the question as if it were a game of charades. He raised one finger and then pointed toward the door. Next, he bent over and walked with a shuffling gate. The clerk knitted his brow, wondering where this was going. Michael put his hands under his chest as if to indicate breasts and then swooped his hands in a wide arc to approximate a fat belly.

The clerk clapped his hands together. He gestured for Michael to stand still while he went through a curtain to the back room.

The next two minutes sounded like a heated argument. Michael almost retreated to the café but recited a silent prayer and stayed put. In another minute, the ruckus settled down. The curtain flew open, and the fat old lady emerged. She swatted the clerk, who retreated to the back room. She then fixed her gaze on Michael.

In his best Italian, he apologized for the intrusion.

"You American?" said the old woman.

"Yes," said Michael, "you speak English?"

The woman sneered. "I speak good English, you bet. I learn at war with soldiers."

"That's wonderful," he said. "I'm American. My family is from here." He waved his arms.

"This my store," said the woman, folding her arms across her bosom.

"No, I meant, from around here, Sicily."

"You want to buy?"

Michael looked around the small shop, then shook his head.

"What you want?" she demanded. The woman started coming around the counter, presumably to throw him out.

"Wait, wait, please," said Michael drawing the photograph from his pocket. "Please, look…"

The woman was muttering something in Italian about money and Americans. She almost pushed him out the door, but Michael succeeded in getting the photo in front of her eyes.

"*Cose'e questo?*" said the woman snatching the picture from his hands.

"It's, uh… *una foto mia nonna,*" he said.

The woman squinted and strained at the photograph before bustling back behind the counter. She picked up a pair of thick glasses and peered at the picture. Then she let out a gasp.

"*Tua Nonna?*" She asked, pointing at the photo.

"*Si, si,*" said Michael, leaning across the counter.

She shoved the picture into his chest and pushed him away! "*Vattene via!*"

Michael stood there, his mouth agape. She was telling him to leave.

"But…"

"*Fuori! Uscire!*" she shouted, waving her fat arm toward the door.

"But, please, listen to me… uh, *per favore…* uh, *ascolta…*"

The woman shuffled out from behind the counter, pushing him toward the door, demanding that he leave and adding several choice epitaphs.

Before he could protest any further, Michael found himself on the sidewalk. The shop door slammed behind him, followed by a resounding click of the door's bolt.

Alphonse witnessed the event from across the street. He jumped to his feet, paused for an extra bite of pasta, and then rushed to Michael's side.

"What happened?" he asked. "So, it wasn't her?"

Michael looked back at the shut door. "It's like a bad tooth, Al. When you hit the right one, you know it! Boy, do you know it!"

"So, what do we do now?"

Michael looked around the square. He pointed at a nearby tower. "We go to church."

– 31 –
Natasha and the Universal Language

They knocked on the door of the first cottage on the outskirts of the small village. Kropotkin raised his finger to his lips and nodded at Clodagh. For her part, Clodagh tried to look like she was a shy country girl. She wasn't sure what that looked like. Hopefully, the people inside the house wouldn't know either.

After Kropotkin's second knock, the cottage door opened. A middle-aged man was standing there.

Kropotkin started speaking in fluent Russian, though Clodagh noticed his speech patterns were rougher than his usual voice. He used his hands a lot in describing their plight. Clodagh didn't know if he was doing so for her benefit or the man's, or both of them. He was a good mime, and she thought he was telling them some sort of story about a car breaking down or an accident or something. The man at the door kept nodding, and his natural suspicion of strangers seemed to be dropping. Kropotkin kept talking and gesturing off in the direction opposite from whence they came. The man started looking off in that direction. But, Kropotkin shoved him back in and seemed to be indicating their plight had occurred miles away, whatever plight that was.

Finally, the man gestured for them to come inside, and he closed the door behind them.

The house was simple but clean. They had entered the kitchen area. A woman, presumably the man's wife, was preparing the evening meal. The man introduced the woman. Kropotkin introduced himself and Clodagh. She only knew this because he pointed at her and said, "Natasha," and then indicated he was Boris. Clodagh smiled. The woman said something and gave Clodagh a strange look. Kropotkin smiled and guided Clodagh to a chair at the table. Then he made some sort of explanation and gestured that somehow Clodagh was dimwitted. Clodagh understood that much and almost responded with a punch on his arm before remembering that was "Natasha's" cover story. So, she just smiled as insipidly as she could and sat down.

The homeowner and Kropotkin talked though Clodagh didn't understand a word of it. Apparently, the man showed concern for the plight of Boris and Natasha, whatever that might be. Not having eaten all day and sitting there in a kitchen filled with food smells made Clodagh's mouth begin to water. She didn't know what was for dinner, but she'd betray their whole ruse for a serving of it. Despite not knowing any Russian, Clodagh's stomach knew the language of hunger: it started growling. Clodagh covered her belly and hunched over in her chair. Her gastric pleas grew louder and more insistent. The woman of the house gave Clodagh a concerned look and leveled a question at her. Clodagh just sat there wide-eyed, feeling like a genuine simpleton.

Kropotkin laughed and answered for her. He then looked at her and nodded, expecting a response.

Clodagh stared at him, wondering which of her two replies he expected. For his part, Kropotkin was just staring at her with raised eyebrows. The man and the woman also seemed to be waiting for what the imbecile Natasha had to say.

She had a fifty-fifty chance. So Clodagh shrugged and guessed: "Nyet?"

"Nyet?" said the woman with surprise.

"Nyet?" repeated the man, similarly astonished.

Kropotkin laughed nervously and kicked Clodagh under the table while making gestures that reinforced that he'd escorted a congenital idiot into their home.

"Da?" said Clodagh.

This caused another round of responses before the woman said something in a definitive tone. She put bowls and plates in front of them, followed by a steaming pot of some sort of stew. Then she ladled out heaping portion in each of their bowls before repeating the procedure for her husband. Finally, she pulled out a large loaf of brown bread and placed it in the center of the table. The man sawed a huge delicious slab of bread, serving Clodagh first, then Kropotkin, and finally himself and his wife.

Clodagh waited using her best American manners, not knowing the protocol in a Russian working-class home. The husband started to eat, dipping his bread in the stew simultaneously with his spoon. She looked across at Kropotkin, who wore a wary expression. For a moment, she was confused until she recalled Kropotkin's allergy to wheat. A few morsels of that bread would make him effectively drunk, risking their safety.

The husband and the wife urged him to have the bread. Kropotkin picked up a piece tentatively. For the first time she had known him, his eyes showed genuine fear. He sat there with a slab of brown bread in his hand, raised halfway to his mouth. His eyes were darting around, apparently looking for a solution.

If she had even a slight grasp of Russian, Clodagh could have said something. As it was, she was effectively mute. She had to do something. His eyes caught hers, and the look in them was pathetic. She didn't speak Russian, but she would have to do something. She decided to communicate in the only universal language she knew: crazy.

Clodagh jumped atop the table and started shouting at the top of her lungs, the only silly thing she could think of at the moment.

"Oooh eehh oooh ahh ahh!"

Her hosts jumped back from the table in shock.

"Bing, bang wallah wallah bing bang!" continued Clodagh, as she stuck out her tongue and flailed her arms.

Kropotkin caught her eye, and she winked at him with her back to the couple.

"Ed-bray! Ixnay on the ed-bray," she shouted, hoping he could translate her Pig Latin. To make sure, she accidentally, on purpose, stomped on the bread. It was a pity as it was such good bread, and she would have enjoyed more of it. But it was better than dealing with an inebriated Kropotkin.

Kropotkin must have understood, for he quickly followed her lead. Offering apologies and explanations to their hosts while trying to calm his looney wife.

Her goal accomplished, Clodagh slowed her gibberish and dropped her arms to her side. She panted and rolled her eyes.

Kropotkin explained his "wife's" condition further and then offered her his hand to help her off the table. The couple, now sheltering in the corner, just watched with bated breath. Clodagh let her tongue dangle from her mouth and took Kropotkin's hand. He spoke in soothing tones. His touch was gentle but strong as he guided her down.

"Da, da," panted Clodagh. It was safe to recover from her seizure now that the bread was no longer fit for consumption. But it was still suitable for one last thing. As she stepped from the table, Clodagh slipped on a smooshed chunk of bread and started falling. Kropotkin's arm grabbed her, preventing her from falling off the table. Unfortunately, it didn't stop Clodagh from tumbling butt-first into the large bowl of stew.

Clodagh's eyes opened wide as the thick mixture soaked through her peasant skirt, engulfing her rear end in a savory mélange. Kropotkin's expression at first was one of surprise but quickly changed to one of amusement. For a moment, his eyes and the corners of his mouth almost betrayed him. But he recovered and replaced the beginnings of mirth with a mock embarrassment.

Using broad gestures, Kropotkin explained his version of what his hosts had just witnessed. He lifted Clodagh out of the stew and used his handkerchief to gently clean off her butt. He then kissed her on the forehead and said something in a soothing and affectionate tone. Then he hugged her before turning to the couple who were still keeping a safe distance from the visiting lunatic and her husband.

Kropotkin held the chair for Clodagh, but before she could sit, the man of the house sprang from his shocked stupor and started talking rapidly. He reached into his pocket, pulled out a set of keys, and pressed them into Kropotkin's hand.

Kropotkin objected and tried to give them back, but the man was insistent. His wife joined in with nervous smiles and urgings. Kropotkin reluctantly agreed finally and took Clodagh by the hand. He looked her in the eye and spoke slowly, explaining apparently what they had just said though, of course, she didn't understand a word of it. He finished by squeezing her hand and saying: "Da?"

Clodagh stared at him for a moment, then nodded and repeated: "Da! Da!"

As they made their way to the door, Kropotkin kept turning and expressing something. The couple, still keeping their visitors at arm's length, spoke hurriedly as it seemed they wanted nothing more to be rid of their guests.

Finally, on the other side of the threshold, Kropotkin once more expressed what appeared to be gratitude. Before he could finish, the homeowner shut the door. Clodagh heard the lock click.

Kropotkin smiled at Clodagh and rushed her away from the house. Once they were safely out of earshot, he dangled the keys in front of her.

"That went well, my dear Natasha," he said. "We now have transportation!"

– 32 –
The Subconscious Need
of a Pillow Fight

"HE DID WHAT?" Verity cried.

Lord Bagnold turned and gave her a puzzled look as he lit his victory cigar.

"'E 'oo?" said Bagnold taking his inaugural puff and waving the match to extinguish it. "I didn't not say no man's name. You going barmy again?"

"I-I'm sorry," said Verity as she slumped into a chair in her father's study at Bagnold Hall. "I thought you said, um, someone else's name."

Her father's eyebrow shot up as he scrutinized his daughter's face. "I don't not know whether to 'ave your ears checked or your sconce examined. I comes in 'ere with the best news I've 'ad in donkey's years, and you starts yowling like a bandleader."

"I think you mean, Banshee, Father."

"And I think you're crackers," said His Lordship. "I knows wot I said. I h'ain't the one oo can't not 'ear."

"The expression is howling like a banshee," said Verity.

"And I knew a bandleader once," said Bagnold. "It was back on me 'oneymoon in Skeggy. Your mother was there, too."

"Nice of you to take her along," muttered Verity. "What girl could resist a romantic excursion to Skegness?"

"We was dancing one night in the seaside ballroom," said Bagnold, miming his dancing prowess, "when this bandleader winks at me wife. Ha! Well, it was the last winking wot 'e did for a while. I gave him a punch up the 'ooter. And..."

"...he yowled like a bandleader," said Verity.

"H'egzactly," said Lord Bagnold. He puffed out his chest like a bantam rooster and looked as if he might crow.

"How nice for mother," said Verity.

"It was," he continued with a smile on his lips. "We went back to our chalet and had quite a romantic time."

Verity put her hands over her ears. "Stop! I don't want to hear it."

Bagnold curled his lip at her. "And they says men h'ain't got no romance. Well, you knows you was born almost precisely nine months later. You might jolly well thank being 'ere today on account of that bandleader's obstetric behavior."

Verity shook her head. He no doubt meant "obstreperous." Most girls started as a gleam in their father's eye. It was a cold revelation that her existence was inspired by the wink in the eye of a rude orchestra conductor. As with most conversations with her father, this one quickly drifted away from the point.

"Sorry, Father," said Verity.

"Sorry? For wot?"

"For yowling like a bandleader," she said, "upon learning your latest bit of news."

His Lordship smiled slyly. "Didn't 'alf put it over. Ha! They thinks they can outwit an old campaigner, does they? But yes, I've got that one neatly sown up, just like wot I said I would. Remember?"

Verity sighed. "I remember your boast that by suing Lorraine Innis, she would wind up agreeing to endorse your products."

Lord Bagnold's chest swelled to an even greater inflation. "It warn't a boast if you can come across, and I comed! Mrs. Lorraine high-and-mighty Innis is going to be squeezing my rolls all over the world. By the time she's done, my toilet paper is going to wipe the globe. I got the best of her high and snotty Yank lawyer, too. That one's packed her bags and went back home!"

"What about the lawsuit with the bearded women?" asked Verity.

"Huh? Wot? Oh, well, yes, I worked that out with 'er lawyer before she left. Ha! That lawyer was glad to see the backside of Mrs. Innis! She did not know 'ow to 'andle 'er, not no 'ow!"

"And you do know how to handle Mrs. Innis, Father?"

Lord Bagnold grinned. "Of course, I does. Women is like plasticine in me 'ands, everyone knows that."

"And you'll be able to handle Mrs. Innis?"

"She's a woman, ain't she?" snorted His Lordship.

Verity bit her lip.

"So, I 'ad to make a settlement on those birds with beards," said Bagnold, "but most important, I gots me a Lorraine Innis! Ha! And you doubted yer old man!"

"I didn't underestimate you, Father," said Verity glumly. She only hoped she hadn't overestimated the character of Lorraine Innis and her Beloved. There must be a good reason Chesney agreed to be the spokesperson for her father's products.

"Um, Father," said Verity, placing her hand on his arm as he puffed his cigar, "about Mrs. Innis...."

"Oh, yes?" said Lord Bagnold. "I knows wot you're thinking, and the answer is a scatological 'No!'"

"You didn't even know what I was going to ask," said Verity.

"Ha! I've known you all your life, even longer," said Bagnold. "I've known you longer than you've known yourself. I can see through you like a picture window."

"You couldn't know what I was going to ask."

Lord Bagnold squinted at her. "I'd bet you that I did, only I'd tell you, then you'd say I was wrong. So, we won't not wager on it. But, just to prove you can't not put nothing over on me, I'll tell you. You was going to ask if you could meet Mrs. Innis."

"I wasn't," said Verity, then paused, "but could I?"

"See? See? I was right, I was," said His Lordship. "And no, you can't not no way no 'ow. You 'ad your chance."

"My chance, what do you mean, Father?"

Bagnold opened his mouth wide, froze, and shut his trap. "No, I can't not tell you wot I means. I'm not allowed."

"Not allowed by whom?"

"I can't not tell you that neither," said Lord Bagnold. "Just suffer it to say that Mrs. Innis is mine, and you can't not 'ave 'er."

Verity rolled her eyes.

"Don't come that look with me, my girl," said Lord Bagnold pointing his cigar at his daughter. "This is business, big business, huge business, even oblique business! This is not the time, and Mrs. Innis h'ain't not the lady to do wot you want."

"What do you think I want to do with Mrs. Innis?"

"Oh, I knows you," said Lord Bagnold putting his hand on his hip in an effeminate pose. "You wants to go shopping, and sip tea, and paint each other's toes, and have pillow fights."

"Pillow fights?"

"It's all very psycho-logic," he said. "You should knows, I paid enough dosh to that university you went to. You is looking for a mother figure, or a big sister, or a best girlfriend. You probably would blame me for that 'ole in your psychic. They blames the father a lot. But let me tell you, you h'ain't not using Lorraine Innis as your substitute mum or sister or whatever."

"More like whatever," muttered Verity.

"Wot?"

"Nothing," said Verity. "I can assure you that the last thing I want to do is paint Lorraine Innis' toes."

"Good, besides, she don't not need her toes painted," said Bagnold.

"How would you know?"

"I means, she don't not need her toes painted to do me adverts," he said. Then he paused and stroked his chin. "Although..."

Verity knew the look, and she wasn't going to encourage his thought process by asking questions.

"Hmmm…" Lord Bagnold's eyes were darting back and forth, almost disappearing under his brow.

"Aren't the dahlias lovely this year?" said Verity looking out the window and hoping to derail his scheming.

"Toes, toes," muttered Bagnold, who was now pacing across the Persian carpet. "Head, shoulder, knees… no, no knees, no shoulders neither, head, toes, hand, yes…."

"The cook said she was preparing lamb chops for tea."

Lord Bagnold wheeled around and slapped his hands together with such force Verity felt as if she'd been shot.

"Yes, that's it," he said. "I've got it."

"Uh, the lamb chops or the dahlias," said Verity, making one last attempt at mental derailment.

"Chops? Dahlias?" he said, having not heard a word. "No, Lorraine Innis is going to work for me."

"Well, as your spokesman, uh, person…."

"That's where it will start," said His Lordship. "But it h'ain't not where it's going to end. I'll make piles of money!"

"I already think of you when I hear the word 'piles,' Father."

"And when I do, I'll make so much money," he said, his eyes glassing over, "that I'll give it to Mrs. Innis."

"Father?"

"I'll buy her, lock, stock, and barrel," he said with a leer. "I'll use her to buy her out. Then I'll own her. Head to toes. She's got that cosmetic muck…."

"A bit too much for my liking…" said Verity.

"They went potty for her perfume," said Bagnold. "And they tell me she's got a whole line of that slop in the States. I'll use her to increase me own pile of dosh, and then I'll buy her out, and I'll own Mrs. Lorraine Innis. From her powered head to her painted toes!"

Verity closed her eyes and said a silent prayer. How could her Beloved get into so much trouble, with even more disaster in-waiting?

– 33 –
When Boris and Natasha Became Nikolai and Clodagh

The engine on the old truck growled several times as if it resented being awoken in the middle of the night. Then, after a few sputters, it chugged reluctantly to life.

"Not the best transportation," said Nikolai Kropotkin, "but we cannot choose as beggars. Let the motor warm up, and then we can get going. And may I add, my dear Natasha, that you were magnificent. They would have given us anything just to rid themselves of their visitor and his lunatic wife. The loan of this tired old truck was a cheap deliverance."

"Glad you approve," said Clodagh. "I just didn't want things to get out of hand. I had to do something."

Kropotkin turned to her. In the dim light of the shed, she could see his warm smile.

"I know why you did that," he said. "You wanted to create a diversion before I was compelled to eat that bread. You know about my condition. Lorruska told you, didn't she?"

"You told me," said Clodagh. "You told the whole world at that press conference, remember? You're the most famous person in the world who can't eat bread. I was afraid if you ate some and had a reaction, that couple would have seen through your disguise."

"Oh, yes," he said, "that was very wise of you, very quick thinking."

Clodagh shrugged. "If I spoke Russian, I would have scolded you for being too fat and not needing to stuff your face with bread. But I don't know Russian, so...."

"So, you made yourself look like a crazy woman to save me," he said.

"My sisters would say I have plenty of practice."

Kropotkin looked down. "I must offer you my deepest gratitude. Things may have gone very badly for me had I been recognized. Oh, yes, and I must apologize for when you slipped and fell in the stew," he said.

Clodagh smiled. "I saw that you almost burst out laughing."

"Forgive me, but the look on your face was very comical," he said, stifling a giggle.

"Well, go ahead," she said, "you can laugh now."

"No," he said, "I couldn't." He sat with a stony expression which only lasted a moment before the hint of a grin snuck out from the corners of his mouth. Kropotkin tried to suppress it, but that only served to force his lips apart. He struggled for another moment and then burst forth with uproarious laughter. "I'm sorry," he gasped between guffaws, "but it was very funny."

Clodagh tried to adopt a severe expression, but this, too, was futile. His laughter, the first she had ever heard from the world leader, was infectious. Soon, she was laughing nearly as hard.

"Stop, stop," he begged, grabbing his sides with mirth. "We're steaming up the windows."

"With that and the way you're jiggling the truck if that couple comes out," laughed Clodagh, "they'll think we're doing something else."

"Da! Da!" agreed Kropotkin wiping the tears from his eyes. "I haven't enjoyed a stew so much in all my life."

Clodagh reached around and pulled on the back of her long skirt. "I think there's still some left."

Kropotkin broke into fresh gales of laughter, and Clodagh quickly joined him for another round.

After a few minutes, Kropotkin started to calm down, taking deep breaths. "Oh, that was enjoyable. I haven't laughed like that since... I can't recall when."

He looked at Clodagh and smiled.

"You know," she said, "that's the first time I've seen you smile."

He shrugged. "World leaders are not afforded many occasions to smile, let alone laugh."

"Don't apologize," said Clodagh. "It's very becoming. It opens a whole dimension of your personality. It's quite... attractive."

Kropotkin gazed into her eyes, and for a moment, she detected a spark she hadn't seen before. They slowly started leaning toward each other until Kropotkin caught himself.

"Oh, and I must offer my sincere apologies," he said.

"What for? You've already apologized for dropping me in the stew and then laughing about it."

He shook his head and blustered in his old way. "No, no, I must apologize for when we were back in the kitchen. I, I kissed you..."

Clodagh looked into his eyes. "No, you kissed Natasha, Boris."

They stared at each other.

"Da, yes, that is correct," he said. "Boris kissed Natasha." He looked down for a moment. When he raised his head again, the severe look was gone, and a small boyish smile appeared. "But would an apology be in order if Nikolai kissed Clodagh?"

Clodagh smiled. "Nikolai will have to try it and find out."

He leaned over and kissed her. Then she kissed him. Then they both kissed. In the middle of the fourth round, she smiled and pushed him away.

"What? What?" he asked.

"You big phony politician," she laughed. "You knew all along my right name! Clott Clodagh! And I believed you!"

He grinned and shrugged.

"Okay," she said, pulling him back toward her, "you can apologize for that one later, Boris!"

– 34 –
Lorraine on
the Half Shell

The lights were blinding. Lorraine Innis had been subject to the illumination of television studios before, but her first encounter with a full-blown film studio was quite overwhelming. Her outfit didn't help, either.

"Is this really appropriate?" Asked Lorraine as she hobbled onto the set.

"Oh, no, lovey," said the director, a tall pre-maturely bald man. "It's all wrong! We were going for something a little bit more daring. He turned to an assistant. "Baz, who put her in that tube top covered with scales? What happened to the seashells?"

An even taller man, the wardrobe designer, rushed to the director's side. "She wouldn't wear them, Chas."

Chas, the director, stared at Lorraine's chest as if she were a mannequin. "Too big, too small?"

"Umm, no," said Baz, cupping his hands inches from Lorraine's breasts, "just right."

"Then what is our problem?"

"Excuse me," said Lorraine, "it's not *his* problem or *your* problem, or even *our* problem. It's *my* problem."

Both Chas and Baz stood mouth agape, surprised that a prop had suddenly been given the power of speech.

"Oh, sorry, lovey," said Chas. "We can fix that. A bit chafing, were they? They really don't make those shells for comfort. Baz can fix it. He's a wizard with costumes. You should be honored. He's been the costume designer on some of the biggest films here. He's been nominated for awards here and in Hollywood. He's an absolute treasure. He'll make it right." Chas turned to his wardrobe designer. "What do you think it was, Baz? Rubbing the nipples the wrong way? See if you can get our girl some pasties." He turned back to Lorraine in a condescending tone. "Don't worry your little head, lovey. Baz will take care of the sensitivity in that area. He designed his very own pasties for that delicate locale. Nothing like the uncouth stickers that strippers wore. He's covered up the nips... uh, that is the biggest areolas in the business, I mean the areolas of some of the biggest stars. We don't want to be uncomfy, do we?"

"We? I seem to be the only one here who isn't 'comfy.' And if Baz or anyone comes near my areo... my chest," said Lorraine, "I promise they won't be comfy for several months and in an even more sensitive area."

Baz threw up his hands, turned, and walked away.

A worried look clouded the director's expression until he forced a smile. He snapped his fingers. A young woman materialized with a chair that she placed behind Lorraine. The director gently urged her to sit. Since she could only take two-inch steps, Lorraine gratefully plopped down in the chair.

"Don't worry, lovey," assured the director. "We'll make sure you're comfortable."

Lorraine glowered at him. "Really? Let's start by getting rid of this ridiculous skirt. My knees are crammed against each other, and I can hardly walk."

"You don't have to walk," said Chas. "All you have to do is..." He lifted his arms slowly over his head. "...rise."

"Rise? I can't even stand up," said Lorraine.

"You'll already be standing," said the director. "I was told to keep this a secret. We want it to be a surprise. But the shooting will start in a few minutes."

"Good, I'll take a double-barreled shotgun."

Chas paused, not sure if Lorraine was serious. Then he forced out a nervous titter. "Oh, yes, quite droll. You Americans and your guns. No, I mean we'll be filming. You haven't seen the script."

"Just my lines," said Lorraine. "I have no idea what paper products have to do with mermaids."

The director crouched down beside Lorraine, nearly cheek to cheek, and pointed off toward the horizon. "Picture this, lovey; it's by the seaside. The dawn is breaking..."

"And I hobble out of the water, a mermaid looking for a toilet roll?" Lorraine snorted.

"*Passe! Passe, mon Cherie,*" said Chas. "No, you rise!"

"You've said that before," noted Lorraine. "I rise out of the water?"

"No, that's the best part," said the director, filled with awe. He stood up and shouted across to a darkened area of the soundstage. "Okay, up with the lights! There! There!"

At the far end of the stage, on a raised platform, was a backdrop of a beach, the sky filled with azure blues and coral pinks.

"There's your beach, and then..." Chas waved his arms, and one of his assistants muttered into a walkie-talkie.

Slowly, something began to rise from the water's edge. At first, she couldn't quite identify it. It looked like a flat stage until it continued to rise and started to taper. Lorraine's mouth dropped open. It was a giant toilet bowl.

"It's a big toilet!" screeched Lorraine.

"Not just a big toilet," said Chas admiringly, "the biggest! The biggest in the world. We've built the world's biggest khazi!"

"And you expect me to stand next to that?"

Chas' face was transfixed with directorial wonder. "No, wait until you see the best part!" He shouted across the stage: "Cue the lid!"

On the director's command, the top of the lid raised slowly. Then a head, followed by shoulders, arms, torso, and legs, of a stagehand emerged as he rose from inside the bowl on an elevated platform. With the lid fully raised, Lorraine could see it was in the shape of a seashell.

"I don't believe it," said Lorraine.

"It is awe-inspiring," agreed Chas.

"Awe-inspiring? It's just awful!"

The director seemed genuinely surprised at Lorraine's reaction. "No, you don't understand. That's just one of the grips. He won't be there when we film."

Lorraine didn't think Lord Bagnold would build a fifty-foot-tall toilet bowl and adorn it with a fat guy in overalls. She gritted her teeth against what she knew was coming next but didn't dare say.

"No, lovey," said Chas, "that will be you. You'll be rising. Just like I promised."

"Sounds more like a threat," muttered Lorraine.

The director ignored her, transfixed by his dubious artistic vision. "The, uh, the convenience rises from the sea, and then the lid slowly lifts, and you rise gloriously!"

"Out of a toilet."

"No, no, well, yes, if you like, but don't you understand, it's really very artistic, it's classic."

"Really?" said Lorraine.

"Of course," he said, "it's that famous painting."

Lorraine stared at him. "Which one would that be? Portrait of a Middle-Aged Woman in the Loo?"

"No, Venus in the Sea Shell, you know, by Michaelangelo."

"It's *Birth of Venus*, by Botticelli," said Lorraine.

"If you like," said Chas dismissively, "but you're Venus, and that's your giant sea shell."

Lorraine sighed and pointed at her legs, encased in sequined fins. "Venus wasn't a mermaid. She emerged naked."

Chas patted Lorraine's shoulder. "I appreciate your dedication to authenticity, lovey, but we'd never get full-frontal past the censors. Toilet paper is a family product, and we want this to air at all hours and all over the world."

"I wasn't offering to do this in the nude; I was just..."

"THAT'S INCREDIBLE! THAT'S WOT THAT IS! THERE H'AIN'T NOT NEVER BEEN ANYTHING LIKE IT! WORTH H'EVERY PENNY!"

Lorraine's explanation was cut off by the bellowing of a boisterous, grammatically disastrous voice. Thankfully, that voice could only emanate from one person. Unfortunately, it meant that he had arrived. She turned to see Lord Bagnold striding across the soundstage up to the giant toilet.

"It's inspiring," he cried, embracing the base. "Look at it. All you's people, I assume you is all working for me. Stop, and just look at this magnificent Oedipus!"

The various hands and technicians stopped and dutifully gazed at Lord Bagnold's giant toilet. There was little appreciation for it since they'd not only been working with it all week, but they had built the darned thing.

"It brings a tear to me eye," said Lord Bagnold, "Damn, to both of me eyes!" He paused to take in the magnificent scene and then realized he was paying a crew of seventy people to stand around staring. "OKAY, H'ART H'APPRECIATION IS OVER! GET BACK TO WORK!"

The crew gave a group shrug and then returned to what they had been doing before their visual potty break.

His Lordship walked toward Lorraine and the director. "They can look at it later on their own time," he muttered.

"Another perk of the job," said Lorraine.

Lord Bagnold squinted at her, not sure if she was being sarcastic. He shook off the comment.

"All set?" Bagnold asked his director. He glanced at Lorraine and then turned to his director. "Wot, no shells?" He pointed to his own chest and then cocked his head in her direction. "Wot's the matter? Is she too big and the shells too small? We can get bigger clams. Or is she too little?"

"*She* is perfectly proportioned," said Lorraine, "and *she* is standing right here. I'm not deaf, and I'm not a mannequin."

His Lordship rolled his eyes, gritted his teeth, and then turned to face her.

"Oh, pardon me," he said, "I did not sees you there, Mrs. Innis. Well, I mean to say, I saws you, but I did not know you were paying h'attention. I thoughts maybe you was studying your lines, mentally like, in your 'ead, so to speak."

"No, I'm here," said Lorraine, "unfortunately."

Bagnold laughed nervously. "Of course, you is, of course." Then he turned to Chas and spoke out of the corner of his mouth. "So, wot happened to the shells?"

Lorraine grabbed him by the shoulder and turned him around. "I'm still here." He looked at her and then looked down at her boobs. "And I'm up here," snapped Lorraine.

"Uh, yes, haw, I knows that," he blustered. "But you is not wearing the costume wot the costume boffin designed for you, based on me own instructions."

"So," said Lorraine, "this is your idea. I should have known. I thought you wanted to sell your paper products, not just get a cheap look at my cleavage."

Lord Bagnold shrugged. "We can do both."

"What?!"

"I means to say," he continued, "one don't not necessarily negate the other. It's wot we calls multi-level marketing."

"Well, let's keep the levels here and here," said Lorraine, pointing to her mouth and her eyes. "And not here," she pointed at her breasts."

"I was not thinking of those, not no 'ow," said Bagnold. "Why would you thinks that?"

Lorraine could feel the blood rushing to her cheeks. She took a deep breath. "I would 'thinks' that because of your track record with women and the dubious, ham-fisted attempts you've made in the past where women are concerned. I know what you've done to... well, women."

Lord Bagnold tilted his head to one side. "'Ow does you know about me and women. You talks like you've got some personal experience. You're a Yank, h'ain't you? I don't not sell in America... not yet. 'Ow would you know?"

Realizing she may have said too much, Lorraine went on the offensive. "How? Uh, how would I know? Of course, I'm an American, but... well, I'm a woman, aren't I? And I've got a brain. I can figure it out. Why else would you need me to try and pedal your toilet paper if you had any sort of rapport with the average woman? And I'm a woman."

"I knows it! Why do you think I wanted you to 'ave them shells? You can't go around bouncing your assets on TV. You is taking this all too personally, you silly cow!"

"Cow?"

Bagnold turned to his director and jerked his thumb at Lorraine. "All the sames, they is. Got one at 'ome like this. Touchy as a stick of dynamite on a block of jelly! If I didn't not knows better, I'd think it was me daughter. Haw!"

Lorraine clenched her fingers into a fist and drew back her arm. "You're asking for it. Have you ever got a bovine punch up the snoot?"

Lorraine swung her arm toward Lord Bagnold's head, but at the last minute, she heard a voice.

"Miss Lorraine, they said I'd find you here..."

Distracted, she turned just enough to miss His Lordship and delivered a haymaker to the speaker's jaw. He fell to the ground like a sack of black puddings.

Lorraine looked down. There lay Purvis Twankey, out cold.

She sighed. "Oh, dear!"

Lord Bagnold, realizing he just dodged a fist, stepped back several yards.

"I shot a boxing picture once," said Chas looking down at the recumbent Twankey. "You could have been a technical consultant."

"I really haven't done that very often," she said. "Unfortunately, every time I do, he's on the receiving end."

– 35 –
A Modest Breakfast

The first rays of sunlight danced upon Valerie Fierro's eyelids. She resisted opening them. She wanted a few more moments in luxury, comfortably ensconced in the suite of one of London's finest hotels. Valerie plumped up the feather pillow, propped herself up to a half-sitting position, and reached for the phone.

"Yes, this is Miss Potts in the Dorset Suite," she said as she fingered the design on her silk nightgown. "Please send up my usual. Thank you."

She hung up the phone and enjoyed a long, languid sigh. Then she giggled. Miss Potts! Valerie couldn't very well call herself Miss Fierro. She wasn't just an international celebrity; she was an international celebrity in hiding. Potts was a good, non-descript name, and since Chesney currently wasn't using it, she doubted if he'd mind her borrowing it for a little while.

Valerie had to keep reminding herself that all this was thanks to the generosity of Albrecht Eckner. It was amazing that the odious cretin, who had been a thorn in her side since high school, had finally matured into a decent human being. No, he wasn't just a decent human being; Albrecht was her greatest help and comfort, and not just for the loan of a luxury hotel suite. Everyone else had abandoned or double-crossed Valerie. Where would she be without Albrecht? He had gone from being a thorn to a genuine rose.

There was a knock at the door. Probably room service with her breakfast. Valerie put on her dressing gown and went to the door.

"Oh, it's you," said Valerie. Albrecht had returned from Gibraltar.

Seeing her in her dressing gown, Albrecht covered his eyes and looked away. "Sorry, I didn't know you wouldn't be dressed. I just got in from Gibraltar and didn't realize the time."

Valerie smiled. The boy who had once climbed trees to take pictures of her in her bedroom was now considering her modesty. What a change had taken place.

"Don't be silly," said Valerie. "I've got my robe on. Come in; I've ordered breakfast."

"Oh, no thanks, I've eaten," he said, entering the suite but still diverting her eyes. "I wouldn't want to take your breakfast."

"You're paying for it," she reminded him.

"Oh, it's nothing, really," he said. "It's the least I can do for an old friend."

"That's very sweet," she said. Valerie asked him to sit down and then started to take a seat.

"Aren't you going to get dressed?" said Albrecht standing. "You don't want room service to see you entertaining a male visitor in your nightgown."

"Okay, okay," laughed Valerie. "That's very considerate. I haven't been shown so much chivalry since the days of Chesney Potts."

Albrecht looked at her and nodded. "You deserve chivalry. You're a fine lady. And if I seem to be going overboard with it, I'm just trying to make amends for the shameless way I behaved in the past. I often made fun of Chesney Potts, but that was wrong, too. He may have been a bit too gushing, but he was a decent guy, and he knew how to treat a lady. If I ever meet him again, I'll apologize and tell him so, too."

For a second, Valerie considered telling Albrecht where Chesney was now but decided against it. It would probably lead to hours of Albrecht asking about Lorraine Innis. Valerie was having too good a time to bring up boring Lorraine. Instead, she just shrugged. "I doubt we'd run into Chesney in London."

She excused herself and went into the bedroom to get dressed. By the time Valerie emerged, her breakfast had arrived. Albrecht had set it out on the table for her.

"Please sit down," said Albrecht. "Enjoy your breakfast. I have something I wanted to discuss with you."

Valerie thanked him, sat down, and proceeded to spread marmalade over a piece of toast.

"I'm starting to hear some buzz in Gibraltar," he said.

"Don't tell me they have bees to go along with those stupid apes," joked Valerie.

Albrecht flashed a brief smile, then his expression turned serious. "Sorry, but this isn't really a laughing matter. It's about you."

"Me? What could they be saying about me on that big rock?"

"It's coming from the States," he explained. "I see all the communication that goes back and forth on the private server. Specifically, the private messages from Robert Valvano."

"Oh?" said Valerie chewing a bit of toast. "I wouldn't think that he would confide in you. He barely trusts his lawyer, Mr. Rosen."

Albrecht lowered his head. "Well, yes, I have more access than Mr. Valvano knows. In my more disreputable days, I stumbled on his passwords."

"Stumbled? How?"

"Okay," admitted Albrecht, "I stole them. I would have destroyed them, and almost did, until your name started cropping up."

Valerie took a sip of coffee and urged him to continue.

"It seems Robert Valvano is obsessed with you and not in a good way. He's asking all his known contacts concerning your whereabouts. He's also trying to find his brother."

"Michael?" Valerie almost spit out her coffee.

Albrecht Eckner nodded. "His brother is missing, or at least unreachable at the moment. He's in Italy or somewhere around there."

"What could he be doing in Italy?" asked Valerie.

"I have no idea," he said. "But that's not important. Robert Valvano is trying to find you."

Valerie nodded. "That's why I can't be seen in public or even use my credit cards. I would have been up shit's creek if I hadn't found you."

Albrecht smiled. "What are friends for? It's the least I can do. Fortunately for you, Robert let his paranoia get ahead of his sense of security. I've read between the lines in the messages, and it seems like he's worried that you might be a rightful member of their family."

Valerie stared at him as she chewed her toast, debating whether she could trust Albrecht with what he already suspected. How could she not? After all she was his guest. He had already done so much for her without asking for anything in return.

"Well," said Valerie after a sip of coffee, "he thinks I'm a member of their family because I am."

Albrecht Eckner sat with his mouth agape. "Really?"

"Apparently so," she said. Valerie related her history with Michael Valvano and how it all fell apart when she met their mutual grandmother.

"And the old lady," concluded Valerie, "wanted to make me the head of the family business, but she died before she could fix it."

Albrecht sat back in his chair. "Wow, well, that explains everything," he said. "It explains why he's paranoid because he should be."

Valerie wiped her mouth on the linen napkin and dropped it on the table. "A fat lot of good it does me. He's holding all the cards, and I don't have a legal leg to stand on. Robert Valvano is sitting there in America enjoying life while I'm hiding out in a crumby London hotel." She glanced at Albrecht, who was looking down sorrowfully. "I didn't mean it that way, Albrecht. I'm very grateful for your help. Before we found each other, I was roaming around England in a teardrop trailer stealing bowties to keep going."

He looked up with a puzzled expression. "Bowties?"

"It's a long story," she said. "I met this loser who promised to bring me to London, only he didn't, so I figured out my own way back here."

Albrecht smiled. "You always were a very resourceful girl, sorry, woman."

Valerie smiled inwardly. The old Albrecht Eckner wouldn't have corrected himself like that. He would have left it at "girl" and probably slapped her on the butt. The new Albrecht was sitting there with his hands folded in his lap.

"Yes," sighed Valerie, "well, I think my resources have finally run out. Here I am relying on your generosity while my rightful place is at the head of the Valvano family. Robert's got all the money and the lawyer."

"What about Michael Valvano?" he asked.

Valerie snorted derisively. "That wimp. He's nowhere to be seen. He dumped me the moment he thought we might be cousins."

"So he believes you're related," nodded Albrecht, "but his brother doesn't."

"Ha! That's an act," she said. "Mr. Robert Valvano believes it more than his spineless brother. Robert is terrified of me. If he wasn't, he wouldn't have tried framing me for the hit on Lorraine."

"And where's your other cousin?"

"Who?"

"Your cousin Lorraine," said Albrecht. "I've read that she's in London, all that trial stuff with those poor women with the beards."

Valerie studied his face. In the past, Albrecht would have had a wonderful time making fun of the afflictions of others.

"And then Lorraine just disappeared for days," he continued, "and now she's emerged again.'

"Yeah, well," said Valerie, "Lorraine's got her own problems, believe me. There's a lot about Lorraine Innis that nobody knows but me."

Valerie paused. She expected Albrecht to start digging for dirt on Lorraine. He never let such an opening go unexplored before. She looked up at him. He was sitting there passively. If this were a cartoon, a halo would have popped up above his head.

"Don't you want to know?" she finally asked.

"About what?"

"About Lorraine."

Albrecht sat there for a moment and then shook his head. "Not if you don't want to tell me. I wouldn't want you to betray a confidence."

Valerie stared at him for a good minute.

"Alright, Albrecht," she snapped, "cut the crap."

"Pardon?"

"Look," she said, "I've known you too long and too well. When did you ever let a secret that seemed even halfway juicy go unsqueezed?"

Albrecht looked at her. Valerie waited a moment to see those piggy eyes squint revealing the old Albrecht, but they didn't. Instead, after a moment, a small, almost imperceptible tear appeared in the corner of his eye. He blinked and turned away.

"Sorry, sorry," he said. When Albrecht turned back, the track of a tear was on his face. He quickly wiped it away. "Again, I don't blame you. I've done horrible things, most of all to you. I don't want to pry into your secrets, well, because I have some of my own. Maybe someday, I'll share them with you when the wounds are a little less raw. When I was little, I remember my father telling me about a bully in his school. He said the best thing that could have happened to that kid was a bigger bully beating him up. Of course, at the time, I didn't think I was a bully. I wasn't, maybe not physically, but I was something worse. I was a psychological bully. And my father was right. The surest way to straighten out bullies is to have them victimized by someone worse than they are. Well, Valerie, if you can believe it, I met someone worse than me, and as big a rat as I was, she was an even bigger one. She sure taught me a lesson."

Albrecht started crying and hunched over, ashamed of his tears. Valerie could never stand to see a man cry. She got up, sat next to him on the sofa and put her arm around him. Albrecht Eckner, the most despicable person she'd ever known, turned and buried his head in her shoulder.

As he blubbered, half-spoken sentences emerged. Words like "sorry" and "ashamed" were muttered into her breast. Something maternal sprang up inside her. Valerie stroked his hair and assured Albrecht Eckner, detestable Albrecht Eckner, that everything would be okay.

– 36 –
Egmont and the Colonic Enema

Patsy Einfalt surveyed the conference table and sighed. It was filled. One side was piled high with business ledgers and the other with bridal catalogs and fabric samples. Fortunately, the table was built from sturdy oak. A lesser table would have given way under the weight.

With these two sides competing for her attention, Patsy would scurry between them. She was trying to organize the books, not only for the charity but also for the bank, in anticipation of the government auditor's arrival. The man had called a few days before announcing a snap inspection. Patsy hadn't understood if his primary interest was examining the charity or the bank. But since they were so closely connected and Patsy had first-hand knowledge of both, she gathered as much information as possible.

The other side of the table was similarly crammed but with bridal paraphernalia. Patsy's wedding consultant was calling. She felt silly having to consult a consultant, but then she figured that's what consultants did best... consult. Growing up, Patsy had always assumed that she and her mother would plan their wedding. But given that she was marrying a singing star like Purvis Twankey and celebrities like Lorraine Innis would be attending, Patsy's mother insisted that they get the services of a professional.

She had already booked the consultant's appointment when the auditor called, announcing an upcoming visit. He wouldn't say when, but from her years in the financial services industry, Patsy knew government auditors were like tornados. They blew in with little or no warning, so it was best to be ready for them. Unlike a twister, however, auditors stayed a lot longer and could be almost as disruptive.

"Well," said Patsy, standing at mid-table, "I'm ready for either of you, I think. I just hope you don't get here at the same time. With Mr. Valvano gone, Lorraine in England, and Valerie... somewhere... I'm the only one left."

She looked out the window toward the east. "Purvis should be in England now. I wish he was here, but..."

Her pondering was disturbed by a knock on the door. She hoped it was the wedding consultant. The door opened, and a man stuck his head in.

"Ms. Einfalt?"

Patsy smiled. "Yes, that's me. Uh, you wouldn't be Madame Fontana, would you? I don't mean that you're a lady. You're obviously not a lady. I mean, you have a mustache. That's not to say a lady can't have a mustache. If you knew my Aunt Mable... Sorry, I meant to ask if you worked for Madame Fontana."

"Madame Fontana?"

"She's the wedding consultant," said Patsy. "Of course, if you knew her, it would mean that you worked for her. But, then, you could know of her without working for her. I mean, I know her, and I don't work for her." Patsy stopped. The man just stared at her. Patsy felt the need to add: "I work here."

The man kept staring at her, and finally, he pulled out a badge. "I don't know of, nor do I work for Madame Fontana. And to the best of my recollection, I have never known or worked for Madame Fontana. I add that disclaimer because my memory is not entirely trustworthy. I work for the federal government. I believe you were notified to expect me."

Patsy blinked several times. "Oh, yes, we, that is I, that is us, we got the call that you were coming. We just didn't know when to expect you."

The man set his briefcase down on the credenza and opened it. "Yes, that is the usual procedure. We like to provide enough notification so that our subjects can get their records together, but not enough for them to..."

"Change them?"

The man grinned, though not at all in amusement. "Yes, something like that. I see you have started to compile your books." He nodded toward the stack on the conference table.

"Oh, yes," said Patsy, "this is our compiling pile. That's what most of it is. I mean, these are the requested documents," she pointed to the other pile, "but these aren't. These are personal, and they're for...."

"Madame Fontana?"

Patsy giggled. "Yes, I can see why you work for the government. You're very clever."

"Thank you," said the man, "your federal government aims to provide maximum value to the taxpayers by hiring the most clever men and women available."

"That's comforting to know, I suppose," said Patsy, her voice quivering.

"Please, Ms. Einfalt," said the man, "I'm from the government, and I'm only here to help."

"Oh, that's a relief," said Patsy. "I think..."

"Yes, we can assist an organization in many ways," he said. "We can assist by rooting out errors or even violations of the regulations. And in the most severe cases, we identify criminals embedded in organizations and prosecute them to the full extent of the law."

"Oh," said Patsy. She bit her fingernail.

"Please, don't be anxious," said the agent. "Think of your charity and your bank as a giant colon, and I'm here like a colonic enema to make sure everything is neat and healthy. Now, doesn't that assuage your anxiety?"

"I guess," said Patsy. "I suppose it feels better when it's all done."

"Like a perfectly cleansed bowel."

"Oh, yes, well, thank you, Mr... I'm sorry, I've forgotten your name."

The man's expression grew even more serious. "No, I haven't introduced myself. Please, can we sit down?"

"Oh, sorry, please sit. Would you like some coffee or tea?"

The agent sat in one of the swivel chairs around the table. "No, thank you, I have to discuss something with you of a very personal nature. This is very difficult, I don't like mixing business with personal matters, but I must do so. In fact, this is the culmination of years of preparation on my part. Please, sit, and wait a moment."

The man pulled a notepad from his briefcase, pulled a pen from his breast pocket, and looked at his watch. Then he jotted down a notation and put away the pen.

"There," he said, "I'm officially off the clock. I'm on personal time now. As I said, I'm loath to mix my personal business with my official duties. It's not fair to the trust the public places in its government servants."

"That's very admirable," said Patsy.

"I treat all aspects of my life - business and private - as a sacred trust," he said. "I take both with the seriousness warranted. And now that I'm on personal time, I can tell you about something that happened to me and another person several years ago in this very city and this very building."

"Really?" she asked. "You've been here before?"

"Yes, I have," he said. "Though my memory is sketchy."

Patsy studied his face. It was average, even pleasant, though that was hard to tell behind the serious expression he now wore. "Have we met?"

The man looked at her intently for a moment before nodding. "Yes, we have."

She scrutinized his face more closely, tilting her head at various angles, then shook her head. "No, I'm sorry, I don't recall. I usually have a good head for faces. That's important for a secretary. We're good with faces. I'm even better with names, Mr..."

The man looked down, bit his lip, and then looked up. "Einfalt, Egmont Einfalt."

Patsy smiled. "What a funny coincidence. That's my name, too!"

"Yes, I know."

"Just the Einfalt, not the Egmont," she said. "Well, it is a small world. You're the first person I ever met with that last name."

"The very first?"

She laughed. "It really isn't a very common name. You're the first, oh, wait, aside from…"

Patsy froze in mid-chuckle. Her mouth remained open, but her smile lines faded. Her mind raced, and though the course was short, it still took a full minute. "The Christmas party…" she whispered.

He nodded. "You remember what I was wearing."

"Santa Claus," Patsy continued, "you were Santa Claus. You were the Santa Claus hired for the party."

"Yes, you remember," said Einfalt. "And you remember what happened?"

"We went to the copier room. We made love on the copier. I had never done it before. You were my first."

Einfalt lowered his eyes. "You… you were my first, too."

"I had my braces…"

He looked at her face. "Your teeth are nice and straight now."

A puzzled look clouded her expression. "No, it wasn't my teeth."

"What? No, of course, I was just noticing what a pretty smile you have. It wasn't your teeth with the braces. It was…"

"My back," she added, "and I still had my boot on."

"Yes, your back, but just one boot," he was quick to add.

"I only broke one foot…"

"Yes, that's what I mean," he said.

A suspicious look, quite out of place for Patsy, crossed her face. "What else do you remember?"

Mr. Einfalt shook his head. "I have to confess, it's still a little hazy. I've been through a terrible ordeal since that night. Do you remember how I left you?"

"We finished making love," she said. "I was a little tipsy, well, very tipsy. And you put on your clothes…"

"Yes, I remember," he said, "the Santa Claus suit. It's coming back. Then what happened?"

"You started out the door," Patsy continued, "and I asked your name. And then you looked at me and said…"

"Einfalt."

"Yes, that's right," she said. "And that's the last I saw you until today."

"I remember," said Mr. Einfalt, snapping his fingers. "What a relief."

"Is it?"

"It's the last bit to the puzzle," he said. "It's all coming back clearly now. I was wearing the Santa Claus suit…"

"And the beard," added Patsy.

"Yes, and the beard. And we made love on the copier. Then I left, but before I did, you asked me my name, and I said 'Einfalt.' Because that's my name. Oh, it's all so clear. You don't know what a relief it is to find you. And what a coincidence that you and I have the same last name."

"Zyobidinski?" she asked.

"Zyobidinski? No, Einfalt."

Patsy shook her head. "No, I changed my name."

"We didn't get married," he said.

"No," she said, "but I thought it best."

"Thank you for your trust," said Mr. Einfalt. "If I had known, I would have been here even sooner," Einfalt stopped. "No, wait, I couldn't have been here sooner, even if I tried. I've spent years trying to find you."

"You have?" said Patsy. Again a wary look returned to her face. "Exactly where were you?"

He sighed. "After we made love, I knew I wanted to marry you. So, I went out to buy an engagement ring. It was night. It was night, right?"

"Yes, it was night," she said. "Don't you recall?"

"I thought it was night, either that or a total eclipse. As I said, my memory was hazy. I ran through the streets looking for a jewelry store. And I finally found one. They weren't too anxious to help me, dressed like Santa Claus, but I got their most expensive diamond ring they had. Nothing but the best for you."

"Wow! Can I see it?"

He shook his head. "No, that's when my trouble started. I was leaving the jewelry store. It was still dark. And a man stopped me and asked the time. When I went to look at my watch, he hit me on the head and stole it."

"He stole your watch?"

"That, too. He stole my watch, the ring, and my wallet."

"How horrible," said Patsy. "What kind of world is it when they steal from Santa Claus and right before Christmas?"

Einfalt shook his head mournfully. "They stole something far more valuable from me than those trifling items."

Patsy gasped. "They stole your pants?"

He reached out and took her hand in his. "No, dear Patsy; they stole my future, my love, they stole you."

Patsy's mouth dropped open.

"You see, sweet Patsy Einfalt, when I was struck on the head, I lost my memory. When I woke up in the hospital, I could only remember your face, the ring, and something about a bank."

"You didn't even know who you were?" she asked. "Where did you go? What did you do?"

He stood and crossed to the window. "Where do you go when you don't know who you are?"

Patsy shrugged. "I don't know. I've always known me."

Einfalt turned and offered her a wry smile. "Then you are greatly blessed, dear Patsy. They kept me in the hospital for a year, in the psychiatric ward, trying every exercise to jog my memory."

"Jogging is good exercise," she agreed.

"For the longest time, all I could recall was your face and the vague notion that you had some connection to a bank. My therapist would take me on field trips to banks, hoping something would help me remember. Finally, they traced my name from a stray hair of the Santa Claus beard I had been wearing. It was a particularly good false beard. They found the costume shop where I had bought it. The shop had a receipt with my name on it."

"And then you knew who you were," said Patsy. "That helps. That's why whenever I call someone on the phone, I say, 'This is Patsy.' That way, we'll both know who I am."

"Very wise, darling Patsy," he agreed. "Yes, I knew my name. I still didn't know why all I could think about was this girl's face, your face, and a ring, and banks. I tried to go back to my old job: professional Santa Claus, and although I was very good at it, it held no joy for me. I knew I wouldn't be complete until I found the missing pieces to the puzzle. I would have to change careers."

"So, you got a job in a bank?"

"That was my first inclination," he said. "But I realized that if I went to work in a bank and it wasn't the bank you were working in, that would be pointless. Then I asked myself, what job allows you to go to many different banks?"

Patsy thought a moment. "Well, I suppose a bank robber would see a lot of different banks, but then he'd also see a lot of prisons."

Einfalt stared at her for a moment. "What? Oh, right, yes, good thinking, and I reached the same conclusion. But I knew you worked in an office, so I thought about it and finally realized the solution."

Patsy leaned forward. "Yes? What did you figure out?"

He stared at her again. He seemed to do a lot of staring. Then he lifted his briefcase. "Bank examiner."

Patsy slapped the side of her head. "Of course, and it must have worked because that's what you are."

"It wasn't easy," he explained. "You can't just walk into a building in Washington and announce you'd like to examine banks. Turns out I had to go back to school and get all kinds of special degrees before they would hire me. It took years. But all through that time, while going to school and going from bank to bank, my memory slowly started to return."

Patsy stopped and studied him for a long moment. Finally, she nodded. "Yes, it could happen."

Mr. Einfalt seemed relieved for some reason.

"But it was all worth it," he said, "because now I found you."

"Here I am," she grinned.

"Can you forgive me," he asked. "I didn't mean to leave you."

She patted his hand. "I can see that. It wasn't your fault that you got robbed, lost your memory, were put in a psychiatric hospital, went back to school, and had to start a new career."

"I'm glad you understand," he said. "It took me years, but I can finally finish what I set out to do." Einfalt reached into his pocket and pulled out a small box. He opened it. Inside was a diamond ring. He took Patsy's hand and started to slide the ring on her finger. Then he stopped when he noticed another ring was already there.

Einfalt's face, which a moment before had been bright and joyful, suddenly sank. "Oh!"

Patsy looked down at the diamond traffic jam on her finger. "Wait," she said, "are you..."

"Asking you to marry me?" he said, his voice quivering. "I suppose I was."

"Oh, this is a problem," she said. "I'm already going to be married in a few months." She pointed at the bridal catalogs on the table. "See?"

"Couldn't you marry me instead?" he asked.

"But I hardly know you."

"Yes, but you've already taken my name," explained Einfalt. "You wouldn't even need to get new stationery."

"I didn't do that for you," she said, "I did that for my daughter."

He sat back in his chair as if he'd been shoved. "You have a daughter? Is she...." He paused and leaned forward.

"A girl?" asked Patsy. "Yes, she is."

"No, I mean, is she mine? That is, is she our daughter?"

"She would have to be. You're the only man I've ever loved," she said. "I mean, physically. I love lots of men, just not..."

"Don't say another word, my darling," he said as he dropped to one knee and took her hand. "This is a doubly joyful day. I've found you and discovered I have a little family too."

Patsy started to speak but was interrupted by a knock on the door.

A middle-aged woman entered carrying a large portfolio.

"Ms. Einfalt," said the woman, "I am Madame Fontana." She stopped and saw Einfalt on one knee. "Oh, and this must be your intended."

"I intended to be her intended," he said, standing.

"I'm always so pleased when I can consult with both halves of the happy couple," said Madame Fontana.

"Thank you," said Einfalt. "You can't know how happy I am." He looked at Patsy. "You're happy, aren't you, Patsy, dear?"

Patsy looked at him, then the wedding consultant, and finally at the pile of papers on the conference table.

"I'm just confused," she said.

- 37 -
The Purloined Pickle

"Purvis, are you okay?" Lorraine knelt beside Purvis Twankey as best she could, given the restrictions of her mermaid tail skirt. She patted his hand. "Purvis, please, wake up. Oh, dear, this seems to happen too often."

"Oo's this mug," asked Lord Bagnold, "some celery stalker?"

Lorraine glowered up at him. "He happens to be one of my dearest friends."

"If 'e's your friend, I hates to see 'ow you 'andled an h'enemy."

"Keep it up," muttered Lorraine, "and you'll get a first-hand demonstration."

"Wot?"

"Nothing," said Lorraine. "Can't someone get me some water?"

Purvis' eyelids began to flutter.

"I think he's coming to," said Chas, the director. "Who is he?"

"He's Purvis Twankey," said Lorraine.

"The singing star?" asked Chas.

Lorraine agreed.

"He looks different lying on the ground than he does standing on the telly," noted Chas.

"He's also the man who invented the *Quandry* perfume."

Lord Bagnold's eyebrow shot up. "Is 'e? No wonder you flattened 'im."

"That was an accident. I was aiming for someone else entirely," said Lorraine. "The perfume wasn't his fault. He's always coming up with novel ideas and wild inventions."

"Creative fellow, is 'e?" muttered Bagnold.

An assistant gave Chas a glass of water, who handed it to Lord Bagnold, who took a drink before realizing it was meant for the man on the floor.

"Oops, sorry," said Bagnold. "Force of 'abit. Peoples is always serving me. 'Orses for courses, you know."

His Lordship crouched down to hand the glass to Lorraine and lingered for a moment at her side. She turned, and he quickly stood up and put his hand in his pocket.

"The chap seems to be coming to," said Lord Bagnold. "I knows what. I'll go see if I can locates a first aid kit. Be right back."

"Purvis, Purvis," said Lorraine wetting his lips with the water, "wake up. It's me, Lorraine."

A wide goofy grin spread across Purvis' face, though his eyes remained closed.

"Purvis, can you hear me?"

"Not now, Patsy," he muttered, "I'm having the funniest dream. I was dreaming, and Miss Lorraine walloped me again."

Lorraine looked up at the studio crew and smiled sheepishly. "Like I said, we have a history. We really are good friends." She shook him by the shoulders. "Purvis, wake up!"

Purvis Twankey's eyes opened slowly as if he were stirring from an afternoon nap. He smacked his lips several times, then focused on Lorraine.

"Hi, Miss Lorraine," he said sleepily, "I was having the strangest dream. It really was daft. I dreamt I was telling Patsy that I was dreaming about you, and you gave me a right clobbering."

"Sorry, that was no dream, Purvis," she said. "I suppose I let my temper get the best of me. I raised my hand in anger. Unfortunately, I brought it down on the wrong target. It's my fault."

Lorraine helped him sit up. Purvis wiggled his jaw back and forth.

"Don't blame yourself, Miss Lorraine," he said with a grin. "I just got to get myself a stronger chin."

Lorraine took him by the hand and pulled Purvis to his feet.

"Eee, Miss Lorraine," said Purvis, "them's some mighty fine arm muscles you got there on your arms. I guess I never saw them before cause I never saw you bare, at least not your arms. I mean, I've nowt seen any parts of you bare except like your face… and your legs… oh, and your fists, of course, I mean, your hands."

Lorraine blushed as she folded her arms, trying to hide her more masculine biceps. "Yes, well, I don't like to show them off; they're not exactly ladylike."

"They're proper champion," he said. "Nothing wrong with a bit of tussle on a lady's muscle. You never know when you'll have to use it." He rubbed his jaw. "I guess you do know when."

"Again, forgive me, Purvis. I can assure you that I don't regularly knock people out."

"Aye," he grinned, "makes me feel extra special." Then he looked down. "But what are you made up for? They told me I'd find you here at this studio. You doing a movie about mermaids, or the ocean, or fish fingers?"

155

"It's a foolish costume for a foolish advertisement," she said.

"It h'aint not foolish," said a voice behind her. Lorraine turned to see Lord Bagnold coming back. "It's 'ighly h'artistic!"

Purvis looked around and did a double take at the sight of a forty-foot-high toilet. He grinned and said to Lorraine in an aside: "Ee, Miss Lorraine, I'd hate to be around when the fella who belongs to that needs to use it."

"I agree, Purvis," said Lorraine, leading him by the elbow away from Lord Bagnold. "I don't want to be near it for any reason. But what are you doing in England? Is Patsy with you?"

"No, she stayed back in the States. I'm just here to record, well, let's just call it a restitution tune."

Lorraine had no idea what a restitution tune was, but she didn't want to ask. Given Purvis Twankey's track record, she estimated the safest place for him was a recording studio. "Well, that sounds... interesting. It doesn't have anything to do with a new invention, does it?"

Purvis scratched his sandy mop of hair. "It couldn't," he said. "They's already invested the microphone and all kinds of recording stuff. But now that you mention it, I did have a dandy new idea."

"Oh," said Lorraine. She meant it more as a groan, but he apparently took it as an invitation for further explanation.

"I've got an idea that will solve the problem of world energy," he beamed.

Another "oh" was all Lorraine could manage.

"Aye, and it's simple," he said, "especially now that I super-charged me granddad's special fertilizer recipe for cucumbers."

Lorraine stared at him. Purvis smiled back, interpreting her confusion as awe.

"That's what I thought, too," said Purvis. "It was so obvious once it was clear!"

Lorraine shook her head. "Sorry, Purvis, I don't think I understand."

He grinned and nodded. "I felt the same way, Miss Lorraine, until it hit me, like that fella sitting under the tree who got hit by the apple."

"Sir Isaac Newton..."

"Aye, him with the figs, too," agreed Purvis. "'cept mine was a cucumber, actually a pickle, but then that's what they get pickles from. And I wasn't sitting under a tree, I was in the kitchen, and it didn't hit me on the head; I bit into it."

"Purvis, this is all getting more confusing," said Lorraine.

"Wait," he said, reaching into his jacket pocket, "I have it all written down." He stopped and started frantically searching all the pockets in his coat. "It's gone. I must have lost it. If I lost it, I don't know what I'd..."

A hand reached from behind them, holding a piece of paper.

"Excuse me," said Lord Bagnold, "did someone drop this?"

Purvis' face lit up.

"Aye! Me!"

They turned, and Lord Bagnold handed Purvis several sheets of loose leaf filled with scribbles.

"I saw it over there," said His Lordship. "There, on the ground, next to where you were knocked out by..." He nodded toward Lorraine.

"Thanks, Mister," said Purvis. "I'd have sooner lost my brains than lost this!"

"Don't mention it," smiled Lord Bagnold before turning to Lorraine. "Mrs. Innis, I just stopped in to see 'ow things were going. I'll leave you in the capable 'ands of Chas, 'ere. I'm sure 'e'll work out any little disagreement you 'ave about the commercial."

His Lordship flashed a hideously broad smile, bowed slightly, and walked away.

"Ee, but don't that fella have a thick accent," noted Purvis.

"Mmm," said Lorraine, "I can get past his accent. It's what's behind it that I find troubling."

– 38 –
The Truth About Lorruska

The rhythmic rumble of the old truck's engine had lulled her to sleep as they drove through the night. Now the morning light coaxed Clodagh Clott's eyelids to open. The first thing she noticed was that her arms were entwined around the strong right arm of the driver, Nikolai Kropotkin. She was also using his bicep as a pillow. As soon as her sleepy mind awoke to this fact, she sat up with a start.

"Oh! Sorry," said Clodagh sliding back to her side of the front seat.

"Good morning," said Kropotkin. He smiled. "You slept well? It sounded like you did."

"It did?" she asked self-consciously. "I wasn't snoring, was I?"

Kropotkin's smile widened. "A little."

"Oh, sorry, when you live alone, you don't know if you snore. I hope I didn't keep you awake."

He laughed. "You did not keep me awake, Clott Clodagh. I was very nicely occupied with driving the truck."

"Oh, yes, of course, how stupid of me. And it's Clodagh Clott. Oh, wait, you said last night you knew that. You were making a joke."

"Forgive me," said Kropotkin. "My jokes are not very good yet. I will have to work on them. But I do enjoy that little one. I hope you don't mind me calling you that."

Clodagh shrugged and waved her hand. "Phht! When you've got a last name like 'Clott,' it's best to get it over with as quickly as possible. So go ahead, knock yourself out. Oh, that's another American expression. It means enjoy yourself."

"Thank you, I shall knock myself out," he agreed, "in moderation, of course."

Clodagh smiled. While not exactly a joke, it was a dry witticism. She was starting to quite enjoy his company. Clodagh looked around at the countryside. They were on a straight road that ran through flat plains.

"Where are we?" she asked.

"We are almost at my birthplace," he said. "The town where I was born. We shall arrive in a few hours. But first, I must take care to get you some breakfast."

"Oh, yes, please," said Clodagh. She hadn't thought of it, but the mention of breakfast suddenly made her ravenous.

Fifteen minutes later, beside a roadside café, Kropotkin handed her a paper cup of coffee and a large crusty roll.

"I thought you would prefer eating in the truck," he said. "It would avoid any language difficulties."

After a sip of coffee and a bite of the roll, she replied with her mouthful. "Mmm, yes, that's fine. This is delicious, and the butter is wonderful."

"Da, this is an agricultural region," he noted. "That is all locally produced."

"I never knew you grew up on a farm," she said. Then Clodagh smirked. "Here I am talking like I've known you for years. Sorry."

Kropotkin swallowed a mouthful of coffee. "No need for apologies, Clott Clodagh. Being thrown together, or should I say 'tied together' in an adventure, often accelerates the feeling of..." He groped for a word.

"...intimacy," offered Clodagh, then winced inwardly at her choice of words.

He nodded. "Yes, that was the word I was thinking of, but I wasn't sure if you would... appreciate it."

They both studied their coffee cups. Both wished the other would address the subject first.

"President Kropotkin," began Clodagh, before correcting herself, "I mean Nikolai..."

"No, please, allow me," he interrupted. "I must apologize for my very rude behavior."

"You've been a perfect gentleman," she said.

"I meant when I first found with whom I was a prisoner."

"Oh, yes, well, you weren't quite yourself then," said Clodagh. "Neither of us was at our best."

"And I wasn't quite a gentleman last night," he said.

"You were perfect," she said with a smile.

He smiled without looking up. "I have enjoyed our time together, as well."

"I think," said Clodagh, "we're ignoring the two-ton elephant in the room."

Nikolai looked up with a confused expression.

"Lorraine," she clarified.

"I thought you were her friend," he said. "And you are of such a similar build to her that they kidnapped you…"

Clodagh raised her hand. "Whoa, that's just another American idiom. It means that we're avoiding what's obvious."

He nodded. "Da, Lorruska. As I said, you are much like her, but you are much more."

"Much less in other areas," said Clodagh under her breath.

"Pardon?"

"Skip it," she said, "I mean, never mind."

"When we are together," he said, "you make me laugh. Oh, Lorruska inspired me. She made me think in new ways. Those are wonderful things for a leader. But you, dear Clott Clodagh, have made me see there is more that a man needs."

He looked down again.

"But," said Clodagh, sensing a wall.

Nikolai looked into her eyes. "See, already you know my mind. You sense my needs. There is a hesitation in my heart. You are not its source. It is…"

Again he paused. Clodagh waited a moment before supplying the ending. "It's Lorraine."

He grimaced and nodded his head. "I have been so devoted, so single-minded towards Lorruska, that now I feel as if I am being unfaithful."

Clodagh took his hands in hers. "Nikolai… Nick… No one knows Lorraine better than I do."

"You have known her since she was a girl, yes?"

Clodagh started to open her mouth and stopped. She didn't want to give away Chesney's secret, especially not to a man with nuclear missiles. At the same time, she couldn't lie to Nikolai Kropotkin.

"I…" she paused. "I have known the person you call 'Lorruska,' since I was a little girl. I grew up with that person, and they are one of my closest friends."

"Then our relationship would cause a break in your friendship, too," he said. "I would not like that."

Clodagh looked away, bit her lip, and then an idea came to her.

"Nick," she said, looking at him, "you say you loved Lorraine, but how did she respond to you?"

He waved his head back and forth. "She was a wonderful friend. Always supportive. Always kind…"

"But romantically, did she ever give you any indication that she viewed you the same way?"

Kropotkin shook his head. "I tried to force myself on her once."

"You got carried away," she said.

"Da, on a stretcher," he admitted. "Lorruska pushed me off a wall into a snow bank."

Clodagh suppressed a giggle, then stroked his cheek. "Nick, I'm going to tell you a secret because I trust you. We haven't known each other very long, but I'm sure what I tell you won't go any further."

"I would not betray a confidence," he said.

"I'm sure of it," said Clodagh. "You're a wonderful man, but Lorraine would never be interested in you."

He started to protest, but she stopped him.

"It's nothing to do with you, Nick," she continued. "But Lorraine isn't attracted to men."

Kropotkin stared at Clodagh.

"I mean," said Clodagh, "she likes women."

"In what way?"

"In every way that counts," she said, "at least where your relationship is concerned."

Kropotkin sat in silence, apparently running this revelation through his mind. He started slowly nodding. Then he stopped and looked at Clodagh.

"And you..." he said slowly. "You Clodagh Clott, do you like men?"

She smiled, set her coffee cup down, took his cup and set it on the dashboard, and then gave him a long, sensuous kiss. When it was done, she whispered. "Now, why don't you take me home, Nick?"

– 39 –
The Multiple Hats of
Egmont Einfalt

Patsy Einfalt sat at her desk and chewed the end of a pencil. She had done a lot of that lately, so much so that she had to order more pencils just for gnawing. Had she been a beaver, Patsy could have constructed three-and-a-half dams in just the last week.

A smiling face popped around the corner.

"Good morning, my darling," he said.

"Hello, Mr. Einfalt," said Patsy. He raised his index finger and grinned. "Sorry," she said, "Egmont."

"That's better," he said, then looked at his watch. "Oops, sorry, it's one minute to nine. I'm nearly on the clock. Wouldn't want to cheat the taxpayers. With the 40 seconds left before I start work, I'll just wish you a happy day, and I'll see you on my break in 90 minutes."

Patsy nodded, and Einfalt disappeared. A few seconds later, she heard the door of the conference room shut. He'd been there for nearly a week examining the books of both the bank and the charity. She went back to chewing her pencil.

Pencils were her only solace. Her other supports were absent. Lorraine was in England, Valerie was missing, and she couldn't very well inform Purvis long-distance that their wedding plans were in jeopardy due to the arrival of a groom with a previous claim. Even her parents were away on a cruise featuring stars of TV shows from the 1950s and 60s. That was just as well. Patsy's father probably would have bought a horse on the off chance that a horsewhip be part of the deal. Egmont Einfalt had upset her life, again, but he didn't deserve a horsewhipping from Mr. Zyobidinski.

It was all so unbelievable, she thought as she gnawed. Still, it had to be true. After all, Egmont was too crazy a name not to be real, plus it was embossed on his government business cards. People didn't go around embossing things unless they were true.

Egmont Einfalt did seem like a nice fellow. He was very kind and attentive to Patsy. And he acted like a gentleman. Aside from their first encounter years ago, Egmont hadn't had sex with her on top of the copier or any other business equipment. He was very respectful in that respect. He didn't even try to kiss her, explaining that he didn't want to take advantage of her.

"I've waited so long to find you," Egmont explained, "that I don't want to rush things. We did that once when we were younger and carried away by passion. I don't want to influence your judgment."

Patsy appreciated that, and since Egmont wasn't in a hurry, neither was she. She didn't even share any details about her relationship with Purvis. Egmont hadn't even asked to meet his daughter.

"I have plenty of time," Egmont told her. "If there's one thing being an auditor taught me is that you must take things slowly and in their proper order. My first job was to find you. My next duty is to examine the finances of the bank and the charity. It would be tempting to forget the exam and just enjoy myself. That wouldn't be fair to the taxpayers of the nation. After all, I wouldn't have found you without them. I became an examiner in hopes of finding you. And now that I have, it would be irresponsible of me not to do my best for them."

Patsy admired Egmont's devotion to duty. He told her that when the exam was completed, he'd be able to show her and their daughter the same degree of commitment. But that would have to wait. He didn't even see her outside of the bank. He was the most focused civil servant she'd ever met. Still, Patsy was terribly torn about what to do. Her daughter, Rachel, needed a father. She thought Purvis would fill that role. But Egmont Einfalt was her real father. For now, all she could do was sit at her desk, worry, and chew pencils.

She was halfway through that morning's number two pencil when she heard a soft rap on her desk. Patsy looked up; there stood Egmont. He wore an uncharacteristic frown.

"Excuse me, Ms. Einfalt," he said with severe formality, "but I need to speak to the president of the bank."

Patsy's brow furrowed. "Why, Egmont, what's wrong?"

He raised his hand. "Please, I'm acting in my official capacity. Please refer to me as Mr. Einfalt, Ms. Einfalt."

"Sorry, Eg... uh, Mr. Einfalt. What was the question?"

"The president of the bank, Ms. Einfalt."

"Oh, yes, sorry, uh, Mr. Einfalt," she said, "but we don't have one. We did, but he resigned, and a new one hasn't been named."

Egmont Einfalt twisted his lip. "Very well, since this also involves the Cross of Lorraine charity, may I speak to the chair of that organization?"

Patsy threw up her hands. "That's Lorraine, I mean, Mrs. Innis, but she's not here either, and before you ask, the next person in line is Valerie Fierro, and she's even more 'not here' than Lorraine."

Egmont took out a small notebook and started to make notations. Then he flipped the book closed. "Very well, Ms. Einfalt, then who is responsible?"

"For what?"

"I mean," he said, "who is in charge?"

Patsy looked around, then shrugged. "I supposed I am on both counts."

Egmont Einfalt nodded, and his expression grew even more serious. "Then I must ask you to accompany me to the conference room."

A gasp escaped from her lips. Patsy rose from her desk and followed Egmont Einfalt into the conference room. Once inside, he locked the door behind them and motioned for her to sit down. After she did so, he sat opposite her behind an impressive stack of ledgers. Several legal pads filled with his notes were strewn around the table along with his laptop computer. It all looked very official and very scary.

She waited for him to say something, but he just sat behind all those documents and notes, wearing the oddest expression. It was simultaneously severe and sympathetic, cruel and compassionate, as if a flurry of conflicting impulses were battling beneath a stoic façade.

"I'm going to wear two hats," he began in measured tones.

Patsy looked around. She didn't see any hats.

"I should only wear one," continued Egmont.

Patsy tilted her head slightly. Since he arrived, she hadn't seen him with any headwear.

"There is my official hat," he said, "my government examiner hat…"

Patsy imagined a peaked cap, like an army officer would wear.

"That should be my only hat," said Egmont. "But despite my official responsibilities to the taxpayers, my heart is wearing a hat as well."

"Oh," laughed Patsy, "you're not talking about real hats. For a minute there, I thought you had a real bank examiner's hat. I was wondering what the other hat was, but when you said you were going to put in on your heart, I realized you're speaking metaphorically."

Egmont Einfalt stared at her for a moment. "Sorry," he said, "for the brief misunderstanding. Yes, I was speaking metaphorically."

"Mind you," said Patsy, "but you would look nice with a hat, especially one of those general's hats. You have a very nicely shaped head." She stopped and shut her mouth tight. It was the first time she had complimented Egmont. She didn't want to sound like she was flirting.

"Yes, well," he sighed. "If I may continue, let me speak directly without the use of…"

"Hats?"

"Hyperbole," he said. "Ms. Einfalt, Patsy, there are problems with the ledgers."

Patsy craned her neck toward them. "Which ones? The bank or the charity?"

"Unfortunately, both," he said.

"Oh."

Egmont rose from the table and started pacing slowly.

"As a government examiner," he said, sounding very much like one of those, "I would say there are serious problems. Ones that would at the very least result in hefty fines."

"At the very least?" she said. "What's at the very most?"

"Life in prison," he said.

"Prison? For Life?" Patsy gasped. "For whom?"

Egmont Einfalt pointed at her. "For you, Ms. Einfalt."

"Me?" she squeaked.

He raised his hands. "You are the only one responsible here."

Patsy lowered her head. She slowly raised her wrists, expecting a pair of handcuffs to be slapped on them. Instead, she felt his hands tenderly clasping hers. Patsy looked up. His severe expression had melted away, and a gentle look filled his eyes.

"That was my official hat," said Egmont.

"The one you wear on your head," she said.

"Yes," he said. "But now, I'll put on the one I wear on my heart."

For a moment, Patsy wondered what a heart hat looked like but then remembered he was still speaking metaphorically. She urged him to continue.

"You are responsible for all of this," said Egmont gesturing to the records of Fourth Fiduciary Trust and the Cross of Lorraine. "I know you didn't make these decisions, and I doubt you were aware of what was going on, but that does not alter the facts of culpability."

"This is your heart hat?" Patsy asked with a puzzled expression.

He raised his palm. "Please let me continue. You, dear Patsy, have been left holding the bag. You've been set up. The people ultimately responsible for this have skipped the country, leaving you in the government's crosshairs. You are the patsy, Patsy, not just by name, but now in a legal sense."

Patsy sat with her mouth agape. She would go to prison. Who would take care of Rachel? Who would marry either Purvis or Egmont? What would her parents say?

"Who's responsible?" she asked. "I mean, yes, I'm responsible, but I mean, who did this? Mr. Liverot? Mr. Valvano? Valerie?" She gasped. "Lorraine?"

Egmont flinched at the mention of that last name. "What? No, not Lorraine. She is even a bigger victim of this than you. I must assure you that Lorraine Innis is innocent, even more innocent than you are."

"I'm innocent?"

"Of course you are," he said.

"But I'll go to prison?"

"Definitely," he said.

Patsy stared at him with wide eyes and then burst into tears.

"Now, now," said Egmont, "calm yourself."

"I'll have plenty of time to calm myself," she wailed, "in jail!"

"It won't come to that."

"But you said that was your heart hat," sobbed Patsy.

Egmont waved his hands back and forth as if he were juggling his hats. "Sorry, I switched too soon," he said. "If I only had my official hat, you'd be in deep trouble. Actually, it was a good thing I had amnesia and went through all that I went through."

"It was?"

"Yes," said Egmont. "If I hadn't been knocked out, we would have gotten married then. And you'd be married to a part-time Santa Claus and another bank examiner..."

"With only one hat?" she guessed.

"Correct, only an official hat. If they had come in to examine your books, he wouldn't care. He wouldn't do what I'm going to do now."

"With your heart hat on?"

"Exactly," he said. "Dry your eyes, dear Patsy, and let your little Eggy fix everything."

"Eggy?" she said. "Oh, you mean you."

Egmont Einfalt nodded and looked at his watch. "It's Friday afternoon. Just leave me your keys and access to all your work accounts. Go home, play with Rebecca..."

"Rachel," said Patsy.

He snapped his fingers. "Yes, of course, Rachel. Go home, enjoy your weekend with our daughter. And I promise you that by Monday morning, everything will be fine."

Patsy wiped her eyes with a tissue. "Are you sure? I don't want to get you into trouble."

"Trouble is my middle name," he said.

She stared at him blankly.

"Everett," he finally said. "Everett is really my middle name."

"Oh," said Patsy, "Everett is a much nicer middle name." And she handed him her keys.

– 40 –
Tickle Me, Dominic,
and Tell Me Elmo

Michael and Alphonse entered the large wooden door of the ancient church.

"Wow," whispered Alphonse looking around the sanctuary, "this place is even more experienced than all the other places we've encountered in Sicily."

"Experienced?" asked Michael.

"I was trying to exercise my vocabulary and not just say it was old. But," conceded Alphonse, "it is indubitably old."

Michael nodded. "It's an old country."

Alphonse slipped into a pew and knelt down.

"What are you doing, Al?"

Alphonse looked around and shrugged. "I was making, uh, supplication," he whispered. Before adding in an even lower voice: "That means praying."

Michael just stared at him.

"Ain't we supplicating?" asked Al. "I mean, when youse said we had to go to church after that fat broad kicked you out of her shop, I figured you wanted to pray about it before we went back and busted up her joint."

"We're not busting up any joints," laughed Mike, "and we didn't come in here to pray, or at least I didn't." He pulled out the photograph. "Now I'm sure that woman is the same one as in this picture. That means we can find out something from the church's records. You know, births, baptisms, that sort of thing. Come on."

Alphonse clambered to his feet and followed Michael to the front of the church.

"Hello," shouted Michael. "Anybody home?"

"Shh, Mikey," said Alphonse cringing as if he were afraid of lightning coming down on them.

"I said, is anyone here?" Michael repeated.

"You are American," said a voice from behind them. They turned to see a young priest. "I can tell by the accent and the manners, or lack of them."

"No disrespect intended, Father," said Michael.

"Tell him you're a priest," whispered Al.

The young priest's eyebrow shot up.

"Former priest," said Michael. "I left holy orders last year."

The young man nodded as if to indicate not a moment too soon.

"Forgive me... Father," said Michael. "I just didn't see anyone, so..."

"You just raised a ruckus..."

"Ruckus," said Alphonse nudging Michael's elbow, "that's a good word."

"Again, I meant no disrespect," said Michael. "And I'd like to add that you speak excellent English."

"I studied in New York for several years," said the priest.

"I'm Michael Valvano, and this is my friend, Alphonse."

"I am Father Dominic," said the priest.

"Father, we're here researching my family's history; specifically, we'd like to see the birth records from around 1940, if you'd be so kind."

Father Dominic smiled. "There's nothing I would like better," said the priest, "but unfortunately, many of the records you seek were destroyed during the war. Your army, I believe."

"Hey, we was liberating you guys," said Al in a loud voice. It echoed off the plaster walls. He clamped his hand over his mouth, then added in a soft voice. "Well, we did."

The young priest shrugged. He started to turn and bid them good day.

"That's a pity," said Michael, "because it involves quite a bit of money. And my family would show their generosity for any assistance that was furnished."

Father Dominic stared at him for a moment. "I'll be right back." On his way out, he paused by a table that had offering envelopes.

"Looks like someone needs to wet their beak," said Michael picking up an envelope and putting a few paper notes in it.

"He's supposed to be a priest," protested Al.

"He is a priest."

"But you didn't do that when you were a father, Father," said Al before adding: "Did you?"

Michael shook his head. "No, not that I didn't have the opportunity."

"It ain't right."

"Lots of things aren't right," said Michael, "but it's how the world works. I just hope..."

He was interrupted by the return of Father Dominic.

"If you'll just go around the corner to the Rectory," he said.

"Thank you, and while we were waiting, I noticed this," Michael nodded at the table. "You've been so helpful. I wouldn't want to leave without making a small offering."

Michael handed Father Dominic the envelope. Father Dominic looked inside and then smiled.

"Glad to be of service," said the young priest. "If you'll just go to the rectory. The housekeeper will be expecting you.

Michael thanked him. Alphonse glowered at him, and they left. Around the corner was the rectory. Michael knocked on the door, and a middle-aged woman answered.

"*Prego, entra,*" she said and led them to a small room. It was musty with the smell of a century of inhabitants and a trace of incense. The curtain was drawn over the only window. For a moment, Michael thought they were alone until he saw the end of a cigar illuminate as the one smoking it inhaled.

"*Entra,*" said a voice that sounded ancient. "You are Americans."

"Yes," said Michael, "My name is Michael Valvano, and this is my associate, Alphonse."

"Mmm, Valvano," said the man. "I've known quite a few by that name. I am Father Elmo."

"You speak excellent English, Father," noted Michael.

"I picked it up during the war. I also was quite proficient in German."

"Proficient," whispered Alphonse. "That's a real good word."

"I am happy you appreciate it, young man," said Elmo. "I've always had a gift for languages. It has served me well, especially during the war when we played host to so many visitors. But I doubt you are searching Sicily for language experts. Please, sit down and tell me how I might be of service to you, my sons."

Michael drew a straight-backed wooden chair alongside the old priest's easy chair.

"Thank you, Father," he said. "I'm looking for information on my family's history. We came here looking for birth and baptismal records but were told they were all destroyed during the war."

The old priest smiled. "Not all; a few remain." He tapped the side of his head with a bony finger. "They survive, for a little while, still."

"I would be grateful for any help," said Michael. "I believe my grandmother came from this town. She left not too long after the war. Her name was Josephina Valvano."

The priest exhaled and closed his eyes. For a moment, Michael thought he had fallen asleep.

"It was 1939 or 40," said Father Elmo, his eyes springing open. "It was one of the first weddings I performed. DiRenzo. She was Josephina DiRenzo. A very beautiful, vibrant young girl." He closed his eyes again and hummed. "Yes, Dante, Dante Valvano. They had a little boy. I baptized him… ah… Giorgio." He opened his eyes, smiled, and took a celebratory puff on his cigar. "At my age, not a lot works. But if I could still exercise one faculty, it would be my mind."

He tapped this side of his head again.

"So, you are the son?"

"Grandson, Father," said Michael.

"Oh, yes, of course," said Father Elmo, pointing at him with his cigar, "you said that. I recall five decades past better than five minutes ago. You spoke of her in the past tense."

"Yes, earlier this year," said Michael. "She passed away."

Father Elmo shook his head. "Shame; I would have liked to see her again." Then he brightened. "Her sister, well, actually her cousin, but they were very close, still lives in the village."

Michael snapped his fingers. "I was right. The woman with the shop, older, quite stout..."

"Fat," laughed the old priest, "she is fat. She has always been that size. She is the best cook on the West coast of Sicily." He jerked his thumb toward the door. "She taught my housekeeper how to cook. Rosa is a chef without peer."

"Rosa," said Michael drawing the photograph from his pocket. "And this is her?"

Father Elmo took the photograph and squinted. He then reached for a magnifying glass and studied the picture through it.

"Ah, yes, that is Rosa and Josephina, the baby..."

"The back of the picture says 'Corrado.'"

"Yes, yes, Corrado, thank you."

"He was my father."

The priest frowned. "Oh, was, another passed away, your father."

"Yes, many years ago," said Michael. "I tried to approach Rosa, but I showed her the photograph, and she threw me out of her shop."

Father Elmo laughed. "Still! She is a fine woman in many ways, but that does not surprise me. With all the rest of the weight she carries, she still finds room for a fifty-year-old grudge. I should not laugh, but it is rather comical."

"She looks cross in the picture," said Michael.

"Cross? Yes, to put it mildly," said the old priest. He picked up the magnifying glass again. "Yes, see, you can tell from the background that they are standing in front of the church. It must have been the day of the baby's baptism. You'd think I would have been in the picture, after all..." He paused and ran his lips across his teeth. "Ha, I couldn't be in the picture. I remember, now."

"You didn't baptize the baby?"

"I did, baptize the baby," said Elmo, "and I also took the picture!"

"I'd like to ask about my grandfather," said Michael.

The smile faded from the old priest's face.

"You must have known my grandfather," said Michael.

Father Elmo was silent for over a minute. Finally, he said: "What did your grandmother tell you?"

"Nothing."

The priest waved his hands. "Then I can't add anything to that."

"But she didn't tell me anything," said Michael. The old man merely shrugged. "I suspect there's more to the story. Certain dates don't match up, and I found letters."

"And what did those tell you, my son?"

"Not enough," said Michael.

"Nor can I," said Father Elmo. "Somethings are family business."

"But there's no family left," argued Michael.

"There is Rosa," said the priest. "She is the family vault, the repository of that privileged information."

"But she won't even talk to me," pleaded Michael. "Can you at least tell me why she won't talk to me?"

The brow of the priest knitted in thought. "They were very close at one time. Rosa even delivered the baby. She brought your father into this world. That was the start of the problem."

"Please," said Michael.

Father Elmo nodded. "Like most family disputes, it was over such a small thing. Smaller than a baby."

"Smaller than a baby?"

"A baby's name."

– 41 –
Better Red Than Dead

It was good to be out in public again. Valerie Fierro had gotten herself a wig. Not a cheap one like the one she had worn when she ran away from Lorraine at Heathrow. This one was very good and very expensive, and, like most things in her life the last few weeks, it came courtesy of Albrecht Eckner. London's best and most discreet wig salon sent their top consultant to Valerie's suite. The goal was to make her look as little like herself as possible.

"Red," said the consultant, a flamboyant man named Henri, "you need to go red!"

Valerie looked at herself in the mirror. "Really? I've always been a brunette. Wouldn't blonde be better?"

"Madame," said Henri trying to adopt an upper crust accent over his Cockney origins, "for your goals, I strongly suggest a flaming auburn, like a forest ablaze in the peak of autumn. It's bold, it's dramatic, it's fabulous, it's *you!*"

Henri fitted a wavy wig on Valerie's head and arranged its tresses around her shoulders.

Valerie studied her face. "It's nice, very nice…"

"It's gorgeous," cooed Henri.

"Yes, but I'm trying to be inconspicuous," she said.

Henri smirked. "Well, you could always rub mud all over yourself and be a bag lady. Darling, you are too beautiful to be inconspicuous. Believe me, love, if you tried to hide your natural assets in a plain wrapper you would draw more attention to yourself. The goal is to be a different woman, a beautiful but different woman. And the vibrance of the auburn will enhance the fire in your eyes while drawing attention away from… less complimentary features."

Valerie knew he was talking about her nose. She almost touched it. But he was right. The red framed her face and drew notice away from her nose. She would have to get a different foundation.

"I'd have to color my brows," she muttered, thinking aloud.

"We can do that for you," added Henri.

"I'll take it," said Valerie. "Oh, charge it to Mr. Eckner."

Henri smiled at her through pursed lips and winked at her. "We already have, lovey."

Now, Valerie was trying out her new look. When she first emerged from the hotel, she almost felt as if she were naked. Were people staring? Valerie watched out of the corner of her eye. They weren't quite staring, but she was getting long, admiring looks. Inwardly, Valerie smiled. It worked. She still was hot, but without being recognized.

Valerie strolled away from the hotel and browsed some nearby high-end stores. She couldn't buy anything, but it was nice to dally amongst the silk and cashmere again.

Valerie looked at her watch. She was supposed to meet Albrecht at a nearby restaurant. He was just back from his latest shuttle to Gibraltar and hadn't yet seen her new look. Valerie decided to have some fun.

Entering the restaurant, Valerie saw Albrecht sitting in the corner, reviewing work papers. Rather than reveal that Albrecht was waiting for her, she asked the maître de to sit her alone at an adjacent table. Once seated, she pretended to study the menu. Valerie glanced up and caught Albrecht's eye. She smiled politely and then went back to her menu. After a second glance, she afforded him a more extended look and a warmer smile. He smiled back. Albrecht hadn't recognized her.

Valerie decided to take it up a notch. She rose from the table and approached him.

"Excuse me," she said, adopting a thick Russian accent, "but you seem terribly alone. May I sit with you?"

Albrecht seemed flustered. "Uh, well, actually, I'm not really alone."

Valerie made a pouty face as she sat down across from him. "Really? I don't see anyone else here. Do you have an imaginary friend?"

Albrecht Eckner took a sip of water and cleared his throat. "Imaginary, heh, no, she's just late."

Valerie raised her red eyebrows. "Oh, a lady? Your wife?"

He ran his finger under his collar. "I… I'm not married."

She reached out and placed her hand atop his.

"Oh, your lover then…"

Albrecht laughed nervously. "No, no, just a friend. One of my dearest friends. We've known each other for years."

Valerie looked around. "Maybe she is not coming."

Albrecht was starting to perspire. "I'm sure she'll be here. She's very reliable. She's the most trustworthy person I know." He glanced at his watch. "I hope nothing's happened to her."

"You are very, how you say, anxious," said Valerie. "She must be very special."

Albrecht forced a smile on his worried face. "She is very special. I'm just afraid something has happened."

Valerie caressed his cheek. "Oh, what could happen?"

He looked around, then leaned in a little closer. "Quite a lot, I'm afraid. You see, my friend has people who would like to harm her. She doesn't usually go out in public. If anything happened to her, I'd never forgive myself."

"You feel responsible for your friend?" she said.

Albrecht nodded. "You do that for a good friend," he said with a quiver in his voice.

Valerie had meant it as a joke, but the last thing she wanted to see was Albrecht Eckner go to pieces in a posh restaurant. She pulled a handkerchief from her purse and dabbed at his eyes.

"Albrecht," she said in her normal voice, "Albrecht, it's me, it's Valerie."

He stared at her for thirty seconds in disbelief, and then slowly, a smile overtook his expression. Fresh tears, these of joy, moistened his eyes.

"Oh, Wow," gasped Albrecht, leaning back in his chair, "for a minute there, I really thought they'd gotten you. I thought for sure they'd somehow traced you through me. I mean, I'm super careful. As far as you-know-who…" He stopped and mouthed "Robert Valvano," though Valerie knew who you-know-who was. "I thought," he continued, "that he'd had me followed."

"Do you think he would?" asked Valerie.

Albrecht thought a moment. "In reality, probably not. I don't think he knows how well we know each other. But he might try to trace you through anyone you may have known. Who knows, he may have even asked Chesney Potts."

Valerie snorted. "Good luck finding him!"

"That's the point," said Albrecht. "If he's looking for you and the trail has gone cold, there's no telling where he might look."

Valerie studied Albrecht. He was genuinely concerned for her, almost paranoid on his behalf. Or was it on his own behalf?

"What would he do to you if he found you were harboring me?" she asked.

Albrecht shrugged. "He couldn't do much to me. I know too much."

"Robert, I mean, you-know-who could have you killed," she noted.

He shook his head. "I've got insurance. After they almost killed Peter Liverot, I set up a little protection for myself. I know they hate me, but they know it's in their best interest to leave me alone."

"But you do not need to worry," she said, returning to her Russian accent. "After all, even you did not recognize me."

Albrecht smiled. "You look fantastic! Like a totally different person. I never knew one woman could be so…" He stopped himself.

"Go on," she said.

He lowered his head. "That one woman could be so beautiful in two different ways."

"How attractive could I be? I flirted with you," she said. "And you didn't even give me a nibble."

"I was more concerned about the real you to notice a Russian redhead."

"Sweet," Valerie whispered. Had she not seen it herself, she wouldn't have believed it. Whoever got to Albrecht Eckner did a thorough job. Whatever trauma he went through changed him completely. They had destroyed the old Albrecht, and he had built a new and better man in his place. Valerie wondered who it had been and what they had done, but as the new Albrecht was respecting her privacy, she could do no less in return. He would tell her when he was ready.

"Well," said Albrecht, "let's order. I'm starving. I left Gibraltar before breakfast, and I haven't eaten a bite all day. And after we order, I have some interesting news."

The waiter came and took their order. When they were alone again, Albrecht leaned closer to Valerie.

"I found a crack in your cousin's setup," he said in a low voice.

"You mean, Robert...," Valerie caught herself and looked around. "You mean you found a vulnerability?"

Albrecht nodded.

"What about Mr. Rosen," she continued, "his lawyer?"

"That's the interesting part," said Albrecht. "I think he, or someone, purposely put it in there. I doubt your cousin knows about it. He probably doesn't have a law background. But someone has left Robert's backdoor open."

"What is it?" she asked eagerly.

Albrecht shook his head. "I can't go into details, but it concerns the set up of Gibraltar bank."

"You mean the subsidiary?"

"Not the subsidiary," said Albrecht. "It looks like the subsidiary, but it's actually the holding company for everything."

"Why would Rob... I mean, my cousin, do that," said Valerie. "As far as I know, he's never even been to Gibraltar."

"He hasn't," said Albrecht, "at least not as long as I've been there, and I was there when they first set up the Gibraltar operation. Like I said, I doubt he knows it, but his lawyer most certainly does. It seems that I'm not the only one who set up some insurance."

"Then you can take it over?" said Valerie.

"No, I can't," he said. Valerie's heart sunk. "But, you can," added Albrecht. "That is if you're really a member of the family."

"Of course I am," she said, "and he knows it." Valerie thought a moment. "That's why he wanted to frame me."

"But why would Mr. Rosen set it up so you could take it over," said Albrecht. "I thought you said that your relationship to the family only came up after the bank was established."

Valerie looked at Albrecht. What he had gained from being a decent human had hobbled his devious side. Fortunately, she could still think that way. "Albrecht, I'm not the only member of the family. Rosen probably set it up that way so if one brother was difficult, he had another brother handy to take over."

A look of illumination spread over Albrecht's face. "Oh, right."

Valerie smirked. "Mr. Rosen likes me, but I doubt he'd double-cross my cousin, not at this stage."

"That's the beauty of it," said Albrecht. "You don't need anyone else. You can do it all by yourself."

Valerie laughed. "Well, then, let's do it. What is it? Some legal document? Where do I sign?"

Albrecht's face fell. "That's the only hitch. You have to sign it in Gibraltar."

– 42 –
A Russian President
Walks Into a Bar

Nikolai Kropotkin opened the passenger door to the truck and helped Clodagh Clott out.

He put his arm around her as they stood on the small hillock overlooking a vista of farms and small towns.

"This is the Chernozem," he said, "the Black Earth. This is the soil I came forth from." There was affection and reverence in his voice.

"It's lovely," said Clodagh softly.

"Over there," he said, pointing to the right. "There is the farm where I worked during school holidays. We grew wheat there."

Clodagh squeezed his bicep. "They grew some beef there, too."

"Mostly dairy," he started, matter-of-factly, before he realized she was making a joke. "Yes, well," he laughed, "as I say, this is where I took root."

Clodagh kissed him on the cheek as he began pointing out the sites of agricultural and biographical interest in the valley below. Finally, Kropotkin stopped and pointed to a group of buildings.

"See that?" he asked, "down there? That long building? That I will have to show you. That is our next stop."

Thirty minutes later, they entered the building, which turned out to be the local tavern. They were still dressed in their rough clothes; Kropotkin in his worker's overalls; Clodagh in her simple dress. He escorted her in with his arm around her. Despite being in strange surroundings, she felt very safe with him. It was around noon, and several men were around the bar. They glanced up at the entering couple but then returned to their drinks. A few men were at a table in the far corner playing cards.

"Do you want me to act mute again, Nick?" she whispered.

Kropotkin looked at her as if the suggestion was odd. "Mute? Nyet, I mean, no, we are in no danger here. I know this place. These are my people."

Kropotkin guided her to a small table and held out her chair. Clodagh sat down. He then crossed to the bar and exchanged words with the bartender.

In a minute, Kropotkin returned with a glass filled with reddish liquid and placed it in front of Clodagh.

"This is kompot," he said.

She held up the glass. "There's something in the bottom."

"Berries," he said, pointing at them. "It's traditional. Everyone likes kompot."

Clodagh sniffed it. "Is it alcoholic? I don't want to get drunk."

He laughed, and his whole face lit up. "No, everyone drinks it. Children drink it. It's very refreshing. And when you're done, you eat the berries. Go on." Kropotkin nodded.

Clodagh smiled, shrugged, and lifted the glass to her lips. It was very sweet and good.

She nodded at the large glass of clear liquid in front of him. "Vodka?"

He laughed again. "Seltzer," he said, "I want to keep my head, too." He glanced around the tavern. A few more men entered.

"Do you see anyone you know?" she asked.

"That is quite unlikely," he explained. "I left here almost thirty years ago to join the army."

"Oh," said Clodagh. "Is your family…"

He shook his head, and a wistful look clouded his eyes. "No, they are all gone now. My only blood relation is my niece, and she is back home in Moscow."

"And your daughter, of course."

"Oh, yes, I was speaking of people who would have known me here," said Kropotkin.

"Your daughter must be worried about you," said Clodagh. "You've been gone for days."

He nodded. "She is accustomed to me traveling. I will give her a call. She is staying with my niece and her husband. I told them to tell her I was on a secret diplomatic mission."

The man behind the bar reached up and turned on the television. A news program was on. Not understanding the language, Clodagh barely gave it any attention. Nikolai Kropotkin, however, was watching intently.

"Nick," said Clodagh, "what is it?"

He waved her to be quiet and then pointed at the screen. "They're going to interview Teplov."

"Teplov? The guy who kidnapped me and knocked you out?"

"Yes, shhh…."

The woman anchor introduced her guest.

"That's him," cried Clodagh. The other patrons turned in her direction. Kropotkin offered a quick explanation in Russian, and the others returned to their games and drinks. Then he urged Clodagh to be quiet so he could listen.

Clodagh watched as Teplov gave lengthy answers. He seemed even more arrogant than he had back in the bunker. She looked over at Nick. His gaze was riveted on the screen. Teplov's speaking grew animated, and as he spoke, Nick was becoming more and more agitated. Finally, the woman said something, apparently ending the interview. By that time, Nick was red in the face. He shouted something in Russian, and all the tavern's patrons stopped and stared at him. Kropotkin stood and started orating in Russian, pointing at the television and waving his arms. Everyone just watched in silence with their mouths agape.

Finally, one of the men at the bar, said something. It sounded like a challenge of some sort.

Nikolai Kropotkin cut the man short, jumped atop his chair, and cried out passionately. Clodagh had no idea what he was saying, but she did understand the last two words.

Beating his chest, and ripping open his coverall, his final words were: "NIKOLAI KROPOTKIN!"

The patrons sat in silent amazement for a moment and then burst into cheers.

– 43 –
The Hovercraft of Venus

Verity Goodhue sat in the library of her father's Eaton Square home in London, reading *Martin Chuzzlewit*. She wanted to revisit the book after Chesney mentioned it was Martina Fergus' favorite Dickens novel. She wished she could have met Martina to thank her for helping to restore her Beloved's sense of sanity after he thought Verity had died. Try as she might, Verity had difficulty concentrating.

Chesney, in the guise of Lorraine, was only miles away filming those silly commercials for her father's toilet tissue. Verity longed to be there, but this was impossible. Chesney's true personality refused to be submerged behind the disguise when she was around. While it kept them apart, it was also encouraging. When he could finally jettison Lorraine Innis, the character wouldn't intrude on them in the future.

Verity also wanted to know why Chesney agreed to make the commercials for her father. Hopefully, he had a good reason. Or, if not, maybe he had lapsed back into Lorraine so deeply he had forgotten all that Lord Bagnold had done to them.

Finally, Verity couldn't visit her Beloved because His Lordship had forbidden his daughter to approach Mrs. Innis. He had ordered the guards at the studio not to admit her. He even had pictures of Verity distributed, warning that any guard that let her on the set would immediately be given the sack.

Verity's concentration was further derailed as she heard the front door slam and her father bellow.

"H'ANYBODY GOING TO COME 'ERE AND TEND TO THE MASTER OF THE FLIPPIN' 'OUSE? ... WELL? IS THEY?"

"I'm in the library, Father," she called.

Moments later the impressive figure of Lord Bagnold filled the doorway.

"Where are them so-called servant wot I pays to run me 'ouse?"

"It's the Carstairs day off, Father," she said.

"Wot? Both of 'em?"

"They are a married couple," she said. "They do like to take their days off simultaneously."

Lord Bagnold rubbed his face. "I don't mind them taking their days off simultaneously. I just don't likes them doing it at the same time."

"Yes, that is quite a liberty," said Verity facetiously.

"'Ad I known that," said His Lordship, "I could 'ave 'ad lunch at me club. Now wot am I supposed to do?"

"I can make fix you some lunch, Father."

His expression softened. "Oh, well, yes, I suppose that's okay, then. I'll 'ave some roast beef and Yorkshire pud."

Verity rose from the easy chair. "I was thinking more of sandwiches. I'll see what's in the refrigerator." She walked past him and started downstairs to the kitchen. Verity turned. "Are you coming?"

Bagnold's eyebrows raised. "Wot? Me eat in the kitchen, like a, a..."

"...Normal human being," she said. "Come on, Father, expand your horizons, she how the other 99 percent live."

He stood tall and pulled down on his waistcoat. "Look me girl, I 'ad expanded 'orizontals before you was even a gleam in me eye! I've noshed in more kitchens than you've 'ad 'omecooked meals."

"Good," she said, "come on. We keep the kitchen downstairs."

Ten minutes later, they were seated at the kitchen table.

"Not bad, not bad at t'all," said Lord Bagnold with his mouthful. "I didn't know you could cook."

Verity smiled. "It's hardly cooking. It's just mixing up some tuna with some other ingredients."

"Credit where it's due," he said. "I means, it h'ain't the Savoy, but it's not bad. You'll make some lucky fella a fine..."

Bagnold stopped in mid-chew, realizing what he'd said. He looked up from his plate to see Verity's piercing stare.

"Uh, yes," he said, wiping his mouth, "I means, uh..." he lowered his eyes and took another bite of the sandwich.

Verity let him stew in his awkwardness for a minute before having a bit of fun.

"You never told me, Father," she began innocently, "how are your ads going with Mrs. Innis? You are filming those this week, aren't you."

Eager to extract himself from the mention of the tragedy he'd engineered, he lept at the change of subject.

"Wot? Oh, yes, Mrs. Innis, yes, well, oh, it's going splendidly."

"That's nice," she said. "So, you enjoy working with Mrs. Innis?"

His Lordship made a sour face, which he hurried to conceal. "Enjoy? Ha, yes, wot's not to enjoy? It's h'ain't work at t'all. It's more like a picnic."

"Oh, that is nice, Father," said Verity sweetly.

"Nice? Of course, it's nice, it's more than nice, it's like an 'oliday." He grimaced. "A real 'oliday. If you got a bossy, naggy woman along 'oo don't not listen to what you're telling 'er to do, the silly cow!"

Verity suppressed a smile. She doubted Chesney would do the ads merely to torment her father. But as long as he had to do them, Verity was glad Chesney wasn't making Lord Bagnold's life any easier.

"Silly cow, Father?" said Verity. "Why I thought you admired Lorraine Innis."

"Yes, well, I does," he said, "from a distance. It h'ain't my fault."

"No, of course not, Father. It couldn't be your fault."

He nodded, missing her sarcasm. "Why you knows me. I gets along with h'everyone."

"Yes, I know you, Father."

"But that woman, that Innis woman is making my director's life a living 'ell. Not to mention the costume designer. She wouldn't wear the costume 'e designed."

Verity gasped in mock surprise. "You don't mean she wanted to do your ad in the nude? Oh, Father, doesn't she realize the level of sophistication you infuse into every sheet of your toilet tissue?"

"Quite right!" said Bagnold. "I'm practically soppy with sophistication! And no, she didn't want to do it in the nude. She just doesn't want to be as classy as wot I am."

"That is a high standard to appreciate, Father."

He nodded. "I envisioned this classy, classical image like wot I saw once in this old masterpiece. I wanted 'er to be like Venus."

"You wanted Mrs. Innis to dress like a planet?" she said, being purposely obtuse.

"Not the planet, the bird," he said, "you know the woman, Venus, like a goddess. I remember this old picture of this Venus bird on a big clam shell stepping out of the water."

"*The Birth of Venus?* By Botticelli?"

"I thinks that's the one," he agreed. "Any road, there's this Venus and this big shell, and angels or something handing this Venus her flowing robes."

"But in the painting, Venus is nude," said Verity trying to hide her amusement.

"I knows it," he said, "that's just the stepping-off point. That was me initial h'inspiration. I knows we couldn't 'ave 'er nude. So I thinks to meself, wot else comes out of the water?"

"A hovercraft, Father?"

"Now 'ow could Mrs. Innis be an 'overcraft? Use yer common sense!"

"Oh, sorry, Father."

"Wot else, I asked meself, could come out of the water that is lovely and woomanly? And I answered meself: a mermaid."

Verity bit her lip and nodded.

"That way, she h'aint naked," continued His Lordship. "So I gets the best costume designer in London to do a beautiful costume, with a lovely scaley tail, and them shells, you knows, to uh…" He gestured to his chest.

"A bra made out of shells?" said Verity.

"Right, one of them contraptions."

"So, you want Mrs. Innis to emerge from the sea dressed like a mermaid?"

Lord Bagnold's face lit up. "No, that's where me brilliance really kicked into 'igh gear! I 'ad to tie it into the product. So, instead of just a big shell, I built the world's biggest khazi!"

"A toilet?"

"That's right!" Bagnold was now standing and waving his arms in majestic gestures. "A forty-foot khazi, only the lid is shaped like a giant shell. It's beautiful! It's all on 'idraulic lifts. It slowly rises from the water, and the giant shell lid rises up, and then, Mrs. Innis rises from the bowl…"

"Dressed as a mermaid?

"H'exactly! And then on wires, angels fly in, just like in the picture."

"Angels fly in and hand Mrs. Innis her robes?"

Lord Bagnold stared at her. "That would be stupid! They flys in and 'ands her flowing rolls of me toilet paper! And then Mrs. Innis the mermaid looks at the camera and says: 'Bagnold's Two-Ply Rolls: the classic wipe!'"

Verity just stared at him with her mouth agape. Finally, she said: "And Mrs. Innis didn't like that?"

"No," said Lord Bagnold. "She didn't like any of it. Not me giant khazi, not her beautiful costume, not me artsy fartsy concept, none of it! Can you believe that! And I thought she was supposed to be classy!"

"Taste is subjective, Father."

"I knows that," he said. "Only I thought she'd recognize true art when she saw it."

Verity thought a moment. This could be the opening she was waiting for. "It is a shame, Father," said Verity. "I'm sure your artistic vision was very tasteful."

Lord Bagnold snapped his fingers. "H'exactly! Tasteful! It's h'ain't not just a big bowl. It's beautiful. Not white, not like your standard hopper. It's more seashell-ish."

"Alabaster."

"I've been called worse, but not by me own daughter."

"I meant the color, alabaster."

"Wot? Oh, right, the color. Yes, something like that on the outside, and then a lovely light pinky color on the inside of the lid, just like a shell. And the backdrop looks just like Skeggy at sunrise."

Verity suppressed a shudder over the image of a giant toilet sitting on the beach at Skegness at any time of the day."

"Yes," she said, "that must be beautiful. I know I'd appreciate it. It must be breathtaking."

"It is, it is," said Bagnold. "Maybe if I took Mrs. Innis down to see Skeggy, she'd h'appreciate me vision."

"Unfortunately, as lovely as it is, she'd never be able to see Skegness through your eyes. After all, you took mother there on your honeymoon, didn't you?"

A warm smile overspread Lord Bagnold's face, which looked all the more hideous since it was genuine. "Ah, I was there with your mother. If it wasn't for Skeggy, you wouldn't be here today."

Verity grimaced as she contemplated the honor of being a daughter of Skegness.

"Yes, well, Father," said Verity as she tried to distance herself from the mental images of the shabby seaside resort. "As I was saying, I doubt a visit to Skeggy would enhance Mrs. Innis' appreciation of your beautiful artistic 40-foot convenience. She's an American. It would take a British woman to fully understand that connection."

Lord Bagnold shook his head sadly. "You is probably right. If only she could see it through British eyes, the eyes of a real English girl."

Verity held her breath, hoping he'd finally reach the conclusion she was guiding him toward. She turned away and said softly to herself. "I'm sure Lorraine Innis would understand it all if she could see Skegness through my eyes..."

She stood there with her back to her father, praying for the penny to drop. Verity held her breath. Then after 30 seconds, the wheels began to turn.

"See it through your eyes," muttered Bagnold. "Maybe, if... no, that wouldn't... but I gots to do something... if she don't do it, I'm left with a giant khazi."

Verity turned. "Pardon, Father, did you say something?"

Lord Bagnold studied her face. It was as if he were weighing her in his mind.

"Father, you have such an odd look on your face," she said. "Is there something the matter?"

He stared at her for another minute before speaking. "Does you think you could do it?"

"Do it? Do what, Father?" she asked. "Did you want me to make you another sandwich?"

His Lordship looked at his plate. "I h'ain't not talking about sandwiches. You been to University and done all them culture h'appreciation courses. I knows; I paid the bills. You knows all about arts and farces, 'ell's bells, you even knew the name of that Venus picture by Bottled Jello."

"Botticelli."

184

"And you knew that, as well," he continued. "And you is a girl, and a woman, to boot. Does you think can talk to this Innis bird on 'er level?"

Verity suppressed the urge to do a handspring. "Oh, well, I mean she's an American, but maybe, that is, perhaps, if you really think it would help you? I might be able to find common ground with her."

Lord Bagnold rose from the table. "Then you gots yourself a deal. Maybe you can reach 'er in a way that snotty director couldn't."

"I'd hate to interfere with your business," said Verity, "but I'll try."

"Good, and that's one problem down, one to go."

"This other problem isn't about Mrs. Innis," said Verity, "is it?"

"Not unless she's the one causing the gum tree root rot," he said.

"The what?"

"The root rot," he said. "Look, toilet paper is approximately 70 percent 'ardwoods, and 30 percent softwoods. Despite wot you may guesses, it's the 'ardwoods that makes the paper softer. I gets me 'ardwoods from me plantation in Borneo, and they is 'aving a root rot outbreak. It could threaten me 'ole crop."

Verity stared at him. She'd seen him more upset over a lost button. "You don't seem particularly perturbed, Father."

The hideous Bagnold grin broke out all the way to his back teeth. "I was perturbed and then some. That is until I found a solution that not only will rescue me from the clutches of the root rot but will revolutionize me paper products empire."

He pulled a folded photocopy from his pocket and flashed it before her eyes before stashing it safely back in his suitcoat.

"I couldn't see it," said Verity. "What is it?"

He waggled his index finger. "Ah, ah, I didn't gets where I am by loose talk, not even to me daughter. You take care of Lorraine Innis. I'll get me business out of the other pickle."

Then Lord Bagnold broke into uproarious laughter as he walked from the kitchen. He muttered something between the guffaws. If she didn't know better, Verity would swear he was congratulating himself on the use of the word "pickle."

Verity shrugged her shoulders. At least she was being allowed to see Lorraine.

- 44 -
Sfogliatella Bombolini, and the Fatal Batch of Marzipan

Michael Valvano straightened Alphonse's necktie.

"Okay, say it again," said Michael, "what's your name?"

"Alphonse," he replied.

Michael rolled his eyes. "No, what are you going to say your name is?"

Alphonse shuffled his feet. "Are you sure of this? This is like lying."

"It isn't like lying, Al," said Michael, "it is lying. I hate to say the ends justify the means, but we have to do this, or we won't know the truth. And if we don't know the truth, we can't find out what's wrong, and if we don't know what's wrong, we can't set it right, can we? So, we have to tell a lie, a temporary lie, to fix the bigger issue."

"Yeah, only I never had a priest, I mean an ex-priest, tell me to commit an obvious fabrication."

"Fabrication," said Michael, "that's a good word."

"Yeah, but it still means a fib," said Alphonse. "I wouldn't do this for nobody else, Mikey."

"I appreciate that, Al," he said. "We can go to confession right after it's done."

"Not with that young priest," said Al. "I like the old one, Father Elmo."

"Okay, we'll go to Father Elmo for absolution, even though we wouldn't be telling this lie without his help. Now, what's your name?"

The hulking henchman looked down, kicked at a pebble, and muttered. "My name is Sfogliatella," said Al.

"The whole thing, the middle name, too."

Alphonse sighed and rubbed his meaty hand across his beefy face. "Sfogliatella Bomboloni Valvano."

Mike patted him on the shoulder. "Good, perfect. Now, say it just like that, like you mean it, and we'll be okay. C'mon, let's go. She has a little apartment around the back of the store."

186

"Who names their kid after Italian pastry?" said Al, following Michael through the dark streets. "I mean, Sfogliatella is those flaky triangles. And Bomboloni is just a donut. Who names a kid that?"

"That's the point, Al," said Michael, "nobody would. But that's what Rosa wanted Nonnia to name my father. That's was the cause of all the trouble."

Alphonse shook his head. "She must be one loony broad, this Rosa."

"It takes all kinds, Al," said Michael as they reached the back of the shop. He knocked on the door and pushed Alphonse forward. "You have to go first. If she opens the door and sees me, she'll slam it in my face."

A bolt was thrown, and a fat woman's face appeared as she opened the door a crack.

"*Chi e la?*" said the woman.

"*Sono io zia,*" said Al as if he were reciting his lesson in a first-year Italian class. "*Tuo nipote dall' America. Il mio nome e... Valvano, Sfogliatella Bomboloni Valvano!*"

The woman's mouth dropped open.

"Sfogliatella... Bomboloni?" She asked.

"*Si,* that's me," said Al, "*uh, sono io.*"

The woman threw open the door, and before he knew it, Alphonse was engulfed in the woman's embrace. She rocked him back and forth, muttering "Sfogliatella Bombolini" over and over again. Alphonse looked back to Michael and shrugged. Michael smiled and gave him a thumbs up. It was working.

"*Zia Rosa,*" said Alphonse, starting to feel like a Sicilian milkshake. "Uh, Aunt Rosa, you speak English, don't you?"

Rosa stopped her rocking and looked up. "English? Why sure, I am top boss English talking!" Her face shone as she looked into his eyes. Then she saw Michael.

"You?" She said, releasing Al and wagging a finger in Michael's face. "You bad, you bad guy, Joe."

"Actually, it's Michael, Michael Valvano," he said.

"You very bad," she continued. "Why you no say you got a brother, a fine big brother, a big brother Sfogliatella Bombolini!"

Michael grinned sheepishly. "You didn't give me a chance."

Rosa waved her hand at Michael. "*Ah! Stupido!*" Then she turned to Alphonse. "*Andiamo!* Come in, Sfogliatella. I make you something to eat." She guided him into the house and turned toward Michael. "Hokay, you can come too."

Rosa led them into the kitchen and escorted Alphonse to the head of the table. She smoothed his curly hair and patted his shoulder. As an afterthought, Rosa nodded at Michael to sit.

Then she crossed to a large pot on the stove and lifted the lid. A wonderful steamy aroma filled the room.

"You're hungry?" she said to Alphonse.

"I ate…" he said.

She shook her head. "You're hungry. A big boy like you can always eat, Sfogliatella Bombolini, especially when your Aunt Rosa makes you her special *Pasta e Ceci!*"

"Nonnia used to make it for us," said Michael.

Rosa stopped, ladle in hand over the pot, and sneered. "That 'Merican!"

Michael laughed. "American? She's from here."

"She was from here," said Rosa, punctuating each point with a flick of her ladle, splattering sauce around the room. "I make the best. I use Sicilian tomatoes and herbs. You can't get that in one of your American super-size markets. And who do you think taught her? And who did most of the cooking when she was running her café? It was me! Rosa! You go tell Josephina that!"

Michael and Alphonse exchanged awkward looks.

"Uh, Aunt Rosa," said Alphonse, "Mrs. Valvano, uh, I mean, Nonnia, is deceased."

Rosa's brow knit. "What's that? Some kind of American thing?"

"It means she's dead, Rosa," said Michael.

Rosa gasped, made a sign of the cross, and leaned against the stove.

"Sorry," said Michael, "I didn't realize that you didn't know. Did we Sfogliatella?"

Alphonse sat motionless until Michael kicked him under the table.

"What? Oh, yeah, that's me," said Al. "No, we didn't know that you didn't know."

Rosa dipped out a big bowl of *Pasta e Ceci* for Alphonse and a smaller bowl for Michael. Al started eating while Michael spoke.

"After Nonnia died," began Michael, "We, that is Sfogliatella and I, wanted to come back here and see if we could find anyone left in the family. We were overjoyed to find you, Aunt Rosa. After all, now you're our matriarch… *la matriarca di famiglia.*

Rosa's face beamed, and her already considerable bosom swelled with pride. *"La matricarca!"* She said with pride. Then she looked at Michael's bowl, grabbed it, and filled it to equal Alphonse's.

"Nonnia, that is, Josephina, felt terrible about what happened between you two," said Michael between spoonfuls.

"She did?" said Rosa. "Why didn't she come and say she was sorry?"

Michael shrugged. "That sort of thing is like a window that's slowly closing. The longer you wait to apologize, the smaller the opening, until, finally…" He raised his hands. "The window's closed. But she made up for it in the only way she knew how." He pointed at Alphonse.

"Sfogliatella," said Rosa, and she patted Al's cheek as he chewed.

"It caused quite a fight," continued Michael. "I was only three when he was born, but I still remember it. I didn't understand until I was older. My parents wanted to name him 'Alphonse.'"

Rosa blew between her pursed lips. "Alphonse? That's no name for a fine boy like my nephew!" Al looked at Michael and kept eating.

"But Nonnia insisted they name him Sfogliatella Bombolini. She didn't say why except that it was for Rosa, to make up for what she did to you. She would never tell us why."

Rosa wiped a tear from her eye with her handkerchief. She fetched a photo album. Opening it to one of the first pages, she pointed to a yellowed photograph of a younger version of herself standing next to a chubby young man.

"That! That's me," said Rosa. "That's me when I was Bombolini, and this is Silvio, my Sfogliatella." She sighed. "He was my first, my only love. He was a baker." She kissed her fingers. "Oh, how he could bake. We fell in love. He called me his Bombolini, and I called him my Sfogliatella. We were going to be married. Then…"

Michael leaned forward. Alphonse stopped chewing. A faraway look appeared in her eyes.

"Then, the war came?" Michael guessed.

"Huh? What?" said Rosa. She waved her hand. "No, the war was already here. Sfogliatella was going to go into the army. He was going to be a cook, but before he went…" Rosa's lip started to quiver. Then she burst into tears and buried her face in her hankie.

Alphonse stopped chewing and looked at Michael. Michael shrugged and reached out to pat Rosa's shoulder.

"It… it was my fault…" she sobbed. "It was the… *MARAZAPANE!*"

Michael and Alphonse exchanged puzzled looks and waited for Rosa to stop crying. After a few minutes, the tears abated, and she continued.

"*Scuzi*," said Rosa. "I haven't cried like that in years. I haven't had to talk about it for even longer."

"You said it was the *marazapane*," said Michael cautiously, not wanting to reopen the sluice gates. "Is that marzipan?"

"Si, si," she sighed. "Marazapane, marzipan was my favorite. And being a baker, Silvio, my Silvo, made the best. He got his orders to join the army, and before he left, he wanted to surprise me."

"With marzipan," said Alphonse.

Rosa nodded. "Silvio. He knew how much I loved marzipan, especially how he made it."

"With almonds," noted Michael.

"And with love," she said, "love for his little Bombolini. My Silvio made a special batch of his marzipan. He wanted it to be a surprise. Silvio went to all the area farms to get enough ingredients. He gathered the honey. He picked the almonds himself so he'd have the best, and lots of them. Then…"

"Silvo didn't make it?" guessed Alphonse.

"He got called up to the army before he finished?" asked Michael.

Rosa shook her head. "Silvio was climbing to the top of an almond tree. He went out on a limb. He was a big boy," she said, looking at Alphonse. "Even bigger than you. The branch, it gave way."

Rosa threw up her hands, then waved them downward before finishing with a sweeping gesture.

"Splat," muttered Alphonse.

"On his head," said Rosa. "*Morto!*"

"I'm sorry," said Michael.

"What about the marzipan?" asked Alphonse.

"I haven't tasted it since," said Rosa.

They sat in silence for a moment.

Michael knew the answer to the question he was about to ask. Father Elmo told him that much, but he didn't want to betray the old priest's confidence. "And that's why you wanted to name Josephina's baby: 'Sfogliatella Bombolina?"

"Si, si," Rosa nodded. "I knew I'd never marry. Silvo was my only love, and I wanted to honor him. I helped your grandmother deliver your father. It was a long, hard delivery. I never left her side. It was the day the American army came. There was chaos all around, but I never left her. I thought she owed me that name."

"Isn't that a lot to ask, though?" said Michael.

Rosa's eyes flared with an anger that had been simmering for over fifty years. "She already had a son, Giorgio. And she could have more. I couldn't have any, and besides, the baby's father..."

She caught herself. Michael held his breath. The truth was smoldering on her lips. He didn't want it extinguished.

"The baby's father, my grandfather," said Michael after a moment. "You mean Dante?"

Rosa stared at him for what seemed like five minutes. Finally, she just waved her hand. "He's not your grandfather."

– 45 –
Needs Must When the Devil Weds

There is no other way," said Valerie Fierro as she paced in the hotel suite. "I've been turning this over in my mind for days, and this is the only solution."

Albrecht Eckner sat on the sofa and shook his head. "It's pretty drastic. You know I'd do anything to help you, but this..."

Valerie had to go to Gibraltar to gain control of the Valvano Family business. Albrecht had found a loophole in the incorporation papers. They assumed Julius Rosen had created it for Michael Valvano without his brother Robert's knowledge. But as a blood relation, Valerie could take advantage of it and wrest control from her cousin. The only hitch was that she had to go to Gibraltar.

"It has to be done with the utmost secrecy," said Valerie. "I'm sure Robert has his minions looking for me all over Europe."

"I told you a few private investigators even came to the office in Gibraltar," said Albrecht.

"Right," said Valerie. "I'm sure they have the airports covered. Robert is nothing if not connected. He's probably paid off the customs and border people. The minute I try to use my passport, he'll probably know it."

"You don't think Robert would kill you? Not really."

Valerie pointed her perfectly manicured nail at him. "Look, Albrecht, they tried to kill Lorraine and pin it on me. Robert would gladly bump me off. He'd have done it already if you hadn't saved my life by hiding me."

"Couldn't you just wait here," said Albrecht with a shrug. "I mean, with your red wig, no one recognizes you. You can go out. You're not a prisoner anymore."

She stared at him. "I'm a prisoner as long as Robert Valvano has the upper hand. Once I sign those papers, I've won. I just have to get to

Gibraltar undetected. I've gone through every possibility, and this is the best solution. You've got to marry me, Albrecht."

Albrecht Eckner squirmed on the sofa. "Can't we just get you a fake passport?"

"I've thought of that," she said. "It's just too risky. I'd be in big trouble if it was spotted. And where are we going to get it? Robert's got connections under every rock. Anyone crooked enough to get a phony passport is probably tapped into his network. No, I've got to have my name changed, legally."

"We could just go have your name changed at a court," he said.

"I looked into that," countered Valerie. "As an American citizen, there's all sorts of red tape and red flags. No, the simplest way is for me to get married. It would draw the least bit of attention."

"Can't we just find someone to marry you?"

Valerie put her hands on her hips. "What's the matter? Don't you want to marry me?"

Albrecht lowered his head. "I just don't want to spoil our friendship."

Valerie sat down beside him. "That's very sweet, but it will only be on paper."

He looked up. "We won't have to complicate it?"

"In what way?" she asked.

For the first time in Valerie's memory, she saw Albrecht Eckner blush. "I mean, we won't have to... consummate the marriage."

Valerie would have laughed if his concern wasn't so sincere. She leaned over and kissed him on the cheek. "No, we'll just be married on paper. We'll get married at a registry office. Then we'll get my passport changed. Then we go to Gibraltar; I sign the papers and take control of the Valvano's total operation."

"And we can get an annulment right after that," he added.

Valerie smiled and nodded. "Sure, we can get it annulled after that. And I'll make sure my ex-husband is well-taken care of in the settlement. After all, I'll need help running everything."

Albrecht just looked at her.

"So," she said, "is it a deal? Will you marry me, Albrecht?"

Albrecht grinned so bashfully that he almost looked like Chesney Potts.

"If it will help you out," he said with a nod, "I will."

– 46 –
Brilliance in the
Second Person Singleton

Lord Bagnold strutted into the research lab like he owned the place... because he did. He was both pleased and annoyed that his entrance went ignored. Pleased because it meant that his scientific staff was all working hard, annoyed because his mere presence should have been a momentous event. He wondered if, in their spare time, these eggheads could invent some sort of monitor that would alert peons when someone important arrived. For now, he would have to resort to his own warning device: his booming voice.

"GLAD TO SEE ME BOFFINS ARE 'ARD AT WORK," bellowed Lord Bagnold.

A collective gasp arose from the stunned scientists, along with the rattle of test tubes.

The head of the lab, a bald, bespectacled man, jumped up from his desk to greet his employer.

"Your Lordship," he said, "we weren't expecting you."

Lord Bagnold squinted at the breast pocket of the man's white lab coat to read his embroidered name. "Yes, well, I was in the area and thought I'd pop in and see 'ow you're getting on, uh, professor... uh, Philbean."

The embroidery was Bagnold's idea, so he could tell them apart. To him, all these scientific types looked alike. They were all weedy with thick glasses and thinning hair, all except for the few women in the lab. They were weedy with even thicker glasses and mousy mops atop their heads. Bagnold liked his scientists to be small and emaciated. He thought it made them smarter, and if they ever turned on him, he could manhandle them.

"Oh, yes," said Professor Philbean scurrying back to his desk, "we have the results of that formula you gave us. Quite remarkable. We were able to conduct a test experiment."

"Really?" Bagnold was surprised. He'd only given them Purvis Twankey's chicken scratch paper a few days before. His Lordship then realized he was in danger of giving his staff too much credit, too quickly, which could make even scientific dweebs ask for more money. "I mean, I really expected nothing less, h'after all, wot does I pay you for?"

Dr. Philbean scratched his head. Not having excelled in liberal arts, he was unaccustomed to rhetorical questions. "Uh, for research?"

"Spot on," said Bagnold, "and you've done it, eh, Polebean, uh, Philbean."

"Yes, sir," said Professor Philbean. He led Lord Bagnold to a room at the rear of the lab. At the door, he handed His Lordship a pair of sunglasses from a tray and took a pair for himself.

"Wots the idea?" asked Bagnold.

"It's not necessary," explained the doctor, "but it may be more comfortable. We've set up this room to simulate the climatic conditions at your plantation. It would be counterproductive to conduct the experiments in a climate of the British Isles only to find it wouldn't translate to the location where the actual growing would occur."

Professor Philbean opened the door and bade Lord Bagnold go in. Once inside, His Lordship was struck by the heat and the bright light. As Philbean had said, it was like stepping onto the plantation in Borneo. Bagnold immediately thought of the expense of the extra heat and electricity. Still, it was cheaper than shipping his eggheads to the Far East.

The room indeed looked like a tropical haven. Bagnold picked up the leaf of a large plant and cast a dubious glance towards his researcher.

"Again, in order to help generate the most accurate climate conditions," explained Philbean, "we've added other plants native to the Indonesian archipelago. Their oxygen output is unique."

Bagnold frowned. "Unique means expensive." He looked around and pointed to several large pots in the center of the room. "I suppose you gots to add these marrows, too. Suppose you're going to tell me they're friends of the cucumbers. Blimey! These is the biggest squashes wot I've ever seen!"

A puzzled look overspread Professor Philbean's face. "You don't understand, your Lordship. Those aren't squashes. Granted, they are of the order *cucurbitales*..."

"I'm the one what gives the orders 'round 'ere, not some cuckoo," spluttered Bagnold as he smacked the giant vegetable. "I knows you all 'ave got more degrees than a thermometer, but remember 'oo's footin' the bill in this overgrown nursery school. Don't go blindin' me with scientific gobbledygook. I don't care what they is, just what they is doing 'ere."

"But your Lordship," said Philbean, "I only meant to say these aren't squashes; these are your cucumbers."

Lord Bagnold's mouth dropped open just as it was preparing for a fresh round of invective. Then slowly, a grotesque smile overspread his lips. He stared at the giant vegetable and reached out to touch it again, this time with awe and reverence.

"You means…" he whispered.

The Professor, realizing his employer had been placated, nodded cautiously. "Yes, sir, we followed your formula precisely, and this is the outcome."

Bagnold's monstrous grin burst into an even more fiendish laugh. "By gum, 'e did it!"

"He? He who?" asked Philbean.

"Wot? Oh, I was speakin' in the second person singleton," said Bagnold. "I means me, of course, this little, uh, big beauty, this h'ain't not the produce of no one's brain but me own. Produce! Ha! Get it? And when my vast brain power produces produce, it's the vastest produce wot ever was produced! Look at it, Pillboat…"

"Philbean, sir."

"Look at it, wot ever your name is," cackled the life peer, "a rose by any other name still smells, and cucumber this big is still a big cucumber, by 'eck!"

"Yes, your Lordship," said Philbean. He handed Bagnold a clipboard holding a lengthy paper crammed with scientific terms. "Now, if you'll just see the staff's notations and recommendations."

Lord Bagnold flipped through the pages. It was even more Greek than Greek to him. He shoved the clipboard back into the doctor's hands. "You worry about that," said Bagnold, "h'actually, you don't not 'ave to worry. Your work is done 'ere…"

"You mean I'm dismissed?"

"Wot? No, no, I means your work on this magnificent project is over, at least the research bit. Now we gets into the practical h'application. Can you make seeds of these things? Will they grow?"

Dr. Philbean adjusted his glasses. "That's the remarkable aspect of this, your Lordship. These are the third generation of the experiment, the grandchildren of the first plant, as it were. We've already harvested the seeds of the first plants…."

Bagnold looked around. "Where is they?"

"They outgrew the room. We had to move them into the loading bay."

His Lordship clapped his hands with glee. "'Ow big? 'Ow big did my beauties get?"

"As we seemed to be entering into new realms, botanically speaking, we thought it wise to move them while we could," Dr. Philbean explained. "The original is approximately twice the size of these, which seems to be the limit of their maturation."

Lord Bagnold slapped the good professor on his back, almost causing Philbean's glasses to fly off his head. "Excellent work, Professor. 'Ow quickly can you start making seeds of these and shipping them out to me plantation in Borneo?"

"Uh, well," said the Professor, "at the rate of growth, I'd say we can start harvesting almost immediately, but you really should look at the research."

"You worries too much, Prof," said Bagnold. "I'll do the worrying. And we can see there's no worries. Does the formula work? Yes. Does the plants grow bigger? Yes, and then some. Can they go to seed? Yes. That's all I needs to know."

Bagnold started for the door with Professor Philbean on his heels.

"But, your Lordship," said the Professor, "I think you should look at the research."

Bagnold turned and stuck his finger in Philbean's chest, almost knocking over the scientist. "You look at it."

"But cucumbers this size…"

"Is a boon to mankind," laughed Lord Bagnold, "especially one particular mankind… me. Besides, no one is going to eat them."

"No?"

Bagnold sneered. "I h'ain't not in the food business, Philpot, not no how. I'm growing these babies to pulp 'em. They's plants, h'ain't they?"

"Well, yes…"

"Then that's all wot you needs to know," said Bagnold. "You boffins is all just a bunch of eggheads. Too much worry will make them fragile shells crack. You're just jealous."

"Jealous, of whom?"

"Of any ordinary bloke wot who doesn't have a fancy price tag from some gooey university coming up with a genius idea. It's normal people like this fellow… uh, I means, like me… who have imagination. You never would 'ave imagined that these could be grown. But 'e, uh, I means me, uh, I didn't not know wot couldn't be done, so I did it. Savvy? Now, you and your bunch of overpriced ice cream men start on them seeds, chop chop!"

Lord Bagnold turned on his heels and left the lab, leaving Professor Philbean to scratch his head and mutter a resigned: "yes, sir."

– 47 –
Patsy and the Stationary Snack

Patsy followed Egmont Everett Einfalt's instructions to the letter. She went home and played all weekend with her daughter, that is, with their daughter. She took his directions so seriously that she played with Rachel more than she usually would. The housework and shopping that typically occupied part of her weekend were postponed. She had her orders: to play with Rachel. And though she doubted that doing so would magically solve whatever problems plagued the bank and the charity, Patsy still felt it was the least she could do. So, she did it.

As she drove to work Monday morning, Patsy thought about Egmont's unusual initials – EEE – and wondered if he had correspondingly wide feet. Then, she recalled that Purvis often used "Eee" as an exclamation. Was that an omen that despite being engaged to Purvis, Patsy was fated to marry Egmont? And if she married Egmont, and since her name was already changed to Einfalt, would that be her maiden name? That would make her initials PEE!

Her maiden name was Zyobidinski. If she used that, her monogrammed towels would read "PZE," but since they usually placed the last name prominently in the middle, that would read "PEZ." At the next red light, she looked through her purse, suddenly having an urge for candy.

Why did Egmont have to come back? If he'd stayed away a little longer, Patsy would have been married to Purvis Twankey, and her initials would be "PET." PET is much nicer than PEE, she concluded.

As she rode up to the office in the elevator, Patsy turned over the problem in her mind. She could just tell Egmont that he would have to sort it out with Purvis. Purvis was so nice, but she was sure he would physically fight for her. The problem was that Purvis was also so scrawny. Once, she noticed Egmont with his suitcoat off. He didn't have bulging muscles, but she was impressed by the hardness of what he did have. In a fight, Egmont would shred Purvis like an soggy Yorkshire pudding.

Patsy could tell Egmont that he was welcome to stay around as Rachel's father but that she was in love with Purvis and would marry him. She couldn't see a job-sharing situation working out. And such an arrangement would only confuse Rachel.

She stepped out of the elevator and walked toward the office. Patsy would just have to tell Egmont that there was only room for one husband in her life and one father in Rachel's. She only hoped that he would realize that wasn't him and gracefully bow out. On the way to her desk, she paused by the copy center. It was there that they had first met. It was there where Egmont first professed his love for her. At least, she thought he had professed his love. That was always a hazy memory. Kids often imagined they saw Santa Claus in the middle of the night. She supposed that she could imagine what Santa said to her while boffing her atop a high-speed copier. Patsy recalled Egmont's harrowing tale of amnesia and his long quest to find her. She hoped her rejection wouldn't plunge his psyche into a relapse.

After hanging up her coat and putting her purse in her desk, Patsy took a deep breath and approached the conference room. She knocked softly and waited for a response. Maybe her knock was too soft. She flexed her knuckles and delivered a firm yet respectful rap. Again there was no reply. Turning the knob, she opened the door a crack without looking inside.

"Egmont," she whispered as soft as her first knock. "I didn't want to disturb you, especially if you're busy. Egmont?"

Patsy craned her neck around the corner. The room was empty; at least, it was devoid of Egmont Einfalt. She stepped inside and closed the door. She glanced at the clock, thinking perhaps she had arrived too early. Then she noticed the large boardroom table. It was empty, or more precisely, half-empty. Gone were the ledgers and reports that had been there when Egmont arrived. Still, there were all of Patsy's bridal books. What could he have done with the bank's records? Maybe he took them back to his hotel or wherever he was staying. He never told her where he went outside of the office. All that was left on the "business" side of the table was an envelope with "Patsy" in typed letters.

She opened it and read:

> Dear Patsy,
>
> I have completed the necessary repairs to the reports and supporting documents of both the bank and the charity. You will not have any difficulty with your upcoming regulatory examinations; I have seen to that. There were several non-compliant issues that I have cleared up for you. I will submit my findings to the necessary agencies.
>
> Please excuse my hasty departure. I received an urgent call to another assignment. I shouldn't be telling you this, but if anyone is owed an

explanation, it is you. I've been called away to an audit of a South American drug cartel. They've recently been expanding their operations in the United States and have realized that they may not be in compliance with federal regulations (outside of illegal drug trafficking). This may sound odd, but ever since the conviction of Al Capone, criminals are loathe to run afoul of tax laws and bureaucratic red tape. The United States government will turn a blind eye to a lot of nefarious activities, but ignoring regulations is not one of them.

I can't tell you where I am going or when I'll be back. But I hope to return soon to re-consummate our relationship and actualize our ongoing interface.

Until then, I shall remain,

E.E. Einfalt

P.S. – Destroy this letter as soon as possible – Eggy

Patsy slumped into the chair. She re-read the letter. Then looked out the window. Then re-re-read the letter. Then she got up and walked around the table twice. Then sat down again and read the letter one more time. A thought occurred to her. The bank's reports! What had happened to those? She rushed from the room back to her work area and opened the filing cabinets. Patsy breathed a sigh of relief. He had not only cleaned up any regulatory problems, but Egmont had cleaned up after himself. Indeed, the office and the board room looked as if he had never been there. Had he been there? She wondered. Of course, he had been there. That was silly, Patsy told herself. Still, just like his first visit years ago, Egmont Einfalt only lingered as a memory. No one else had seen him. He had been careful about that, and now Patsy realized why. A government regulator couldn't very well be seen fixing the problems he was supposed to be finding. There was no evidence he'd even been there except for…

Patsy gasped. Egmont's letter. The one he had told her to destroy. She had left it on the conference room table. Patsy rushed back into the room. Thankfully, it was still there. She closed the door and locked it behind her. Then she sat down and hurriedly read it twice, trying to commit it to memory. Then, as she had seen in countless spy movies, Patsy ate the letter.

– 48 –
The Mediterranean Trousseau of Mrs. Aloysius Chaircurtain

Hope was renewed! Lord Bagnold had allowed Verity Goodhue to view the rushes of Lorraine Innis' commercials. She could tell Chesney was purposely sabotaging them. After seeing them, Verity had fresh assurance that everything would work out.

It was in this frame of mind that Verity decided to go shopping for their honeymoon. She didn't know when that would be, but she had faith in her man, even if he still was stuck in skirts for the time being.

Verity was at one of the nicer shops in London. She didn't usually spend a lot on herself, despite her father's incredible wealth. But she decided to splurge, wanting to look her best when she and Chesney would finally be man and wife. Not knowing where they were going, Verity had no firm idea what to look for. Would they be going somewhere tropical? Or perhaps an Alpine honeymoon? She laughed to herself about her father's ideal of a romantic getaway: a week in Skegness.

Suddenly, as she perused a rack of cruise wear, Verity was distracted by a familiar voice with an American accent.

"Don't you have anything a little more expensive," said the voice. "This is supposed to be one of London's finer shops. I mean, I'm getting married in this. Don't you have any better silk?"

"I can assure you, madam," said the shop assistant, "that we only carry Mulberry."

Verity turned around. There was a redhead glowering at the assistant. The redhead was very familiar.

"Mulberry silk," continued the assistant, "is the finest silk available. It's called Mulberry because the farmers cultivate the mulberry trees specifically for the purpose of having the silkworms feed on and inhabit them. The combination produces the finest…"

The redhead's eyes grew as fiery as her hair color. "I know that," she snapped. "I know that the worms like those trees. Everyone knows that the mulberry bush, I mean tree, they're the ones that farmers use. I didn't ask for a lesson on what worms eat. Everyone knows what they like to eat. Anyone in this shop…"

The woman turned toward Verity and stopped.

Verity recognized her and called out: "Valerie…"

Before Verity could add the name "Fierro," the redhead, who was none other than Valerie Fierro, launched into a spasm of loud coughs. The shop assistant, fearing she had provoked a customer into an apoplectic fit, produced a chair and rushed to get the victim a glass of water.

Verity rushed to Valerie's side.

"Are you all right, Valerie," she said. The woman's eyes grew large in a combination of panic and anger. Verity wondered if the woman who sounded exactly like Valerie Fierro and looked almost exactly like Valerie Fierro wasn't Valerie Fierro. "Aren't you Valerie Fi…"

Verity's question was cut short by a swift kick to her ankle. She looked down to see the point of the woman's stiletto poised for a second jab.

"Shut up," whispered the woman from behind gritted teeth.

"Pardon me," said Verity, "but I could have sworn you were…OW!"

A second kick had been delivered.

"There's no need for assault. I just thought you were…" Verity instinctively jumped to the side, avoiding another kick.

The redhead's eyes darted side to side, then she said in a low voice. "Yeah, okay, it's me. Just don't say my name."

"Sorry." Verity looked around. "Are you hiding from someone?"

"Hiding?" Valerie forced a titter. "Why would you think I was hiding?"

Verity shrugged. "Well, your appearance is different…"

"So?!" snapped Valerie. "Didn't you ever change your hair or your appearance? No, I suppose you didn't. You're one of those lucky women who finds what works for them when they're in kindergarten."

Verity fought the urge to slap her. She was a lady, this was one of London's more genteel shops, and most of all, she may learn something useful to Chesney. It was obvious that Valerie was traveling incognito. Was she hiding from Lorraine, or was there something else going on? Verity forced a smile onto her face.

"Kindergarten? Oh, yes, I suppose I am rather plain. We all can't be glamorous. That must be why so many women look up to you."

The shop assistant returned with a glass of water. Valerie shooed her away and stood up.

"I couldn't help overhearing," said Verity, "that you're looking for a dress… for your wedding."

"What? No, I mean, yes, that's right," said Valerie.

"That must be why you're keeping a low profile," continued Verity. "I'm sure you have enough to do without the press hounding your every step."

Valerie tossed back her vibrant red locks. "Yes, it is quite a bore. You know how intrusive the paparazzi can be. Oh, no, I suppose you don't. You don't know how lucky you are being able to stand unnoticed among the masses."

"How is your cousin?"

Valerie's eyes widened. A look of panic crossed her face, and she looked around.

"Your cousin Lorraine," clarified Verity.

"What? Oh, yes, of course," said Valerie with a nervous chuckle. "Oh, Lorraine is fine. She's, uh, she's taking a break, you know, after all that trial upset. She's on vacation, in, uh... Wales."

"Wales? Really?" said Verity realizing now that Valerie Fierro had no inkling of where Lorraine was.

"Oh, yes," said Valerie, "I turned her on to Wales. I discovered a wonderful little place. It's called Caerphilly. Ever been?"

"No, is it nice?"

"Oh, yes, it's marvelous," said Valerie, "very exclusive, you know. It's where all the smart set is going."

"I'm sure Lorraine will be coming back," said Verity.

Valerie's eyes shifted back and forth. "Oh, yes, well, you can't stay on holiday forever."

"Even in a paradise like Caerphilly," noted Verity.

"Oh, yes, even Wales gets tiresome eventually."

Verity suppressed a smile. This was too much fun. "What I meant, however, is that Lorraine will be coming back for your wedding."

"Oh, I hope not," blurted Valerie, "that is, I wish she could, but her busy schedule won't allow it. That's Lorraine, busy, busy, busy."

"Maybe you'll see her in Caerphilly," said Verity, "when you're on your honeymoon."

Valerie snorted. "As if I'd go back to... that is, no, we're not going to Wales on our honeymoon."

"But you said all the smart set is there."

"Yes, well," said Valerie, "it's quickly wearing out its trendiness. It's become so popular that no one who's anyone is going there anymore. No, I'll be honeymooning in, uh, in Canada."

The sales assistant who had been bringing out samples for Valerie stopped and looked at her. "I thought you said you wanted appropriate fashions for Gibraltar."

"Gibraltar?" said Verity.

Valerie looked back and forth between the salesgirl and Verity. "Yes, I said Gibraltar," she said to the shopgirl before turning to Verity. "No, I'm going to Lake Louise in Canada."

"I'll go get our winter collection," said the girl.

"No, wait, this is fine," said Valerie, pointing at the more tropical clothing.

"You'd be awfully chilly in these in Canada," said Verity fingering the lightweight fabric.

Valerie gritted her teeth. "I'll rough it."

Verity smiled. "You'll be on your honeymoon. You'll have your love to keep you warm."

A sour expression crossed Valerie's face, which she quickly hid behind a phony smile. "Oh, yes, there will be lots of love snuggles. I doubt we'll get out of the hotel suite."

"You and," Verity paused. "Oh, I'm sorry, you didn't tell me your husband's name."

"Al..." Valerie stopped herself.

"Just 'Al?'"

"Uh, no, of course not, it's short for... Aloysius. Yes, Aloysius is very important in business."

"Oh? My father has a few associates named Aloysius," said Verity. "What's his last name?"

Valerie's eyes darted around the room. "His last name? Uh... Chair... uh... curtain. Yes, that's it, Aloysius Chaircurtain."

"Chaircurtain," repeated Verity. "What an unusual name. I've never heard of it before."

"Yes, well, it is rare," said Valerie. "It's anglicized. Originally it's German."

"German."

"Yes, or Dutch, or Spanish, one of those places not England," said Valerie grasping. She looked at the salesgirl walking away with the garments she had just brought out. "Where are you going with those? I want to try those on!"

The salesgirl stopped. "But I thought you wanted winter clothes."

"No, I don't," snapped Valerie, "You said that, you stupid girl. I want to try these on. And it's none of your business what I say to someone else. You'd better watch yourself. I'm sure your manager wouldn't want to hear about how you've been eavesdropping. First, you lecture me about worms, and then I catch you snooping into my private conversations."

Valerie snatched the garments from the girl's arms and stalked off to the fitting room. The salesgirl's eyes filled with tears. Verity put her arm around the girl's shoulder.

"It's not my fault," said the girl, holding back her tears. "Do you really think she'll complain to my manager? I really need this job."

"I'm sure she's just got pre-bridal jitters," assured Verity. "If it helps, maybe I can have a word with Miss Fierro."

"Who?"

Verity nodded in the direction of the fitting room. "Miss Fierro, the woman you're waiting on."

The girl's anxious expression was replaced by one of confusion. She reached into her pocket and fished out a card. "That's not her name. At least, it's not the one the bill goes to." The girl handed Verity a business card.

"Albrecht Eckner," read Verity aloud.

"She said to send the bill to that name and address," said the girl. "She said that was who she was marrying."

"She's marrying him?"

The salesgirl nodded at the card. "She bragged that she was getting married to this big wheel banker and that they were going to Gibraltar where his bank is. So, she's getting a whole new Mediterranean wardrobe."

– 49 –
The Aberglaubish Attorney

"You gonna divulge him everything, Mikey?" Alphonse asked Michael Valvano as he parked the car outside Julius Rosen's office.

"Everything, Alphonse," said Michael getting out of the car. He started to close the door. "You coming along?"

"Me? You want me to go in? I thought it was like a family type of confabulation."

Michael laughed. "I think you're family, at least you are to me. And you are to our great Aunt Rosa. Aren't you, Sfogliatella?"

Alphonse climbed out of the car. "I am honored for that august designation." Then he pulled a stubby pencil from his pocket and made a note. "I keep forgetting to mention that at my next confession, you know about lying to that old lady about being her nephew."

Michael reached up and clapped him across the shoulders. "If I had to adopt you formally into the family, I would, Alphonse. And besides, as we've learned, the Valvano family is a pretty elastic group."

He held the door for Alphonse, and they went in.

"Gee," whispered Alphonse in the same voice he used when entering a church, "who knew Mr. Rosen had an office, just like a real lawyer."

"He is a real lawyer," said Michael. "Did you see Robert's car outside?"

Alphonse confessed that he hadn't. They entered the anteroom of an office unmarked except for a number on the door. A secretary greeted them and announced them over an intercom. Then she told them to go in.

"Michael," said Julius Rosen standing to shake his hand.

"You remember Alphonse, Julie?"

"Oh, yes," said Rosen looking over the top of his spectacles at the hulking figure of the former hitman. "Yes, Alphonse, of course, he was engaged in a different area of the family concerns."

"No, Mr. Rosen," corrected Alphonse, "Michael here was the one who was engaged, only that didn't work out. But now…"

Michael placed his hand on Al's forearm. "We'll get to that, Alphonse."

Rosen invited them to sit down. There were only two chairs in front of the desk. Michael looked around.

"My brother is late," said Michael.

Rosen sighed. "Yes, well, Robert was called away on business. But, as the family retainer, I fully represent him."

"Shame," said Michael, "I really wanted to see his face when we shared our bit of news. It concerns Nonnia's estate."

Rosen smiled and shook his head. "I thought it might. Forgive me, but as much as I sympathize with your plight, the conditions of the will are sacrosanct. Robert is the legal heir to all of your grandmother's holdings."

Alphonse raised his hand. "'Cuse me, Mr. Rosen. What's sacrosanct?"

"What? Oh, um, it means too important to be interfered with or invalidated," said Rosen.

Alphonse smiled, pulled a small notebook from his pocket, and jotted the new word down.

"But," said Michael, "Robert's not mentioned in the will by name, is he?"

"No," said Rosen, "the rightful heir is the oldest living Valvano. I hope you're not trying to convince me that you are somehow older than your older brother."

"Of course not," said Michael, "but there is Miss Fierro."

"Ah, Miss Fierro," said the lawyer. "I know you believe that Miss Fierro was the child of…" He stopped to leaf through a file on his desk. "Giorgio Fierro, born Giorgio Valvano. I am sympathetic to that view. If it made any difference, I would add that I believe she is your departed grandmother's granddaughter. But Miss Fierro is even younger than you are, so her claim on the estate is even less valid."

Michael took a deep breath. "Yes, well, I've learned that Miss Fierro is actually the valid heir of our grandmother. You see, Robert and I are not really Valvanos."

In all his years of knowing Julius Rosen, Michael never recalled the attorney laughing; even a smile was a rarity. Now, however, Rosen emitted such a hearty guffaw that it was scary. It was like seeing a dog fly or a cow sing opera. Michael sat stoically until the lawyer calmed down.

"Sorry, sorry," said Rosen, "but you…" He searched Michael's eyes, then his expression turned serious. "Wait, you're not joking."

"Not at all," said Michael.

"You're trying to tell me that you and your brother are not the grandsons of the late Mrs. Valvano? Excuse me for my unprofessional outburst just now, but the idea is ridiculous. Why the family resemblance alone…"

"I didn't say Nonnia wasn't our grandmother," said Michael. "I said we weren't Valvanos." He reached into his breast pocket and pulled out a sheath of papers. "We have no Valvano blood. Our grandfather is a German pilot by the name of Zimmer. It's all there, and we've been all over Europe confirming it." He handed Rosen the documents.

Michael described how he was first suspicious after going through Nonnia's photo albums. Then he detailed their trip to Sicily and their meeting with Rosa. Rosa had confessed that Nonnia had gotten pregnant by a German in the Luftwaffe. What followed were trips throughout Germany until they finally discovered the identity of the mysterious airman.

"Herr Zimmer died in the war," said Michael, "but not until he had taken Giorgio Valvano, thinking he was an orphan, to his wife's family's farm in Bavaria."

Julius Rosen sat with his mouth agape as he examined the documents. "This is fantastic."

"*Aberglaubish*," noted Alphonse proudly.

Rosen looked at him.

"Just a German word he picked up," explained Michael.

"We heard that one extensively," said Alphonse. "It might even be…" he glanced at his notepad, "sacrosanct! It means beyond belief."

"I'd tend to agree," muttered Rosen.

"That last document is a DNA test," said Michael. "It verifies that I'm half-German, on my father's side. I'm sure if Robert were to be tested, the results would be the same."

Julius Rosen silently studied the documents for several minutes. Finally, he looked up.

"It would seem," concluded Rosen, "that Miss Fierro satisfies the conditions of the late Mrs. Valvano's estate. She is the rightful heir."

Michael raised his eyebrows. "Really? I thought you'd put up a stronger fight."

Rosen leaned back in his chair. "Michael, you've known me long enough to know that I represent the Valvano family interests. My primary duty is to the family. Because of my decades-long service as the family's legal retainer, I naturally had to work most closely with your brother, Robert. He hired me, but not as his personal attorney. And as the legal trustee of her estate, as outlined by your late grandmother, I work for the estate and whoever is legally designated as the estate's beneficiary."

"*Aberglaubish*," muttered Alphonse.

"I'm glad to hear that," said Michael. "I just thought that Robert would put up a bigger fight."

"I'm sure he will," said the lawyer, "but I will not be the person wielding his weapons. As I said, I work for the estate. Your brother couldn't hire me now if he wanted to, at least not to fight this. I will conduct my own investigation to verify what you've told me, but at face value, the evidence seems conclusive. Have you informed Miss Fierro of your findings?"

Michael shook his head. "No, I don't even know where she is. Somewhere in England, the last anyone heard."

"Just as well," said Rosen. "I wouldn't want her to be informed until I've confirmed everything. And then it will be my responsibility."

The lawyer paused, and an uncharacteristic smile overspread his face. "Miss Fierro will most likely find herself a wealthy woman. And if I may add on a personal note, given that you only share one common grandparent, I believe that any impediment to your nuptials would be removed."

Alphonse's brow lowered in thought. "Impediments? Nuptials?"

Michael turned to his friend. "He means we could be married."

Alphonse took out a notepad and pencil. "I kinda surmised that," he said, licking the end of the pencil and scribbling down the new words.

"Yes," said Michael to Rosen, "I thought of that, as well. Too bad we didn't know that at the time. Of course, Nonnia knew about the German but never admitted it for obvious reasons. We're going to England to try and find Valerie. That's the last place she was seen."

Rosen pulled a file from his desk drawer and handed it to Michael. "This may be of use. Your brother was trying to find Miss Fierro, as well. There's an investigator working on the case. Here's his card…"

"Streatham?" said Michael reading the card.

"It's a suburb of London," said Rosen. "That's where his office is."

Michael stood. "Okay, Mr. Rosen, I'll be in touch. If I find Valerie first, I'll let you know. If you find her first, I'd appreciate you telling me."

"It will be my pleasure," said the lawyer, without a trace of joy.

"And, of course," said Michael, "I'll let you tell my brother the news, as well."

"That," Julius Rosen said slowly, "will be interesting."

– 50 –
Romance in the Third Person

Verity Goodhue entered the foyer of the film studio on the outskirts of London.

"Hello," she said to the receptionist, "I'm here to…"

"There you is," boomed her father's voice.

Verity turned. "Hello, Father, I'm a few minutes early. I didn't know about the traffic."

"Haw!" Snorted Lord Bagnold. "I almost h'expected you to be camped out on the doorstep overnight."

"Why would I…"

"You is so damned keen to meet the bane of my existence."

"You mean Lorraine Innis?" said Verity. "I thought you were eager to have her as your spokesman, uh, spokeswoman."

Lord Bagnold flicked at his mustache. "Yes, well, be careful of wots you wishes for, as I'm sure you'll find out once you meet 'er. She's the most difficult woman wot ever I was up against."

"Meaning Mrs. Innis has standard, scruples, morals…"

His Lordship nodded. "You makes it out like I'm some sort of beast. I don't not mind people, even women, 'aving morals, as long as they keep them to themselves and don't jam 'em into the wheels of industry, especially me own industry!"

"Sorry, Father," she said.

"C'mon," he said, guiding her by the elbow through a security door. "That's wot you're 'ere for. I only agreed to let you talk to Mrs. Pain-in-the-Bum so you could try to talk some sense into 'er. You know, bring 'er around to me own way of thinking."

Verity nodded. "Yes, I remember. Though I don't see how I can convince Mrs. Innis to go against her good taste and conscience."

Bagnold bent down, coming nose to nose with his daughter. "Look 'ere, missy, I gots a lot riding on this, and you'll do as you're told."

Verity could feel the blood rising to her temples. She took a deep breath. It would be satisfying to tell off her father, but it might cause more trouble for her Beloved.

"All right, Father... dear," she said sweetly.

"Wot?"

"I'm ready to meet Mrs. Innis."

Lord Bagnold studied her face for a moment, then shrugged. He led her to a doorway. "Okay, she's in 'ere."

Verity paused with her hand on the doorknob. "Did you tell her I was coming?"

"Wot for? I told 'er I wanted 'er to meet someone," said Bagnold. "I did not say 'oo, because she don't not know you from the doorpost."

"Oh, yes," she said, "of course. I suppose Mrs. Innis meets so many people."

"Round 'ere she meets 'ooever I tells 'er to meet," he said.

"Oh, yes, of course, you're in charge, Father," said Verity.

"Now, if you could convince Mrs. Lorraine 'Igh-and-Mighty Innis of that, I would be much obliged." He started to turn away.

"Father, aren't you coming in?"

"Wot? Oh, no, I, uh, I've gots to do something, somewhere," he looked around furtively. "But you goes ahead, 'ave your nice little girly chat. That's wot you wanted."

"But don't you want to know how it goes," she said.

"Wot? I'll know," he coughed. "That is to say, I trusts you, me own daughter. You goes ahead."

Verity started to turn the knob and watched as her father started down the hall. He stopped at the next door down and reached for the doorknob. Then he glanced back at her and motioned for her to go ahead. That confirmed her suspicion.

She went inside the conference room. Lorraine was sitting there. She was wearing a simple rose-colored suit. Her face lit up as soon as she saw Verity. She jumped up and was about to speak when Verity interrupted.

"Hello, Mrs. Innis," she said, "my name is Verity Goodhue. I'm Lord Bagnold's daughter. I've been so anxious to meet you."

Verity's eyes darted around the room, toward the ceiling and the wall, and then subtly tapped her ear. Lorraine nodded.

"My father wished he could be here, to formally introduce us," said Verity, "but he had pressing business nearby."

"Nearby?" repeated Lorraine.

"Quite nearby," said Verity.

"Marvelous," said Lorraine grimly. "I mean, your father must be a marvelous comfort to you, especially being so close."

"You have no idea."

"Oh, I think I do," said Lorraine. "It's been quite an experience working closely with him. I only hope I can deliver everything he deserves."

"That's why I'm here, or at least part of the reason," said Verity. "Father wanted me to encourage you to, well, to do your best on those advertisements for him."

"Yes, I'm sure he would have asked himself, but he's such a shy, retiring man," said Lorraine. "Don't worry, I'll give your father exactly what's coming to him. But you said that's only part of the reason. Why else are you here, Miss Goodhue?"

Verity smiled. "I've always admired you, Mrs. Innis. I've followed your career very closely. When father said he was working with you, I told him I'd very much like to meet you."

"But I've been working for your father for weeks now," Lorraine said. "Were you away?"

"No, Father didn't want me to meet you," said Verity. "That is, he didn't want me to distract you."

Lorraine smiled, and Verity could see Chesney's love shining through. "Your father is right," said Lorraine. "That would have been a distraction. But, I'm glad you came in today." Lorraine pointed at Verity's hand. "Oh, I see you're engaged."

"Yes," she said, "that is, I was supposed to get married. Then there was an accident, and my Beloved, well, he went away."

"I'm sure he loves you very much," said Lorraine.

"And I love him just as much," said Verity, "and more every day."

"I'm sure that he knows that, wherever he is. I know you'll see him again, and you'll be with him forever."

"I know that," said Verity. They stared longingly into each other's eyes across the table. Verity wanted to say so much more but was cognizant that they were being eavesdropped upon. Finally, she decided she should say something, lest her listening father become suspicious. "Oh, speaking of weddings, I saw a friend of yours or at least a relative... Miss Fierro."

"Valerie?" Lorraine leaned forward. "Really? I haven't seen her since I came to England, and aside from a single postcard, I haven't heard from her. Where did you see her? Is she all right?"

"I saw her in London," said Verity. "She was shopping."

Lorraine's brows knitted. "Really? I would have thought she'd have contacted me, or at the very least, her reappearance would have made the gossip columns."

Verity bit her lip. This wasn't the time or place to air her suspicions about Valerie. Apparently, poor Chesney still had a blind spot where Valerie Fierro was concerned. To delve any deeper might indicate to those listening that Verity had a relationship with Lorraine. Fortunately, Verity had anticipated not being able to speak freely with Lorraine, and she had formulated a backup communications plan.

"Maybe I was mistaken," said Verity. "I did meet your cousin, but that was months ago. I probably was confused."

Lorraine studied Verity's face.

"On an entirely different subject," said Verity reaching into her handbag, "I know, that is, I read in the papers, that you're quite a devotee of Charles Dickens."

"You know," Lorraine said before catching herself, "that is, yes, I am."

Verity smiled. "Oh, good, because I got you a rare edition of one of his novels." She reached across the table and handed Lorraine a paperback book. "It's *Martin Chuzzlewitt*."

Lorraine picked up the book and studied it. It was a recent mass-market printing and obviously not rare. She looked up with a puzzled expression.

"I think you'll find the annotated comments especially enlightening," said Verity.

Lorraine thumbed open the book, and then her face lit up.

"Oh, yes, this is excellent," she said. "This edition will bring an entirely new perspective to it. I'm looking forward to studying it."

Verity smiled. "I thought you would." She glanced at her watch and then at Lorraine. Though she wished she could stay for hours, it was clear that meeting this way was putting a strain on Chesney. She saw subtle clues that he was having difficulty maintaining his feminine façade the longer she stayed.

"Well," said Verity, standing, "I'd better be going. I know you must be terribly busy doing what you're doing for father; for whatever reason you're doing it." Verity grimaced. That last comment was ill-conceived. And while she wondered why Chesney had agreed to work for Lord Bagnold, this was not the time or the place to discuss it. Especially not with her father listening in the next room.

"I, uh, that is, your father..." Lorraine was fumbling for an answer.

"I mean," said Verity, "that your work for my father will greatly benefit your various charities. Well, I really must go. It was a pleasure to meet you, Mrs. Innis."

Lorraine stood. "Yes, it was delightful to see you, that is, to meet you, too, Miss Goodhue. I hope I can see you soon, uh, after I read this book. Thank you again."

Verity paused, fighting the urge to rush across the room and hug Lorraine. She looked down and noticed Lorraine had a white-knuckle hold on the table, evidentially battling the same desire. Instead, she just waved and rushed out the door.

In the hallway, Verity leaned against the door and took a deep breath. That was more difficult than she imagined. She only hoped the meeting hadn't made her Beloved's situation worse.

"Thanks a fat lot!"

Verity turned to see her father standing beside her. He didn't look happy.

"Thank you, for what, Father?"

"Haw! Thank you for nothing," snorted Lord Bagnold. "Your little chat with Mrs. Innis didn't not do me a bit of good, no 'ow!"

Verity stood up straight and looked at the door.

"Could you please do a good job for me Dad?" whined Bagnold, imitating Verity in a high-pitched voice.

"How do you know what I said to Mrs. Innis?" said Verity. "There's only one entrance into that room, and I just left it. Unless you've learned to slither under doors."

"To think that me own flash of blood is comparing me to a snake!"

"To think that my own father would eavesdrop on his daughter's private conversations," Verity retorted.

"Wot? Well, yes, I mean no," flustered Bagnold. "I means this is a production 'ouse. All the rooms is wired for sound. I just 'appened into a room next door, and the mikes was on."

Verity stared at him long enough to make him squirm. "Yes, of course." She started towards the exit.

"I means it," said Lord Bagnold, following her.

"I said 'of course.'"

"I am innocent," he said.

"I believe you," said Verity with scant conviction. She reached the entrance to the building.

"You does? Well, good," said Lord Bagnold, "cause it's true. But, let's not change the subject. I sends you in there to get that Innis bird to straighten up and fly right, and you hold some sort of girl's book club."

Verity turned and stuck her finger in his face. "Well, then, we both were disappointed, weren't we? You wanted me to get Lorraine to tow your line, and I wanted a simple meeting with her away from prying ears!"

Verity walked out of the building with her father on her heels.

"I'll talk to 'er," said His Lordship, "I'll tell 'er you said that she should go along…"

"It's bad enough you were eavesdropping, Father," said Verity. "Now you want to lie and put words in my mouth. If you'll excuse me, my ride is waiting."

Lord Bagnold looked over to the visitors' parking.

"WOT! 'IM?" His face turned a shade of purple that would have been lovely in a watercolor sunset. On his face, not so much.

"What?" Verity looked around and saw the cause of her father's agitation. "That's my friend, Mr. Li. You've seen him before. I know you don't like him, but…"

"Don't likes him?" Spluttered Lord Bagnold. "No, I don't 'ave an 'abit of getting chummy with blokes wot picks up famous women on the 'ighway. Wot did you just call me? A slithering thing? Now, you is the one who's going all snakey! Me own daughter. I'm 'arboring a wiper in me bosom!"

"What are you talking about?" said Verity.

"You don't knows?" said Bagnold. "Well, either you're in caboose with kidnappers, or you're the grade-A prize chump of the year, me girl!"

"I don't understand?"

Lord Bagnold leaned over, nose to nose, with his daughter. "You don't, eh? Well, just to give me own spawn the benefits of the doubt, I'll let you beat it before I call the cops and have you knicked, both of you, for conspiring to kidnap! Maybe I'm the chump, letting you in to see me little goldmine! But you'd better make yourself scarce, you and Mr. Wu. If I sees you near Mrs. Innis again, I'll give you the same treatment that Chinaman is supposed to get. And tell 'im I could have 'im arrested for breaking 'is part of the bargain! Now, I'm going to see Lorraine 'Igh-and-Mighty Innis and tell 'er 'ow it's going to be!"

With that, Lord Bagnold turned on his heels and stormed back into the building.

Verity stood with her mouth agape. She looked at her father as he departed and then over to where Li Gao was waiting. And suddenly, she understood why Chesney had agreed to work for her father.

"I suppose, my Beloved," she muttered while looking at the building, "I've got to do the next part alone."

– 51 –
The Chalet of Magical Delights

Robert Valvano stood outside the weathered wooden building. He looked both ways. He couldn't afford to be seen, not here, not by anyone he knew. His lawyer, Julius Rosen, would call it an unprofitable urge. His wife, Megan, would want to know why he wasn't satisfied with what she brought to their marriage. His business associates and rivals, well, it didn't bear thinking about what they'd do if they knew. It was just something Robert had to do. It was a higher priority than meeting his brother. Michael probably wanted to beg for money after being left out of Nonnia's will.

Robert took one last furtive look and slipped into the building. There were no other patrons around, not at this time of the day, only the older woman at the counter. She looked up from the magazine she was reading.

"Back again," she noted. Robert Valvano was a regular, but she only knew him by his face. He always paid cash.

"Yeah," he said, "I mean, yes." He took some bills from his wallet and handed them to the woman.

The woman rang up the amount on her old cash register and handed him a small paper receipt in faint purple ink.

"I don't have to give you directions," she said, nodding towards a heavy velvet curtain.

"Thanks," said Robert. He pulled back the curtain, plunging into his secret world. Inside it was dark. It was sometimes, depending on when you entered. He looked up at the ceiling. Tiny lights embedded in the black ceiling panels approximated starlight. He looked down. There were the lights of the villages, farms, freight yards, and towns, all in precise miniature scale. He stood by the entrance for a moment, waiting for the simulated dawn. Slowly, the lights came up on another new day in the world of the Choo-Choo Chalet. He exhaled as the detail came into breathtaking fullness.

Robert Valvano had always loved model railroads. One of the few happy memories of his childhood came here at the Choo-Choo Chalet. He remembered the first time he was taken there. He was six years old. It was magical. He asked for a train set of his own for his next birthday. While he got it, his parents never encouraged him in the hobby. When he asked his father to help him build a larger layout, his father told him it was frivolous and not something a grown man should do. It was a toy and a waste of time. So, he never got beyond the simple oval of track, the one little engine, the boxcar, the coal car, the passenger car, and the caboose. Still, he would sit transfixed, watching his little trains go around, imagining the magical world he would build if only he could. When the family ventured out around Lancaster, which was rare, Robert would beg to be taken for a visit to the Choo-Choo Chalet. Sometimes, grudgingly, his pleas would be answered, but never for as long a visit as he would like. Robert would try to move as slowly as possible, absorbing every detail. Still, he would be prodded along like a truculent calf and then back out through the curtain.

"You're too old for that," Robert was told sharply when he was ten. Then his younger brother, Michael, accidentally broke his train. If he was too old to visit the Choo-Choo Chalet, a replacement train was out of the question. He hated Michael for taking that small pleasure from him, even though he knew it was an accident. In the rush to groom him for adult responsibilities, Robert's love of model railroads went dormant for years. Then, one day while in college, Robert was exiting a diner after a late night of partying with his friends. In the restaurant foyer, in a rack filled with local tourist brochures, he saw the flyer for the Choo-Choo Chalet. Through bleary eyes, he drank in the glory of his childhood in glossy, four-color printing. His friends came out, and he quickly stashed the brochure in his pocket. He would not risk being told again that he was "too old for that," especially not by his peers.

Now, Robert looked around the large room where he was the afternoon's only visitor. It hadn't changed much in the years since. The walls were still covered with 1960s wood paneling. Aside from a two-foot wide walkway around the edges, the area was filled with the elaborate scale model layout of hills, valleys, town, bridges, tunnels, back roads, highways, and most importantly, trains. The entire world rested on a four-foot high platform, shielded from grasping younger hands by a plexiglass barrier. Off to the side, raised behind darkened glass, was what Robert assumed was a control room, though the entire layout ran on an automated schedule.

When first he was married, Robert brought his wife there, hopefully, to share in his wonderment. Meghan's reaction was even harsher than his father's had been. Though she didn't put it into words, the look on her face spoke more deeply than any words of derision ever could. Since then, it was Robert's private escape, a place only he could appreciate, and he came to prefer it that way. The Choo-Choo Chalet allowed Robert to decompress, to recharge his inner child so he could be the ruthless bastard he needed to be the rest of the time.

As he watched the orderly world pass by, the regular arrival and departure of the miniature trains, Robert thought of his own world. Valerie Fierro's arrival may have upset his timetable, and now her departure further confused his plans. Still, he was confident that he would set her straight. There was time for that later. This was Robert's time in his private world.

Robert was losing himself in watching a passenger train stop at a small suburban station when his private world was invaded by the ringing of his cellphone. If it had been human, he would have strangled it. As it was electronic, he fumbled to answer it as quickly as possible. It was Julius Rosen.

"What the hell do you want," Robert growled in a whisper. "I told you I wasn't to be disturbed."

"I thought you'd want to know about my meeting with Michael," said the lawyer.

"Not particularly; that's why I've got a lawyer to toss out the garbage," said Robert.

There was a pause.

"You there, Julie," said Robert. "Are we done?"

"I'm not quite done," said the lawyer, "but suffice it to say, you are."

Robert laughed. "Yeah, right; did my sniveling brother threaten to sue me for a piece of the business?"

"He doesn't want any of it," said Julius.

"Good, 'cause he ain't getting any!"

"And there's a lot of that going around," said the lawyer cryptically.

Robert stared at the phone. Figuring out what lawyers meant was a waste of time. "Yeah, well, want did he want?"

"Michael wanted," said Rosen, "to give you information."

"Don't tell me he's dropping a dime on that Fierro bitch," said Robert. "Where did he find her?"

"He found her place in the Valvano family tree," said Rosen.

"I've heard that tune before, Julie. But it's a load of shit. She's not in my family."

"You're right; she's not in your family, at least not fully, Mr. Zimmer."

"Zimmer? Who the f**k is Zimmer?"

"As it turns out," said Rosen, "you are, along with your brother. At least that was the name of the German pilot who was your grandfather."

"This isn't funny," growled Robert.

"Which is why no one is laughing. Nevertheless, it is true."

The thoughts raced through Robert Valvano's mind as he watched the model trains speed through the miniature world in front of him.

"We can buy him off," said Robert thinking aloud.

"Who?"

"Who do you think?" snapped Robert. "My rat of a brother."

"Unfortunately," said the lawyer, "he's not looking for a payout. He's looking for the truth."

"I always knew he was too good for my own good," said Robert. "So, who do we buy off, the Fierro bitch?"

"I doubt you could buy her off," said Rosen. "Besides, the estate is hers. You can't pay her with what's already hers."

"The dirty bitch," snarled Robert.

"And you and your brothers are bastards," noted Julius Rosen, "at least half-bastards, once removed."

"We can fight it," said Robert, "we have to fight it. We'll say it's fake."

Rosen was silent for ten seconds. "I doubt that would hold up in court. Your brother has the proof."

"Yeah, but did he tell Fierro?"

"Not yet. He was going to England to find her and relate the news."

"Julius, Julie," Robert pleaded, "You gotta figure a way around this. You're a slick lawyer... you're my lawyer."

Robert heard a sigh. "Actually, I represent the estate. As long as Miss Fierro is the legal heir, I take direction from her. I'm sorry, Robert."

Robert stared at the phone after the lawyer hung up. "You're gonna be sorry. Jew bastard! After all I did for you! Estate's lawyer. As long as that bitch is the legal..." Robert angrily tossed the cell phone across the room, over the plexiglass barrier, and into the display. The phone bounced off a miniature barn and into the freight train, derailing it. The intrusion of the phone upset the illusion of the otherwise perfect little realm. Though Robert was the only visitor this weekday afternoon, the tiny world was overseen by an operating deity in a raised control booth. On the rare occasion of a malfunction, a man would emerge from the booth, open one of the trap doors in the platform, crawl beneath it to one of the access panels cleverly camouflaged across the layout, and set things right again. Robert had only seen it happen a few times in all the years he'd been visiting the Choo-Choo Chalet.

After the train derailed, a buzzer could be heard in the control booth. The dozens of trains came to a stop. The sound of someone descending steps followed, and the door opened. At the same time, the lights began to dim as the layout approached its nighttime scene. A shadowy figure emerged and quickly disappeared through a nearby access hatch. Robert watched, following the sound of the man scuffling beneath the platform. Then a piece of the landscape, shifted as if by an earthquake before lifting up and sliding back from underneath the platform. A man's head appeared like some subterranean giant emerging from his grotto. He reached up for the derailed engine and carefully placed it back on the track. Then he sank back down, below the surface, concurrent with the lights slowly increasing with the approaching dawn. Just as the man's head ducked under the landscape, the controller turned his face toward Robert.

Robert Valvano recoiled at the face, uncertain he had seen it. With the lights low, it was evident Robert couldn't be seen, even if the man had been looking in that direction. As he heard the man rumble through the substrata of the layout, Robert hurried to the access door.

As the man emerged, Robert grasped his hand to help him out.

"Thanks, pal," said the man, standing. His last syllable was pinched as Robert squeezed him by the Adam's apple.

"Shorty Long," Robert growled.

"M-M-Mr. Valvano," the man, who indeed was Shorty Long, squeaked as best as he could through his constrained windpipe.

"I thought you were dead," said Robert.

"I-I can explain," said Shorty.

"Go ahead," said Robert relaxing his grip but still holding on to Shorty with his other hand.

"Um, well," Shorty looked around the room and then back at his captor. "I'm not?"

"Obviously," said Robert with more than a bit of displeasure. It was bad enough that Shorty Long, a man he had ordered killed, was still alive, but to find him here, violated the sanctity of the Choo-Choo Chalet.

"I'm sorry," said Shorty, "uh... I think."

"Don't apologize," said Robert, without any sense of absolution for the hapless Shorty Long. "You didn't mess up your own execution."

"It wasn't Alphonse's fault, neither," said Shorty, not wanting to get his would-be assassin into deeper trouble.

"No? What did he do, miss?"

"Heh, heh," laughed Shorty nervously, "no, that's a good one, no, he didn't miss. I guess he was talked out of it, but it's okay. Your brother, Michael, told him to let me go. So, it's okay."

Robert grabbed Shorty by the throat and pushed him against the plexiglass barrier.

"It's okay, huh?" said Robert. "If it's so okay, I suppose that's why you're hiding out here, huh? Because it's okay?"

"Hiding?" Shorty Long stammered. "No, no, I ain't hiding. My cousin's got a friend, and his family runs the place, and they gave me a job. It's nice and quiet."

"And outta the way for a guy who's supposed to be dead twenty miles from here."

Shorty had no response except to hang there against the plexiglass. That's why Alphonse hadn't been around, Robert thought. He assumed that the big idiot had gone to ground after disposing of Shorty. Now, he knew the truth. Alphonse was with Michael.

"Uh, Mr. Valvano..." whispered Shorty.

Robert looked at Shorty Long and relaxed his grip. He studied Shorty's shifty features. Shorty had done a good job blowing up Lorraine Innis' car and helping to pin it on Valerie. Having Alphonse dispose of him was just to tie up loose ends. Perhaps a live Shorty was advantageous in light of what Julius Rosen had just told him.

"Shorty, Shorty," said Robert, a smile returning to his face.

Shorty Long smiled nervously. "Uh, yeah, Mr. Valvano."

"Shorty, I think we've got something for you in the organization."

"Another job, Mr. V?"

"Let's say it's more than a job," said Robert. "It's more like a full-time position. An opening has just opened up."

– 52 –
Evelyn and Her Lethal Paperclip

I appreciate the update, Agent MacKay," said Paul Rocher as they sat in his hotel suite. "I want to give Mrs. Innis her space and not feel like the government is hovering over her."

Margie MacKay smiled. "But you're retired now, Sir. You're no longer a government agent."

Rocher nodded. "Technically, I am still working. My retirement starts in another six months. I've accumulated so much time over the years that I'm officially on vacation."

"Without your family?"

"My wife talked about coming over in a little bit, but she…"

"Understands?"

"It's essential to have an understanding spouse," said Rocher in an avuncular tone. "If you're still in the service when you get married, you'd be well to remember that."

"Yes, sir."

"Sorry, I didn't mean to lecture you. And please, drop the 'sir' stuff. I told you, you can call me Paul."

"Yes, sir, uh, Paul."

Rocher rose. "So, I'm on vacation, and you're on a leave of absence. Any idea when Mrs. Innis will return to the States?"

"She has to complete those commercials for Lord Bagnold. And presumably, that will wrap up the lawsuit, her reason for coming here."

Rocher shook his head. "Still hard to believe with all the classy endorsements she's done and the high standards that she's set, Mrs. Innis would hawk toilet paper for a guy like Bagnold."

"I don't understand it either," said MacKay. "Lorraine, Mrs. Innis, is often a mystery to me, too."

"You've essentially put your career on hold to protect her," said Rocher. "If she doesn't confide in you, who does she open up to?"

"She was close to her cousin, Valerie Fierro, and her chief-of-staff, Clodagh Clott," said Margie. "But both have gone missing. One of the reasons I stick close to Lorraine is so the same thing doesn't happen to her. I hate to sound like some conspiracy kook. It's almost like someone is working behind the scene, causing all these strange situations."

"Yes, well, I'm sure there's a good explanation for this without jumping into the realm of mysterious cabals and nefarious plots," Rocher laughed. He only hoped his laughter didn't betray his nervousness. He looked at his watch to change the subject. "Oh, hey, look at the time. Didn't you say you were picking up Mrs. Innis?"

Margie MacKay jumped up. "Oh, you're right. I'd better go." She crossed to the door of the suite. "I'll let you know if I hear anything... about anything."

A moment after she left, Rocher heard a knock on the door. He opened it, expecting to see Margie. "Did you forget something..."

A chambermaid was standing there.

"Oh, sorry, I thought you were someone else."

"I came to turn down the bed, sir," she said. There was something odd but familiar about her voice.

Rocher looked at his watch again. "Turn down the bed? At two o'clock in the afternoon? Why..."

Before he could finish his sentence, the maid shoved him inside and shut the door. Rocher's eyes widened as he looked into the maid's face.

"You?"

"I couldn't very well be the bellhop again," said Vyvan Lily.

"Well, I knew you were a master of disguises," said Rocher, "but I never saw this side of you before."

"Shut up," said Lily, "or the bed won't be the only thing I turn down!"

Rocher looked over the rogue agent from head to toe and nodded in grudging admiration. "It's a perfect disguise. You look like an average woman, an average woman who could kill a man with nothing more than a paperclip, but an average woman."

Lily stared at him, and for a moment, Rocher wondered if this chambermaid was carrying a paperclip with his name on it. Loathe to let Lily see him sweat, Rocher quickly changed the subject.

"Well, I'm glad you dropped by," said Rocher. "Yes, and like I said, that's a very impressive disguise."

"Cut the crap," sneered Lily. "This isn't a social visit. Sit down."

Rocher did so. "Yeah, I didn't think it was. What can I do for you..." He leaned forward to look at the nametag on the uniform. "...Evelyn."

Lily paced back and forth in front of the sofa before sitting opposite him.

"What can you do for me?" snorted Lily. "It's what I can do for you? Like not maiming you right here. You sent me on a wild goose chase to Delaware. Delaware of all places."

"Delaware's not so bad," said Rocher.

"Yeah, it's delightful, except for months with a vowel in them. I was looking for Lorraine, and she was in London all the time."

"Yes, we know that now," said Rocher. "During your last visit, I had no idea where Mrs. Innis was. I don't exactly have your phone number, RR. Besides, it soon was common knowledge after she was rescued."

"By Nigel Verve," muttered Lily.

"You know him?"

"I know of him," said Lily with a hint of professional jealousy. "He's got a reputation for being a slick ladies' man."

Rocher looked at Lily's legs and shook his head. "Don't worry, I think you're safe, Evelyn."

Lily's eyes turned steely. "If I saw even the hint of a grin, I'd take care of you right now."

Rocher raised his hands. "Look, it wasn't my idea for you to go to Delaware."

"You mentioned the money," said Lily.

"If you recall, I said that to myself," said Rocher. "I was thinking aloud, and even then, not very loudly. You were the one who jumped on the lead."

Lily stood and tugged at his apron. "Fortunately, it wasn't a complete waste of time. Egmont Einfalt took care of that."

"Who?"

"Never mind. Some hinky things were going on there. I fixed those before they could hurt us."

"Us?"

"Lorraine and I," said Lily.

"You're a team then?"

"Zip it," snarled the ersatz chambermaid, "you know what I mean. I, that is, we created Lorraine Innis."

"Do I have to keep reminding you that we only supported her backstory? You're not her father, or mother, despite present appearances to the contrary."

Lily ran his lower lip against his teeth. "I know I'm not her father or mother, smart ass, but I might as well be. There's more to Lorraine than meets the eye. I still don't know who erased her past when we first met her, but they did a first-class job of it. It's disturbing enough to find out there's someone as good as you in the field, but then someone, probably the same person or persons, managed to torpedo her vice presidential nomination. I hate playing defense."

Rocher leaned back in his seat. "So, you go on offense, running around the globe shooting up Russian bunkers and hacking into financial records, and who knows what else."

Lily stared at him. "So, what's your point?"

Rocher shook his head. "Nothing. Actually, it's probably a normal day for you. I'm just mystified to understand your motivation."

"My motivation?" Lily looked around the room, "You're the one on leave looking out for her. Of course, I know your motivation. You're trying to relive the great love of your life."

Rocher's fists clenched.

"Take it easy, Paul," continued Lily. "I know you're too much of a straight shooter, the epitome of the clean-cut 1950 G-man. It's not like that. I know you too well."

"She's, well, she's like a daughter to me."

Lily slapped his hands together. "See, we're on the same page. Lorraine Innis is the daughter you never had, and she's the daughter I practically built from scratch. We're both looking out for her. Of course, we have different approaches to our duty. You prefer to stay close and protect her from immediate threats. You're like a good strong lock on the front door."

"And you?"

Lily smiled. "I'm the early warning system, the satellite that scans the world for incoming missiles, and when I find one, I take it out before it can come close to the target. Neat and clean."

"I see," nodded Rocher, "but I just want to protect Lorraine so she can enjoy a happy life after all this. What's your endgame, Evelyn?"

The cold stare of Vyvian Lily turned frigid as his eyes narrowed. "I just want what's best for us."

Paul Rocher was about to ask Lily's definition of "us" when a knock was heard at the door. Rocher turned his head. Lily jumped to his feet and rushed back to the bathroom.

Rocher opened the door to find Margie Mackay.

"Forget something?" he asked, glancing over his shoulder toward the bathroom.

"No," said Margie, "Lorraine called me. She's having dinner tonight with that British agent."

"Nigel Verve?"

"Yes, him," she said. "I know there's supposed to be a certain comradery between people in our line of work, but that man gives me the creeps. Sorry, that sounds pretty unprofessional."

"I don't think so," said Rocher. "Instincts are an important part of our profession."

"And it's not his professional credentials that bug me," continued Margie. "After all, Verve did find Lorraine."

"But?"

"Oh, I don't know," she said, sitting on the sofa, "I hate to say it, but it's a woman thing. He just looks at every member of the opposite sex like he's God's gift to them. Mrs. Innis thinks so, too."

224

Rocher craned his neck, trying to see back to where Lily was. "Mrs. Innis said that?"

"Not in so many words," said Margie, "but I know Verve was flirting with her if you can call it that. That's one woman you don't want to treat like an object of conquest."

"Lorraine? Uh, no, definitely not," said Rocher, looking down the hall.

"I've known guys like Verve, not on such a grand scale, but he probably takes that as a challenge, like some kind of foreplay, and... is there something going on? You keep looking down the hall?"

"What? No," said Rocher, "it's just we're not alone; the, uh, the maid is back there."

"Oh, sorry," said Margie, "did I say anything I shouldn't have had?"

"Probably not," said Rocher, "I guess I'm always a bit paranoid after years of looking over my shoulder."

"All done, sir," said Lily, coming down the hall, carrying a load of towels.

Margie Mackay turned around. She scanned the maid from head to toe and then looked back at Rocher. "Well, I should be going. If Mrs. Innis doesn't need me, I'm going to do a little bit of shopping. Oh, may I use your restroom before I go?"

"Certainly," said Rocher, "it's just down the hall."

"Thanks," said Margie. She started down the hall but paused as she passed the chambermaid. "Excuse me, Miss..."

It happened so quickly. Lily had made the first move, grabbing Mackay by the wrist and attempting to twist it behind her back. Margie Mackay suspected something wasn't quite right and was ready with a flip that sent Lily on his back. Before Margie could take advantage of this, Lily countered with a double kick to Margie's stomach. The force of this would have sent Margie flying, but she hit the wall instead and used that to propel herself back in her attacker's direction. Lily was too quick and rolled to the side. Margie landed on the floor, and Lily sprang atop her and put his hand around her neck. Rocher grabbed a candlestick from the mantel and rushed to take out the ex-operative. Lily turned just in time to see his old friend swing. Lily ducked and avoided the candlestick, but the moment of distraction allowed Margie to break her attacker's chokehold by grabbing the maid's uniform and tearing it.

Apparently, seeing that his old friend was now a new enemy, Lily took the opportunity to retreat. He elbowed Margie's head, disengaging himself from her long enough to dash for the door. The entire action took less than 30 seconds.

Rocher helped Margie to her feet.

"Let me get you a drink," he said, heading for the bar.

Margie nodded as she panted. "I could use one. Know him?"

Rocher looked up. "Him? You knew, I mean, how did you know?" He handed her a tumbler of whiskey.

225

"Thanks," she said, downing the drink in one swig. "Well, either the hotel is hiring Olympic lady wrestlers with anger issues, or that was a professional. I haven't seen moves like that since I went through hand-to-hand combat training. Besides…" She bent down and stood up again, holding a flesh-colored prosthetic. "He left behind one of his boobs."

– 53 –
The Odiferous Osculation
of the Little Housewife

Lorraine Innis was led down the oak-paneled hallway by a man wearing a uniform of sorts. He wasn't a maître de and certainly not a waiter. She'd never been in private gentlemen's club before, and this one was undoubtedly one of the most private. Its exclusivity was underlined by the fact that its entrance looked like an ordinary door down a quiet street in London's Mayfair section. She had been chauffeured there in a Rolls Royce no less.

"In here, Miss," said her guide as he unlocked the door to a private dining room. "Rudolph will be here, momentarily."

Lorraine almost said she wasn't there to meet Rudolph and that she must be in the wrong room. But before she could say so, the captain, majordomo, or whoever he was, had exited. Almost simultaneously, another door opened, and a man who looked like a waiter, albeit a very high-class one, entered.

"Rudolph?" said Lorraine.

"Yes, ma'am," he said. "May I offer you an aperitif?"

"No, thank you," said Lorraine.

Rudolph bowed out of the room.

Lorraine looked around. There were framed 18th and 19th Century prints on the paneled walls. She wondered what great British statesmen had dined in this room over the years.

After a quick review of the artwork, ending with a depiction of the Siege of Sevastopol, Lorraine sat down at the imitate table set for two. She glanced at her watch. She was early. She wished she was late. In fact, Lorraine wished she had declined the invitation and would have if she hadn't needed something. Still, she wasn't going in blindly. Lorraine opened her purse and took out a small capsule filled with a fatal liquid. Lorraine surreptitiously tucked the capsule toward the back of her mouth, between her gums and her cheek. She felt it with her tongue. It would be there if she needed it.

Lorraine then reached into her purse and pulled out the paperback copy of *Martin Chuzzlewitt* Verity had given her. She smiled at Verity's cleverness. Knowing that her father would either be present or monitoring their meeting, Verity had written Chesney an extensive letter in the margins of the Dickens novel.

My Beloved (the letter began), *I so long to be with you. Know that I think of you in all my waking moments. I will do everything possible to assist you in your goals and hasten the day when we can start our forever.*

That was Lorraine's favorite part of the letter. She wrote alongside it in the margins, "as do I."

Next, Verity expressed confusion as to why Lorraine had agreed to be a spokesperson for her father's paper products. Despite this, she affirmed her trust in her Beloved's judgment. Lorraine wished she could explain to Verity that she agreed to hawk Bagnold's toilet paper to protect Li Gao and ultimately, Verity. She hoped that one day soon, she could explain it all.

Verity went on to tell how she had seen Valerie Fierro, essentially in disguise, shopping for her wedding trousseau. Even more puzzling was the news that Valerie was going to be married to Albrecht Eckner. Chesney didn't doubt what Verity had told her. He just couldn't understand it. Is that why Valerie had disappeared? Verity noted that though Valerie tried to conceal the fact, she was going with Eckner to Gibraltar. Gibraltar! That must be the key to it all. It went back to what Peter Liverot had said on his deathbed; that Albrecht Eckner had requested that Martina go to Chicago. Lorraine couldn't go to Gibraltar to investigate. She was too famous. Her presence there would draw too much attention. Besides, this called for a professional investigator. That's why she was now in this intimate dining room of this exclusive gentlemen's club.

The door opened.

"Good evening, my dear," the smooth baritone voice of Nigel Verve slid into the room. "I'm so glad you accepted my invitation to this cozy *tete-a-tete.*"

"As long as it's just a tete-a-tete," said Lorraine. An uncharacteristic look of confusion darkened Verve's confident expression. "It's just a conversation between two people," she explained, "a tete-a-tete, it's French, literally translated it means 'head to head.'"

"Of course," said Verve regaining his assurance. "I speak French, along with eleven other languages. So, I assume we can continue our conversation in French. It's a much more sensual… tongue."

"You'd be speaking to yourself," said Lorraine. "Aside from the etymology of a handful of words and phrases, I don't speak French. Nor will there be any tongue, sensual or otherwise, Mr. Verve."

"Please," he smiled as he sat across from her, "Mr. Verve is so formal. Please, just call me 'Verve.'"

Verve reached out and took Lorraine's hand. She took it back.

"Ah, the thrust and parry," he said with a sly grin.

"Not at all," said Lorraine, "I'm not here for parrying and certainly not for thrusting."

"No, of course not," he said. "So, it's the debonaire agent and the chaste virgin."

"No, it's not," said Lorraine. "I can assure you, I'm not flirting."

Verve raised one eyebrow. "Although not flirting can be a form of flirting."

"I promise you," she said firmly, "that I'm not flirting, and my not flirting is definitely not a form of flirting. I didn't accept your invitation for any amorous intents. I need your assistance."

"Champagne?" said Nigel Verve. He raised a finger, and suddenly a waiter slid in from the shadows with a magnum of champagne in a silver bucket. Without looking at the waiter, Verve nodded, and the man seemed to evaporate as silently as he had appeared. Nigel Verve removed the crown from the bottle and popped the cork in a way that suggested the task was second-nature to him.

He poured a glass and offered it to Lorraine.

"Sorry, I don't drink," said Lorraine. She didn't want to present even the slightest opening to his well-rehearsed tactics.

"Pity," he said, downing the champagne and quickly pouring himself a refill. After he took the first sip, he leaned back in his chair. "So, beautiful woman, in need of assistance. What is your dilemma?"

Lorraine rolled her eyes and took a deep breath.

"I need information," she said. "It's sensitive information. I would have pursued it through regular channels, but it's in Gibraltar."

Nigel Verve smiled. "Ah, the virtuous Mrs. Innis needs some dirty work done."

Lorraine started to protest but then shut her mouth and nodded.

"I see," said Verve. "Intelligence is non-unlike sewer work. Everyone needs it, but no one wants to get their clean clothes soiled. I'm not criticizing you; far from it. It's what I do exceedingly well. Anything from a simple wiretap to, well, eliminations. It is amusing that you would come to me rather than an American. There are plenty of agents from your country who could do such a job. Admittedly, not with the same panache of yours truly."

"I thought that as Gibraltar is a UK territory, an American might not do it," said Lorraine.

Verve laughed. "How quaint. You really are the innocent. Those in my profession have no borders, Mrs. Innis. The world is our workshop. You really are quite amusing. You're like the little housewife who calls for the exterminator when she sees a mouse in her pantry. But then is scandalized when she learns she's contracted a professional killer."

"It doesn't involve murder," she said. "I could never agree to that."

"Yes, of course," said Verve, but the look on his face told Lorraine that he still thought she was naïve. "Now, perhaps you tell me what you require."

Lorraine explained she had a friend who was connected to a bank in Gibraltar but was killed. The reasons for her friend's death stopped at a man named "Albrecht Eckner."

Nigel Verve sipped his champagne as Lorraine spoke. He sat placidly as if he were all alone.

"Well, that's quite simple," said Verve. "I've gone to far worse places. Gibraltar isn't the most exciting locale, but I get can in some sun during the day and visit the gaming tables at night."

"What about..."

Nigel Verve raised his hand. "And, of course, never neglecting your concerns, Mrs. Innis. Remember my analogy of the exterminator? Well, this is far easier than killing a mouse. You're merely asking me to investigate the pantry and look for indications of a rodent infestation. As I said, quite simple."

"How will..."

"How will I proceed?" said Verve smugly. "With my customary aplomb and style. Please, don't ask me what I'll do. You've contracted a professional, Mrs. Innis. Let me exercise my skills in my usual way."

Lorraine nodded her head. "Yes, of course, forgive me. I just don't want to be misunderstood. I'm only seeking information. This is very important to my goals."

"Goals? I see, and you think this man, Eckner is in the way of your goals?" said Verve.

"He may be," said Lorraine.

"And you want to prove this man Eckner is culpable in your friend's death, so you can neutralize him?"

"I think you misunderstand," said Lorraine. "It's just a vow I made to myself, and I can't retire before I learn the truth. That's my goal."

"To be a lady of leisure," said Verve.

"To disappear completely," said Lorraine. "So, you see, this is very important to me. But, please, I just want the information. I wouldn't want anyone else killed."

Verve smiled. "You've seen too many spy films, Mrs. Innis. I don't execute justice."

Lorraine stood. "Thank you, I appreciate that, and I appreciate your assistance. I didn't want to imply that men such as yourself went through life leaving behind a trail of corpses."

Nigel Verve stood and took Lorraine's hand. "Nor do we leave a trail of romantic conquests, at least not unsatisfied ones."

Lorraine tried to pull her hand back, but despite Verve holding what appeared to be a loose grip, it was practically escape-proof.

"Mr. Verve..."

"Please, Verve," he said, leaning forward.

"I'm not..."

"Mrs. Innis," he whispered in her ear. "I've agreed to your assignment. I respect your chastity, but I do insist on at least one kiss... to seal our arrangement."

Lorraine smiled nervously as her tongue fished around for the capsule she'd hidden there as a precaution. As his lips approached hers, Lorraine positioned the capsule over her back molars and bit down. It was just in time as Nigel Verve leaned Lorraine back and forced his lips against hers. He purred as his tongue penetrated her mouth. His technique was rehearsed but seemed spontaneous; passionate but practiced. It was the neatest sloppy kiss Lorraine had ever encountered. The work of a true professional, or at least it would have been. The liquid contents of the broken capsule spread quickly, reaching the amorous tongue of Nigel Verve in a second. His eyes went from being sensually closed to flying open like a pair of window shades with busted springs.

"Oh, my," Verve recoiled, trying to retain his suave exterior.

"Is there something wrong, Mr. Verve?" said Lorraine innocently.

"What? No, no," said the British agent, trying to shield his nose from the full olfactory assault of a concentrated garlic capsule.

"I know you must have kissed thousands of women," she said.

"What? Oh, no, yes, I mean," he backed away as subtly as he could. "I can honestly say I've never had a kiss like that."

Lorraine feigned modesty. "Oh, Verve, you're so kind."

"Quite."

She leaned forward. "Would you like another? I mean, I need to thank you for the investigation."

Nigel Verve practically jumped backward. "No! I mean, no need to thank me. One kiss was plenty."

Lorraine batted her lashes at the spy. "Perhaps you can have another when you complete the assignment."

By now, Verve was at the door. "I, uh, I'll mail you the results, or I'll phone."

"But what about our dinner?" said Lorraine pointing to the table.

"Oh, no, no time to eat," he stammered. "Have to get to work. Gibraltar, you know."

"I understand," she said, feigning disappointment but greatly relieved.

He opened the door and glanced back at the table. "You haven't eaten already, have you?"

"No, I haven't eaten all day," said Lorraine. "Why?"

"No reason," he muttered, then looked up. "Enjoy a Mediterranean cuisine, do you?"

"Well, I am part Italian on my father's side," she said. "My maiden name is 'Ammaccappane.' But I doubt the Italian shows much."

"Oh, breeding has a way of coming to the surface," he said as he ducked out the door with his handkerchief over his nose.

Lorraine smiled, then raised her hand for a whiff of her own breath. She recoiled and hoped she had plenty of mouthwash back at her hotel.

- 54 -
Are These Nuptuals Necessary?

Valerie Fierro looked at her Versace original in the mirror and sighed. She knew it was only a marriage of convenience, but she had always envisioned her wedding day very differently. The dress was beautiful – it should be, it cost enough - but it wasn't a wedding dress. And there wouldn't be a fancy reception at the duPont Country Club. The Delaware and Philadelphia papers' society pages wouldn't be filled with the details of what a beautiful bride she was. Maybe when she got married someday to a real man in a real wedding with all the trimmings to which she was entitled, she would have all those things. But for now, it was a simple ceremony in a London registry office. Followed by a quick trip to Gibraltar to claim her rightful place at the top of the Valvano family and then a fast divorce. Divorce? She wouldn't even need a divorce. An annulment would do the trick.

Valerie adjusted the neckline and stopped to stare at the charm her father had given her.

"Daddy," said Valerie as she fingered the necklace, "the things we have to go through to get what's ours. If only we had known years ago. All this was rightfully yours. You wouldn't have had to…"

Valerie stopped. In her mind, she completed the sentence, but she still couldn't say the words aloud. Her father had died from overwork, earning money for her prom dress. That thought summoned up other memories of that fateful night. Albrecht Eckner had been part of that, too. Now he was helping to set it all right. Albrecht's transformation had been nothing short of astounding, but Valerie knew it was genuine. No one, not even Albrecht, was that good an actor. And, after all, she had to convince him to marry her just to get a quick name change and a new passport.

Valerie still had to remind herself how different Albrecht was now. He was kind, considerate, and not even the hint of an ulterior motive.

Once she had talked him into it, Albrecht made all the arrangements. Even getting married in a registry office had its share of paperwork and red tape. According to Albrecht, his work visa for Gibraltar and England made the process much easier.

There was a knock at the bedroom door. "Are you ready?" asked Albrecht from the other side.

Valerie went to the door. Albrecht was standing there in a dark blue suit. He was holding a bunch of flowers.

"Oh, you didn't need to get me a bouquet," said Valerie.

Albrecht shrugged. "I know, it's all just for show, but I did want you to look nice." He looked up and down her dress. "I mean, even nicer, you look beautiful."

Valerie smiled and felt a slight blush rise to her cheeks. "Thank you, you look nice too, Albrecht."

"Yeah, well," he said bashfully, "I thought we should do our best to blend in, you know, look like a couple getting married for real."

"We are getting married for real," she said, "but I know what you mean. We don't want to attract attention."

"I always thought you were the prettiest girl in Delaware," he said, looking at his feet. "You can't help but attract attention."

Valerie kissed him on the cheek. She was surprised at her lack of hesitation, but his transformation was so genuine and rather appealing. Instead of kissing her in return, Albecht just grinned shyly and turned away.

"We really should get going," he said, changing the subject. "The registry office is only a few blocks away, but we don't want to be late. The ceremony is pretty straightforward. It only takes about ten minutes."

And one hour later, Valerie Fierro was Mrs. Albrecht Eckner. Albrecht was actually cute. He had to be coaxed, twice, to kiss the bride, and then his lips barely touched hers. On the way out, only after seeing other couples cuddling in the waiting area, Albrecht put his arm around Valerie. She locked arms with him and pulled him closer. Valerie paused at a table in the vestibule and picked up a brochure titled "Your Registry Office."

"What do you want that for?" asked Albrecht.

She shrugged as she shoved it into her purse. "Oh, I don't know, for a souvenir; just a reminder of the first time I got married and the very gallant man who made it possible."

"Temporarily," he was quick to add.

"Yes, temporarily," she agreed.

Outside, he hailed a cab. "And now," he said as they climbed in, "let's go consummate our marriage."

Valerie's eyes widened.

"With brunch at one of London's best restaurants," he added.

She smiled.

"Uh, and I have a little surprise," he said, lowering his head.

"Oh?"

"It's sort of a wedding present," he said bashfully.

"You already gave me this beautiful ring, Albrecht," she said, waving the diamond.

"And that's yours to keep," he said. "It's not only a wedding present; it's sort of an apology, you know, for all the rotten things I did in the past."

"You don't have to apologize," she said, "again."

"Yeah, well," he said, "still, I got us a honeymoon..."

Valerie felt her throat tightening. "Honeymoon?"

"For outward appearances," he said. "I booked us separate rooms."

"Won't that look a bit strange for newlyweds?"

"I booked one in my name and the other in your maiden name," Albrecht explained. "I just thought you deserved a break after all you've been through. And it will give you time to relax and figure out your next move after we, that is, you get to Gibraltar. It's in the Bahamas."

"The Bahamas," Valerie squealed and then caught herself. "But what about my passport?"

"I've got it all set at the American embassy," he said. "Right after brunch, we'll go there. And now that we have the marriage license, they can issue your new passport... Mrs. Eckner."

– 55 –
Off Into the Wild Blue Plimsolls

I appreciate you accompanying me to the airport, Gao," said Verity Goodhue. "It really wasn't necessary. I could have gotten a cab."

Li Gao smiled. "It is not just a pleasure. It is a duty. Now, may I get you some tea?"

He excused himself and left Verity seated in the departure lounge at Heathrow. He returned in a few minutes with two cups of tea.

"This recalls the departure of your Chesney many years ago," said Gao. "I believe we waited in approximately the same spot."

Verity nodded. "My poor Beloved. He was going home after the passing of Elinor."

"And believing you had also died," added Gao. "But excuse me, partings are melancholy enough without such recollections."

"It breaks my heart to think how sad he must have been," she continued. "At least he had you to console him." Verity patted Li Gao's hand.

"And our dear friend, Postlewaite," said Gao. "Though his contribution was ill-managed…"

"But well-meaning, I'm sure," said Verity.

"I was about to qualify that," said Gao with a wistful grin. "He bought Chesney an odd collection of magazines and a bag of crisps for the journey."

"Dear, Mr. Postlewaite," said Verity. "Have you heard from him lately?"

Li Gao shrugged. "The poor fellow. He went on a holiday around Britain to visit the homes of his comic heroes. Poor chap."

"Oh, no," she said. "Nothing happened to him, did it?"

"Something always happens to Postlewaite, it would appear. It seems he befriended a young lady in distress. Then after several days, the girl absconded with a piece of memorabilia that Postlewaite had just secured at auction."

"How terrible," said Verity. "Was it very valuable?"

Li Gao shook his head. "I do not know the monetary value, but knowing the mind of our friend, it was more valuable than gold. He was quite distraught. He is back at his shop in Norfolk. I will go visit him to console him on his loss."

Verity looked down at the ticket in her hand. "I only wish I could go with you. But I must try and find out whatever I can in Gibraltar. My Beloved can't go for obvious reasons. And I have the perfect excuse. I convinced my father that opening some accounts in Gibraltar may be profitable for tax purposes. Representing such a large potential client will give me a plausible reason to ask questions without arousing too much suspicion."

Li Gao nodded. "And Chesney believes the answers reside at this institution?"

"Martina was supposed to examine that bank," Verity explained, "but then this Albrecht Eckner had her sent to Chicago instead. That's where she died. I just need to find out what was so important to cover up that it could lead to her death."

Gao bowed his head. "I will pray for you. If this person was the cause of one death, there is little doubt that they would not hesitate to repeat their actions."

Verity placed her hand on his. "That's very much appreciated. I don't think I'm in danger. For one thing, they were expecting Martina to uncover whatever they were up to. I'm just a client doing due diligence. Still, after I realized what my Beloved did on my behalf... our behalf."

"Then you know," said Gao looking up.

She nodded. "At first, I was very cross when I learned Lorraine Innis would be doing commercials for my father. But after I met with Lorraine and saw my father's reaction to you being there, I understood."

"Chesney only agreed to do it to protect me from prosecution. They wished to charge me with abduction. And then, when your father saw me, he began to suspect you were involved. Only Chesney agreeing to appear in the advertisement caused your father to relent. Part of the agreement was that Lorraine Innis would have no contact with either of us."

"And Father only agreed to let me meet Lorraine when he couldn't handle her." Verity laughed. "I suppose it's working out. Shakespeare said the course of true love never did run smooth."

Gao smiled. "And even greater than the Bard, St. Paul wrote to the Romans that God works all things for the good of those who love him, who have been called according to his purpose."

Verity sighed. "Well, I'm glad it's not just up to me, but I still have to do what I can."

"And I'm sure that is a great deal," said Gao. He looked up at the departure screen. "But I believe your flight is boarding, my dear. You don't want to have to run for it."

Verity stood up and grabbed her carry-on bag. "No, but I do have on my new plimsolls." She stuck out her right foot. "Sky blue, Chesney's favorite color. Much comfier for flying and walking."

She leaned over and kissed Li Gao on the cheek. "Thank you again for seeing me off. Wish me luck."

He hugged her. "More than that, you are in my earnest prayers."

– 56 –
The Toilet Roll
That Saved the World

Lorraine Innis smoothed out the skirt of her tweed suit and sat down. She looked back at the subdued lighting of the television stage and smiled inwardly.

"Okay, Luvie," said Chas, the director of the television commercial, "all set; you've had a chance to read the new copy?"

"The new copy of what?" asked Lorraine.

Chas flashed a patronizing smile. "The lines, your script, Luv."

"Oh, yes, sorry," said Lorraine. "You'd think I'd be used to all these terms by now."

"One would," sighed Chas, turning away, "we've only been trying to shoot one spot for weeks now."

Lorraine tried to look contrite, but it didn't matter. The director was now across the studio, conferring with the technicians. She didn't know Chas' opinion of the giant toilet bowl or the mermaid costume. She suspected he didn't care as long as he and the crew were paid. Lorraine's sabotaging of the horrible concept of Venus rising from the loo had resulted in many hours of lucrative overtime for them at Lord Bagnold's expense.

If there had been a trophy for wooden acting in a television ad, Lorraine certainly would have been given a lifetime achievement award. Her portrayal of Venus in a mermaid suit was awful. It took quite a bit of acting to perform so badly and make it seem that she was so genuinely bereft of talent.

Lorraine thought back to their previous meeting a few days ago. As they reviewed the rushes, she savored Lord Bagnold's pained reactions.

"That one wasn't too bad," Lorraine said innocently, "was it?"

His Lordship fumed but was loathe to lose his temper, apparently still believing there was gold in Lorraine's endorsement of his paper products. Finally, after scores of botched performances, Bagnold admitted defeat.

"Wotcha think, Chas," he asked his director as they finished reviewing the two hundred and eighty-second take.

The director puffed out his cheeks and then exhaled slowly like a leaky balloon. "I don't think it's useable yet, your Lordship." He turned to Lorraine and added, "no offense, Mrs. Innis. I know you're trying."

"Is she?" mumbled Lord Bagnold. "If you plays this one," he pointed at the screen, "and then looks at the first one, I could swear she's getting worse."

Lorraine suppressed a smile. Her bad acting skills had improved. "Well," she offered, "could you use the first one."

Both Bagnold and Chas stared at her. Lorraine's ads were abysmal from the start, and they both knew it.

"No, no, not no 'ow," said Bagnold, his frustration rising. He caught himself and forced a smile. "Mrs. Innis, you is beloved…"

Lorraine smiled. "That's very kind of you to say so, your Lordship."

Bagnold wiped his face with his palm. "I means, you is a beloved public figure. You is loved the 'ole world over. That's why I wants you to do my ads. But if we were to run the best of this muck, you would be immediately 'ated 'round the world, and me sales would go right down the 'opper!"

Lorraine giggled. "How ironic, you see, because that's what ultimately happens to toilet tissue, isn't it?"

"I don'ts 'ave the luxury of being h'ironic," said Bagnold, "when it hits me bottom line."

"Bottom line," said Lorraine, "another pun, your Lordship."

"This h'ain't not no laughing matter, Mrs. Innis," he said, "wot I'm getting at is that everyone loves you all over the place. Even me, I likes you, which is why I wanted you to be me spokes wheel. I've seen you on the telly before, and you is very lovely. Wot is mystifying me and the director, and just about everyone on the crew, is how could you be so likable then and so bad now."

Lorraine pretended to ponder the question for a minute. "I suppose it's because I was just being myself in those other places. I'm not an actress. I'm just Lorraine Innis. Who else would I be?"

"'Oo else would you be," Lord Bagnold repeated.

Chas nodded. "She right, your Lordship. Any woman could rise out of a giant toilet…"

"'Cept 'er," said Bagnold jerking his thumb toward Lorraine.

"Well, any actress," clarified Chas, "but Mrs. Innis isn't famous for acting or being a mermaid or Venus, or whatever. People love her because she's herself. She's honest. Rather than try to make her be something she's not, you should have her talk truthfully about your product."

Lord Bagnold blanched. "Truth? In a telly advert?"

"It would be novel," noted the director.

Bagnold turned to Lorraine. "Okay, Miss Trustworthy, say something about me product." He grabbed a roll of toilet paper and pushed it across the table to Lorraine. She picked it up and examined it.

"Well," said Lorraine, "I hadn't used it until I came to England because we don't have your brand in the States. But I have used it since I arrived. It's the brand used at my hotel."

Lord Bagnold snapped his fingers. "The elite toilet paper used at the finest hotels!"

Lorraine shrugged. "That may be true, but I doubt many people go to a five-star hotel because of the toilet tissue." She examined the roll more closely. "It's good toilet paper. I mean, it does the job. But it didn't make my daily ablutions a transcendent experience. I confess I didn't think much about it. It's a product that one only notices if it's poor quality. I doubt I could honestly wax rhapsodically about it. If I did, that would seem phony."

Chas nodded. "There you have it, the famous Innis truthfulness."

Lord Bagnold sneered.

"I'm sorry," said Lorraine, "but toilet tissue is a very nice thing to have. But it's not exactly going to save the world, is it?"

His Lordship stewed for a moment until his right eyebrow suddenly shot up. This was followed seconds later by his left eyebrow. Then a ghastly grin overspread his lips which parted to reveal his mismatched teeth.

"Save the world?" he muttered. Then he said it aloud. Finally, he shouted it. "SAVE THE WORLD!"

"Are you all right, your Lordship," asked the director.

"All right?" cried Bagnold, "I h'am jolly well not all right. I'm bloody marvelous. I'm tickety boo, and a 'alf!" He sprang from his seat and pointed at Chas. "You gets it ready. We don't needs no forty-foot khazie. Just 'er 'ere, sitting in a chair." He swung his finger toward Lorraine. "And you, you just needs to be yourself. Dress like wot you normally does, and get ready! Me and me toilet paper is going to save the world."

Lorraine pointed back at him. "I won't lie for you."

"You don't not 'ave to lie," said Bagnold.

"Nor will I prevaricate," she added.

"Wot you does in private don't not matter," said Bagnold. "You will just tell the truth. Now I've gots to go and get your words together." He paused by the door and sneered a frightfully cheerful sneer. "I h'am going to save the world, I h'am!"

Now, days later, Lorraine sat in her tasteful suit against a plain but tastefully lit backdrop. Thankfully the giant toilet, the mermaid suit, and angels draping tissue were nowhere to be seen. She was still loathe to do an ad for Lord Bagnold, but at least she had battled him to do it her way, and she had won.

Lorraine was surprised by the new text of the ad. And while it might not save the world, it did seem like a planet-friendly initiative from the last man she would have expected one.

"All set, Luv," said Chas. "It's straightforward. Just look into the camera and read the copy, that is, the lines as they appear on the prompter over the camera."

"Yes, thank you," said Lorraine.

"Right then," said the director. He called for quiet, then a woman with a clapper appeared and announced take one number. And Chas called "action."

"Hello, I'm Lorraine Innis," she began. "We're all concerned with the responsible use of our resources. I'm delighted to announce a new product from a brand you've all known for many years. To be honest, it's less a new product and more a new process."

Lorraine held up a roll of green-colored toilet tissue.

"This is the new Green World tissue roll. It's made from 100% sustainable material using a new process. Previously, bathroom tissue was made from a combination of softwoods and hardwoods. It would take years for trees to grow, all for a disposable product. Green World is made in a process using the finest plant material that is practically grown overnight. And no dyes or perfumes are used. This is its natural color and its fresh, natural scent. Green World is better for the planet, and that's good for all of us."

Lorraine smiled until the director called "cut!"

"Was that okay?" she asked. "Do I need to do it again?"

"Luv," said Chase, "no need, that was perfect! You just needed to be yourself."

"Who else could I be?" asked Lorraine.

"That's wot I said all alongs," interrupted the voice of Lord Bagnold.

"You did?" said Lorraine.

"Course I did," said Bagnold walking down from the control booth. "It's these experts wot told me we needed a flash production."

Chas gave him a withering look, then glanced at Lorraine. They both knew the giant toilet was His Lordship's idea.

"Keep it simple," said Bagnold. "A good product don't not need a lot of tosh to sell it."

"No, of course not," said Lorraine with a roll of her eyes. "By the way, do you think your daughter will like the ad?"

"Wot she gots to do with it?"

"Oh, nothing," said Lorraine, "it's just that in our brief meeting, she impressed me as a woman of exceptional refinement. I thought perhaps she provided some input."

Bagnold snorted. "Haw! Any polish wot like she's got she gets from me."

"Obviously," muttered Lorraine.

"But she's got nothing to do with me business," he said. "Oh, well, I means, she didn't usually. To be perfectly 'onest, like wot I always am, me daughter is taking a greater interest in me empire."

"Oh?"

"Well, even a magnum of industry can't not live forever," he said.

"Pity," said Lorraine.

"Quite," agreed Bagnold, "but time and tide marches on. When I goes, someone's got to follow in me footpaths. In fact, right now, she's on 'er way to do some business for me."

"Verity?" said Lorraine.

Lord Bagnold looked puzzled. "She's the only daughter wot I got. Of course. Why?"

"Uh, ah, no reason," said Lorraine. "I just hoped that when I was done filming your commercial, I could get together with her, um, for some girl talk."

"Well, if you likes to speak Spanish, she's down there."

"Verity's in Spain?" asked Lorraine anxiously.

"No, not Spain," said Bagnold, "past Spain."

"Morocco? Africa?"

"No, wot would she do there?" he said. "She's down in Gibraltar."

"Oh, no," said Lorraine falling back into the chair.

"It was 'er idea," said Lord Bagnold with a shrug. "She's looking into banks. She says they got better bank laws there." He gestured, hiding his wallet in his coat, and winked.

"This is terrible," said Lorraine jumping up and hurrying off the set.

"Wait, it's all legal," said Bagnold calling after her. "So don't get no ideas of telling the Inland Revenue." Lorraine rushed out the door. His Lordship turned to Chas. "It is all legal… probably… anyway, it h'ain't no business of 'ers no 'ow."

– 57 –
The Marks of a
Successful Wedding Night

I won't carry you over the threshold," said Albrecht Eckner. "I mean, we're not really married." He fumbled with the key to the suite.

"Yes, we are married," said Valerie Fierro Eckner. "You don't have to keep saying it like that. I know it makes you uncomfortable, but it was my idea. Technically, I proposed to you."

"It's all a technicality," said Albrecht, opening the door. "As soon as we get to Gibraltar, we'll have this annulled." He held the door for her, and Valerie went in.

"Oh, this is a beautiful suite," she said.

Albrecht shook his head. "I told them I wanted separate rooms."

Valerie looked around the spacious suite and inspected the adjoining bedrooms. "There are separate bedrooms, Albrecht."

"Yeah, well, I guess that's okay," he said, throwing the key on the coffee table.

"Back in your suite in London," she said, "you gave me the bedroom, and you slept on the sofa."

"That's before we were married," he said. Albrecht stopped and smirked, realizing the absurdity of that statement.

Valerie laughed. "Really, this is fine. And it was very nice of you to surprise me with this lovely honeymoon."

"Vacation," corrected Albrecht, "it's more of a vacation. I mean, we're not going to do honeymoon things. I just thought that after hiding out for weeks in cold, dreary London, you could probably do with some time on the beach."

Valerie opened the sliding door to the balcony and admired the azure waters of the Caribbean. She did want to get to Gibraltar and assume legal control over the Valvano family business, but Albrecht was right. She did deserve a vacation.

There was a knock on the door. Albrecht answered it. It was the bellhop with their suitcases. Right behind him was a waiter pushing a cart with dinner and champagne. Albrecht directed the bellhop to place Valerie's luggage in the bedroom with the sea view. Then he tipped them both generously and whispered something to the waiter on his way out. The waiter nodded.

"What was that?" asked Valerie, who had been watching from the balcony.

"I had asked for a rose," said Albrecht shyly. "You know, I wanted it to look like we're really…"

Valerie smiled and nodded. His hesitancy was cute. She lifted the dome on the lid. "Lobsters," she cried, "and champagne."

Albrecht picked up the bottle and began unwrapping the foil from the top. "Shall I pour you a glass?"

She headed toward the bedroom and then stopped in the doorway. "Let me slip into something more comfortable."

"Not too comfortable," called Albrecht as she closed the door.

A few minutes later, Valerie emerged in a lace peignoir. She stood by the doorway for effect. She didn't want to excite Albrecht, but she would have made a dramatic entrance even if no one was there. He looked up, and his eyes grew wide. He almost spilled the champagne he was pouring.

"Wow," said Albrecht, "you look… uh, very nice."

Valerie shrugged. "Not exactly the reaction a girl wants on her wedding night."

Now Albrecht knocked over the glass and scrambled for a napkin. "Cut it out, Valerie. It's not your wedding night. Okay, yeah, it is, sort of, but you know."

Valerie nodded. "Yeah, I know. Sorry, I'm not trying to excite you. It's just the outfit goes with the setting. The sea, the suite, the setting sun…"

Albrecht coughed. "Uh, yeah, you look nice, really nice. Green, isn't it?"

Valerie did a half-twirl, holding out the skirt of her peignoir. "Sea foam, actually." She looked in the large wall mirror and admired herself. Before leaving London, she had ditched the wig and had her hair dyed the same color. "I don't usually wear any shade of green, but it goes with the auburn…"

"Auburn?"

"My hair," she said. "As long as I have to be a redhead, I want to have complimentary colors." Valerie fussed with her locks. "When I go back to my natural color, I'll have them add red highlights."

"What? Oh, highlights? Sure, I guess," he said. "Uh, let's have some lobster."

"And champagne," Valerie said sitting down beside him on the sofa.

"What? Oh, right, champagne," Albrecht handed her a glass and held up the bottle. "I hope it's good. I don't know a lot about champagne."

Valerie raised her glass. At first, Albrecht just stared, and then he realized she expected him to clink glasses.

"Right, right," he said raising his glass to hers. "Sorry, this is all new to me."

She smiled. "Oh, you've never been married before?"

"What? No, of course not."

"Albrecht," she said, "I'm kidding."

"Oh, right, sorry."

"Well," said Valerie, "here's to a happy…"

"…and brief…"

"And brief marriage," she said. She clinked his glass and took a sip. It was good. She finished her glass. He refilled it.

♦

The following day Valerie awoke in bed. She sat up with a start and immediately grabbed her head.

"Oww, whoa, I must have had too much champagne," she said, slowly rising from the bed. Her first thought was that Albrecht had gotten her drunk and had his way with her. Valerie glanced back at the bed. Only one side was disturbed. No, she thought, he hadn't done anything. She didn't remember going to bed. And she was wearing her peignoir, the outer robe included. Perhaps he put her to bed.

Valerie shuffled into the living room and looked over at his bedroom. The door was open, and the bed was made. The coffee table in front of the sofa was cleared of last night's lobster and champagne. A glance at the mantel clock told her it was just before noon.

"Girl," Valerie muttered, "when you tie one on, you really tie one on…"

The only thing out of place was a note on the table. She picked it up.

Dear Valerie,
    Didn't want to wake you. Went for a walk on the beach. Be back soon.

It wasn't signed, but it obviously was from Albrecht. She let the note flutter back to the table and went to take a shower.

Valerie slid out of her peignoir and turned on the water. While waiting for it to get warm, she looked in the mirror. After a cursory glance, she did a double-take and examined her torso more closely. There were lines on it. For a moment, she thought they were just the lines left on her skin from sleeping on folds in the sheets, but they weren't like that. These lines were deeper and more even, like the marks her bra left around her chest. But she hadn't worn a bra since last evening, and besides which, those lines ran parallel to the floor. These lines were as deep but ran down her body, from under her breasts to her waist. It was almost as if…

Valerie gasped. How could he? No, he couldn't. Could he? She dashed from the bathroom, grabbed her robe, and went into Albrecht's bedroom. Opening the dresser drawers, all she found were his clothes neatly arranged.

Valerie shut the drawers and looked around for his suitcase. Finding it in the closet, she hefted it in her hands. It was empty, or nearly so. Something was loose inside. Valerie set the case on the bed and flipped the latches. It was locked. Fortunately, it was one of those three-digit locks. Her sister Rose had one of those, and Valerie had learned they're not that hard to crack.

Pulling the suitcase to the edge of the bed, Valerie knelt beside it with her ear to the lock. Starting with the first digit on the left, she turned the wheel slowly. On most suitcases, you could hear the click when the correct number was reached. 1... 2... 3... 4... 5... click! Valerie smiled. With the first number in place, it was just a matter of repeating the process on the other two.

In less than a minute, she flipped back the latches. Inside was a bag from one of London's upscale department stores. Valerie opened the bag and slid out a heavy surgical corset. She held it up to her body. Its boning was a perfect match for the marks on her torso.

"You little bastard," she muttered. "You can take the pervert out of Delaware, but you can't..." she stopped. That didn't make sense, but Valerie knew what she meant. Albrecht Eckner hadn't changed, at least not in that respect or lack of respect.

Valerie sat on the edge of the bed and thought. Albrecht must had drugged the champagne. Then probably, he had carried her into the bedroom, treated her like his own dress-up doll, and played Kinky Barbie all night. She started to imagine the depths of depravity to which Albrecht Eckner could sink but stopped herself. Albrecht's perversion wasn't a rabbit hole; it was a bottomless pit. If Valerie let herself wander through his degrading wonderland, she would probably murder him.

Valerie returned the corset to the bag and re-locked the suitcase. Then she hurried back to her room and locked the door. A shower wouldn't do. She needed a hot bath to purge away the icky feelings that were crawling all over her skin. As she soaked in the tub, Valerie reached up and fingered the charm her father had given her.

"I'll take care of myself, Daddy," she promised as the steam rose from the tub. "I won't let on that I know anything about what went on last night. And once we get to Gibraltar and I take over, I'll settle the account of Mr. Albrecht Eckner... once and for all."

– 58 –
Sleuthing in Streatham

Michael Valvano looked out of the window of the mini-cab as it traveled south from Waterloo Station. Julius Rosen had given them the name of the private investigator Michael's brother had hired. At first, Michael was surprised by Rosen's cooperation. Then he realized that Rosen's loyalty belonged to the estate and not Robert. Now, Rosen's interest was finding Valerie Fierro. With that goal, Michael was in complete agreement.

He had called the private eye but had to leave a message. The detective was based in a suburb called...

"OW! Watch it, Al," said Michael, shoving his companion's elbow from his ribs.

"Oh, sorry, Mike," said Alphonse, "only I was unwrapping this chocolate bar. You know this ain't the biggest cab I've ever inhabited."

The driver eyed them suspiciously in the rear-view mirror.

"How much further is it to..." Michael took out the scrap of paper. "Streatham?"

"Not much further," said the cabbie, a black man about forty.

"It's amusing, ain't it?" whispered Alphonse.

"What?"

Al nodded towards the driver. "He talks like he's a limey."

"He is a lime... uh, he is English," whispered Mike.

"Yeah, but..."

"Pardon?" said the driver, who obviously had overheard thanks to the vehicle's small size.

"I was just saying," said Alphonse, "you talk like people here do."

"I was born here," said the driver. "In Brixton. We just went through it."

"Yeah," said Al, "I don't mean to be rude or nothing, but you don't talk like the black folks back in America."

"What a coincidence," said the driver, "you don't talk like the white folks here."

"I didn't mean nothing, pal," said Alphonse.

"Well, then you've succeeded admirably," said the driver.

Alphonse took out his notebook and started scribbling. "That's a good one."

"What's a good one?" said the driver.

"Admirably."

Michael leaned forward. "Don't take notice of my friend. He collects words. He's improving his vocabulary."

"Well, I could give him some more choice selections," said the driver pulling up on the parking brake, "but we're here."

They were on a busy main street. There, between a laundry and an Indian takeaway, was a narrow shopfront. The windows were curtained, but a sign in the window announced: "G. Marino – Investigations."

After paying the cabbie, Mike Valvano entered the storefront with Alphonse bringing up the rear. A dark-haired woman with small round glasses was sitting behind the desk.

"We have an appointment with Mr. Marino," said Mike. "The name's Valvano."

The woman stood. "I'm sorry, Mr. Marino is dead."

Mike looked at Alphonse and then back at the woman.

"Dead?"

"About seven years ago," she explained.

Mike took a paper from his pocket to verify the information that Julius Rosen had given him. "There must be some mistake. This is the Marino Investigation Agency."

"It is," said the woman. "My father founded the agency. I'm Geraldine Marino."

"But you're a woman," said Alphonse.

She looked at Al and then at Michael. "I'm surprised you hired me, Mr. Valvano when your friend is such a perceptive detective."

Alphonse took out his pad. "Perceptive, that's another good one." He looked at Michael. "They've got a lot of good English words here in England."

"You'll have to forgive us, Ms. Marino. We didn't know who we'd be meeting. I'm Michael Valvano. My brother, Robert Valvano, was probably the one who hired you."

"Actually, it was a Mr. Rosen who secured my services," she said.

Alphonse's face lit up, and he scribbled while mumbling, "secured services, wow, that's really great."

Geraldine peered at Alphonse over her glasses. Michael shrugged. "He's improving his vocabulary. Anyway, if Mr. Rosen hired you, that explains a lot. Robert, my brother, wouldn't have hired a woman."

"Oh, is he a male chauvinist?"

"Yes, and you forgot 'pig,' too," said Michael. "But, I want to assure you that makes no difference to me. In fact, it makes sense."

"How so, Mr. Valvano?"

"If you want to find a woman, it seems logical to put a woman on the case."

"Yes, well, quite," she said. "Fortunately, I've developed the necessary expertise to handle cases of both sexes."

Michael almost explained he didn't mean anything by his comment but decided that the wisest course of action would be silence.

Geraldine reached into a desk drawer and pulled out a file.

"You wanted to locate Valerie Fierro," she said.

"Yes, yes, very much," agreed Michael.

Geraldine Marino nodded. "When I was first contacted by Mr. Rosen, I thought it was an interesting coincidence. Trying to find someone by the same name as the famous cousin of Lorraine Innis. Then Mr. Rosen informed me it was no coincidence, but the actual person of notoriety."

She looked up. Alfonse was scribbling in his notepad.

"It's not necessary for your associate to take notes," said Geraldine. "I'll give you a copy of my report."

Michael shook his head. "It's the vocabulary."

"Extraordinary," said Geraldine. Alphonse's eyes lit up, and he wrote even more furiously. "I see. Well, in the pursuit of brevity, I'll try to confine my findings to the simplest terms."

"Probably a good idea," Mike agreed.

"I located her," she said.

"That's great," he said, "can I see her?"

"I assume so," said Geraldine, "if you go where she is."

"You mean she's not here?" said Alphonse.

Geraldine shook her head. "I have no powers of detention, my dear fellow. I was merely asked to find Miss Fierro. I was able to track her movements from her leaving Heathrow Airport to her return."

"Her return?" asked Michael, "to America?"

"To Heathrow," said Geraldine.

"We coulda just waited at the airport for that, Mikey," said Alphonse.

"Quiet, Al," said Michael turning to Ms. Marino. "Where has she been?"

Geraldine adjusted her glasses, took a deep breath, and started. "She initially went to Wales."

"The fish?" asked Al.

"The country," she said, "a besides which, whales are not fish, they're aquatic mammals."

"Yeah… aquatic," muttered Al, putting pencil to paper. "A-K-W-A-T-I-C…"

"Quite," said Geraldine, casting a wary eye at Alphonse, "I was able to reconstruct her itinerary."

Michael reached up and pushed Alphonse's hand away from the notepad. Geraldine offered an appreciative smile.

"It seems that Miss Fierro took quite a circuitous route. She spent several days in Caerphilly, in Wales, then seemed to disappear for a time. It was only through interviewing an antique dealer in London that I was able to ascertain that she'd been in the north of the country where she obtained some curious Victorian personal implements which she offered him to sell to a third party."

"Victorian personal implements?" asked Michael.

Geraldine flipped the page. "Umm, yes, nose straighteners, to be precise. Granted, I was able to piece that together by an inquiry of hotels throughout Britain. I learned a young woman matching Miss Fierro's general description had entered one of the better establishments in the city. But she had not checked in, nor did she leave. I constructed the rest via well-placed bribes to hotel personnel. People don't realize how much the hotel staff observes and retains against the opportunity to convert that information into a bit of dosh."

"Dosh?" asked Alphonse.

"Sorry," she said, "it's a local slang term referring to cash."

"So, you found Valerie," said Michael.

"I found where I thought she was," said Geraldine. "At this stage, I relied on the testimony of the hotel staff, none of whom knew her name. They also relayed the name of the antique dealer who had brought her to the hotel. They also confirmed the young woman bore a striking resemblance to Miss Fierro."

"So you didn't actually see Valerie," said Michael.

"Not at first," I had to surveil the lobby for over a week until I observed her first-hand. She was wearing dark glasses, but I was confident it was her."

"How could you tell?"

Geraldine tapped her nose. "A slight kink in her nose. She apparently did not put her trust in those Victorian implements, either that, or they didn't prove efficacious."

Alphonse leaned over and whispered to Michael. "What words I could learn just followin' around this broad!" Michael shushed him.

"I shadowed the clandestinely adorned woman to various retail establishments. Oh, I neglected an important detail; she is now a redhead."

"Redhead?" said Michael.

"Just so, then she went to lunch with this man." She handed Michael a photograph.

"No," said Michael shaking his head, "I don't know him."

"That's Eckner," said Alphonse. He pointed at the photo. "I seen him a few times. He used to work for Mr. Liverot."

"Albrecht Eckner?" said Michael.

"Precisely," said Geraldine.

"I know of him," said Michael, "but Eckner had already moved on by the time I came to the bank. He was in…"

"Gibraltar," said Geraldine. "He is the president of a bank there, a subsidiary of Fourth Fiduciary Trust."

Michael stroked his chin. "Valerie worked with him in Delaware. I suppose she went to him for help."

Geraldine Marino smirked. "And she received quite a bit of succor. Miss Fierro then was observed visiting several upscale stores and apparently charged a considerable amount to Mr. Eckner."

"And then they went to Gibraltar?"

"No," she said, "then they went to the Bahamas, but not before visiting a local registry office and the U.S. Embassy."

"Why would they go there?"

Gerald closed the file. "I'm not certain why she went to the embassy. I didn't want to make direct inquiries there. Usually, nationals visit their own embassy in a foreign country to replace a passport."

"And why do people go to a registry office?" asked Alphonse.

"The most common reason," said Geraldine, "is to get married."

– 59 –
Clean a Piece of the Rock

The flight from London only took three hours. Stepping off the plane, Verity Goodhue was glad she had worn something light. After the cool temperatures of England, the warm Mediterranean sun felt like a different world. She was also glad she had worn her favorite plimsolls, sky blue, to match her dress. Gibraltar wasn't very large, and its narrow streets were best navigated on foot.

After dropping off her portmanteau at her hotel, Verity made her way to the offices of Fourth Fiduciary Trust, Ltd. The Gibraltar subsidiary of the Delaware bank. The building was small but still impressive. She stared at the façade. Somewhere in that building, Verity hoped, would be the answer to the mystery of Martina Fergus' death. She would go in asking about opening an account on her father's behalf. Being a high-profile client should gain her access to the financial statements of the institution… maybe… she hoped.

Taking a deep breath, Verity steeled herself for the task, and walked up the marble steps and into the lobby. A woman sat at the desk just inside the door.

"Yes," said the woman standing. She peered at Verity from head to toe over the top of her glasses. The woman stopped at Verity's feet, pausing there before moving back to her face.

"You're early," said the woman.

"Am I?"

"The advertisement clearly said interviews would start at 3 p.m."

Verity started to object but stopped herself. Interviews: that indicated a job. Investigating the bank would be even easier if she were working there. She had a little bit of finance in her education and had certainly heard her father hurling business terms around the house. If she could bluff her way inside the organization…

"Well?" said the woman.

Verity glanced at her wristwatch. "Oh, yes, three, I'm sorry. I am early. I hope that won't be held against me. I really do need the job…"

Before she could complete her apology, the woman had picked up the phone. She spoke in hushed tones and kept glancing at Verity.

"They'll see you now," said the woman hanging up. She reached under her desk and pressed a button. An electric buzz was heard. "Through there. Second door on the right."

"Oh, yes, thank you," said Verity, "again, I'm sorry I'm early, but as I said, I really…"

"Second door on the right," repeated the woman, making every effort to dispense with Verity.

The door was marked "Personnel." Verity tapped on it, and a voice bid her enter. The room was small and windowless; a woman sat behind the desk.

"Hello, I'm Ms. Gort. Please have a seat…"

"Goodhue, Verity Goodhue," said Verity sitting down. "I'm sorry I don't have a resume with me."

The woman smiled indulgently. "I rarely ask for a CV for a cleaning woman."

"Cleaning woman?"

Ms. Gort rolled her eyes. "Sorry, that's what we called it in my day. I suppose I should have called you an environmental engineer."

"Oh, no, I just, I mean, yes, I'd be happy to be a cleaning woman. That would be fine."

"Good," said Ms. Gort. "Actually, when I started in business, they were called 'charwomen.'"

Verity nodded. Being a cleaning lady would be perfect, even better than a financial position. She would have access to every facet of the bank and after hours when the staff had left. "It doesn't bother me what the position is called," said Verity. "I imagine the work is the same."

Ms. Gort put on a pair of eyeglasses that had been sitting on the desk. She scrutinized Verity.

"Is there anything wrong?" asked Verity.

Gort lowered her glasses and put one of the frame tips in her mouth. "No, it's just, well, you speak rather posh."

Verity shrugged. Had she known it was a janitorial position, she would have come in doing an imitation of her father.

"Do you have references?"

"References?" Verity squirmed. "No, not per se; I mean not really. I used to do the cleaning and housekeeping for an elderly gentleman back in England. He died recently. It was on an estate. I suppose that's where I picked up me, I mean, my posh way of talking."

Ms. Gort studied her another moment and then relaxed. "I suppose there's nothing wrong with having a cleaning woman with refinement. Not that you'll have much opportunity to chat. You'll work after normal business hours when most of the staff is gone."

"Perfect," said Verity.

"What?"

"I mean," said Verity, "I prefer cleaning alone. I do a better job without distractions."

"Oh, yes, of course," said Gort. "Well, you won't have many distractions." She looked at her desk calendar. "Well, even though you were early, we haven't had any other applicants. So if you want the job, it's yours, contingent on a background check."

"Background check?"

"Yes, we are a bank," she explained. "We don't leave piles of cash lying around, but all of our employees, from the president to the lowest member of staff, which would be you, have complete a background check. It's routine."

Ms. Gort handed Verity an application form to fill out. Verity left the address vacant, explaining that she was looking at rooms to rent this afternoon. After that, Ms. Gort explained her wages and outlined her duties.

"The background check takes a day or two," said Gort. "We use an agency that verifies the data and checks for any problems."

"Problems?"

"Like felonies."

"Oh, yes, of course," Verity smiled. "Thankfully, I've never even gotten a traffic ticket."

"Good, though you won't be driving much more than a cleaning cart here," said Gort. "You'll get a few pinnies, and you can wear your own shoes. Those plimsolls look just the thing." She pointed at Verity's shoes.

Verity thanked her, promised to do a good job, and left. Once out in the street, she decided she should look for a more humble address, one that matched the wages of a cleaning lady.

She was in!

– 60 –
The Non-Violent Display of Affection

Lorraine Innis sat in her hotel suite that evening, deep in thought. It was strange that Valerie would go to Gibraltar, even stranger that she would marry Albrecht Eckner. Perhaps Valerie was also trying to get information about who was responsible for Martina's death. And now, Verity was off to Gibraltar as well. Even after securing Nigel Verve's services, Lorraine felt impotent. The two most important women in her life were going to battle for her, and she was stuck in London in skirts. It was a terrible blow to her manhood. Lorraine couldn't go to Gibraltar without a good reason. She couldn't go as Chesney Potts because she didn't have his passport. When she came to England, she didn't even know there was a person named Chesney Potts, let alone that he was her.

Lorraine was about to brush her teeth and get ready for bed when she heard a knock on the door of her suite. Cinching her robe around her waist, she walked to the door and looked through the peephole. Through the fisheye lens, she saw the elongated face of Purvis Twankey. Somehow the distortion enhanced his natural looks.

Lorraine opened the door. "Hello, Purvis."

"How do, Miss Lorraine," he smiled. Then he looked down. "Oh, gosh, I'm sorry, I didn't get you up, did I? Only it's not even ten yet."

"No, Purvis," she said. "Come in. How is Patsy?"

He scratched his sandy hair. "I don't rightly know, Miss Lorraine. She's back in the States. When I call her, she doesn't talk back much. I don't mean to talk back, like being sassy. She just don't say much in return."

"Maybe it's just pre-wedding jitters," she said. "I'm sure Patsy has a lot on her mind. It's also difficult with you being over here, and she's back in Delaware. I hope that puts your mind at ease."

"Oh, heck," he grinned, "I've always had an easy mind. That's not why I come over, Miss Lorraine. I wanted you to have the first one of these." He pulled a 45 rpm record from his coat and handed it to her.

Lorraine studied the label. "'*My Gal with the Face Full of Hair*?'"

He grinned. "Aye! I did it for you, Miss Lorraine."

Lorraine felt her own cheeks. "Uh, thank you, Purvis, but I don't have a hairy face anymore; I mean, I don't have a hairy face."

Purvis laughed. "It's not about you. Heck, you're a real smoothie, at least in the hairy face department. It's about them women what grew beards because they used me perfume. You recollect? The one that got you all kinds of sued."

"Yeah, I recollect," muttered Lorraine. "But I don't think they'll want to be reminded of their plight in a song."

"They don't have to," he explained. "The song just says that all girls are beautiful kinds of females, no matter what's sprouting out of their faces. And all the money the record makes will go to help them women, at least the ones that don't fancy their whiskers anymore."

"That's very sweet, Purvis," she said. "But Lord Bagnold is supposed to be paying for that."

"Him what was there when you were doing that TV ad?"

"Yes, that's him," said Lorraine. "And he's also the one that took your perfume formula and caused the problem. One of the reasons I agreed to do that commercial was so he'd do the right thing for those poor women."

Purvis scratched his head. "Well, I hope he learned his lesson that it's not right to steal another fella's idea without his permission. Anyway, I'll still give any proceeds from this record to them fuzzy women."

Lorraine looked at the record again. "Well, I'm sure they'll appreciate it, Purvis. Now I suppose you'll be getting back home to Patsy."

"Aye," said Purvis, "and working on me next project. Remember, I got me idea for the solution to world energy." He rubbed his jaw.

"Oh, right," said Lorraine, "you mentioned that the last time I decked you. Something about cucumbers?"

"Pickles," he beamed, "big ones and fast growers, too. That's the key to it all."

Lorraine smiled patronizingly. "That's wonderful."

"Aye, it is. I'm ready to announce it," said Purvis. "It's such a momentous idea; I want to do it somewhere special. Where it will get lots of attention, like the top of the Empire State Building, or the Eifel Tower, or the pyramids."

"Or the Rock of Gibraltar!" said Lorraine.

"Do what?"

"The Rock of Gibraltar," she repeated. She needed an excuse to go to Gibraltar and help Verity. She could travel there as Lorraine, then change to Chesney and work unobserved. "It's very dramatic, awe-inspiring, just the type of backdrop you'd want for your announcement."

Purvis sat down and closed his eyes, apparently deep in thought; either that or he had fallen asleep. After a minute, he opened one eye and looked at Lorraine."Where is this Rock of Gibraltar?"

"Um, in Gibraltar," she said. "That's near Spain."

"Do I have to do it in Spanish?" said Puvis. "Only, I don't speak Spanish."

"It's at the southern tip of Spain," she explained, "but it's British territory. They speak English there," said Lorraine, "just like in England."

"That's good," he said with a nod. "Most of England speaks so what you can understand. Except for them Geordies around the Tyne. I have a hard time understanding them blokes."

Lorraine assured Purvis that he would understand the residents of Gibraltar, and they would probably understand him. Then she added. "I've always wanted to go to Gibraltar. I could go with you. It would help draw attention to your announcement."

Purvis just smiled his usual innocent smile without saying a word. She wished he would have said something. His silence allowed her conscience to start talking to her. She would be using him. It was like lying to a small child or playing a trick on a trusting Labrador. Lorraine smiled back, but he just kept looking at her with those devoted eyes. Finally, after only 30 seconds, Lorraine cracked.

"I'm lying to you," she cried. "I'm sorry, Purvis, but it's a lie."

Purvis' expression went from contented to confused. "Lying, Miss Lorraine?" It was as if the concept and the name couldn't share the same sentence.

"Yes, Purvis, I'm terribly sorry. I'm a horrible person. I lied to you about Gibraltar."

"You mean it ain't near Spain?" he asked.

"No," said Lorraine, "I lied about wanting to go there."

He scratched the side of his head. "Oh, so you don't want to go?"

"No, I do want to go," she said, "I need to go."

"But you don't want to go with me?" he asked, trying to understand.

"I would gladly go with you," said Lorraine.

"Oh," he said. His eyes rolled upward, deep in thought. "So, you do want to go, and you want to go with me."

"Yes, that's right."

"But you're lying about it?" He sat down and slapped his knees. "Nope, sorry, Miss Lorraine, you're wrong. I don't see the fib."

Lorraine sat down beside him. "I need to go to Gibraltar on a very personal matter."

She paused. Most people would have asked for more details, but Purvis just sat there with a blank expression.

"...a personal matter," she continued. "But it would be difficult for me just to go there. I'm under such public scrutiny; people would wonder what I was doing there."

Again, she paused, waiting for a question. When none came, she continued.

"...so I thought if I got you to go to Gibraltar, that would be my excuse for tagging along."

"That would be champion," he said.

"No, but you see, I was deceiving you," she pleaded. "You don't need Gibraltar or me to make your big announcement. I was using you for my own selfish ends."

Purvis sat quietly for a minute, turning over her confession in the corn popper of his mind. Then he smiled and nodded. "Okay, then."

"You forgive me?"

"Ya what? Oh, that, sure I do, no, I was figuring out how we're going to do this."

"You mean that you not only forgive me, but you're going to help me?"

"Course," he said, "you're one of me best friends."

"But I lied to you."

He waved his hand. "No, you didn't. You tried to, but you didn't. Now, if you had lied to me and I didn't find out, then I'd be mighty sore. But as you didn't lie to me, and I found out, then there's nowt more to it. So, let's figure out how we're getting to Gibraltar."

Lorraine threw her arms around him and hugged him.

The hug was enough, causing Purvis Twankey to blush.

"Gosh, Miss Lorraine," he muttered as a blush rose to his cheeks, "that the most affection we ever swapped without me winding up on the floor!"

– 61 –
The Gift That Stops Giving

This is swell of you, Mr. V.," said Shorty Long as they made their way through customs in Gibraltar.

"Yeah, yeah," muttered Robert Valvano, "get out your passport."

Shorty waved it in front of him. "Right here."

Robert grabbed it and examined the photograph. "Ha, I knew you were an ugly bastard, but you're even worse in front of a camera."

Shorty sighed. "Yeah, my mom wouldn't even frame my school pictures. The only good picture I ever took was my mugshot."

"Must be the numbers across your chest distracting from the rest of your repulsive puss." Robert stopped and took a second look at the passport. "Sheldon?"

He blushed. "You don't think my parents named me 'Shorty,' do you?"

Robert handed him back the passport. "They might as well have. I mean, Shorty fits you."

"My father was six-foot-three, and my mother was five-ten," noted Shorty.

Robert scanned his traveling companion's slight frame. "Yeah, well, they must have used up all the height before they got to you."

After clearing customs, Robert turned to Shorty.

"Okay, Sheldon," he said in mocking tones, "let's get you outfitted."

Shorty shook his head. "I wish I coulda brought my tools and equipment."

"Yeah, well, customs agents have a funny way of frowning on bomb-making gear, to say nothing of the airlines," he hailed a taxi.

A cab stopped, and the pair climbed in. Robert gave the driver instructions.

A few minutes later, they were wandering the aisles of one of Gibraltar's hardware stores.

"You know what you need?" asked Robert.

"Oh, yeah," said Shorty tapping the side of his head. "It's all up here. I didn't think it would be too smart to write it down. I gotta tell you, Mr. V.," said Shorty as he examined a selection of wire. "This is gonna be a challenge. I never made a bomb so small."

Robert grabbed Shorty's collar. "Don't use that word, especially not in public. Call it a... a *gift*."

Shorty shrugged. "Okay, I never made a *gift* so small."

"Can't you do it? You said you could do it," said Robert. "Or am I just wasting a Mediterranean vacation on a runny-nosed twerp?"

"Oh, I can do it," said Shorty. "Only, this is a little different. I never did a gift for a person."

"That's what you're known for. You've made a lot of gifts."

Shorty raised an index finger. "Not for people. I did gifts for cars. They just happened to have people sitting in them. There's a difference."

"Look, *stunad*, nobody has a vendetta against automobiles. You give a gift to a car, and the people in them enjoy it, too."

"Yeah," agreed Shorty, "but what I'm saying is that the people insides were what you can a byproduct. Lighting a car is easy, but now you just want a small gift to take out one person. I never done that before. I guess you could say it's expanding my professional horizons. I'm going from the sledgehammer to the scalpel. You, know, finesse."

"You're a real artist, Picasso," snarled Robert. "Just get what you need. Only don't get all of it now. You don't want to make your intentions obvious."

"Oh, right. So's nobody will figure I'm making a gift."

After selecting some tools for fine work and an assortment of wire, the pair made their purchases and left.

"Next time, we'll go to a different store," said Robert. "Spread it out, so it doesn't draw attention." He looked up and down the street, searching for his next stop.

"Can I be of assistance, sir?" a voice with a British accent asked.

Robert turned around and almost told the inquisitor to get lost when he saw it was a cop.

"What? Uh, no, I mean, yes, officer," said Robert. "I was just saying to my friend..." He turned to where Shorty had been standing. That space was now vacant, and Shorty Long was nowhere to be seen. "The little rat..."

"Excuse me, sir?" said the cop.

"I mean, my friend, he was wearing a little hat. He must have gone into a shop," said Robert with a forced smile. "We're out looking for an anniversary present for my wife." He held up his hand and pointed at his wedding ring. "Maybe you can help. My wife is nuts about fancy makeup, you know, expensive designer cosmetics. Got any places like that around here?"

The officer eyed him carefully for a moment before breaking into a smile.

"Yes, sir, my wife is the same way; she likes the sort of things a husband doesn't know anything about."

Robert laughed nervously. "Right, pal, I mean, officer, dames, uh, wives, always sending us out..."

"... into uncharted territory," said the cop.

"Yeah, right," Robert laughed.

"For mine, it's fancy knickers," said the cop in a low voice.

"What?"

"You know, lingerie."

"Oh, yeah, ha, sure," said Robert. "I guess mine is letting me off easy just getting her fancy make-up."

The office nodded and pointed down the street.

In a few minutes, Robert Valvano was standing outside an upscale cosmetics boutique. He was about to enter when he felt a tug at his elbow. It was Shorty Long.

"You little chiseler," growled Robert as he lifted him by his collar.

"Take it easy, Mr. V.," said Shorty, "only I thought we was getting pinched."

"And you left me to take the rap," said Robert.

"Naw, it ain't like that," pleaded Shorty. "Only, I know you're a smooth talker and a classy guy. I thought me being there might make the whole deal look hinky."

Robert released him. "Yeah, okay, you do bring down the tone of any gathering. But don't do that again. You bail on me, and I'll make some anonymous calls on your behalf to several enforcement jurisdictions. Get me?"

"Right," assured Shorty.

"Now, come on in here and keep your mouth shut." Robert opened the door, and Shorty followed him in. They were greeted by a young woman wearing a generous amount of cosmetics.

"Gentlemen, how may I help you?" asked the woman.

"We, that is I, would like to buy some make-up for my wife," said Robert. "It's our anniversary, and I want to deck her out with all the best gear. Can you do that?"

"Looks like she's wearing most of the stock already," noted Shorty under his breath. Robert elbowed him in the ribs.

"You'll have to excuse my, uh, my brother-in-law," said Robert. "He's not very couth. But like I said, as it's a special occasion, I want the best stuff you got."

"I'm sure we can accommodate you," said the girl, "what brand does your wife use?"

Robert's mouth hung open. "Use? Uh, shit, I mean, well, ha, you know how husbands are…"

"Sorry, I'm not married."

"I mean, the average stiff doesn't know what crap, uh, cosmetics his wife uses. I just know it's good stuff. I know; I pay the bills. Just give me an assortment of all of it."

The woman led them to a nearby counter. "We carry all the best brands. I'm sure your wife will be pleased with all the products we provide."

"Yeah, right, I'm sure, too," said Robert.

"What are your wife's colors?"

"She's white," said Robert.

"I meant her shades," said the woman.

Robert turned and looked at Shorty, who raised his sunglasses from his breast pocket.

"Not those kinds of shade, dickhead," said Robert before catching himself. "Ha, my brother-in-law, always the little clown."

"Perhaps he can help," said the woman turning to Shorty. "What tones does your sister have."

Shorty looked at her blankly. "I ain't got a sister, lady." Robert jabbed his ribs again. "Oh, yeah, my sister. I didn't finish. I ain't got a sister, 'cept the one who married him."

"He doesn't know from tones," said Robert, who was just as unfamiliar with the term. "I'm sure you could explain it to him better than I could."

"Well, each complexion has a different quality, such as warm, neutral, and cool. Then with those, there are varying hues: gold, yellow, pink, rose…"

Robert slapped Shorty on the arm. "See, just like I told you."

"Your brother-in-law," she said, indicating Robert, "is a warm peach."

"Yeah, we've always said that," said Shorty, "now this makes it official."

"Shut up," growled Robert under his breath.

"Excuse me?" said the saleswoman.

"Nothing, nothing," said Robert. "Look, my wife's tone is just like her brother's here."

The woman examined Shorty's face. "I see, then she's a cool pink."

"Sure," said Robert, "what do you got in a cool pink?"

The saleswoman started pulling out different lotions and explaining their various qualities.

"Yeah, well," said Robert cutting her off, "she pretty well set for that stuff. I'm looking to stock up her handbag, you know, with whatever you ladies like to stow away in those. Show us what you got in that line."

The woman thought a moment and began placing several items on the counter. "I would imagine she'd need the essentials: a lipstick, a mascara, a powder compact."

Shorty's eyes narrowed as he picked up the compact and examined it.

"Whatya think?" Robert said to Shorty. He noticed the woman's puzzled expression. "I mean, would 'Sis' like it?"

"Got anything bigger?" Shorty asked the saleswoman.

"Bigger?" the woman was non-plussed. "All our compacts are approximately that size.

"That's why they're called compacts," said Robert, "you know, like a car."

"These are all smaller than a compact car," noted Shorty. "I could really do a job with a compact car."

Robert jabbed his ribs. "Yeah, but can you make this work?" The woman gave him a puzzled look. "I mean, would your sister like this?"

Shorty shrugged. "I guess she'll have to. Get those other things, too." He pointed to the lipstick and the mascara. "Just to be safe."

"Yeah, we'll take those," said Robert. "Oh, and just to cover all our bases, give us two of each, and so we make sure we got what she already uses, give us that in your three top lines."

"Wouldn't it be easier to find out what brand she already uses?" asked the woman.

Robert smiled. "Naw, it's going to be a surprise."

"A big surprise," added Shorty.

– 62 –
The Temporary Blonde with a Moral Dilemma

Lorraine Innis pulled the floppy hat further down over her head. It was a difficult fit. Lorraine already had a large noggin thanks to her full hairdo, but on top of that, she wore a long blonde wig. An oversized pair of sunglasses helped complete the disguise.

She had slipped out of the hotel unnoticed by a side entrance. Rather than take a cab, she jumped on one of the city's red double-decker buses. She rode this to the familiar neighborhood in Marylebone, around the corner from Aunt Elinor's old flat.

Lorraine climbed the two flights of stairs in the old building and knocked on the door. Lorraine glanced over her shoulder. There was no one following her. She heard the click of the door latch.

"Come in," said Li Gao, "I am most honored for your visit."

Lorraine thanked him and, with one more backward glance, hurried inside. He closed the door behind her and locked it.

"Tea?" asked Gao as he led her into a small but comfortable sitting room.

"Yes, please," said Lorraine. She took off her sunglasses and hat. But the blonde wig came off with the hat. "Oh!"

"Ah, a wig," noted Li Gao, "I wondered if you had dyed your own hair, but then your own hair is not that long. I presume this was to remain undetected."

"Yes," said Lorraine undoing her trench coat. "I didn't want to be noticed, especially not by Lord Bagnold's minions."

"Does Verity's father have minions?"

Lorraine shook her head. "I wouldn't put it past him, but I didn't want to find out. I've gotten you in enough hot water."

"Fortunately, some of that hot water has been appropriated for the tea," said Gao pouring her a cup. "Biscuit?"

Lorraine started to reach for a cookie but stopped. "No, sorry, I still have a figure to watch. It's not easy being a woman. I'm not only scrutinized by the public, but I have to watch every morsel I put in my mouth."

Li Gao smiled.

"What?" asked Lorraine.

"Nothing," he said, "it is quite reminiscent of your dear aunt. I can almost hear Elinor saying similar words. You do look and sound very much alike. As much as I pray for the day of your liberation, I must confess I have enjoyed seeing her again by way of this similitude."

"At least one consequence of all this is happy, then," said Lorraine sipping her tea.

"Do not be troubled, my dear, excuse me, my boy," said Li Gao. "I have every confidence that it will all work out well."

"You do?"

Gao smiled enigmatically. "Eventually. But, let us not be sidetracked into a theological discussion, as pleasant an occupation as that may be. I have procured those items you requested." He went into the next room and returned with a small parcel. "I was uncertain how you wanted to carry them, so I wrapped them thusly."

"Thank you," said Lorraine taking the package. "While there are definite disadvantages to womanhood, one plus is the use of an oversized handbag." She pulled out a shoulder bag and placed the bundle inside.

Gao took a piece of paper from his breast pocket. "All the items you requested are there. I encountered minimal difficulty acquiring them as they are quite common."

Lorraine smiled and took his hand. "Thank you, my friend. How much do I owe you?"

Li Gao smiled. "I could not take money from…" he stopped.

Lorraine smirked. "Yeah, I know, you couldn't take money from a lady."

"Forgive me, Chesney," said Gao, "but your transformation is quite convincing, even to those who know the real you."

Lorraine stood. "I'm sure that's a compliment. Let's just say that a man who looks quite like me will settle up when he sees you soon."

"That is a transaction I eagerly anticipate," said Gao.

Lorraine reached the door and stopped.

"Oh, I forgot my blonde hair," she said. Lorraine sat down and started arranging the hairpiece. She stopped and looked up. "I forgot something else, too."

"Your sunglasses?"

Lorraine sighed. "No, I wish it were as easy as taking off a pair of glasses. But, it involves when I cease being Lorraine Innis."

"As I understand it," said Gao, "you have not made any permanent changes."

"No, thankfully not," said Lorraine. "It's not a physical predicament."

Li Gao nodded. "Rather a moral one?"

"Precisely," she said with a nod. "How do I get rid of Lorraine Innis? I have been living a lie to the world. Do I owe them the truth?"

"Do you?" asked Gao without a hint of his position on the subject.

"If this had all gone according to the original plan," she continued, "I wouldn't owe anyone an explanation. I was going to get justice for Martina and the only one affected was the recipient of that justice. But now, millions of people believe in me. Lorraine Innis has become an icon against my wishes. People have donated money and bought products based on a sham of a person. I feel like I owe those people an explanation."

Li Gao sat down, folded his hand across his chest, and closed his eyes.

"Or maybe, I don't," continued Lorraine. She had hoped he would offer her sage advice. Instead, he just sat placidly. "If I didn't confess it all, I'd have to go around the rest of my life with that on my conscience. I don't know how that would affect me in the long term. Would that be fair to Verity?" She paused again, waiting for a glimmer of a reply. "Or, if I told the world the truth, would that make things even worse? The world might not like the truth. Things could get nasty. That would be all I deserved, and I could face those consequences, but again, I have to think about Verity." Lorraine stopped. Li Gao remained perfectly still, with his eyes shut. "Or..." Lorraine said, tailing off, "maybe no one would care."

She almost wondered if Gao had fallen asleep. His breathing was steady, though not in a slumbering way. She was about to reach over and nudge him when his eyes opened, and he smiled.

"I believe," he said thoughtfully, "I believe you are correct."

"About what?" asked Lorraine.

"All of it," said Gao standing and taking Lorraine by the elbow. "Now, the time grows late, and there is much to do."

"But what shall I do?" she said.

He smiled. "That depends on the outcome you are seeking."

"I just want to do the best thing."

"For whom?"

Lorraine looked into his eyes and nodded.

"Let that thought guide you," said Gao as he led her to the door. He paused with his hand on the knob. "Recall the words of Paul: 'do nothing out of selfish ambition or vain conceit. Rather in humility, value others above yourself, not looking to your own interests but to the interests of others.'"

"Thank you," said Lorraine. "Thank you for everything. And I hope I see you soon, in a better way."

– 63 –
Three Little Words
and Three Little Letters

Clodagh Clott couldn't understand what Nikolai Kropotkin was saying as he addressed the small crowd in Russian. But his audience seemed to approve enthusiastically.

Since he was back in his home region, Kropotkin felt confident in dropping his disguise and announcing his true identity. His rival, Gregor Teplov, calling him out on television, spurred on Kropotkin. At first, the bar patrons looked on in stunned silence and then erupted in wild cheers. After accepting the congratulations of the crowd, Kropotkin asked to use the telephone.

"I called my office in Moscow and spoke to my assistant, Yuri," Kropotkin explained to Clodagh. "When I left, I hadn't told Yuri where I was going or when I would be back."

"He must have been worried," said Clodagh.

"Da," agreed Kropotkin, "especially when Teplov started nosing around concerning my whereabouts."

"But Teplov knew where you were," said Clodagh.

"He knew where he'd left me, that is, us," he said. "I can only surmise that he returned to the bunker, found his guards dead, and his prisoners gone. Yuri said he's been asking if he'd heard from me. Fortunately, Yuri had no idea. Teplov is wily, like a serpent. If Yuri had known, Teplov would soon have tricked it out of him."

"So, are you going back to Moscow?"

Kropotkin smiled. "No, we are going back to Moscow."

Clodagh almost responded pedantically that since she had never been to Moscow, she couldn't return there. But that was too much of a Lorraine Innis answer, and she felt Nikolai needed a healthy alternative to Lorraine. Instead, she just smiled.

"They are sending a car and an airplane," said Kropotkin.

"Okay, I'll take the car, and you can have the plane, Nick," she said.

A confused look crossed his face. He opened his mouth, presumably to explain, and then stopped. A broad smile broke out across his face, followed by a hearty laugh. "Another joke," he said. "You are a treasure, Miss Clott. You get kidnapped, traipse around the wilds of Russia like a fugitive, sleep in cars, wear stolen clothes, and you still have that wonderful sense of humor."

"I guess that comes from being an American," she said.

"I've known many Americans," said Nikolai, "and a sense of humor is not an inborn trait. No, that is uniquely you, darling Clodagh."

Kropotkin embraced her and gave her a passionate kiss. Clodagh enjoyed it for a few seconds until she opened her eyes and saw the tavern patrons standing around grinning.

"Nick, I don't think this is exactly the place..." said Clodagh, though her words were garbled, spoken as they were into his mouth.

"What?" said Kropotkin coming up for air. He opened his eyes, looked around, and smiled. The crowd burst into enthusiastic cheers.

One man shouted out something in Russian.

Kropotkin replied jubilantly in Russian, which led to even louder cheers. He then made another announcement eliciting a third round of shouts, and they all turned to the bar.

"I told them I was buying the next round of drinks," Kropotkin explained.

"There were two rounds of cheering," said Clodagh. "What was the other one for?"

Kropotkin turned red and grinned bashfully. "Oh, that was something else."

"I figured that," said Clodagh. She poked her finger into his side and twisted it. "You said it, and then they all looked at me. Come on, Nick, what did you tell them?"

"Oh, that," he said. "Someone asked if you were my girlfriend."

"Ha, and I suppose you told them I was."

Another broad smile broke out on Kropotkin's face. "No, I said you weren't."

Clodagh's face dropped. "Oh."

"I told them you were my future wife," he said. He looked at her for a moment. Clodagh's face was expressionless. A worried look darkened his eyes. "If you would... please? I love you."

Clodagh felt as if she must have stared at him for several minutes as a thousand thoughts raced through her mind. Marry him? She always figured she would get married someday; at least, she thought that when she was younger. But, with no serious boyfriend for years, that assumption had grown dimmer. She was used to being on her own. Marriage was no longer a requirement to complete her life. She was content now. But, she hadn't closed the door on the possibility either, if the right person would come along.

She looked into the hopeful face of Nick Kropotkin as he waited for an answer. She did enjoy her adventure with him. He really was a nice guy once she had pierced his politician's shell. She had gone through a lot with him in a very short time. Was that enough on which to build a lasting relationship? And beyond the man himself, he was the president of a world power. Could she be the wife of a world leader? She'd have to move to Russia. She'd have to learn the language. She'd have no friends. It would be like moving to a new planet.

Kropotkin's eyes grew anxious as these and many more thoughts raced through her mind. He was waiting for some kind of response.

"I… uh, wow…" was all Clodagh managed.

"I have upset you," said Nick.

"No, no, it's just, well, it's unexpected," she said. "Can I think about it?"

"Yes, yes, of course," he said. "Forgive me; I am a fool."

"No…"

"Not for wanting to marry you," he said. "I am so impetuous. I let my emotion carry me away without thinking."

"Yeah, not the best habit to develop," she said, "not for a guy withhis own army."

Kropotkin paused a moment and then laughed.

"Yes," said Clodagh, "it was a joke."

"And I am getting better at laughing," he said. "That is just one of the reasons that, well…"

Clodagh kissed him on the cheek. "Yes, I'm getting better at this, too."

In about an hour, a man in a chauffeur's livery entered and saluted Kropotkin.

"Ah, the car is here to take us to the plane," he said. "Please…" he held out his arm, and Clodagh took it.

The chauffeur opened the rear door. Kropotkin gestured that Clodagh should get in. She did so. Nick walked to the other door and climbed in while the chauffeur reached in to secure Clodagh's seatbelt. As he clipped the belt, she looked at him. He smiled warmly and said something in Russian. She smiled back and thanked him in English. Then as his hand drew away, Clodagh noticed something on his wrist. It was a small tattoo.

Inside the back of the limo was a small bar, a phone, and a few writing implements on a counter. It was just what you'd expect in the limo of a top executive or leader. Kropotkin gave an order in Russian. She noticed the manner was much harsher than the one she had grown accustomed to. The driver replied in an obsequious tone. Kropotkin was seated behind the driver with Clodagh on the passenger side. Nick couldn't see it from his vantage point, but though the driver sounded subservient, a sly smile appeared on his lips after he spoke. Clodagh thought it odd. She started to say something to Nick, but she saw the driver eyeing her in the rear view mirror.

Nikolai Kropotkin picked up the phone. "I must call my assistant and tell him we're on the way."

Clodagh looked at the driver. He kept glancing back at her. She just smiled.

"I think," she said, picking up a pencil and notepad, "I'm going to write to my sister."

Kropotkin nodded and started speaking Russian on the phone. Although she was no artist, Clodagh sketched a rough approximation of the tattoo she had seen. It was a dagger or something and some sort of crest or shield. Underneath the drawing, she wrote: "On his wrist."

As they drove, Clodagh tried to think of a way to show it to Nick. He was absorbed in his phone call. The driver kept glancing back in a way that gave Clodagh the creeps. Finally, she put her hand on his.

"Excuse me, Nick," she said, "but I'm writing to my sister. Did I get the name right of the village we were in?"

"What, please, Clo…" Kropotkin looked down at the paper, and a look of concern darkened his expression. His eyes darted briefly toward the driver. Clodagh nodded.

"Did I get that wrong?" Clodagh asked with a subtle nod.

"Ah, you have the letters reversed," he said before taking the pad. He took a pen from his pocket. "Let me correct it for you, my dear."

On the pad, he wrote: "Sword and Shield… KGB."

– 64 –
The Vase That
Aspired to Be an Urn

Valerie Fierro stepped out of the cab and paid the driver. She looked up at the façade of the Gibraltar subsidiary of Fourth Fiduciary Trust and nodded. It was an old building, but so were most of the buildings on the street. The tall columns projected a feeling of stability and wealth. Valerie liked that, especially the wealth part. She hadn't been there on her previous visit when she was supposed to audit the company accounts. Now, audits didn't matter. In a few minutes, it would all be hers.

She was meeting Albrecht in his office. After their celibate honeymoon, they had flown back to London and hopped the connecting flight to Gibraltar. Albrecht had offered Valerie the spare room in his apartment, but she declined. After drugging her and using her as his personal mannequin, she didn't trust him as far as a flea could throw him. He was perverted enough in a hotel. Who knew what secret cameras and peepholes Albrecht had installed in his home? Valerie hadn't let on that she knew what Albrecht had done to her with his collection of kinky corsetry. She would wait until she had complete control of the Valvano operation. Then she would thank Albrecht for helping her secure it and then make him pay severely for including her in his debauched hobby.

Valerie stopped at the front reception desk.

"I'm here to see…"

"Oh, yes," said the woman jumping to her feet, "yes, we've been expecting you, Mrs. Eckner."

Valerie gritted her teeth. She hadn't gotten used to being called that; fortunately, she wouldn't have to.

"On behalf of the entire staff," the woman reached under the desk and pulled out a large bouquet wrapped in cellophane. "We'd like to extend our congratulations."

Valerie took the flowers in her arms. "Yeah, well..."

"And we all wish you many happy years of bliss," continued the receptionist.

"Not until after the divorce case..." muttered Valerie.

"Pardon?"

"Oh, I said, of course, could you put these in a vase," said Valerie speaking up. She smiled broadly and handed back the flowers. "Please?"

"Yes, absolutely."

"And now I'd like to see my darling husband."

The woman looked at Valerie and sighed. "It must be wonderful to be a newlywed."

"Words can't express how I feel," said Valerie. The woman continued to beam at her. Valerie sighed. "My husband? Mr. Eckner? Where is he?"

"Oh, sorry," said the woman, putting down the flowers. "Right this way, Mrs. Eckner."

Valerie followed, making a mental note that this woman would be one of the first to go, if for no other reason than those "Mrs. Eckner" references.

She followed the woman through a security door, down a hallway, and then up an elevator to the top floor.

"This is your husband's office," said the woman as she stopped in front of a door marked "private."

"Roberta," the woman said to another woman sitting behind a desk, "this is Mrs. Eckner."

"I'm delighted to meet you, Mrs. Eckner," said the secretary.

"Please, call me Valerie." Anything but Mrs. Eckner, she thought.

"Yes, ma'am," said Roberta, pressing the intercom. "Mr. Eckner, Mrs. Eckner is here..."

"My mother?" Albrecht's voice replied.

"That's it," snapped Valerie and barged through the door to his inner office. She slammed it behind her. "It's bad enough using your name temporarily..."

"That was your idea," said Albrecht.

"But don't even intimate that I spawned you!"

Albrecht grinned. "I guess I'm not used to having a wife."

Valerie slapped her purse on the desk and sat down. "Yeah, well don't get used to it."

Albrecht picked up the phone. "Shall I order us some tea?"

"Tea? No, I don't want tea, or coffee, or a ham sandwich," Valerie said. "I want to sign those papers."

He just looked at her. "What papers?"

Valerie exhaled. "The papers, the ownership papers, the ones that will drive a tank through the Valvano's loophole. The only reason I'm back on this damned rock. So give me what I have to sign."

His blank expression intensified.

"The papers that will turn everything over to me," said Valerie raising her voice. "The ones you told me about."

"I told you?" he said, feigning the innocence only a pathological liar could muster.

Valerie dove over the desk and put her fingers around his throat. "Yes, you told me, back in London."

Albrecht gurgled something barely intelligible. It may have been "you're choking me" because she was.

"I'm going to release this stranglehold just enough to understand you," she said. "But if I don't like what I hear, normal strangulation will resume immediately."

"Uh, I have to explain," said Albrecht.

"Go on," she said.

"There's a glitch," he said.

Valerie released his throat. "What kind of a glitch?'

"Uh, well, not exactly a glitch. More like a slight miscalculation."

Valerie climbed off the desk and straightened her blouse. "How slight?"

Albrecht stepped back behind his desk chair. "Not at all slight. Actually, I was wrong. Completely wrong."

Valerie started to raise her hands like two claws ready to strike.

"But it's okay," he said.

She inched toward him.

"Don't worry," sputtered Albrecht, "we can work it out. I-I mean, would I go through all this for nothing?"

"You got something," she said, pointing to her wedding ring. "You got me."

He smiled. "And you got me, too, dearest. I've read that newlyweds often go through a period of adjustment."

"The only thing that's going to need adjustment is your spine, if you have one, after I throw you out that window."

"Ah, remember, this was your idea to get married," he raised his finger. "Technically, I'm a kept man."

"Kept maybe," she said, "but a man… never. And it wasn't actually my idea to get married. You were the one who said I had to come to Gibraltar, that I needed to get a passport in another name. Oh, and while we're on the subject of our nuptials," Valerie reached into her purse and pulled out a pamphlet. "I picked this up on the way out of the registry office."

"Oh, as a souvenir of our wedding?"

Valerie stared at him. "More like a warning not to do it again." She flipped through the pamphlet. "According to this, you need to give notice for a registry office wedding."

"Yes, I know," said Albrecht with a smile. "I did that. It was all legal if that's what you're worried about."

"I'm not worried," she said, "but you should be. You need to give notice no less than 28 days before the wedding."

"I told you, I took care of everything."

"Our wedding was two weeks after I suggested it," said Valerie. She shoved the booklet in his face. "You would have had to register the wedding before I even thought of it."

Albrecht took the pamphlet and pretended to read it. "Well, this is news to me. What do you think happened?"

"I know exactly what happened," shouted Valerie. "This is another in a long line of Albrecht Eckner manipulations, presented by the king of scheming, conniving, low-life worms! I'll get you for this. First, I'm going to call a lawyer and get this sham of a marriage annulled. Then, I don't know exactly how yet, but then I'm going to get you for everything, Albrecht, all the way back to the first time I saw you in high school!"

Valerie turned to leave.

"Stop, wait," said Albrecht, "you don't understand. I... I did it all to protect you."

Valerie stopped at the door and turned back.

"I can help you," Albrecht pleaded. "I know things. I know all about the inner workings of the Valvanos, intimate details."

Valerie smiled and walked slowly back to him. Albrecht relaxed.

"Intimate details," she said. "Thank you for reminding me. I know all about what you did to me on our honeymoon. You've been faking all this. I bet you even recognized me in that restaurant the first time when I went out with red hair. Didn't you?"

Albrecht tried to suppress a grin.

"I thought so," she said before rearing back and delivering a hard right to Albrecht's soft belly. His usually narrow eyes widened as the wind left him, and he fell against the wall and slid down to the floor.

"That," said Valerie, "is a down payment."

There was a knock at the door, and Valerie opened it. The receptionist from the front lobby was there with the bouquet in a vase.

"I put your flowers in a vase, Mrs. Eckner."

Valerie thanked her, took the flowers, and shut the door. She walked over to where Albrecht was slumped, took the flowers out of the vase, poured the water over him, and smacked his head with the bouquet. Valerie raised the vase over her head, and Albrecht cringed into a fetal ball.

"Nah," said Valerie, examining the vase. "It's too nice a vase to waste on a snake like you." She placed it on the desk and walked to the door. There she stopped and looked back at him. "Who knows, I may need it as a cremation urn for my husband."

– 65 –
The Pencil is Mightier
Than the Fighter Jet

KGB? Clodagh Clott bit her lip. She had almost cried the name out loud. She looked at Nick Kropotkin. A determined, steely look filled his eyes. He gently patted her hand and nodded slightly.

Kropotkin asked the driver a question in Russian.

"I asked how long until we get to the airfield," said Kropotkin, translating.

"I good English speak," said the driver.

"Oh, yes, very good," said Clodagh. She tried to suppress the nervous quiver in her voice.

"So how long until we get there?" asked Nick.

Clodagh could see his hideous smile in the rearview mirror. "You will arrive at your final destination very soon… very soon, Mr. President."

"Oh?" said Clodagh.

"You sound nervous, dear woman," said the driver.

"I-I'm afraid of flying," said Clodagh.

"Do not worry, my dear," said Kropotkin. "I trust you're a good driver."

"Driver?" said Clodagh. "Yes, I've driven since I was a teenager."

"Good, good," said Kropotkin. He leaned over the front seat. "You see, my friend, I have asked this lady to marry me. And as I've gotten so used to being chauffeured around, I must have a wife who can jump in to take the wheel… like NOW!"

Kropotkin put his left arm around the driver's neck while holding out his right hand.

"Give me the pencil," he shouted.

"But you have a pen," she said.

"I NEED THE PENCIL!"

Without finding out why he was so particular about his writing implement, Clodagh placed the pencil in his outstretched palm. Being an ex-KGB agent, the chauffeur's reflexes were well trained. He reached back, trying to gouge out Kropotkin's eyes. Kropotkin smashed his forehead against the back of the driver's headrest to counter the move. With his right hand, Kropotkin held the pencil like a dagger and struggled to maneuver it under the driver's chin.

With the driver otherwise occupied, the vehicle weaved back and forth across the two-lane road. Clodagh was torn about whether she should help Nick fight or try to gain control of the car. Kropotkin's had said take the wheel, so she leaned over the front seat and reached for the steering wheel. The struggle going on in front of her made this nearly impossible, and she only managed to grab it for a moment at a time. Each time she got hold of it, the driver broke her hold with his elbow.

Kropotkin nearly had the pencil poised under the man's chin. It looked like he was trying to thrust it upwards rather than down into the man's throat. As they struggled, the KGB agent twisted the pencil to the side, away from its intended target. A hideous look of triumph crossed his lips. Kropotkin seemed to be losing his hold around the younger man's neck. Instinctively, Clodagh leaned over and grabbed the man's wrist, and then over his KGB tattoo, she opened her mouth wide and bit him as hard as she could. The man gasped, and in the moment of distraction, Kropotkin spun the pencil around and aimed it toward the bottom of the man's jaw. Just as Kropotkin was about to thrust the pencil upward, the driver, realizing his fate, jerked his head to one side. The pencil went upward, piercing the driver's cheek.

Clodagh fell into the front seat. She clutched the wheel, but the man's foot was still on the accelerator.

"I can't stop it," cried Clodagh. The heaviness of the vehicle and the speed at which they were traveling made steering difficult.

"Just steer," shouted Kropotkin.

"I am... oh, HOLD ON, NICK!" They reached a bend in the road, and Clodagh pulled on the wheel, but to no avail. They kept going straight and careened off the highway and down a grassy slope.

"Just a minute," said Kropotkin as he managed to release the driver's seatbelt and then leaned forward to open the driver's door. At that speed, the wind resistance kept pushing the door shut. Finally, Kropotkin pushed the door open while shoving the driver's head to the side to keep it open. Then he leaned over and, with a mighty shove, flung the driver out of the car.

With the driver's seat empty, Clodagh could steer better, but they were nearing two obstacles: a large tree and a hedgerow. She didn't have time to stop, not that she could, given their inertia down the hill. The choice was obvious: hit the hedgerow, and hopefully, that would bring them to a stop.

The limo hit the hedgerow at 60 miles per hour, and while the impact slowed the vehicle, the muddy pond on the other side completed the task.

Kropotkin shoved the door open and pulled Clodagh from the car and into a mucky quagmire.

Then he scrambled up on the embankment and pulled her onto the grassy bank. They sat there, the only sound being their heavy breathing.

Finally, Nick Kropotkin looked at her.

"I suppose," Clodagh said, "you'll have to get a new pencil."

Kropotkin laughed. "Yes, maybe the next car will come with one. I was trying to kill the man."

"With a pencil?"

Kropotkin reached out with his muddy hand and placed his index finger just behind the point of her chin. "Here," he said, "here is a soft spot. A thrust upward right there avoids any bone and goes through the soft palate and into the victim's brain. I learned that in my military training."

"My Dad was in the Air Force," she noted.

Kropotkin nodded. "Yes, failing the availability of a pencil, a fighter jet will do in a pinch. He turned his head, and I missed. We will go back and take him prisoner."

She nodded.

"You were magnificent," said Kropotkin after several moments of silence. "You saved our lives."

Clodagh stared at the limo, sinking in the mud. "Well," she said, "I suppose then I'll have to marry you now."

– 66 –
The Gift That Keeps on Shiving

Valerie fumed. She had been duped again by Albrecht Eckner. Whenever she thought she had outsmarted him, he was at least one move ahead of her. This wasn't just the prom or losing her virginity to the slug. Now she was married to him.

She felt the gold charm around her neck that her father had given her. *Prima I dente, poi I parenti!* First, your teeth, then your family, was the exact translation. It meant: look out for number one!.

"Don't worry, Daddy," muttered Valerie, "I'll get him!"

"Excuse me, Miss?"

"Huh?" Valerie looked up and saw the cabbie's eyes in his rearview mirror.

"You told me not to worry," said the driver, "but how did you know my name was 'Danny?'"

"What? Oh, no, I was saying, oh, never mind," said Valerie.

"Right," said the driver stopping at her hotel, "we're here."

Valerie got out, paid the driver, and went inside to the front desk. She cringed when she asked for the key to her suite and was given it with a polite: "Yes, Mrs. Eckner."

Valerie gritted her teeth and started toward the elevator when a delightful thought struck her. She pivoted on her four-inch Louboutins and returned to the desk.

"Oh, by the way," said Valerie in her sweetest voice, "my husband has arranged for everything, hasn't he? I mean, he's given you his credit card information."

"Yes, Mrs. Eckner," said the manager, "Mr. Eckner has a long-standing account with us. We're very appreciative for the business he and his bank have given us."

Valerie nodded. "Yeah, he's given me the business plenty of times too."

"Pardon?"

"Skip it," she said. "Mr. Eckner, my dear husband, likes to entertain, does he?" Valerie could only imagine the depravities carried out by Albrecht.

"Mr. Eckner is a wonderful client and very generous to the hotel and the staff."

"Generous to a fault," agreed Valerie, thinking, and he's got plenty of those.

"Yes, Mrs. Eckner," agreed the manager.

"You know we're newlyweds," said Valerie, "dear Albrecht and I."

"Yes, congratulations."

"And, I do appreciate your hospitality," she continued. "I'll be staying here while renovations are completed on my husband's apartment. You know, converting it from a bachelor pad to something more appropriate for a newly married couple."

The manager smiled and nodded. "I hope your stay will be comfortable and your marriage long and joyful."

"That's it exactly," said Valerie, "Joyful. We're so deliriously happy, Brecky... that is Albrecht, Mr. Eckner, my dear husband, wants to share that joy. How many guests have you got staying here now?"

"I cannot divulge the exact number," said the manager, "but we are almost at full occupancy."

"Wonderful," said Valerie leaning across the counter to pat the man's hand. "Could you arrange for a little celebration for your guests?"

"Celebration?"

"Oh, nothing elaborate," cooed Valerie. "I mean, my husband is as shy as he is generous. We wouldn't want to throw a party, but we'd like to give each guest their own little celebration. Could we have a bottle of your best champagne along with a box of your best chocolates and a nice floral arrangement sent to each room? And charge it to my husband."

"My, that is most generous," said the manager. "And what should we put on the card?"

"Oh, something like, 'Hope you enjoy this half as much as I've enjoyed letting you have it.' And just sign my name."

"And your husband's, too?" asked the manager.

Valerie smiled. "Oh, no, as I said, he's much too modest. Believe me, he'll get all the thanks he deserves in his own humble way." When he gets the bill, she thought.

"It must be wonderful being married to such a generous man," he said.

"He's generous in ways he hasn't even imagined yet," said Valerie, "but he will."

– 67 –
A Woman is a Woman
But a Bomb is a Blast

With the utmost care, Shorty Long packed the explosive concoction into the plastic tube. He wasn't used to constructing so small a bomb. He much preferred cars. This device had to be effective over a small area. Shorty had combed various shops for the elements of the bomb, being careful not to purchase everything from one source and thus raise suspicion.

He'd never made a bomb in a mascara tube before. In fact, mascara was a foreign subject to him. When you're a short, ugly guy for whom the term "goon" seems to have been coined, you don't have much experience with women. That was okay with Shorty Long. He preferred explosions to romance. A well-executed detonation was more satisfying than a relationship with a member of the opposite sex. After all, a woman was a woman, but a good bomb was a blast.

Shorty had already made a bomb out of the powder compact, though it was messy. With its round, flat shape, the compact reminded Shorty of a land mine. While the tube of mascara was more like a little stick of dynamite. He liked dynamite.

Holding his breath, Shorty slid the Detcord into the explosive. This was a critical step requiring a steady hand. One false move...

"YOU DONE YET?"

Though Robert Valvano had spoken at a normal level, he had done so right in Shorty's ear. Shorty fumbled with the explosive-packed tube for a split second before clutching it to his chest.

"No, I'm not done," said Shorty through gritted teeth.

"Temperamental," snorted Robert. "That's what I get for hiring an artist. I tried to come in quietly, so I didn't disturb you."

"You could have knocked," said Shorty.

"I don't need to knock. I'm paying for your room."

Robert looked around. It was the smallest, cheapest room in the hotel. Fortunately, he had a much nicer room. It was on another floor on the opposite end of the hotel. That way, if Shorty accidentally blew himself up, Robert would be as far away as possible.

"Yeah, well, this is delicate work. You could have blown us both up," said Shorty.

"I only want this bomb to blow up one person," said Robert. "I ain't no mass murderer or some psycho nut job."

"That's why it can be detonated remotely," said Shorty proudly. "That's the beauty of my design. See this here? The bottom of the tube? That's where the make-up crap, the mascara, usually is. I cleaned that out and packed it with the explosive. But see this, this bristly brush that comes out of it? I've replaced some of the nylon bristles with these metal ones." He fingered the bristles. "Now, I run the Detcord up through the insides of the brush to the metal bristles. When the top is on the thing, that hooks it up with the relay, you know, like the plunger on a load of TNT. And that has the electronic connection that is activated by the remote."

Robert looked at the mascara tube. "And that's got enough pop to pop my cousin?"

"I'm sure of it."

"Yeah," muttered Robert as he walked to the room's mini-fridge. He took out a beer and opened it. "but it's no good unless we actually plant it in her handbag."

Shorty shrugged. "That's easy. I used to do some dipping in my day before I learned a real trade."

"You don't get it," said Robert. "Your skills as a pickpocket don't help if we don't know where she is. I've been to the bank. She's not there. I went in and asked, but they didn't give out the information."

"But don'tcha own the place?"

Robert stared at him. "Yeah, I own it, or I thought I did until this hereditary legal crap turned up. That's part of the problem. We own it, but it's like silent ownership. No one at the bank knows I own it. I can't just waltz in there and act like the boss. Nobody there knows me, and that's how it's got to be."

"What about that private dick in London?" asked Shorty. "I thought she said your cousin married Eckner."

"Why do you think we're here, stupid?" Snapped Robert. "They gotta turn up here eventually."

"Does your cousin know she's the one coming into all dough?"

Robert shrugged. "I don't care if she does. Once she meets the cosmetic surprise you're making, it won't matter. It doesn't matter to a corpse either way."

Shorty Long looked down at his handiwork. "Yeah, this is really the nicest bomb I ever did. You know, it's got class."

"Yeah, any woman would be tickled to death to get it," said Robert. "But it's just for one broad if she ever shows up. You keep working. I'm going back to watch the front of the bank."

Robert started for the door when there came a knock. Both he and Shorty froze and looked at each other.

"Who's that?" whispered Shorty.

"How the hell should I know," said Robert. "You haven't been out?"

"Not since I bought all the stuff," he nodded at his tabletop workbench. "I haven't even let a maid in to clean up."

A second knock came.

"Yeah?" said Robert, "who is it?"

"Room service."

Robert turned and glared at Shorty.

Shorty threw up his hands. "I didn't order nothing. You told me not to."

"Just a minute," said Robert. He nodded at the table, and Shorty covered his tools with a towel.

Robert opened the door. A bellhop was standing there, holding a large gift basket and a bouquet of flowers.

"What's this? We didn't order none of this shit," said Robert scanning the items.

"Oh, no, sir, this is a special gift," said the bellhop. "From one of the guests."

"Guests? We don't know anyone else here."

"It's a special gift. One of the guests just got married..."

"Oh, yeah?" said Robert.

"Yes, and they're sharing their happiness with all the other guests." He handed Robert the basket. "There's a card."

"Good," said Robert reaching for it. "I mean, that was good of this person..."

"Lady," corrected the bellhop.

"Even better," said Robert, opening the card and reading it. "'Hope you enjoy this half as much as I've enjoyed letting you have it...Valerie Eckner.'" He turned to Shorty and smiled.

"Well, isn't that nice," said Robert. "And you say this Mrs. Eckner is staying here?"

"Yes, she is."

"Honeymoon suite?" asked Robert.

"Well, we're not supposed to divulge..." said the bellhop.

Robert reached into his pocket and pulled out a large bankroll. He peeled off several bills and stuck them in the bellhop's pocket.

"No, she's here alone," said the bellhop. "In a private suite..."

Robert stuck another bill in the bellhop's pocket.

"Suite 804," said the bellhop.

"Nice," said Robert. "I just wanted to know where to send the thank you note. Just put that crap on the dresser."

The bellhop did so, thanked Robert, and left.

Shorty Long looked at the champagne and chocolates. "Wow, if she sent this to everyone in the joint, it must have cost your cousin a ton!"

"Maybe she thinks she can afford it now," muttered Robert. "She might as well enjoy the dough now because she won't be around to enjoy it much longer."

– 68 –
Alone on Top

There was a knock at the door of her suite; when Valerie opened it, all she could see was a large basket containing a bottle of champagne, a box of expensive Belgian chocolates, and a floral bouquet. On closer inspection, she saw a man's hands clutch the basket.

"Oh, I wasn't supposed to get this," said Valerie, "but what the hell, bring it in. I'm not paying for it."

"Really?" said a familiar voice as it crossed the threshold. "Your name's on the card…" The basket lowered; there stood Michael Valvano. "… Mrs. Eckner."

Valerie stood with her mouth agape. "Michael."

The hulking frame of Alphonse popped around the corner.

"And me, too," said Alphonse.

"Don't you go anywhere without this lunkhead?" snorted Valerie.

"No, it's 'lummox,'" corrected Al. "Remember?"

"Shut up," said Valerie.

"May we come in?" said Michael.

Valerie looked around and shrugged. "Sure, what the hell."

She waved them in and pointed to the sofa. Alphonse sat down and opened the box of chocolates. Valerie cleared her throat.

"Do you mind?" she said.

"Those are Al's," said Michael. "They were delivered to his room."

"Oh, yeah, sorry," said Valerie.

"That's okay," said Alphonse, "and may I take this opportunity to render my most felicitous gratitude for your confectionary largess."

"What?"

"He's thanking you for the chocolates," translated Michael.

"Don't mention it," muttered Valerie.

Alphonse stopped with a truffle halfway to his mouth. "But I already did."

"Eat your candy, Al," said Michael. "We didn't come here to…"

Valerie leaned forward. "Yeah, why did you come here? Was it to dump me? Hmm, no, you already did that? Was it to warn me about your brother? Yeah, well, I know all about that. What else could it be, Mr. Michael Valvano?"

"Zimmer," said Michael.

"What?"

"He said 'Zimmer,'" mumbled Alphonse with a mouthful of chocolate.

"Shut up," said Valerie.

"My real name is Zimmer, Michael Zimmer," said Michael. "If you go by ancestry or genetics. That's why Alphonse and I are here. We found evidence in Nonnia's effects."

Valerie shook her head. "Wait, so you're saying she wasn't your grandmother."

"No, she was," explained Michael. "But she had an affair during the war with a German named 'Zimmer.' So, I'm not really a Valvano."

Dozens of thoughts flew through Valerie's mind. One came to the front. "But we're still cousins."

"Actually, we're half-cousins."

Valerie stared at him for a minute. "What does that mean for us?"

Michael grimaced. "Legally, we could have gotten married."

"Could have?" said Valerie. "We still can…"

Michael pointed at her wedding ring. "Mrs. Eckner…"

Valerie took the ring off her finger and threw it across the room. "There, problem solved."

Michael got up, retrieved the ring, and handed it back to Valerie. She slapped it onto the coffee table.

"I don't understand you," she snapped. "First, you won't marry me because your grandmother says so, and now you won't because…"

"…you're already married?" Offered Michael.

"I can get a divorce," said Valerie.

"You know how I feel about divorce," he said.

She brightened. "Divorce? Hell, I don't need a divorce. I can get an annulment. It was only a marriage of convenience."

"Convenience," muttered Alphonse, writing the word in his notebook.

"Zip it, chimp," said Valerie before turning back to Michael. "I can get an annulment, right?"

Michael reached up to his neck as if touching his former priestly collar. "There are three grounds for an annulment: lack of capacity; lack of consent; and lack of form."

"I'll take any of those," she said.

He shook his head. "I doubt either of you entered this unwillingly, and I don't doubt your sanity… usually."

"Form," said Valerie, snapping her fingers. "We were only married in a registry office, not a church."

There was the sound of a key in the lock, and Albrecht Eckner entered.

"What are you doing here?" snapped Valerie. "And how'd you get that key?"

Albrecht smiled and waved the key before placing it in his pocket. "That's a fine way to greet your husband." He walked over to Michael and extended his hand. "Albrecht Eckner."

Michael shook it reluctantly. "Michael Valvano and this is my friend, Alphonse."

"Oh, Mr. Valvano," said Albrecht. "I've always wanted to meet you. Thank you for coming all the way over here to congratulate us. If you'd like, you may kiss the bride... on the cheek, mind you."

"Look, why don't you beat it," said Valerie to Albrecht. "We have important things to discuss."

Albrecht smiled and walked to the door. For a second, she thought he was actually going to leave. "Like any good married couple, newlyweds, if you will, we have no secrets." He put his ear against the door and winked.

"You were eavesdropping?" said Valerie.

Albrecht raised his palms as if to admit it, though without a shred of contrition. He sat on the arm of Valerie's chair and put his arm around her shoulder. She shrugged it away.

"Now, dear, what's this about an annulment? Haven't I given you everything?"

Valerie snorted. "Everything? Ha! We haven't even consummated the marriage."

Eckner smiled. "No, not since prom night."

"Prom night?" said Alphonse.

Albrecht nodded. "Yes, it was quite romantic. Two virgins experiencing the first blush of love. We were each other's first."

Valerie glanced at Michael. When he came in, he wasn't acting very warmly. Now, he was looking at her like she emitted an offensive odor. Valerie felt the blood rising to her cheeks.

"Alright," she said, "I've had about enough of all this from all of you."

"But.." Michael started to protest.

"What did you come here for anyway? To give me the good news that we're not as closely related as you thought? What? So you could tell me you would take me back? Ha! That's rich! Even if I wasn't married to this flaccid blimp, which I won't be for long, I wouldn't marry you, Michael Valvano, or Saurkraut, or whatever your real name is, not if you were the last man on earth."

"You don't understand," said Michael calmly. His serenity only turned up the thermostat on her ire.

"Oh, I don't," she snapped. "Well, why don't you tell me. Wait," she turned to Alphonse. "Why not let your mouthpiece explain it all."

"Hey, lady," said Al, "we've been all over Europe, and Sicily, and Germany, and everywhere looking out for you."

"Listen, imbecile," said Valerie. "You both can go to hell and back, but I don't need you, or him or any man, to look out for me. Got that?"

Michael stood up. "Come on, Alphonse, let's go. We're not welcome here. Besides, we wanted to tour Spain before we went home."

"But..." said Alphonse.

"We need to go," repeated Michael. He went to the door and opened it. "Spain awaits."

"Aren't you going to tell her about her inheritance?" said Alphonse.

"She's not interested," said Michael exiting.

Alphonse was almost out the door. Valerie grabbed his arm.

"Inheritance? What inheritance?" said Valerie.

Alphonse paused and looked down the hall. He turned back to Valerie. "Mikey and his brother ain't full Valvanos. 'Cause of that, all of it goes to you."

"What?"

Alphonse shrugged. "Yeah, I don't get it either, but all the family business is yours." He went out the door and then stuck his head back in. "But you didn't hear that from me? Okay?" he whispered. He closed the door behind him, only to open it again.

"What?" snapped Valerie.

Alphonse held up his notebook. "That word you used a minute ago, 'flaccid,' that's a good one. What's it mean?"

Valerie pushed the door closed and locked it. She stood there pondering what she had just heard. It was all hers. She had finally done it, just like her father had told her. Look out for number one, and you'd wind up on top. Nonnia said the same thing. Valerie was the smart one. She controlled the Valvano business.

She turned and saw Albrecht Eckner looking at her with a smug expression.

"See?" said Albrecht. "I told you there was a loophole. Now we're in charge."

The blood in her cheeks that had started to abate rushed once more to the top, making her see red. Valerie opened the door. Then, she grabbed Albrecht by the collar and the seat of his trousers, frog-marched him into the hall, and threw him down.

"Loophole? You little pervert. You didn't know anything about that. And you're not in charge. I'm the boss now. I'm the boss of you all!"

Valerie slammed the door and locked it. She crossed to the table, opened the bottle of champagne, and raised it.

"Daddy, Nonnia... to us," she said as she took a swig from the bottle.

– 69 –
Mr. Pocket's Pocket

Vyvan Lily recognized his target sitting at a small café in Gibraltar. He tipped his straw trilby and nodded at the empty chair across the table.

"May I?"

Nigel Verve looked up from his copy of *The Times*. "I'd rather..."

"Please..." he lowered his voice, "...Mr. Verve."

Nigel Verve arched his eyebrows and then nodded. Lily sat down.

"Pocket..." said Lily.

Verve looked down at the breast pocket of his sports coat.

"...Waldo Pocket, Mr. Verve. NSA."

Verve put down his newspaper and studied his companion's face.

"Have we met before, Mr. Pocket?" said Verve. "You look familiar."

"I dare say we've probably seen each other in the course of our mutual travels," said Lily.

"One can't help bumping into familiar spirits in our profession," said Verve with a wry smile.

"I make it a point not to do any bumping, Mr. Verve. That can lead to complications."

"Quite," said Nigel. "Please, call me Verve."

"And you may call me Pocket."

"Tea, Pocket?" said Verve signaling for the waiter.

"Mineral water," Pocket told the waiter. He watched the waiter walk away before continuing. "I believe we have an overlapping interest, Verve."

Verve adopted a nonchalant air. "Oh, do we, dear Pocket?"

"Yes, we do." He gently slid Verve's copy of *The Times* out of his hands, laid it on the table, and turned it over. There was a story about Lorraine Innis.

"I'm not sure I catch your drift, Pocket," said Nigel Verve. "I'm here in a private capacity. Technically, I'm on holiday."

Lily smiled. "I know you're not on assignment, Nigel. But as my Daddy used to say, don't piss down my leg and tell me it's raining."

Verve shifted in his seat and adjusted his tie. "My, what an unusual turn of phrase your father employed."

"Just like that lady," he pointed at Lorraine's picture, "employed you."

"How do…"

"You boys in the UK don't have a monopoly on information," said Lily. "I know how unsettling it can be when you're in the intelligence racket and find someone else looking over your shoulder."

"Quite," said Verve looking as if he wanted to make a quick exit.

"Settle down, partner," said Lily. "I don't mean any harm, but we're after the same thing. Like I said, I don't like bumping into anyone while I'm working. I think our interests are mutual."

"Are they?" said Nigel Verve with an aloof air.

"Yes, they are," said Lily. "We both want to visit a certain institution here in Gibraltar, after hours and undetected."

"Look, Pocket, old man," said Verve in a piqued tone. "For all I know, you're throwing darts in the dark and just happen to be making educated guesses. I prefer to make my business forays alone, especially at night."

"Yeah, I've heard you public school boys did a lot of meat slapping."

Nigel Verve stood up. "I'll slap your meat, you loathsome oaf."

"Sit down," said Lily. "And calm down. I didn't mean it. I apologize. I'll let you in on a professional secret since we're both in the business. Your private club, where you took Mrs…. uh, your client…"

"Yes?"

"I was the waiter that night."

"Good lord!" Verve's mouth dropped open.

"Yeah, well," said Lily. "I won't tell anyone about that night if you won't. And by the way, you're a good tipper. But I say that because I trust you. I know what you're looking for and where it is, so let's go there together. I like you even if you are a limey snob, no offense."

"None taken," said Verve icily.

"Good. As I said, I like you, and I wouldn't want you to go through all hassle of busting a box only to find I was already there."

"You're sure of yourself, aren't you, Pocket?"

Lily smirked and shrugged. "Got to be. It ain't bragging if it's true."

Nigel Verve eyed him sideways.

"So whatcha say, Verve, old pal?"

"Share information?"

"Right down the middle," said Lily. "Of course, we're looking for different things."

"And what are you looking for, Pocket?"

"Ha, if I told you that, you'd know as much as me," said Lily. "But I'll tell you this much. I don't mean any harm to our mutual friend. Hey, isn't that one of your old limey books?"

"Yes, Charles Limey, uh, I mean, Charles Dickens," said Verve. "*Our Mutual Friend.*"

"Great," said Lily. "See, I read, too. And like I said, I'm working on our friend's behalf, or at least, for her best interests."

"So, you don't know her?"

"Let's say I've met her a few times, though she doesn't know she's met me. So, is it a deal?" Lily extended his hand.

Nigel Verve looked at it for a moment and then shook the hand of Waldo Pocket.

"Terrific," said Lily as he reached into his coat. "Now, let's see what's in Mr. Pocket's pocket. Ah, it looks like a plan..."

– 70 –
The Head Cheese

Valerie was awakened by the knocking. She opened her eyes and squinted at the morning light. Raising her head, she saw the large bottle of champagne, now empty and on its side atop the coffee table.

"Now I remember," muttered Valerie. She sat up and immediately regretted the move. "Oh, my head." The last time she'd woken up like this, she discovered Albrecht had used her as a kinky mannequin. The only regret she'd have this time was a hangover.

There was another knock on the door, accompanied by a familiar voice.

"Valerie, it's me. I'd like to talk."

Valerie's anger cut through the ache in her head. Michael was back. What did he want now? She thought she'd made herself quite clear yesterday.

Crossing to the door, Valerie threw it open.

"Look, I told you yesterday… you?"

Standing there was Robert Valvano. He grinned.

"Sorry, I wasn't here yesterday," he said.

"What? No, no, you weren't. I thought you were your brother, Michael. You sort of sounded like him through the door."

"Yeah," snorted Robert. "Only he's not as charming. That's a joke."

"I'll remember that and laugh later," said Valerie. "What do you want?"

"Well, first off, can I come in?"

"Sure, why not," she said, waving him in. "All alone? No goon?"

"Goon?"

"Your brother doesn't go anywhere without his," said Valerie. "I thought it might be a Valvano trait… oh, sorry, I mean Zimmer."

Robert seemed surprised for a second but quickly retrieved his smile. "Oh, yeah, some shit, huh? So, I'm a kraut or half a kraut. If I had the legs for them, I'd have to get those funny leather shorts."

He sat down in the easy chair.

"So you know about Nonnia's will and all that?" said Valerie.

"Yup," said Robert, "that's why I'm here."

Valerie sat on the sofa. "What, no lawyer? I thought you'd have come in with Mr. Rosen, your attorney."

Robert pointed at her. "Correction, your attorney. Julie works for the family first, and as you are the rightful head of the family, he's your lawyer now. I came to Gibraltar to sort out some matters with the bank's subsidiary to transfer the operation to you. I didn't know you were here."

Valerie stroked her chin. "And you haven't been trying to find me? I mean, before this whole thing about me being the rightful heir came up?"

He threw up his hands. "What for? I mean, yeah, after Michael came back with the news about our ancestry, we wondered where you were, but before that, I figured you were off with your cousin."

"Why would I be off with my cousin?" she said. "Michael dumped me."

"Your cousin Lorraine," said Robert.

"What? Oh, yeah, her," said Valerie. She kept forgetting everyone thought Lorraine was her cousin. "So, you came here not knowing where I was."

"That's right."

"So, how did you find me?" she asked.

Robert reached over and set the champagne bottle upright. "You found me, Cuz. Oh, and thank you for the gift basket. It was really thoughtful. And it wasn't cheap shit, either." He hefted the empty bottle and noted the absence of a glass. "Congratulations on your wedding. You must have been doing some real celebrating last night."

"Yeah, thanks," mumbled Valerie.

"No, I mean it," said Robert. He stopped and looked at her sideways. "What? Are the marriage seas a bit rocky?"

"None of your business," she said. "Besides, if I recall, you didn't think much of Albrecht Eckner."

"Yeah, but I never met him," said Robert. "That was strictly business. I knew he was a chiseler, but he's a penny-ante worm. You expect that in our line of work... sorry... your line of work. You are the head of the family now."

"Yes," said Valerie suppressing a smile, "I am. And finally, I have total control over that puffy little slug."

"Whoa," laughed Robert. "When I said something about rocky marriage seas, I didn't think it was a full force hurricane. Sorry, it's none of my business if you went in for the big rebound."

"It wasn't a rebound," snapped Valerie. "And you're right; it's not your business. The little rat tricked me. If you must know, I thought I could get at you if I married him."

Robert seemed surprised. "Me? What would you want to get at me for?"

Valerie just stared at him.

"Yeah, okay," said Robert, "point taken. I admit I haven't always been the best cousin."

Valerie snorted.

"But, hey," Robert continued, "like the other shit, that was business. You do what you have to in business. As you proved when you married a creep just for business. But there are some boundaries that you can't fight; legal ones."

"Like Nonnia's will?" Valerie said as she picked at a piece of chocolate.

"Precisely," said Robert. "So, what are you going to do with your new husband?"

She looked up. "Do you want the contract on him?"

Robert laughed uproariously. "*Marone!* You must really hate that guy. Contract? No, I don't do that sort of thing. I'm flattered that you think I would. That's another business tip: don't let your opponent think you won't bump off someone if you have to. They'll think twice if they think you're capable of murder."

Valerie nodded and nonchalantly bit into a raspberry truffle. She rolled the Belgian chocolate around on her tongue for thirty seconds and then spoke. "Oh, like the job you did trying to kill Lorraine and then framing me for it?"

Robert stared at her with his mouth agape.

Valerie took another bite of truffle. "Michael told me about it," she said with her mouthful.

"That bastard," muttered Robert.

"So, it's true?"

"No, it's not true," he said. "I guess that bit about letting people think you could kill for money should come with a warning. It's not too helpful when your own brother thinks you're capable of it."

"What about Sheldon?" asked Valerie.

"Sheldon? Who's Sheldon?"

"Sheldon 'Shorty' Long."

Robert seemed to be searching his memory. Then he snapped his fingers. "Oh, yeah, the client of that shit, Peter Liverot. What about him?"

Valerie smiled. "According to Michael, you hired Shorty Long to blow up Lorraine's car and then frame me for it."

Robert shook his head in disbelief. "Whoa, my brother must have been overdoing the sacramental wine. Where does he come up with that shit? If you recall, Julie Rosen and I warned you against meeting with him. Remember?"

She nodded slowly. "Yeah, you did."

Robert stood and started pacing. "I love my brother, but that *gavone* is seriously mental. Where does he get that? Who is he trying to screw? You or me?"

"Or both of us," said Valerie.

He snapped his fingers. "Yeah, right, both of us. Somebody stuck a dick in his ear and f—ked up his brain! I mean, there you were, nice job as the president of the bank, and then you disappear. And if you recall, we didn't know anything about German grandfathers or any of that stuff." He looked at the ceiling. "Michael, what the hell's the matter with you?"

"Wait," said Valerie smelling a rat. "Are you saying you think the whole inheritance being mine is fake?"

"What? No, as nutty as some of his shit is, Michael was right about that. What do they say, a stopped clock being right twice a day? No, it's just he's got that choirboy face and smooth voice. He can say the most outrageous crap, and he's halfway there. Me, I got stuck with this angry-looking mug and a longshoreman's pipes. When he came back with all that stuff, we checked it out. Julie went over all the evidence Michael brought back from Sicily and Germany. Nonnia was doing the dirty dance with that slab of German sausage. You are the rightful heir to it all. Michael even got a prick."

"He what?"

"You know, the jab, the blood test for the DNA crap."

"Did you, too?"

Robert shrugged his shoulder. "I will if you want me to. But like I said, Julie went over it all. He's the lawyer for the estate. If he's convinced, what's one more blood test going to prove?"

Valerie eyed her cousin. What was he up to? "And what do you get?"

"Me?" Robert laughed. "I get *ugatz!* That's the way it goes."

"And you're not going to contest this?" said Valerie.

Robert reached into his breast pocket and pulled out a sheath of papers. "For what? When my own lawyer says it's no use, what am I going to do? That's why I had him draw up this. It relinquishes any claim I might have to the Valvano business."

He handed it to Valerie. She read it and fingered her father's charm as she did so. She suppressed the urge to jump up and down.

Valerie looked up. "This appears legal. Can I get it checked out?"

"Sure, do whatever you want," he said.

"And Mr. Rosen is my attorney now?" she said.

"He's the estate's mouthpiece," said Robert. "And as you are reigning queen of the castle, he's your lawyer, too. Of course, you might want to consult another attorney. Not that you can't trust Julie, but he wrote that."

Valerie folded it up and put it in her handbag. "Thanks, I will. So, what about you?"

He leaned back in his chair and laughed. "I guess I gotta go get a job. I mean, if you want to hire me, I know the business. I'd be glad to be an employee. It means a hell of a lot fewer headaches. You're the big cheese now, Cuz."

For the first time, Valerie felt as if this was really true. "Yes, I am. I am the boss." A wicked grin spread over her face as she thought of Albrecht Eckner, now completely in her power.

"Uh, oh," said Robert, "I know that look. I've seen it in the mirror enough times. Hey, don't let this go to your head. Take it slow. You want to settle some score, but go easy on Michael."

"Michael?"

"Yeah," he said, "I know it didn't work out romantically, but the guy is your cousin and my brother. If it wasn't for him, you wouldn't have met Nonnia; God rest her soul. And if it wasn't for Michael, you wouldn't have found out you were the head cheese. So, take it easy."

Valerie shook her head. "I wasn't thinking about Michael."

Robert studied her face for a moment. "Oh, yeah," he laughed. "Eckner." She nodded.

"Well," said Robert, "he ain't family. You can do whatever you like to that little prick."

"Yes," Valerie smiled, "yes, I can."

– 71 –
Distracting Stewie

Robert Valvano entered Shorty Long's room. Shorty was asleep on the sofa. He kicked the bottom of Shorty's feet.

"I wasn't anywhere near there," muttered Shorty as he was roused from his slumber.

Robert snorted. "What do you do, dream of alibis?"

Running his fingers through his hair, Shorty sat up. "I dreamt I was pinched."

"Yeah, well, you can get arrested in your dreams," said Robert sitting in the chair beside him. "Only don't get pinched over here, and certainly not for what you did today. You did do it, didn't you?"

Shorty nodded. "You didn't see me?"

"No."

A proud grin overspread Shorty's face. "I told you I was good, and that's with you looking for me."

"Fix me a drink," said Robert, pointing to the minibar.

Shorty crossed and opened a bottle. "How did you get her to go to lunch with you?"

"Are you kidding? I'm her new best friend," bragged Robert.

"Kissin' cousins, huh?"

"Don't be disgusting," said Robert. "Incest might be best for Michael, but I don't go in for that. And I sure don't go around picking up his sloppy seconds."

Shorty handed him a drink. Robert took a sip.

"Yeah, we're real pals, now," said Robert. "Miss Fierro and me."

"Isn't she a Valvano now?"

Robert shrugged. "Who cares? Only the guy who has to chisel it on her tombstone."

"I would have thought she'd want to be cremated," said Shorty. "I mean getting blown up, if it's done right, don't leave a lot to lay out. You especially wouldn't want an open casket."

Robert smiled. "Yeah, well, I guess that's up to me. I'll probably be next of kin."

"Unless that Lorraine dame steps in to do it," said Shorty.

"Yeah, I like that even better," said Robert. "No muss, no fuss. All I'll have to do is send a nice wreath. So, you're sure you planted it?"

"Oh, sure," nodded Shorty. "I know her. I know you. You were sitting there at the sidewalk café. That was a nice touch; real easy to get lost in a crowd. I waited until the one guy showed up with the wine…"

"Steward, you jackass."

"How was I supposed to know the wine guy's name?" said Shorty. "Anyway, Stewie shows up with the wine just as the waiter comes to take your order. Then with all that going on and everyone looking at the menus and stuff, I slipped it way down in her purse. The plain black leather one. It was one of them big jobbies."

"Perfect," said Robert taking a sip of his drink.

Shorty fidgeted in his seat, wringing his hands.

"What?" asked Robert.

"So, when do I get to…" He put his hands in a ball, and then spread them apart, accompanied by the sound of an explosion.

"When I say so," said Robert. "I've got to give her some space."

Shorty laughed. "Yeah, especially when I press the detonator… KAPOW! You don't want to be within ten feet."

Robert gave him a withering stare. "I've got to build up her confidence in me. She needs to think that I've resigned myself to it, and I'm a good sport."

"Good sport!" Shorty giggled.

"Shut up. I am a good sport," he said. "Because I never lose. Show me a good loser, and I'll show you a loser. Yeah, I'll be her loyal cousin… half-cousin."

"And when I set off that surprise package in her purse, you'll be lucky to find a tenth of a cousin," said Shorty.

Robert rolled his eyes. He had come to the realization that people who blow up other people for a living can be pretty strange.

"I've got to make sure I'm there to pick up the pieces," said Robert.

"And there will be plenty to pick up," said Shorty.

"I'm in line to inherit what was rightfully mine anyway." Robert crossed to the window and looked out. "I got to make sure she doesn't have a will. Not many single broads her age have wills. They think they're going to be young and cute forever. I'll have to ask Julie about that. He's done legal work for her."

– 72 –
Memo to the Cleaning Woman: Be Sure to Get Under the Desk

Verity Goodhue buttoned up her smock, wrapped the scarf around her hair, and checked her appearance in the mirror. She looked like a cleaning woman. That's because she was a cleaning woman. Verity had been a cleaning woman before. But now she was getting paid for it. She wore similar clothes and wrapped her hair like this when she used to do the cleaning at her grandfather's cottage. Once her father saw her in the middle of her chores and scolded her.

"Wot are you doing?" Lord Bagnold shouted.

"I'm cleaning the house, Father," she replied. "What did you think I was doing?"

"I didn't not know," he said. "I thought you were going to some fancy dress party as a charwoman."

Verity looked at her watch. "At nine o'clock in the morning, Father?"

Lord Bagnold rubbed his hand over his face in exasperation. "To think that a Lord of the realm, like wot I am, would 'ave a daughter cleaning bogs!"

"Someone has to do it, Father," she smiled and then went about her chores.

Verity closed her locker in the cleaning closet of the bank. "Oh, Father, if you could see me now."

She wheeled her cleaning cart into the hallway toward the lift. Most evenings, aside from Bert, the old security guard, she was alone in the building. Bert was good company. After she cleaned the first floor, where Bert was stationed, she'd share a cup of tea from her Thermos flask.

They'd chat about old days, Bert's old days, that is. Verity would share stories about her dear grandfather without divulging he was the famous

Hugh Goode. Quite often, upon returning from the upper floors, she would find Bert dozing at his desk. She'd only wake him to tell him she was done, so he could see her out and lock up behind her. It was a pleasant enough work environment, thought Verity, especially for undercover espionage.

Not long after Verity started at the bank, Albrecht Eckner returned from his honeymoon. She'd only seen him once, but based on Chesney's recollections, Verity immediately disliked him. Not that her beloved's testimony prejudiced her much. It only took a few minutes in his presence to form her own opinion on Eckner's lack of virtue. The way he looked: at her, at others; at the world in general verified everything Chesney had told her. His eyes were filled with disdain, and envy. An overheard phone conversation, apparently with Valerie Fierro, only solidified this impression. The way he spoke to her indicated he thought he almost possessed her, but not quite, and that added a cruel edge to his voice. It was as if everything he saw he simultaneously hated and wanted. Eckner was one of life's vandals, despising what he didn't have and seeking to mar it to keep others from enjoying it.

"You," said Eckner dismissively as he noticed Verity dusting the bookshelf, "you can go and finish when I've left."

Verity didn't need to be asked twice to leave that viper's den. As she closed the door behind her, she could hear Eckner snort in the phone: "It wasn't anyone important, just the cleaning woman."

If Albrecht Eckner weren't responsible for Martina Fergus' death, Verity concluded, it wouldn't be because of any higher morals he had.

"Hello, Bert," said Verity as she pushed her cleaning cart past his guard desk.

"Hello, Luv," said Bert. "All done?"

"Done with the first floor," she said, raising her Thermos. "Got time for a cuppa?"

"Nothing but time, darling," said Bert pulling a mug from his desk drawer.

"Shall I be mother," said Verity filling his mug with the hot tea and then pouring herself one in the plastic cup that topped the flask. "How's the missus?" she asked after her first sip.

Bert shared the nightly litany of his wife's complaints and threw in his own aches and pains. Verity never minded. It was charming, almost bittersweet, to listen to the daily news of a couple who had shared nearly fifty years of marriage. She wondered if she and Chesney would one day have the luxury of growing old together along with its accompanying challenges.

Sometimes Bert would ask Verity about her young man. Verity would respond with vague details, which were plenty for Bert.

"Here," he said, pointing to his copy of the evening paper, "guess who's coming here, to the Rock."

"The Queen?" guessed Verity.

"No," said Bert, then became sidetracked in his thoughts, as he often did. "Here, I've seen Her Majesty once. When we were living in London. Not me and the Queen, me and the wife, though the Queen was living there, too."

He then launched into a detailed reminiscence of the 1977 Silver Jubilee, including how he and his wife had stayed out half the night to reserve a front row seat on the parade route.

After nearly ten minutes, Bert's recollection ended in a smile. "Happy times," he said, then his expression grew confused. "What was I talking about?" He looked around and then down at his paper. "Oh, yes, I asked if you knew who's coming to Gibraltar. Her what's all famous," he said, and then snapped his fingers, "Oh, you know, what's her name."

Verity held her breath. She was afraid she knew the name Bert was grasping for.

"Oh, you know..." Then he remembered that the name was right in front of him, and he held up the newspaper. "Lorraine Innis!"

"Oh," said Verity trying to sound enthused. "She's very nice."

"The missus loves her," said Bert pointing at the picture of Lorraine. "She even had her hair done like her."

"Oh, so she could look like Mrs. Innis?"

"More like Mrs. Innis in another 40 years," said Bert. "But then I'm no Cary Grant, either."

Verity looked at her watch. "Well, I doubt Mrs. Innis is coming to visit us, but still, if she did, we wouldn't want her to find a dirty bank."

"Huh?"

"I mean, I need to get on with my cleaning. I still have the offices upstairs to do."

"Right-o," said Bert, who went back to his paper.

Verity pushed her cart toward the lift. She hoped Lorraine wasn't coming to Gibraltar to visit the bank. She hoped Lorraine wasn't coming to see her, especially not now. In short, she hoped Lorraine wasn't coming. Verity hadn't had much chance to go through the files. She had been looking for weaknesses in the bank's security. All it would take would be a drawer or file cabinet left unlocked or a computer password scribbled on someone's notepad. Then she would be able to delve deeper into whatever it was the Albrecht Eckner was hiding, specifically, as it related to Martina Fergus.

Verity had cleaned the executive offices, doing a quick but thorough job. She looked at her watch. She had at least 30 minutes before Bert might wonder where she was. Parking her cleaning cart in a storage closet, Verity entered Albrecht Eckner's office, turned on the desk lamp, and started sorting through the drawers. There was a wall safe. Perhaps she could find a combination.

She had barely begun when she heard a sound in the hallway. If it was Eckner, she would have difficulty explaining since her cleaning supplies were nowhere to be seen. Quickly, Verity turned off the light and hid under Eckner's large desk.

Verity heard the door open, and a sliver of light shone across the floor. Then the door closed.

"Draw the curtains," said a distinctly American voice, "and we can turn on the lights."

"The guard..." began a British voice.

"Will be out for at least an hour," said the American.

"You're sure, Pocket?"

The American snorted. "Look, Nigel, it was a piece of cake. I pretended to be a delivery man. I gave him a dummy package that he signed for. Like most watchmen, he had a cup of coffee, or, in his case, being a Limey, tea. I distracted him, slipped my special mix in his brew, left, and waited a few minutes. I undid the catch on the way out. Then I slipped back inside and waited for you."

"Yes, of course," said the man named Nigel. "And he won't recognize you?"

"I wore the fake stash and glasses," said the man identified as "Pocket." "Besides, he will hardly remember me. Like I said, it's my special mixture."

"Ingenious," said Nigel. "You'll have to share the recipe."

"Yeah, I could," Pocket laughed, "but then I'd have to kill you."

Nigel laughed, though there was a trace of nervousness in his laugh.

She heard the drapes being closed. Then the lights came on.

"The safe is in this bookcase," said the Brit. "Shall I, or would you prefer."

Verity held her breath and she saw two sets of feet in front of her. Both men wore rubber-soled shoes and black trousers. Fortunately, the desk was large with a closed front. She squeezed against the front panel, trying to make herself as tiny as possible.

"Oh," said Pocket, the American, "go ahead. That's a pretty basic lock; shouldn't take a pro more than a minute. So, let's see what you got."

"Certainly," said the Brit.

There was silence for about thirty seconds. A pair of legs, presumably belonging to the American, leaned against the desk only two feet away from Verity. She could hear the Brit making small grunts as he worked on the safe.

After two minutes, the American said: "Ding! Time's up."

"What," said Nigel.

"You're taking too long," said Pocket. "Move over."

"Steady on..." said Nigel. His legs appeared in front of the desk, presumably having been pushed aside by his partner.

Pocket started whistling, and in less than a minute, Verity heard the sound of the safe handle being thrown open. "There you go!"

"I say, that was remarkably rapid," said the Brit. "How did..."

"Trade secret," said Pocket. "I'd be glad to teach you the trick..."

"Thanks, awfully…"

"…but then I'd have to kill you," snickered Pocket.

"Ha, yes, jolly jape," muttered Nigel. "Now, let's see what we have here."

"Back off, pal," said Pocket. "You're out of line. I'm on official business for the government."

Verity had thought the two burglars were working together. She wondered now what the government had to do with it, and it seemed Pocket was working for the United States. Oh, Chesney, she thought, what have you gotten yourself into?

"I'm on official business, too," said the Brit.

"Don't bullshit me, Chauncey," said Pocket. "Your day job may be for MI six-and-seven-eights. But don't forget I was there when Mrs. Innis asked you to do this little caper as a personal favor. So, I get the first look at what's here."

Personal favor? Verity bit her lip. Lorraine Innis had British Intelligence working on her behalf?

"I assume you're looking for illegal activity or something that compromises national security," said Nigel. "I'm sure you'd share that with my superiors via proper channels. But my main concern is discovering what Mrs. Innis wants to…"

"This looks interesting," said Pocket.

"What?"

"This envelope marked 'Valerie Insurance,' that's her cousin's name, ain't it?"

"Probably just a policy," said Nigel. "Miss Fierro used to work for the bank, and she recently married the man whose safe that is."

Verity listened as the envelope was opened.

"Insurance policy?" said Pocket. "I don't think so. It's just a letter and copies of a letter." She could hear the paper being unfolded as Pocket began to read: "'*Dearest Valerie, although I've already thanked you for the shower and the thoughtful gift…*' This is a woman's handwriting."

Pocket began to mumble as he read through the letter, stopping to clearly enunciate words like "clinic" and "procedure."

"Let me see," said the Brit.

"Here, have one," said Pocket. "This Eckner guy made plenty of copies."

Pocket tossed a few copies toward Nigel. Several fluttered to the floor, one under the desk just by Verity's hand.

"Pick that up," said Pocket.

Nigel reached down, and Verity pressed her body hard against the desk. Fortunately, from his vantage point, Nigel couldn't see her, her body shielded by the right-hand side desk drawers. He picked up two copies, but a third, the one nearest Verity, went unnoticed.

"According to the signature, this was written by some dame named 'Martina,'" said Pocket. "She mentions a guy named Chesney. Ha, sounds like some geek from your neck of the woods. Chesney!"

There was more muttering from Pocket. Then he laughed. "Looks like Mrs. Innis' cousin got knocked up and had a little disposal done in this Martina chick's name."

"And somehow this cad, Albrecht Eckner acquired this letter," surmised Nigel.

Verity's mind raced as she followed the implications of Valerie's actions. Valerie had an abortion but stole Martina's identity to do it? Then, Martina found out and wrote to expose the deception? Did Valerie arrange the events that ultimately resulted in Martina's death? Verity had seen hints of toxicity in Chesney's friendship with Valerie Fierro. Was it so poisonous that it killed Martina Fergus? Poor Martina! Poor Chesney!

"Yeah, well," said Pocket, interrupting Verity's thoughts, "there's something juicy there, but it's not what I'm looking for. Gimme that letter, and I'll put it back in the safe."

"Actually," said Nigel, "I think this would be very interesting to Mrs. Innis. It may be exactly what she is looking for. She mentioned the death of someone close to her. I'd like to share it with her."

There was a slight pause before Pocket replied. "Oh, yeah? Sure, okay. This Eckner clown's got so many copies, not sure why, but I doubt he'd notice one missing."

Verity's heart raced. She itched to pick up that letter inches from her fingers, but fear of being discovered immobilized her.

"That looks like it," said Pocket after searching the safe for about five minutes. "Sorry, we didn't find what we were looking for."

"Perhaps you didn't, my dear, Pocket," said the Brit. "But the more I peruse this letter, the more I'm convinced it's precisely what Mrs. Innis needed."

"Yeah? Needed for what?" said Pocket.

"I'm not exactly sure how it's connected or what her motivation is," said Nigel. "But Mrs. Innis has expressed a desire to retire. She wants to become something of a recluse."

The lights were turned off, and Verity could hear the sound of the drapes being opened as they prepared to leave.

As they opened the door, Verity heard the American speak.

"So, you're going to give her that letter?"

"Yes," said the Brit, "it may be what she's looking for."

"Yeah, how?"

"I could tell you," Nigel said jokingly, "but then I'd have to kill you."

The American chuckled. "Yeah. Good one."

- 73 -
The Selective Hearing of Julius Rosen

Valerie Fierro lay on the sofa in her hotel suite, sipping a glass of champagne, as she picked up the phone.

"Get me a long-distance line," she said. "I'm calling America." After giving them the number, she put down the receiver.

Valerie had considered making this call from the bank. Since the bill for her suite was going to Albrecht, she enjoyed making him pay for the call that would put the final nail in his coffin.

"Oh, I'm going to enjoy this," said Valerie, running her tongue over her lips. "Albrecht, I'm going to make you pay for everything; for every conniving little trick you subjected me to since high school. I'm going to get you double for everything you did to me, my father, my dog, my..."

The phone buzzed.

"Your call to America, Mrs. Eckner," said the hotel operator. "Go ahead."

"Mrs. Eckner?" the voice belonged to Julius Rosen. "No one informed me that you'd gotten married."

"Yeah, well," said Valerie, "that can be one of your first cases as my attorney, Julie." For a moment, she felt odd using the familiar term that Robert Valvano used. But then she realized she was the boss now, and could call anyone anything she liked.

"I don't usually handle divorce cases," said Julius, "but I'll ensure you get a good attorney."

"The best," said Valerie, "I want the best. I'm sure I can afford it. Oh, and it's not going to be a divorce. I think an annulment would be more appropriate."

"I see," said Rosen in his usual non-committal tone. "Well, I will certainly get you the best for the situation."

"Good," she said, "but that's not why I called you. My cousin, Robert, informed me that I'm the rightful heir to our grandmother's estate."

"With what Michael uncovered, I would say that neither he nor Robert can lay claim to satisfying the conditions of Mrs. Valvano's will."

"I see," said Valerie, "good. And you're my attorney now."

"I'm the family's attorney," said Rosen.

"And I'm the head of the family," said Valerie. "Look, I don't want to rush anything, but I don't want to wait, either. There are a few things I want to take care of sooner than later. First Robert..."

"Yes," said Rosen without emotion.

"I want him kept on," said Valerie. "He's been very helpful."

Rosen was silent.

"Are you still there?" she asked.

"Yes, Miss Fierro, um, Valvano, I mean Eckner..."

"Use Fierro for now," said Valerie. "I'm used to it."

"As you wish," said Rosen. "I'm a bit surprised, given your history with Robert."

"Look, Julie, Mr. Rosen," she said, "he's a businessman. I'm sure I'll make some changes once I get my feet under the desk. But he is my cousin, well, half-cousin, and I don't want to throw him out as long as he remembers who's boss."

"Very generous of you, Miss Fierro."

"I can afford to be generous... with Robert," she said.

"I see."

"And with you, too, Mr. Rosen," continued Valerie.

"And your other cousin?" asked Rosen.

Valerie paused a moment. "Nothing."

"I see."

"He didn't want anything from Robert, so I'll continue Michael Valvano's wishes in that area. He will get nothing from me."

"Just as you wish, Miss Fierro," he said.

Valerie laughed. She was really in charge.

"But that's not the main thing," said Valerie. "It's about the bank here in Gibraltar."

"What about it, Miss Fierro?"

"I'm in charge, right?"

"That's correct."

"Good," she said. "I need something in writing to that effect."

Rosen paused. "It's not direct ownership. For legal matters and concerns about, well, shall we say, privacy, your position is well guarded."

Valerie gritted her teeth. "Look, I don't want to undo any of that stuff. I just need some proof that I'm in control. It's a personal thing."

"Michael already is aware of that fact."

"Damn it, Julie," she snapped, "it's not for Michael. It's for someone at the bank. I just need something to show that, without a doubt, I'm the one in charge. Can you do that?"

"I'm sure I can draft something to that effect," said Rosen.

"Good boy," said Valerie, "I mean, thank you, Julie, uh, Mr. Rosen." She didn't want to antagonize her lawyer, at least not yet.

"I'll put something together right away, Miss Fierro."

"Thank you," said Valerie. "I'm sorry, I'm still adjusting to all this. It's a lot to get used to."

"I'm sure it is," said Rosen. "I'm at your service and look forward to seeing you when you return."

"Thanks. Oh, and not now, but eventually, we'll have to find a new house for Robert and his family. I want to redo that family place and probably move my mother in. She can have Nonnia's old room. Rose will be so jealous."

"Rose?"

"Yeah," laughed Valerie, "my sister, I used to call her 'Big Fat Rose, with her Big Fat Nose."

"I wasn't aware you had a sister," said Rosen.

"No?" said Valerie, "well, yes, we're not that close. You know how older sisters can be."

"You're the older sister?"

"No, do I look like I would be an older sister, Julius? Rose is two years older than me. She will go green with envy when she..."

"Pardon me, Miss Fierro..."

"Yeah, what, Julie?"

"If you have an older sibling," said Rosen, "then they're the rightful heir."

Valerie felt the blood drain from her face.

"Michael never told me you had an older sister," said Rosen.

"Uh, yeah, well, I never brought it up," stammered Valerie. "We're not that close. She was very mean to me. And she's not that older..."

"You said she was two years older."

Valerie's mind raced. She clutched her pendant. Her father would want her to be the heir. Nonnia would want her to be the heir.

"Mr. Rosen," she said in a more deferential tone, "my grandmother told me I would run the family business. She told me that the night we met."

"Yes," said Rosen, "I don't doubt that."

"Good!"

"But what she said to you, and what I believe she said to you, doesn't matter in terms of the law. If that's what she wanted, she should have changed the terms of her will."

"She would have, but she died that night," said Valerie.

"And unfortunately, before she could change her will," said Rosen.

Valerie thought. "Well, if you believe that's what she wanted, and I'm practically the oldest Valvano, we could just not tell my sister. We're not all that close anyway."

"I didn't hear that," said the attorney.

"I SAID WE DON'T HAVE TO TELL MY SISTER," shouted Valerie.

"I heard you," he said, "what I meant is that I would pretend I didn't hear you asking me to lie in order to circumvent the terms of the will."

"Oh," Valerie was close to tears. Why? Why was it that every time she almost had something, it was always yanked away from her? It's not fair, she thought, and then said it aloud. "It's not fair!"

"Wills and estates rarely are," said Rosen.

"But I know the family business better than Rose, especially the bank stuff. She doesn't even know she had a grandmother or another family. How can she be the head of the Valvanos when she doesn't even know they're alive?" A thought crossed her mind. "Oh, well, I guess I can tell her, okay?"

"As executor of the estate," said Julius Rosen, "that's my duty. But if you like, I can tell your sister about your connection to the family business. Perhaps she would welcome your support in managing it."

"Work for Rose?" Valerie snorted. "Yeah, that would work."

"I'll leave that to you," he said. "Now, what's your sister's full name? Is she married?"

"Not likely," grumbled Valerie.

"Fine," said Rosen, "So I assume her name is Rose Fierro."

"Sure, whatever."

"And where can I contact her?"

Valerie stared at the phone. "Just stick your head out the window and yell: 'BIG FAT ROSE WITH THE BIG F**KIN' NOSE!'"

Valerie slammed down the receiver and threw her champagne glass against the wall.

- 74 -
Too Much Information Can Be Dangerous to Your Health

S orry, Pocket, old chap," said Nigel Verve as he closed the door of his rented room. "Our little evening foray didn't yield any information for you." He held up a bottle. "Spot of brandy? I always reward myself with a tincture after an exercise."

Vyvan Lily sat down in an easy chair. "Never touch the stuff. Slows my responses."

Verve shrugged and poured himself a snifter. Then he turned to his guest and raised the glass. "To your good health."

"Yeah, thanks," said Lily. "And you're wrong about not finding out anything useful. I found out exactly what I wanted to know, or rather, I had it confirmed."

A puzzled look crossed Verve's face. "Really, Pocket? Was there something in the safe that I didn't see?"

Lily shook his head. "Nope. But I wasn't looking for anything stored in a safe." He tapped the side of his head and then pointed at Verve's own head.

"Something I said, dear chap?"

"Exactly."

Nigel Verve pondered for a moment. "Can't think what it could be."

Lily smiled. "I needed to be sure of Mrs. Innis' plans."

"What? That she wanted to retire?" said Verve. Lily nodded. "But you already knew that, my dear fellow."

"True," said Lily, "but I didn't know if she would do it or if she would be able to do it. You see, Nigel, old bean, I'm not with the NSA."

"No?"

"I'm what you call a soul adrift. Ex-agency. I helped create Lorraine Innis."

Verve took another sip of brandy and snorted. "Don't tell me she's some sort of cyborg."

"Oh, no, she's all woman," said Lily. "But no one knows who she really is. In fact, I don't think she really knows."

Nigel Verve shook his head. "But there's an extensive background. She has a history."

Lily tapped his chest. "Not until I created it. Lorraine Innis is a cypher, a non-person. I built her identity after some covert interviews. She's not even aware of it. And after all that, I don't want her to retire. I've grown accustomed to her, her influence, her very being. I thought how interesting it would be for a person so loved and popular to reach the pinnacle of leadership, controlled by someone else and unaware of that fact. Lorraine Innis is like my daughter; I just won't let her go. And I'm concerned that if you give her that letter, she might cease to be. You see, I'd go to any lengths to keep her around."

"Extraordinary," said Verve pulling the letter from his breast pocket.

"Yes, isn't it?" said Lily. He smiled. "And I could tell you all that, but then I'd have to kill you."

Nigel Verve looked at him with a puzzled expression. "But you just told me, my dear chap."

Lily thought for a moment. "You're right. I did…"

He drew a small pistol from his pocket and fired two shots into Verve's head, killing him.

Then he slipped on a pair of gloves. Wiped his prints off the gun and placed it in Verve's hand. Removed the letter from Verve's other hand. And slipped out the window.

– 75 –
An Offensive Occurrence in a Respectable House

Verity Goodhue sat in the dark, crouched underneath Albrecht Eckner's desk. She dared not emerge from her hiding place until she was sure the two safecrackers had left the building. When one is crammed under a piece of furniture, myriad desires spring to mind. Her first impulse was to read that letter. But without a flashlight or night vision goggles, this was impossible. Next, she thought of Bert, the watchman. From their conversation, it sounded like one of them, the American, had drugged Bert. She didn't think it would have been a fatal mixture; at least, she hoped not. The fact that Pocket had worn a disguise indicated that he didn't mean Bert any lasting harm. Otherwise, he would have simply killed him. Finally, overtaking both of these thoughts was her need to use the loo. In the dark, she couldn't see her wristwatch. She wondered how long she had been there. It felt like ten minutes, though with her mind racing, it could have been thirty seconds or maybe an hour.

Finally, Verity could wait no longer... for any of it. She crawled out from under the desk, stood up, massaged her stiff legs, stretched her aching back, and went to the window. Down the street, there was a tower with a clock on it. She had been under the desk for at least an hour, and her sacroiliac attested to every moment of it.

Verity patted the pocket of her smock to verify that the copy of the letter was secure. Then she inched toward the door and put her ear to it. Not a sound. She slowly opened the door and looked into the empty hallway. Then she scurried toward the closet where she had left her cart, got halfway there, and quickly turned around and ran the opposite way to the ladies' room.

A few minutes later, she exited the lift on the ground floor. Verity returned her cart to the cleaning cupboard and went to the guard's station.

She recoiled when she saw old Bert sprawled in his chair, his head tilted back, completely motionless. That American had killed him. She inched closer and reached out to touch his wrist. As she did so, Bert gave a loud snort, and Verity let out a cry.

"What? Who? Huh?" said Bert sitting up and rubbing his eyes. He looked at Verity. "Oh, it's you, dear. I must have fallen asleep. You won't tell anyone, will you?"

Verity smiled and promised she wouldn't. She'd seen Bert napping before and had never whispered a word about it.

"Are you feeling well, Bert?" she asked.

Bert smacked his lips a few times. "What? Oh, right as rain."

"Any visitors?"

A puzzled look crossed his face, and Bert looked around as if he'd misplaced something. Then he scratched his head. "Must have dreamt it," he muttered to himself. "Visitors? No, not a soul. Why were you expecting anyone?"

Verity shook her head. Then she poured him a cup of tea and watched as he drank it. When she was sure he had suffered no lasting effects from Pocket's potion, Verity announced she had finished and was going home.

Back in her rented room, Verity sat down and pulled out the letter. She read it several times. Then she made a cup of tea and sat down and reread it. She reached the same conclusion the British agent had come to back in the office. This was the missing piece of the puzzle Chesney had been looking for. According to Chesney, Valerie had been scheduled to go on that business trip. But her plans were changed at the last minute, and Martina had been sent in her place. Verity wasn't exactly sure how or why. Apparently, it had something to do with Valerie assuming Martina's identity to have an abortion in her name. It was clear that Martina had discovered the secret and was forgiving Valerie. From the date at the top of the letter and mention of the proximity of the wedding, the letter may have been written just before Martina's death. It was highly improbable that Valerie had Martina killed. But it did answer Chesney's question: who had arranged for Martina to go to Chicago.

Chesney would probably be able to fill in the pieces. She had to show him the letter.

The first tracings of dawn were appearing over the eastern sky as Verity Goodhue lay down after a long night. She fell quickly asleep but was awakened just a few hours later by the sound of commotion out in the hallway of the small rooming house. She pulled on a robe and opened her door to see two paramedics and a woman going up the corridor. Verity concluded the woman was a doctor from the small black satchel in her hand. Her landlady was standing in the doorway two doors down, wringing her hands.

The landlady saw Verity and scurried to her side.

"Oh, it's horrible," said the landlady. "I never would have rented to him if I'd had the slightest inkling."

"What is it, Mrs. Cryer?"

"This is a respectable house," continued the woman. "Respectable people come here to stay. They get a clean room and breakfast for a decent price. If I had only known."

"Known what?"

"This is a decent house," said Mrs. Cryer. "You don't ask when people come in if they're planning to do that."

"Do what, Mrs. Cryer."

"I only ask for a week in advance and a previous address. And he looked so clean and dignified, something respectable, like a postman or a civil servant. Maybe I'm naïve, but you don't ask prospective tenants if they're planning to top themselves. Maybe I should."

"Top themselves?"

Mrs. Cryer pointed down the hallway. "I go in to knock him up; he asked for a morning call. That's a sick joke to play on a respectable woman running a respectable rooming house. Go in to bring them a cup of tea and find them sitting in the chair, dead as a door knocker, holding some sort of pistol."

"Dead," said Verity holding her hand to her mouth. "How horrible."

"Not a very nice thing for Mr. Nigel to do. This is a decent house."

"Mr. Nigel?" One of the safecrackers was named Nigel. "That was his first name?"

"He gave that as his last name," said Mrs. Cryer. "It was just Mr. Nigel."

The paramedics were removing the body on a stretcher. Verity and Mrs. Cryer pressed against the wall to let them by. Though most of the corpse was covered with a sheet, the feet, and lower legs were in view. The same black trousers and rubber souled shoes she had seen from under the desk.

Immediately the words of the American, Pocket, came to mind: "I could tell you, but then I'd have to kill you."

Verity excused herself, went back into her room, and locked the door. This was becoming more dangerous. She had to warn Chesney.

- 76 -
The Waste of a Perfectly Good Push-Up Bra

Valerie tugged on her suit jacket and took a deep breath as she entered the bank. She had bought the new power suit just for this occasion. It was fiery red. Fiery, like her name "Fierro." She'd probably never find out how Daddy had wound up with that as a last name. Now she learned she was really a Valvano. That would have been great if she had been an only child. Her inheritance was snatched away from her by her older sister, Rose. Rose wouldn't know what to do with a shady family business. It needed someone that was essentially honest but knew how to be just dishonest enough to outsmart the really evil people. Someone like Valerie. Valerie assured herself she was a good person but knew how to be devious when she had to be, like now. When last she saw Albrecht, he thought she had inherited the whole Valvano business. As far as Albrecht knew, he was entirely at her mercy. She just needed a few minutes in control to move some assets.

Valerie approached the reception desk in the lobby.

"Good morning," said Valerie. "Is my... is Mr. Eckner in?"

"Yes," said the woman, "shall I announce you?"

"No," smiled Valerie, "I want to surprise him. Just buzz me in."

The woman unlocked the door leading to the bank's private area. Valerie proceeded down the hallway to the elevator. As she rode the elevator to the top floor, Valerie pushed her breasts up for maximum cleavage. She needed all the bolstering possible to bluff her way through this showdown with Albrecht Eckner. Albrecht, the little pervert, wasn't particularly a boob man like most healthy men. Still, Valerie wanted to go in with all her weapons on display.

Reaching the executive floor, Valerie breezed past Albrecht's secretary before the woman had a chance to react. Albrecht was studying something on his computer. He looked up and then did a double-take.

"Oh, hello... dear?" he said.

Valerie smiled to herself. She had him off guard, just as she wanted it.

"Good morning," said Valerie sweetly, "you loathsome little slug."

"I wasn't expecting you," said Albrecht.

"No, I bet you weren't," she said.

"Can I get you something?" he said, standing. "Coffee, tea..."

"A divorce?" said Valerie.

Albrecht laughed nervously. "Ha, yes, you were always a wonderful kidder. Of course, if you really wanted to dissolve our sacred union..."

Valerie snorted. "More like an unholy alliance. I think you realize things are different now."

Albrecht glanced at his computer screen. "Yes," he said slowly. "Things are quite a bit different and very quickly."

"I know all the news must have come as quite a shock to you," said Valerie. "I know you're probably worried. Let me assure you..." Valerie leaned over the desk and executed her most piercing stare. "...I will treat you exactly as you deserve."

Albrecht looked back at the screen. "Quite different," he muttered without looking at Valerie.

"To put it as succinctly as I can," said Valerie striding toward the window. "This kingdom has a new ruler. Long live the queen!"

She stared out the window toward the sea, waiting for Albrecht to grovel to her side on his hands and knees. Valerie doubted he would, but she paused a moment just in case.

"The kingdom ain't what it used to be," said Albrecht calmly.

"What?" Valerie turned.

Albrecht smiled. "Sorry, your majesty," he said, "but it seems that your kingdom is nearly bankrupt."

Valerie rushed to the desk and looked over Albrecht's shoulder. The figures on the screen seemed a blur to her. But there could only be one answer.

"Rose! Big Fat Rose," she muttered behind her clenched teeth. "She didn't waste any time, did she?"

"Sorry?"

"So what do you mean, bankrupt?" snapped Valerie.

Albrecht pointed to the screen. "The Valvano holdings in this bank have been reallocated. This institution now rests solely on the much more insignificant assets of the average depositor."

"That bitch," said Valerie.

"Not a very nice way to talk about your cousin," said Albrecht.

Valerie grabbed Albrecht by the collar. "Not my cousin, you stinkbug, my sister."

"Lorraine Innis is your sister?"

"No! Will you listen, you sea slug," said Valerie. "My sister did this, my older sister, Rose."

"What? How could…"

Valerie slumped into the chair and sighed. "I'm not the heir. It turns out my sister Rose is in control."

Albrecht looked puzzled for a moment, then his eyes narrowed, and a knowing smile crossed his lips. "Ah, ah, ah," he wagged his stubby finger at her. "You were trying to con me just now. I should have realized it. The power suit, the four-inch heels… are you wearing a push-up bra?"

"Shut up!"

"Yes, you are," he laughed. "You had the rug pulled out from under you, and you thought I didn't know."

"Okay, smart ass," she said, "you didn't know. I just told you."

"You told me the cause," said Albrecht smugly, "but I already knew the effect."

Valerie put her head in her hands. "How did she do that so quickly?" she muttered. "She couldn't have found out more than a few hours ago. It was like she knew. But there would have had to be papers to sign and accounts to transfer. Rose couldn't have done it in so little time."

Albrecht looked at the screen. "So, your sister is the Valvano heir."

"Yes."

"And you found out when?"

"What?" said Valerie distractedly. "Oh, yesterday. I opened my big mouth to the estate's lawyer that I had an older sister."

"Nope," Albrecht was shaking his head.

Valerie looked up. "What do you mean, nope? Rose couldn't have known until yesterday after I spoke to the lawyer."

"Then why were these transactions done way before that?"

Valerie pushed Albrecht aside. "Where? What transactions?"

Albrecht gently moved Valerie to the side. "These here, and this one, and this one. They were done when we were in London and when we were on our…" he smiled. "…honeymoon."

Valerie punched Albrecht on the shoulder. "You idiot, you should have seen this, but you were too busy with your little perverted schemes."

Albrecht raised his index finger: "First, I don't have access to these accounts. I don't monitor them since they're your 'family' holdings, and I'm not supposed to look at them."

"But you do."

"Hey," he said, "I want to ensure that nothing too illegal is going on. Besides, I have to have my excuses ready in case we get examined."

"Plus, knowing the big operations they're pulling makes it easier for you to get away with your petty thieving," she said.

"Correct," said Albrecht without a trace of remorse. "And, I would not call my activities perverted. Let's just say I have alternative interests."

"Whatever," she said with a shudder. "What I want to know is: who did this, and what did they do?"

"Knowing what they did may answer that first question," said Albrecht. He pointed at the screen. "Someone has gone through and laundered or un-laundered these accounts. Someone has taken all the dirt out of the operation and made the Valvano's activities completely legitimate. And then, they moved the money out, and cleaned out the Valvanos."

Valerie grabbed Albrecht by his lapels and shook him. "And where's the money?"

Albrecht gently removed her hands from his suit and pointed at the screen. "It's all been transferred into another bank on behalf of your cousin."

No wonder, Valerie thought, Robert Valvano had acquiesced to turning over the business. He had transferred the money first. Valerie sat down in the chair and banged the desk with her first. "Robert!" she seethed.

"Not Robert," said Albrecht.

"Michael?"

"No, your other cousin," he said, pointing at the wire transfer confirmation.

Valerie looked at the computer. The total of the Valvano assets had been wired to The Cross of Lorraine. She stared at it for a moment, and slowly a smile overspread her lips.

"That's perfect," she said. "I'm on the board, and I'm one of the signers on the charity's accounts. Ha! Thank you, cousin Lorraine!"

"You're a signer on all the accounts?" he asked.

"Sure, why?"

He sat down at the computer and typed in a quick search. "Because according to this, that account was opened when you were still hiding out in my London hotel suite."

Valerie stared at the screen, the date, and the bank where the account resided. It was true. It was a new account. An account with millions, but one she couldn't access.

"Shit!" spat Valerie. "I'll get him for this!"

– 77 –
How to Blow Up Wives,
and Influence Weasels

N o shit!" said Robert Valvano. Shorty Long looked up from the newspaper he was reading as his boss continued his telephone call. "Yeah, well, that definitely screws my plans... What?... No, you don't need to know my plans, Julie, you Jew bastard. You ain't my lawyer now. Any client-attorney privilege is right down the crapper."

He slammed down the receiver and glowered at Shorty. He wasn't angry at Shorty, but there was no one else to glower at, and he needed a good glower.

Shorty Long was even shorter on courage than he was on height and quickly crumbled under Robert's gaze. "I didn't do it!" Shorty cried.

Robert stared at him for a moment, then turned away. "Michael's got a hand in this or that Fierro slut."

Realizing he wasn't the object of his boss's ire, Shorty relaxed. "Yeah, it's one of them."

Robert turned back to Shorty. "Didn't I just say that?"

"Yeah, yeah, you did," agreed Shorty. "It's either your brother or your cousin that did it. Uh, what did they do?"

Robert sat down and drummed his fingers on the arm of the chair. "What did they do? According to my former mouthpiece, Julius Rosen, esquire, one of those two *stunads* cleaned out all my bank accounts."

"Your accounts, Boss?"

Robert waved him away. "Yeah, well, they were mine once. The family accounts, the business accounts."

"So, you're busted?"

"Practically," said Robert, "I'm probably down to a half million in my personal account."

Shorty laughed. "A half a rock? Gee, I wish I had half a rock. Hell, I'd settle for half of a half a rock!"

Robert stared at him. "I'll give you a full rock upside your f**kin' head, you *gavone!*" He sat down, deep in thought, muttering to himself.

"Why don't you get it back, boss?" asked Shorty.

"Gee, why didn't I think of that," snapped Robert. "They did it with computers. Someone took all my dough and put it in that Lorraine charity account. And that's where it's sitting. Michael doesn't have the head for that kind of operation."

"What about your cousin?"

Robert nodded. "Yeah, it could have been her or that little weasel she married. Sure, that little scumwad, Eckner. He's conniving enough to do it. If anyone helped Valerie, it was him. It makes sense."

"Yeah?" asked Shorty. "How?"

"It's simple," said Robert, "Valerie thought she was getting control of the family bizzo. But she's got this sister no one knew about. So, when Julie Rosen finds out, he tells Valerie 'no dice.' So rather than go begging to her sister, Valerie and Eckner steal it."

Shorty scratched his head. "So they actually stole it from the sister."

Robert bared his teeth. "No, they stole it from me. And I'm going to get it back."

"I didn't know you knew computers," said Shorty.

"I don't," he said, "computers are for geeks and pointy heads. But I know how to scare a weasel."

Shorty looked at the detonation device in his hand. "Aw, so I don't get to blow her up?"

Robert grinned. "Oh, you get to blow her up. Once you blow up his new wife, Eckner will be happy to use his little computer to swipe all the money back. Not to the family business, but to me, just me."

– 78 –
It Takes a Rat to Smell a Rat

Y ou got me into this," said Valerie, "and you're going to help me get what I deserve."

Albrecht Eckner looked at her with his piggy eyes and smiled. "Excuse me? I got you into this? No, sorry, not me, babe. I've done a lot over the years, all from the most honorable intentions…"

Valerie snorted loudly.

"…but," he continued, "I didn't make you a Valvano. I didn't write some old twat's will, and I wasn't your older sister."

Valerie folded her arms across her chest and grumbled. Albrecht was right; damn him. She almost objected to him calling her grandmother an old twat. But at the moment, Valerie wasn't particularly well disposed toward Nonnia.

"But, as your devoted husband," began Albrecht.

Valerie rolled her eyes.

"I will help you," he concluded. "Someone moved all the family fortune and stuck it in the charity. Who could have done that? You have to see who had access to the accounts. One of the Valvanos?"

Valerie thought about it. Michael or Robert would probably have access to the accounts, but why would either do that? It put the money further from them than before.

"Who else had access to both sides of the organizations?" asked Albrecht.

Valerie shrugged. "Just Patsy."

Albrecht nodded his head. "There you go."

"Really?"

"Sure, if Patsy had a pet Labrador Retriever or knew a clever monkey, she would have been able to do it. Come on, Valerie, be serious. Patsy can barely transfer a sneeze onto her hankie. There's only one other person it could be."

"Yeah," said Valerie. "Patsy's too stupid. But Lorraine is too honest."

"I've only seen her on TV," said Albrecht, "but I wouldn't be surprised if she's putting up a false front."

"Two false fronts, and a false behind, too," muttered Valerie.

"What?"

"Nothing," she said.

"And your cousin Lorraine is the only one with access to the new account. Maybe she found out who blew up her car."

"The Clott!" said Valerie. "She could have done it. I never trusted her."

"And she was blown up in the car."

"No, she wasn't," said Valerie. "The FBI said it was a man. And no one's seen her since."

Albrecht got up from the desk. "Look, it doesn't matter who did it. We know where the money is. What you have to do is get back on Lorraine's good side and get access to that money. Then you could have it all. The charity's money and the Valvano's money."

"You're probably right," said Valerie. "I don't know how Lorraine feels about me now. I did abandon her in London."

"Because you were afraid that Robert Valvano was after you," said Albrecht. "You have to go into every situation in life with at least one excuse ready."

Valerie bit her lip. "Yeah, Lorraine would fall for that."

Albrecht slapped his hands together. "I know you can sell it. Then we'll be on easy street."

"We? What do you mean 'we?'"

Albrecht Eckner grinned his porcine smile. "We're in this together, my dear."

"You wish," snorted Valerie and started to leave.

"I don't wish," he said. "I know too much. I don't think your cousin Lorraine would like to hear all I know about you and your designs on her money."

Valerie waved her hand dismissively. "Like she'd believe you. She hates you, always has."

A suspicious look crossed Albrecht's face. "I've never met your cousin."

Valerie stood with her mouth agape. Chesney loathed Albrecht. She wished she had one of those excuses Albrecht advised a few minutes earlier.

"That's okay," said Albrecht with a smile.

"Uh, it is?"

"Sure," he said, "it's enough that I know you're hiding something from me. Now that I know the gun is loaded, I don't have to pull the trigger yet."

Valerie seethed. "I hate you."

"Just like your cousin, Lorraine," he replied. "Now I know we can come to an amicable arrangement. See? This proves that you need my labyrinthian mind."

"Twisted mind!"

"Precisely," said Albrecht. "You're in a devious neighborhood and need an experienced guide."

"And what do I get out of this?" said Valerie.

"You get the money and power," said Albrecht. "Well, most of the money, and you can keep all the power. That's too much work."

"I want more," she said. "I want a divorce."

"That goes without saying, my dear," he said. "Once I've got my money, our marriage license is just excess paper."

Valerie nodded. "You'll make me the happiest girl in the world." She turned to leave and then stopped. If she was going to get back in Lorraine's good graces, Valerie would need to destroy Martina's letter. "Speaking of excess paper, I want that letter."

Albrecht feigned forgetfulness. "Letter? Letter? Oh, yes, that letter from the late Miss Fergus. Yes, you can have that... as part of our completed agreement."

"How do I know you're not bluffing? I bet you don't even have it anymore," said Valerie.

"*Au Contraire!*" said Albrecht.

"Let's see it," she said.

"After all we've meant to each other, don't you trust me?"

"After all we've meant to each other," replied Valerie, "certainly not!"

He stood and crossed to the bookcase. "I have it in the safe. Stand over there. I don't want you grabbing it and trying to run away."

Valerie sighed and stepped to the other side of the room.

Albrecht slid open the panel to reveal his wall safe. He started to enter the combination, then stopped and turned to her. "You don't have any matches on you? I don't want you diving across the room to burn it."

"Not a match, not a lighter," said Valerie.

He smiled. "Not even a flame thrower?"

"If I had a flame thrower, you would be a crispy critter right now."

Albrecht twirled his finger. "Turn around while I enter the combination."

Valerie shook her head but did as he asked.

"It's not that I don't trust you," said Albrecht. She could hear the clicking of the safe's dial. "You can't be too careful in my line of work."

"You mean the extortion racket?" said Valerie. "No, I imagine not."

"Ha, ha, very droll," said Albrecht. "There!"

Valerie heard him throw back the handle. She turned around. Albrecht extracted a manila envelope from the safe.

"It's all in here," he said.

Valerie took a step toward him. He threw up his hand. "Not any closer." Albrecht undid the clasp and opened up the envelope. "All here, nice, and…"

He stopped. A worried look overspread Albrecht's face. At least, Valerie thought it was worry. She'd never seen him exhibit anything like it. Valerie was used to seeing smugness, lasciviousness, greed, and avarice. But she'd never seen him look like he did now.

"What is it," asked Valerie, as Albrecht rifled through the pages in the envelope. "Don't you have the letter?"

"What? Letter? Yes, I have the letter. But, I don't have all the copies," he said. Albrecht looked in the safe, on the desk, and then under the desk.

"So, if you have the original…"

Albrecht counted the papers and recounted them, then shook his head. "There were eight copies. The original and eight copies."

"I don't see what…"

"Now there are only six," he said, his voice raising an octave. He closed the envelope, reopened it, and counted the papers again. Then he put them back, sealed the envelope, put it back in the safe, shut the door, and spun the lock.

Albrecht slumped in his chair.

"Look, if you have the one…"

"Don't you see what this means?" he cried.

"Frankly, no," said Valerie. "Big deal you miscounted or misplaced…"

Albrecht shook his head violently. "No, no, I couldn't. I audit the contents of the safe every week. Every week that envelope has one original letter and eight copies."

"Why do you need eight copies?" she asked.

He looked at her as if she were a slow child. "In case the original is lost. I have copies."

"And now you still have the original," Valerie reasoned. "So your system works. You lost some copies, and you have extras."

"But where did they go?" he said. "No one has access to that safe but me."

"Has anyone else been in your office?"

"Not without me here as well," he said, pulling at his hair.

Valerie shrugged.

Albrecht stared at her. "You don't get it, do you? If someone else has a copy, it means someone's been in my private safe." His mouth dropped open, and he jumped to his feet. Hurriedly he entered the combination and reopened the safe. In less than thirty seconds, he sorted through every item it contained. Then he shut the safe again.

"Everything there?" she asked.

"Yes, except for two copies of that letter," he said. "You should be more worried than I."

"Why?"

"It means you have a potential blackmailer out there," said Albrecht. "If you're going to be devious, you'd better start thinking like a..."

"Rat?"

"If you like," he said. "But maybe, just maybe, someone else has that letter. Someone who isn't looking out for your best interests, like I am."

Valerie started to laugh and then stopped. Albrecht was right. It was a case of the devil she knew. Who knew what someone else, an unknown enemy, might do with that letter? But, she thought, who would want the letter? And besides, the only person who would care was Lorraine, and Lorraine wasn't mentioned in the letter. If someone stole the letter, it would only be of use to them if they knew that Lorraine and Chesney were the same person.

"Valerie!" snapped Albrecht. "Are you listening to me? It's disconcerting to think someone out there may be playing the same game as me, though why they'd want that letter is a mystery. I doubt old Chimney Potts could crack a safe."

"No," said Valerie, "probably not. Look, who else has access to your office?"

"My secretary," said Albrecht, "but I can't see her doing it. No one else is in here during the day. And at night, it's just the old guard and the cleaning woman. The guard's been here for years, and I've only seen the woman once. She's new."

"New?"

Albrecht crossed to a filing cabinet and pulled out a file. "Yes, only a few weeks. They hired her when we were on our honeymoon. Here she is."

He opened the file and handed it to Valerie.

"Her?" gasped Valerie. "I know her. She's rich. She's the daughter of some English Lord. And I saw her in London when I was shopping. She knew about the wedding, but I didn't tell her who I was marrying."

Albrecht looked puzzled. "So, why should she care? And why would she want that letter?"

Valerie's eyes narrowed. "I don't know, but I'm damn well going to find out!"

– 79 –
The Mona Lisa of Cabbies

Margie Mackay stood on the balcony overlooking Gibraltar. She had just arrived in advance of Lorraine Innis. She turned to Paul Rocher. "Are you sure he's here?"

Rocher folded the newspaper he was reading and turned it toward Margie. He pointed at a headline.

"BRITISH MAN FOUND DEAD; PROBABLE SUICIDE."

"I'm certain of it," said Rocher.

Margie scanned the story's first paragraph, then looked up at Rocher quizzically.

"That British man was an agent," said Rocher. "Though it gives a different name and says he was a businessman, that's standard cover in these situations. That man was Nigel Verve."

"The agent who rescued Lorraine from her abductors?"

"The same."

Margie nibbled the end of a pen. "Why would your friend assassinate a British agent?"

"I'm sure you're using 'friend' euphemistically," said Rocher. "At best, we were acquaintances. Lily has no friends. You trust friends."

"And he trusts no one?"

Rocher shrugged. "Only as far as is necessary. And I'm afraid that distance has grown considerably shorter of late. He was once one of the best agents in the field. But he's become terribly short-sighted, or maybe it's tunnel vision. I don't know. I'm not good with metaphors, but it gets hard to see someone's reasoning when he goes around the bend."

"You think he's gone mad?"

Rocher held up the paper again. "This is not the act of a sane individual. He probably saw Verve as a threat to..." He fell silent.

325

"To what?"

"I can't get into particulars," said Rocher. "Let's just say he's become obsessed with Lorraine."

"Romantically?" she said.

Rocher shook his head. "No, it's more paternal. Actually, it goes beyond that. If I had to guess, I'd say Lily fancies himself as Pygmalion, the ancient sculptor who fell in love with the statue he had carved."

Margie laughed. "But Lorraine isn't a statue, and Lily didn't create her."

Rocher started to speak but stopped himself. Then he looked at his watch. "Didn't you say you wanted to check on the security at the hotel Lorraine will be staying at?"

"Oh, yes," said Margie.

Margie Mackay grabbed her purse and left. Lorraine was arriving in Gibraltar for some sort of announcement. It was a different hotel a few blocks from the one where she and Rocher had rooms. She started down the street when a cab pulled up alongside her.

"Taxi, lady?" said the driver.

"No, thank you," said Margie. "I'm just going a short distance."

The taxi crawled along at her pace.

"Special offer, Miss," said the cabby. "Free today for government workers... Miss Mackay."

Margie stopped and looked into the vehicle. The driver wore an enigmatic smile, like the Mona Lisa of cabbies. There was also something familiar about his eyes. She had last seen those eyes in London on a kung-fu chambermaid.

"Uh, no," said Margie looking around. "Thanks anyway."

The driver put the cab in park and leaned toward her. "Don't worry, Miss Mackay. You're not in any danger. If you were, I wouldn't have told you."

"What do you want?" asked Margie. She looked up and down the street for a policeman, though she realized they would be of little help.

"I just want to talk," he said.

"Why didn't you come up to Mr. Rocher's room?"

Lily shook his head. "Lately, Paul and I and hotel rooms don't get along well. And I'd hate to have furniture breakage put on his bill, even if you are staying in a second-class hotel. Don't take that personally. I know what government paychecks are like. Besides, I wanted to talk to you."

Margie eyed the rear of the cab. Who knew if she got in where she'd get out, or even if she'd get out alive. She shook her head. "You want to talk? Let's go down the street to that coffee shop."

"Okay," he said with a shoulder shrug, "but it's your treat."

Margie walked down to the coffee shop while Lily parked his cab. While she sat waiting for him, Margie wondered where he got the taxi. Whether he stole it or if he killed the owner to get it.

A minute later, Lily entered and sat down.

"Nice public place," he said. "Feel better?"

"My mother always warned me against getting into cars with strange operatives."

Lily laughed. "Wow, old Paul must have told you some tales about me."

She shook her head. "No, not really. I learned all I needed to know while kickboxing a chambermaid in London."

He smiled. "You were pretty good."

"Thanks," she said, "and you have nice legs. But I don't think you wanted to hear my opinion in that area."

"No," said Lily, "you're right. I wanted to do you a favor."

"Me?"

"You and my old pal, Mr. Rocher," he continued. "I know why you're here. You were in the protection detail for a certain lady, and I know your assignment has ended. So, I doubt you're just here on holiday. It must be personal, just like it is for Mr. Rocher."

Margie just looked at him. She was there because Lorraine Innis had become a friend. Margie had wondered what Paul Rocher's interest was. She assumed it was a sense of duty.

Lily noted her hesitation. "He had an old girlfriend. You might want to call her the one that got away; a dead ringer for our person of mutual interest."

It was as if he had read the question running through her mind. His next statement only reinforced that feeling.

"No," said Lily, "it's not the same girl. The original died a few years ago. Some broad, pardon me, some woman named 'Potoski.' They went to school together. And that dame, uh, woman, is no relation to that certain lady."

"Oh," was all Margie managed to say.

"Yeah, so, you're doing what you're doing because you're a dedicated agent. Paulie's doing it because he's fulfilling a wet dream that dried up years ago."

Margie's lip curled.

"Excuse the crudity," he said. "I'm used to speaking like I did when all the G-Men had tackle commensurate with their title. Anyway, I just wanted to let you know I'm moving on because of that certain lady's plans."

"So, you know," said Margie.

"Yes, I know," he said. "She plans to retire."

Margie nodded and then caught herself. Had she just been tricked into divulging Lorraine's plans?

"Don't worry," said Lily. "You didn't tell me."

"No?"

He smiled that Mona Lisa smile. "Nah, you just confirmed it, that's all."

Margie clenched her fists. Lily noticed.

"Hey," he said, "it's okay. Like I said, I can move on. Looks like we all can move on, except maybe your Mr. Rocher." He started to stand. "Okay, so, that's that. I got what I wanted, and you got what you wanted."

"Me?" said Margie, "what did I want?"

Lily paused and gave her a puzzled look. "You get to go back to whatever you were doing. You get to tell your boss that he came to Gibraltar on a wild goose chase. To tell you the truth," he suppressed a laugh, "I was on my way to Africa. I only stopped here because I couldn't resist yanking Paulie's chain for old times' sake."

Margie relaxed for a moment, then a thought occurred to her. Unfortunately, she let it slip out of her mouth. "What about that British agent?"

Lily raised his eyebrows. "He thinks that I... Hey, no, I read about that in the paper. There's no percentage in dead limeys."

"But he knew Lorraine," said Margie.

"So, did lots of people," he said with a shrug. "A lot of people in England know her, too, and if you want to check my passport, it will show you that's where I was. I didn't get to this Rock until after he got whacked."

"The papers said it was a suicide," said Margie.

"And you'll read the same about me someday," noted Lily. "The majority of agents buy it in supposed suicides. But I don't know a single one who actually killed themselves."

He stared at her for a moment. "Any more questions? Only there's a flight to Nairobi that I need to be on. And if I miss that, several connecting flights will get screwed up. Look, you're a good agent and a hell of a good fighter. If you retire, forced or otherwise, look me up. I can always use a good wingman, uh, lady. On second thought, you won't be able to look me up, but if you're interested, I'll find out." He looked around, then looked at his watch. "Okay, I need to get that hack back to the guy I rented it from. Good thing, too, he can give me a lift to the airport."

– 80 –
The Russian Cincinnatus

The presidential limousine, the genuine one, entered the outskirts of Moscow.

"We will be there soon," said Nikolai Kropotkin.

Clodagh Clott looked at her borrowed peasant clothing, now even worse for the wear. "There won't be reporters there, will there?"

Kropotkin shrugged. "Probably. The story is out that I'm returning after Teplov reported me missing."

Clodagh fingered the torn skirt, dirty with mud. "I look like a mess," she muttered.

Kropotkin took her chin in his hand and turned it toward him. He kissed her gently. "You look like an angel to me."

He fell silent for a moment and then chuckled to himself.

"What?" asked Clodagh.

"I seem to recall saying those exact words to Lorruska," he said, "after she saved my life. And now you've saved my life by spotting that KGB driver."

Clodagh smiled. "Well, Nick, if you're going to keep having your life saved by American girls, you'll have to come up with a new line."

Kropotkin laughed and pointed at her. "Yes, that is a joke. I know that!"

She nodded her approval.

"And I do not plan on needing any more rescuing, but just to make certain, I will keep you on permanent retainer. Henceforth you shall not leave my side!"

Clodagh glanced up toward the driver, whose eyes were on the road. She leaned over and kissed him and then slid back to her side of the seat.

"Don't you want to sit close to me?" he asked.

"Of course I do, Nick," said Clodagh, "but I think you need to take care of the more immediate issues before you tell the world we're getting married." She nodded toward the rear window of the vehicle. Behind them was an army ambulance containing the handcuffed driver of the crashed limo.

"You're right," said Kropotkin. "I have to settle accounts with Teplov. That jackal he sent to abduct us confessed…" Kropotkin shook his head. "Most ex-KGB men would have killed themselves."

"I guess you're lucky he didn't," she said.

Kropotkin shrugged. "In the old days, if a plot like that failed, the victorious party, me, would have taken care of justice much more quickly. Teplov would have just disappeared."

"I'm glad things are different now," said Clodagh.

He smiled wryly. "Things are not different, not that much. It is I who am different. Thanks to…" he stopped.

Clodagh took his hand in hers. "I know, Lorraine."

"You are not jealous?"

She laughed. "Jealous that a person who could never be competition would make the real you emerge?"

"The real me?" Kropotkin bristled slightly.

"Yes," continued Clodagh, "the real you. Lorraine Innis didn't turn you into a kind, decent person. She just made it possible for the real you to come out. She helped you realize this stupid game of power politics, both in Russia and internationally, ultimately had no winners. The old Nikolai Kropotkin would have probably taken his competition out and had them shot. Teplov would be dead, and you would be a cold-blooded murderer. Even if you won, you'd be no better than some gangster. You would be feared, even by those closest to you."

Kropotkin looked out the window, deep in thought.

"And I wouldn't be here," said Clodagh. "I couldn't love Nikolai Kropotkin."

He turned and looked at her with surprise.

"But," she continued, "I do love my sweet Nick."

Kropotkin smiled and nodded.

"You are wise, much like your friend," he admitted. "You must have come from a very brilliant neighborhood."

"Oh, yeah," she said, "we even had a kid who ate dirt and bugs."

He stared at her for a moment and then smiled. "Ah, another joke. I'm getting better."

"Yes," she said, "you are."

When they arrived at the Kremlin, a battery of cameras and reporters were waiting. There was a tsunami of shouted questions about his whereabouts, his appearance, and the woman at his side.

"I will have a complete statement soon," Kropotkin told them. "And that will answer most of your questions." Then he excused himself and escorted Clodagh into the building.

"What are you going to tell them?" asked Clodagh as she followed him down the corridor.

"The truth," he said.

Clodagh noticed that in these halls of power, Kropotkin seemed to grow. He was more commanding. Those he encountered stepped to one side and snapped to attention. Clodagh wondered if this attitude would eclipse the man she had grown to love and if she had made a mistake in agreeing to marry him.

They went up an elevator and into a large, ornate office. A short fat man greeted Kropotkin.

"Uncle President," said the man with tears in his eyes. "How happy I am to see you. I feared..."

"Yuri," said Kropotkin, "this is Miss Clott. Clodagh, this is Yuri, my nephew, and my aide. Yuri, please get Miss Clott some refreshments and contact a lady's outfitter."

"A lady's outfitter?" said Yuri. "What for?"

Kropotkin smiled and pointed at Clodagh. "Why to outfit a lady, of course, my dear boy."

Yuri stood with his mouth agape as if he expected a verbal tongue lashing but received a gentle joke instead. His mouth moved up and down for a moment before speaking. "Can I get you something to eat or drink, Miss Clott?"

Clodagh thanked him and asked for some mineral water.

Yuri bowed and started backing away. "Yes, Miss Clott, and I will see about a lady's outfitter."

"Oh, and Yuri," said Kropotkin, as Yuri reached the door, "A Cherry Coke for me, with ice." He paused and patted his belly. "Make it a diet one... please."

Yuri's mouth dropped open. He simply nodded and then excused himself.

"My nephew," noted Kropotkin, "by marriage, but a good fellow." After offering Clodagh a seat, Kropotkin picked up the phone and made several orders in Russian. He put down the phone, looked out the window, and sighed.

"You work so long and so hard for something," he said, "and even when you want to let go of it, it is difficult."

Clodagh came up behind him a put her arms around him. "Letting go?"

He nodded. "Yes, of all this. I just ordered my lifelong rival arrested. It was he who had you kidnapped, who held us captive, who sent that last assassin to kill us."

She said nothing but squeezed him tighter.

"I will resign," he said. "I don't have to, but..."

Kropotkin fell silent for thirty seconds.

"...but you feel you need to?" she said.

He nodded. "I want to rid my country of that vermin. But at the same time, I do not want my motives to seem political. Perhaps that will break the cycle of cutthroat politics that have plagued us for so long."

"Sort of like George Washington retiring instead of letting them make him king," she said.

He turned and looked at her. "A very apt description, though your Washington was following the example set by the Roman statesman, Cincinnatus. I have done all I can; perhaps the best service I can render my country is to see it through this crisis and then hand over the reins to someone else."

Clodagh kissed him. "You know, Nick, you are a remarkable guy, and that's why I love you."

Their embrace was broken by the sound of someone clearing his throat. They turned to see Yuri standing there with a tray containing their refreshments.

"Excuse me, President, Sir," said Yuri. He set the tray on a table and turned to leave.

"Wait a minute, Yuri," said Kropotkin sternly. The aide stiffened. Kropotkin smiled. "You didn't bring anything for yourself. Won't you join us?"

Yuri's face melted into surprise and then delight. "Yes, sir, thank you. I'll go get something." He dashed from the room.

"I'm guessing he's seeing a new side to you, as well," said Clodagh.

Kropotkin nodded. "Now, we have several announcements to work on. First my resignation, then we will have to announce our wedding. The first we can do right away. Second, before making it public, I want to tell our mutual friend the news. How do you think she will react?"

"Lorraine?" said Clodagh. "I'm sure she will be surprised and happy. Very surprised and very happy... for us."

Yuri returned with an extra bottle and a glass for himself. Kropotkin put his finger to his lips. "Nothing to anyone," he whispered to Clodagh, "until we tell, you know who."

Yuri poured their respective beverages and handed each one their glass.

"To our journeys," said Kropotkin raising his glass.

"You just returned," Yuri exclaimed. "Where are you going?"

Kropotkin opened his mouth and then shut it. He turned to Clodagh. "She is in America, I assume."

"She was the last time I saw her," said Clodagh, "but that was weeks ago."

Yuri looked back and forth between them and then nodded. "If you are speaking of Mrs. Innis, she is going to Gibraltar."

– 81 –
The Post-Nuptial Team Building Exercise

Valerie Fierro opened the door of her hotel suite and smirked.

"That's not a very warm reception for a newlywed bride to give her husband," said Albrecht Eckner with his usual snarky tone. "Don't tell me the romance is gone from our marriage already?"

She stared at him with a look that would wither the strongest human. Unfortunately, he was made of altogether different stuff.

"Are you going to invite me in?" he asked.

"I suppose I have no choice," she said, waving him in.

Albrecht entered with a gait that could only be described as a "sashay."

"You always have a choice," said Albrecht, sitting on the sofa. "But since I'm paying for this suite, you obviously made the wise decision." Albrecht placed a leather portfolio beside him and patted it. "And once you see what I've brought you, you would have welcomed me with a bottle of vintage champagne and a box of Belgian chocolates."

Valerie winced.

"Yes," he hissed, "I just got the bill for our little gift to everyone else in the hotel. Very generous…"

"Look, Albrecht," she began.

"A generosity I heartily approve of," he continued.

"You what?"

Albrecht smiled, much like a python being introduced to a mouse who hadn't visited the gym in several months.

"I'm very touched," he said, "that you wanted to share your happy delirium, your deep ecstasy with those around you. It was quite expensive, but an expense that will be far outweighed by our future profits; the profits from our charitable endeavors."

Valerie sat down across from him. "Ours?"

"Yes, my dear," he said, reaching into his portfolio. "I've drawn up a little deal between us. Let's call it a post-nuptial agreement."

He handed the paper to Valerie, who scanned it.

"I get a divorce," she said gleefully.

"Though it contradicts your recent gifts to strangers, celebrating our marriage," he said melodramatically. "But I know it's what you wanted."

"And you get..." Valerie sprang to her feet. "Fifty percent?!"

Albrecht passively examined his fingernails.

"Half?" she cried. "You expect me to hand you half of the charity?"

He shrugged. "Not outright. It's not like you're going to hand me cash."

Valerie looked back at the document. "No, just an equal controlling interest."

"Better than cash," he said. "We'll be able to invest how we please, set up off-shore accounts, and so on. The opportunities are limitless once I, that is, we have the capital."

"But..."

"And we'll make sure those snotty-nosed masses we're supposed to be helping won't be deprived. After all, we have to look like we're doing good."

"Oh, we do, do we," said Valerie.

"Of course," he said, "so big-hearted contributors will keep giving to the saintly Cross of Lorraine."

"And what about the saintly Lorraine?" she asked.

"I'm sure you can handle her," he said. "She loves you."

Valerie snorted. "He, uh, I mean she hates your guts."

"So you've mentioned," he said. "And yet, you married me. Your cousin Lorraine will understand the fiery swings that passionate couples like us go through."

Valerie started to crumple the agreement.

"Ah, ah, ah," he said, wagging his finger. "I didn't expect you to agree outright. As they say in television commercials: 'wait, there's more.'" Albrecht held up the portfolio.

"What do you have in there," she asked, "a receipt for your pre-paid cremation?"

He smiled. "Now, like any good husband, I'm sensitive to every desire my dear wife may have. You wanted to know about that cleaning woman, didn't you?"

Valerie's eyes lit up. "Yeah? What? What is she up to?"

Albrecht's eyes narrowed. "It's fascinating, and it involves someone you know."

"Who?" Valerie thought. "Her father? Lord Windbag, or whatever his name is?"

"Nope," said Albrecht, "you'll never guess. Even I was surprised. You can imagine my shock when I was conducting a routine search of her purse."

"How did..."

"It was while she was on her rounds, cleaning up the third floor," he said. "After hours. I just happened by her locker in the cleaning closet and wanted to ensure all her personal belongings were secure."

"So, you broke in," said Valerie.

"I'd never break into an employee's personal locker," he said, "not while I have a duplicate key."

Valerie shook her head. She might have known. Anyone who would climb a tree to take pictures of her with the family dog would have no qualms about violating a cleaning woman's privacy.

"Okay," she said, reaching for the portfolio, "so what did you find out?"

Albrecht pulled it away. "No dessert until you eat your veggies, darling." He held up their partnership agreement.

Valerie looked at the document and then at the portfolio. She hated to give Albrecht a cut of the charity, but curiosity was itching away at her mind. She could always figure out a way to double-cross him later. Valerie snatched the paper from his hand, picked up a pen, and signed the agreement. She shoved the document back at him. Albrecht read her signature and smiled. Then he carefully folded it and put it in his pocket.

"I cherish this even more than our marriage license," he said.

"I'll bet you do," she sneered, "now, what's her big secret? Why did that Verity chick want that letter?"

Albrecht shrugged. "Dunno."

"WHAT? You lied to me... again!" She leaned over him, reaching for his pocket. "Give me back that agreement."

Albrecht leaned away. "Hold on. I didn't say I knew why she wanted the letter, not directly. But I have information that is, at the very least, quite juicy and intriguing. My cleaning woman, the daughter of some English lord, is romantically involved. You might even say she is in love."

"Yeah?" Valerie snorted. She thought of the plain appearance of Verity Goodhue. "So, what, whoever it is must be a real drip."

Albrecht smiled. He reached into the portfolio and pulled out a photograph. "Truer words were never spoken. Meet her Mr. Drippy."

He handed Valerie the photograph. It was of Verity Goodhue and Chesney Potts. Valerie gasped.

"See," said Albrecht, "I told you it was juicy. You didn't know where old Cheese Pot was. He's got himself a woman in to clean his pipes."

Valerie just stared at the photograph. She knew Chesney was supposed to marry some English girl, but she died. When did he have the chance to go back for another girl? The photo showed Verity looking much as she did now, but Chesney looked like his pudgy, pre-Lorraine self. She turned over the back. There was a date written in ink. It was before she met him, before Martina got him the job with the bank.

Valerie flipped the photo over again. Verity Goodhue must be the girl who was supposed to have died but obviously wasn't dead.

Albrecht was saying something, but Valerie's thoughts drowned him out. That's why Verity was so set on meeting Lorraine. She obviously knew Lorraine was Chesney. Verity knew, and she had played Valerie for a sucker. And now she had that letter. Why did she care about Martina? If Valerie was in Verity's shoes, she wouldn't care about some dead girl her boyfriend had been engaged to. But, she reminded herself, she wasn't like Verity. Verity had no style. She was plain. Then she thought about her own assessment of Verity and Chesney. Valerie told her they were like bookends when she and Verity had dinner back in London. If Verity was so intent on getting information about Martina's death, she must have met up again with Chesney. But how?

It had to be after they returned to England after Valerie ran off to Wales. She snapped her fingers.

"What?" said Albrecht.

"Huh?"

"You're sitting there like some zombie," he said.

"Shut up," she said, "I'm thinking."

Lorraine was being sued by Verity's father. Then Lorraine fainted at the trial, then disappeared for several days. Somehow, somewhere Verity got a hold of him. Chesney must have told her the whole reason for being Lorraine, and Verity was now helping him. Chesney must have told her about Albrecht and Gibraltar, and...

"You've got to stop her," said Valerie.

"What?"

"You want your cut of the charity? Then earn it," said Valerie. "If we don't get that letter back, it will all be over for me. And if it's over for me, it's over for you! We've got to stop her before she leaves Gibraltar."

"Leave Gibraltar?" he asked. "To go where?"

"Back to England," said Valerie. "She going back to show that letter to, uh, to Lorraine."

"She won't have to go back to England," said Albrecht. "Your cousin will be here tomorrow." He pulled the morning newspaper from his case and handed it to Valerie.

"Lorraine Innis Visits Gibraltar!" read the headline.

"Okay," snapped Valerie Fierro, "I've got to get to Lorraine before she does. You just run interference."

Albrecht Eckner snorted. "That's easy I can make sure that Goodhue the charlady won't be near her tomorrow."

Valerie folded her arms. "And how can you be so sure?"

"You think you're dealing with an amateur?" said Albrecht. "By the time your cousin lands, I'll have the Goodhue girl in Marbella."

"How..."

"I'll call it a team building exercise, or a staff outing. I'll put her on the bus myself," said Albrecht, "along with the rest of the bank employees. I'll call it day trip for employee appreciation."

Valerie gasped. "You'd close the bank for a day and spring for everyone to have a holiday?"

Albrecht smiled. "An all-expense holiday. I'll paid for the bus, their lunch, and spending money. You have to spend money to steal money. That's chicken feed compared to our payday when we completely control that charity."

Valerie nodded. Albrecht was right. It was crucial to keep Chesney and Verity Goodhue far apart.

"Don't worry, I'll take care of Lorraine," said Valerie. I'll take care of you all, she thought.

– 82 –
The Final Flight of
Lorraine Innis?

Lorraine Inns stepped off the plane onto the mobile stairway. Below, on the tarmac, were a phalanx of reporters and photographers to greet her. She smiled broadly, not for the media. Instead, she was hopeful that this was the last trip Lorraine Innis would ever make. If all went well, she would be leaving Gibraltar as Chesney Potts. With Nigel Verve, the ace of British espionage, on the case, the mystery of who was responsible for Martina's death would soon be solved. And the need for Lorraine would be gone.

"Powerful glad you came with me, Miss Lorraine," said Purvis Twankey emerging from the plane carrying his guitar.

"I've told you, Purvis," said Lorraine, "you're helping me more than you'll know."

Purvis shrugged. "Well, if I'll never know, I'll just have to take your word for it. I'm just glad you shared this with me."

Lorraine smiled. "I'm glad, too, Purvis, and thank you for that big bag of M&M's. It's very sweet, but you didn't need to give it to me."

"Heck," he said, "I always take plenty of snacks when I get on an airplane, in case they don't feed you on the flight or if the plane goes down on a deserted island. That's the biggest sack they sell. You never know when it might come in handy."

"Thankfully, they gave us lunch," Lorraine laughed, "and we avoided crashes. So, I'll save the candy for later."

Purvis looked down on the tarmac. "Eee, but there's a lot of reporters down there. That's another reason I'm might grateful. I wouldn't know what to say to all these folks."

"But you're a celebrity in your own right," she noted. "You have all those hit records."

Purvis scratched his head. "Aye, but that's singing. You can't sing a press conference."

Lorraine patted his hand, "Just leave everything to me, Purvis." She looked into his puppy dog expression and felt a twinge of sadness. She would miss Purvis when Lorraine ceased to be.

They walked down the plane's stairs to a podium. Reporters shouted out their questions. Lorraine smiled and waited for them to calm down.

"I want to thank you all for this warm welcome to Gibraltar," she said. "I'm sure you all know Purvis Twankey. I'm mainly here to support Mr. Twankey as he prepares for his exciting announcement."

"You going into record promotion, Mrs. Innis?" shouted one reporter.

Lorraine chuckled. "Even though you've all enjoyed Mr. Twankey's music. The nature of his announcement is not related to that phase of his career."

"Are you two getting married?" asked one woman reporter.

"NO!" screamed a voice from the back of the crowd.

The reporters turned, and there in the back was Patsy Einfalt.

"Patsy," cried Purvis with delight. "Patsy!"

Patsy elbowed her way through the media and put her arms around Purvis. They kissed.

"As you can see," said Lorraine, "I am not the subject of Mr. Twankey's romantic affections."

The reporters shouted out more questions. Lorraine nudged Purvis to the microphone with Patsy still hanging on his arm.

"How do," said Purvis. "This is a surprise. This is my fancy, I mean my fiancée. This is the gal I'm gonna marry. Ain't that right, Patsy?"

Patsy redirected her gaze from Purvis to the assembled media, and her eyes widened.

"Uh, I think so," she muttered.

Purvis did a double take. "Do what? What do you mean, Patsy? Don't you love me no more?"

"Of course I do," said Patsy looking at him. "Only there's something I need to talk to you about."

He put his arm around her shoulder. "Sure enough! Shoot!"

Patsy glanced at the reporters. "In private."

Lorraine turned to an airport official. "I'm sure you can find a private place for Mr. Twankey to speak with his young lady."

The airport liaison escorted Purvis and Patsy away. Lorraine turned back to the podium. "As I said, I'm here mainly to support Mr. Twankey. He has an important announcement he promises will be of great interest."

"What's it about, Mrs. Innis?" shouted a British reporter.

"Yeah, give us the straight dope, Lorraine," said an American.

Lorraine forced a smile. "I'll leave that up to Mr. Twankey. But I don't think he'd mind if I told you that he's devised a strategy to alleviate the world energy situation. He is something of an inventor."

"Yeah," said another American, "he's the guy who grew beards on those dames in England."

Lorraine felt herself blushing. "Well, yes, that was an accident and not entirely his fault. And I'm sure you've heard his latest hit song, the proceeds of which will go to those women. Purvis Twankey's heart is always in the right place."

"Too bad his head ain't," said the American.

"His head isn't," said Lorraine, correcting the grammar.

"Yeah, whatever," said the reporter.

"So, are you vouching for this new scheme?" said another reporter.

"I don't know if I'd call it a scheme," said Lorraine. "That's a pejorative term." All she knew about Purvis' idea was that it had something to do with pickles, but she wasn't going to broadcast that. "I really don't know the details, so any comment I make would be unfair."

"Then what are you doing here," asked another reporter.

Lorraine couldn't very well explain her true motive. "I'm here because I'm supporting a friend." She thought of Martina. "A very, very, dear friend. And I'm hoping for a satisfactory resolution for everyone."

– 83 –
The Consistent Devotion
of a Dumbbell

The airport representative showed Purvis and Patsy to a private lounge.

"If there's anything you need," said the woman.

"Oh?" Purvis' eyes lit up. "That's mighty nice of you, ma'am. I got a busted E."

"A what?" she said.

"E, the string on my guitar, it busted," He held up his guitar. "I must have been the change in air pressure when we landed."

The woman just stared at him with a lost look in her eyes.

"Purvis," said Patsy, "I think you misunderstood. She meant a cup of tea or a sandwich."

Purvis suppressed a giggle that buzzed out from between his lips. "Don't be daft," he said to Patsy. "You can't replace a guitar string with a cup of tea or a sandwich!"

"Silly me," said Patsy before turning to the woman. "We're fine, thank you."

The woman excused herself and closed the door behind her.

"Imagine that," said Purvis, "putting a sandwich where an E string ought to be. A B or a G, maybe, but not an E. For one thing, the E is too thin. Hey, there's an idea, a musical instrument what you can eat! I mean, there's been lots of groups that smash up their instruments on stage, but it would be a real novelty to eat your guitar at the end of a show."

"Purvis…" said Patsy.

"Course, you'd have to be pretty hungry to eat a whole guitar," he continued, fascinated with the concept. It wouldn't do to start on the neck and not be able to finish. That would be a real letdown for the audience. I could skip lunch and dinner. That would build up an appetite. Course,

I could do a uke, not a tenor uke, a soprano uke. I reckon I could eat a soprano uke just about any time." He paused and looked at the door. "Wonder what kind of sandwiches she had."

Patsy tried to contain herself, but the talk of edible guitars busted her last string. She sat down on the settee and broke into tears. Purvis sat beside her and put his arm around her shoulder.

"There, there, pet," he said. "I can get you a sandwich."

"Oh, Purvis," she said, looking up at him, her eyes wet with tears, "do you always have to be such a dumbbell?"

He shrugged. "I am what I am, but I do love you no matter what I am."

She buried her head in his shoulder and cried. He patted her head.

"When I was a lad and would get hurt," he said, "our mum used to pat me head like this. And she'd say over and over again, 'there, there.'"

Patsy looked up at him. "Did it help?" she sniffed.

"Well, it was distracting," said Purvis. "She'd say: 'there, there.' And so, I'd stop crying and look around trying to see what was there that she was referring to."

Patsy laughed.

"Sorry I'm such a noddy-head," he said. "But at least I'm good for a laugh. You'll keep me around for that much, I hope."

She looked into his eyes. "I'll keep you around if you'll stay."

Purvis snorted. "Stay? I'll stay forever. Why would you say something like that?"

Patsy daubed her eyes with a hankie. "Purvis, while you were in England, a man showed up. Rachel's father, Mr. Einfalt."

Purvis sat dead still for several minutes, staring forward, unblinking with a vacant look in his eyes. Finally, Patsy nudged him.

"Ya what?!" said Purvis, as if he had been roused from a deep sleep.

"Purvis, dear, are you alright?"

Purvis looked around the room and then at Patsy. "Aye. Have you ever been smacked full in the face with a cast iron skillet?"

"No, I haven't," said Patsy.

"Oh," he said as if that were somehow unusual. "Well, that's what this feels like."

"Purvis, darling," she said, putting her arm around him, "that's how I felt, too."

"I thought you said you'd nowt been smacked full in the face with a cast iron skillet."

She nodded. "I mean, I had a similar reaction when Mr. Einfalt showed up. I was shocked."

He nodded in agreement. "Aye, shocked."

"And stunned," she added.

"Yeah, stunned." Purvis looked at the ceiling. "And gobsmacked," he added.

"I'm not familiar with that term, but if you say you're blobsmacked..."

"Gobsmacked," he corrected.

"Sorry, gobsmacked," said Patsy, "if you say you're that, then I must be too."

Patsy took a fresh hankie from her purse, wiped her eyes, blew her nose, and then proceeded to tell Purvis about the arrival, stay, and departure of Egmont Einfalt.

Purvis listened attentively for the entire twenty minutes. As far as Patsy could recall, it was the longest he had ever paid attention to anything without looking out of a window, asking for a snack, or falling asleep. When she finished, Purvis had a look that for him could only be described as "contemplative," though on most other people, it would be termed "bilious."

They sat in silence for another minute, then Patsy spoke. "So, what do you think?"

"'Bout what?"

Patsy wished she had that aforementioned cast iron frying pan. "About what I just told you all about."

"This fella," said Purvis, "this Einfalt guy what thought he was Santa Claus, do you believe him? I don't mean about him being the real Santa Claus. I mean, about him being Rachel's daddy?"

Patsy shrugged. "I sort of did..."

"But?"

"Well," said Patsy, "for a guy who came back because he supposedly was Rachel's father, he never asked to meet her. Isn't that odd?"

Purvis stroked his chin. "I'd say so. My daddy said he always wished he could un-meet me. He was foolin'... I think. But that's not natural. If I was someone's daddy, I'd want to see my sprout as much as I could."

"And then there was the way he treated me," continued Patsy.

"He wasn't mean, or nothin', was he?"

"Not at all," said Patsy.

Purvis gritted his teeth. "He didn't get fresher with you, did he?"

"Fresher?"

"Well, you know," said Purvis, "he was already right fresh before. So, he couldn't get a whole lot fresher. I mean, you know..." He made smoochy faces.

Patsy shook her head. "He didn't even kiss me. He was more interested in the books, the accounts, and the ledgers of the bank. And I did let him violate..."

Purvis gasped.

"I let him violate the security of the bank and charity computers," she continued. "I gave him my password. He said he didn't want me to get in trouble, and he wanted to fix things so the regulators wouldn't put me in jail."

Purvis thought hard, so hard he had to remove his hat. "Do you think maybe he was a crook?"

Patsy shook her head. "No, that's the odd thing. The charity's finances are better than ever. If anything, he straightened them out. The accounts have never looked better." She thought for a moment. "No, it was the strangest visit. He said a lot of words, but there was no emotion, no action behind them. Then he just disappeared, and I haven't heard a word from him since. I'm starting to feel like a real dope; like he was a con man, but then he didn't take anything."

Purvis looked down. "Not even your heart?"

Patsy put her arm around him. "He couldn't take my heart."

"No?" said Purvis looking up.

"How could he? You've had it all along."

- 84 -
The Mascara and M&M Reunion

Valerie fumed at the back of the crowd at Gibraltar's airport. Living on the edge of Lorraine's celebrity was annoying. A flock of reporters and photographers buzzed in front of Valerie, completely ignoring her. Admittedly, she was sporting her new hair color and was hiding under a large-brimmed hat and a pair of oversized sunglasses. Fine, she thought, let Lorraine get the glory for now. Soon she would have all of it, just as she'd promised herself and her father.

Lorraine's plane landed and taxied toward them. The media contingent buzzed more loudly. Valerie shook her head. She wanted to grab Lorraine in private. Turning toward the terminal, she spotted a woman in an airport uniform.

"Excuse me," said Valerie, "do you have a private room?"

The young woman looked at her oddly. "No, I share with my two roommates."

Valerie exhaled. "How wonderful for the three of you. I meant, does the airport have a VIP lounge?"

"Yes, they do, but it's not open to the general public," said the woman.

Valerie thrust back her shoulders. "I am *not* the general public."

"No?"

"I am Valerie Fierro; that's me!"

The woman nodded. "I, Valerie, me... well, how wonderful for the three of you."

"*The* Valerie Fierro!"

The woman just gave her a blank stare.

Valerie pointed toward the jet that had just landed. "The celebrity cousin of Lorraine Innis!"

"Oh."

"And I'd like a private room to greet my cousin out of the media glare."

The woman nodded and went to a nearby courtesy phone. After a minute, she hung up. "Allow me to show you to our private guest lounge."

"Thank you," said Valerie frostily, following the woman.

"Do you really know Lorraine Innis?" said the woman excitedly. "Oh, of course, you do; you're her cousin. That was a silly question, wasn't it?"

"Right both times," muttered Valerie.

The woman escorted Valerie to a private room on the second floor overlooking the runway. She took out her card, jotted a note on the back, and handed it to the woman with instructions to give it to Lorraine.

From the window, Valerie saw Lorraine exit the plane along with Purvis Twankey.

"Oh, please," Valerie said to herself, "don't bring that Brit-head with you."

She was then surprised to see Patsy Einfalt emerge from the crowd of reporters.

"Oh great," said Valerie, "is there anybody left in Delaware, or is Gibraltar hosting a doofus convention?"

Valerie sat down and waited, reviewing the plan in her mind. She wondered what version of Lorraine she'd encounter. When she last saw her, Lorraine was convinced she was really a woman and without any knowledge of Chesney Potts. She hoped this wouldn't be the person greeting her. The all-female Lorraine was much savvier than the half-and-half version.

After about ten minutes, there was a knock on the door. An airport official announced Lorraine. After she entered, the official excused himself, leaving them alone.

"Valerie," said Lorraine hurrying to embrace her.

Valerie returned the hug and then held Lorraine at arm's length. She searched her eyes, wondering who exactly she was hugging, or more precisely, who thought they were hugging her.

Lorraine knitted her eyebrows. "What? What's wrong?"

"Nothing, I just haven't seen you in a while," said Valerie, before adding: "...Chesney."

"Hey," whispered Lorraine, "watch that Chesney stuff."

"Why?"

"You don't know who may be listening," said Lorraine out of the corner of her mouth.

Valerie smiled. "Then it is you, really you."

Lorraine rolled her eyes. "Who did you think it was? Oh, I know what you're talking about. There were some times recently when I, well, that I forgot myself, you know... my other self."

"But you know who you are now, don't you?" said Valerie tentatively.

"Yes, you see, I was hypnotized," said Lorraine. "Clodagh..."

Valerie slapped her hand. "I should have known. I never did trust that chick. Are you sure you're okay? She didn't permanently scramble your brain, did she?"

"I'm fine," said Lorraine. "And I've known Clodagh since I was a little boy…" she looked around. "…I mean, girl. Besides, the hypnosis was my idea. Then when my car blew up, I thought she was dead. But then the evidence said the remains belonged to a man."

"Are you sure she was really a woman?" said Valerie hoping that the Clott woman was the corpse in the car.

"Certainly, she was," said Lorraine. "How could she be anything but a woman?"

Valerie just stared at her.

"Oh, right," said Lorraine. "But Clodagh is one of my oldest friends."

Valerie nodded. "Yeah, right, and she sure disappeared in a hurry. Maybe she was the one who blew up your car."

Lorraine sat down on the lounge sofa. "No," she shook her head. "Clodagh wouldn't have done that. In fact, she was borrowing my car. She said she knew who was responsible for Martina's death."

Valerie's eyes opened wide. "And she told you who it was?"

Lorraine shook her head. "No, she said she knew but was going out to get the proof. And that's the last anyone has heard of her."

Valerie heaved a sigh of relief. "Thank goodness!"

"What?"

"Uh, I mean, thank goodness she wasn't the one in the car," Valerie said. She sat beside Lorraine and put her arm around her. "But still, the Clott woman was probably lying. After all, why would she disappear like that if she really cared?"

Lorraine paused in thought. "But you disappeared, too."

Valerie sat with her mouth agape, wracking her brain for a comeback.

"Yeah, well, uh, I, I was on the run," she said. "My life was in danger."

Lorraine kept looking at her, not critically, but with that look Chesney had always had: trusting.

"The Valvanos were after me," she said.

"Michael?"

"Actually, his brother," said Valerie, "but Michael's no saint in this equation, either."

"And that's why you changed your hair," noted Lorraine. "It's very becoming."

"Thank you."

"And that's why you came to Gibraltar, I guess," said Lorraine.

"Right, yes, that's right." Valerie relaxed. It was good to have old trusting Chesney back. He always assumed the best in her and filled in the blanks. Lying to him was so effortless. He did most of the heavy lifting for her.

"But I can't figure out why you had to marry Albrecht Eckner," said Lorraine.

Hearing Lorraine say that was like a sock to her jaw. Valerie didn't know that Lorraine knew about her marriage.

"Oh," said Valerie, lowering her head, "you heard about that, huh?"

"Yes, someone told me about it," said Lorraine.

Valerie thought for a second. Who could have told? Then she recalled meeting Verity Goodhue while she was shopping. Wait, she could use that.

"Verity," said Valerie.

Lorraine looked around, genuinely surprised. "How did…"

Valerie smiled. "I've known Verity for months. We've had girls' nights out and everything."

"Really? She didn't say," said Lorraine, "not that we discussed that. We had other things to talk about."

"She's here," said Valerie, "in Gibraltar."

"You knew? Where? Where is she? Is she all right?"

"She's fine," assured Valerie. "In fact, uh, we've been working together… for you."

"About Martina?"

"Yes," said Valerie, "in fact, I got a note that she found out some very interesting things. Verity wouldn't tell me what, but she said it was the answer you were looking for."

"For which you were looking," corrected Lorraine, "oh, what am I saying? Grammar doesn't matter at a time like this. That's why I came to Gibraltar, to find Verity. We're going to be married."

Valerie looked at her. "Which one of you is going to wear the wedding gown?"

A puzzled look crossed Lorraine's face. "Verity, of course. No, don't you see? This is why I became Lorraine, to get justice for Martina. And as soon as I find out who's responsible for Martina's death, I can stop being Lorraine."

"Forever?" said Valerie. She thought about the charity. Without Lorraine, contributions would dry up. Still, there had to be billions there. Enough for her to invest and skim off the top. She could do it without Lorraine. In fact, if Lorraine disappeared, Valerie would be left in complete control.

"Of course, forever," said Lorraine. "I can't wait to ditch it all."

"Going to burn your bra, huh?" joked Valerie.

"In a manner of speaking, yes," said Lorraine, "along with all the other accouterments of Lorraine Innis."

In her mind, Valerie was doing backflips. Outwardly, she adopted a look of concern. "Wait, but… who will run the charity? Who will carry on all the wonderful things you've achieved?"

Lorraine shrugged. "Does it matter?"

Valerie gasped. "The Cross of Lorraine, without Lorraine?"

"Valerie," said Lorraine, "it's all a lie. There is no Lorraine Innis, not really. The world got along without Lorraine Innis before, and when she disappears, it will get over her in about five minutes, if not less. The charity can go on, just without me. Any imbecile could run it."

Valerie held her breath. There was no deficit of imbeciles around Lorraine. She bit her lip and hoped Lorraine wouldn't suggest Patsy Einfalt or Purvis Twankey.

"It doesn't matter," said Lorraine. "If you're so concerned about the charity, you run it!"

Valerie tried to register her best look of surprise. "What? Me?"

"Sure, why not," said Lorraine, though with scant enthusiasm. It was evident Lorraine just wanted out of the whole mess. That was fine with Valerie. In fact, it was perfect.

"Oh, well, if you think I could do it," said Valerie modestly. "I mean, it would be such a great responsibility and honor to follow in your footsteps."

"Great," said Lorraine, again with very little conviction. "Follow in my footsteps. You can even have my shoes. I won't need them anymore."

Valerie pretended to giggle at the lame joke. Inwardly, she wouldn't be caught dead in Lorraine's shoes. They were definitely middle-market.

"I'd love to have your hand-me-downs," said Valerie, thinking she would burn them or, better yet, auction them off to some desperate Lorraine fan. "I guess we'll need to get that in writing."

Lorraine looked puzzled. "You can just go over to my house and empty out my closet. You don't need it in writing."

"Yes, of course," said Valerie. "I meant the charity. We'd need to get that in writing."

"Sure, whatever," said Lorraine. "But we can do that after I settle the reason for being Lorraine. You said Verity had some proof? Where is she? When can I meet her and get this all settled?"

Valerie smiled. "She has a cute little place, but you can't go there." Valerie had the address from Verity's bank employment records. She hadn't been there but imagined it was as drab and plain as its occupant.

"What? Why not?

Valerie tapped her on the side of the head. "Hello, Earth to Chesney... Lorraine Innis is the most famous woman in the world. You just can't go visiting."

"So, what am I supposed to do?"

Valerie smiled. "Don't worry. I've figured it all out. I've arranged a secret rendezvous for you. There are plenty of caves up on the Rock. You just need to write a note to Verity. I'll take it to her, and then you can meet."

Lorraine's face lit up. "That's a wonderful idea. I'll write it right now." She looked around. There was a desk in the corner of the room. Lorraine crossed to it and sat down. She opened the drawer. There were envelopes and sheets of writing paper but no pen. She turned to Valerie. "Do you have a pen?"

Valerie rooted through her oversized handbag. "I'm sure I do..." Reaching to the bottom, there was something that felt like a pen. Pulling it out, she found it was a tube of mascara, unopened with a seal upon it. It wasn't her brand. Valerie stared at it for a moment.

"What's that?" asked Lorraine.

"What? Oh, I picked this up… for you," said Valerie. She wouldn't use it, so she may as well look like she was being thoughtful. "A girl can't have too much good cosmetics."

Lorraine took it and nodded. "Thanks, though hopefully I won't be a girl or need mascara too much longer. Still, that was very thoughtful of you."

"Yes, it was," said Valerie. "You know me. I'm always thinking of nice things I can do for you."

Lorraine reached for her purse and put the mascara inside. "Oh, here's a little something for you, too. It's not designer makeup, but I guess I'm not as thoughtful."

She pulled out a large bag of M&Ms and handed it to Valerie.

"How sweet, thank you," said Valerie, trying to look enthused. She stuck the bag of candy deep in her large handbag. "Oh, here's that pen…"

"Thank you," said Lorraine, and she began to write.

– 85 –
The Eve of Forever

Verity Goodhue sat in her rented room and read the morning paper. There were several pages of stories covering Lorraine Innis' arrival in Gibraltar. The article said Lorraine was there in support of a major announcement by Purvis Twankey. Though he was a county singer, Twankey had supposedly discovered a significant breakthrough in the energy field. That was as unclear as it was odd. Verity knew that Lorraine had launched Twankey in his musical career, but she couldn't help but think this was just an excuse to come to Gibraltar. Fortunately, Verity had the proof needed to solve the mystery of Martina's death, or at least why she had replaced Valerie Fierro on that ill-fated trip to Chicago. She only hoped Chesney would understand, given his blind devotion to Valerie.

Verity had longed to be at the airport but realized this might have put Chesney in danger. Besides, she was bundled off with the rest of the staff on a last-minute outing for the bank's employees. Verity had only attended to avoid blowing her cover and arousing suspicion.

She looked at the photographs of Lorraine and covered up the shoulder-length hair with her fingers. Despite the layer of cosmetics on his face, it was easier to see her Beloved that way. Verity picked up the copy of the letter and re-read it. How could Valerie steal Martina's identity to terminate an unwanted pregnancy? The grace and forgiveness Martina extended to Valerie shone through even more strongly. It wasn't Martina's intention to ever let Chesney know the truth, but now it was imperative to tell him. Verity seethed when she thought that not only had Valerie done that to Martina but allowed Chesney to launch into the crazy Lorraine Innis scheme to find the truth. It all could have been avoided.

Verity clenched her fists, thinking of Valerie's subterfuge. But then she thought of her conversations with Li Gao. Ultimately, Valerie wouldn't get away with it. There was still a sovereign God who guided their destinies. And if there hadn't been a Lorraine Innis, Verity and Chesney never would have known the other was still alive. She took a deep breath and closed her eyes.

At that moment, she heard a slight scuffing sound. She opened her eyes and looked toward the door. An envelope had been pushed under it.

Maybe it was the landlady's weekly bill. Rising to her feet, she saw her name on the envelope written in a familiar hand; it was the handwriting of her Beloved!

Verity opened the door and looked up and down the hallway, but it was empty. Chesney probably hadn't delivered the note himself, not in his guise as Lorraine Innis. He must have had a courier deliver it. She closed the door and sat in the armchair beside her bed.

Her heart beat faster as she opened the envelope and unfolded the single piece of light blue stationery.

> *My Dearest Verity,*
>
> *I learned from Gao that you had come to Gibraltar in search of the solution to the mystery of Martina's death. I feared for your safety, as we don't know the forces with which we're dealing. But in my present mode, traveling undetected is impossible. I had to find an excuse to travel here, and now that I have, I am close to you.*
>
> *I long to be with you, but given the fame of that certain "lady," that is impossible without drawing attention to us. An ally has arranged for us to meet discreetly in one of the many carved-out passages in the Rock. I will be there waiting for you tomorrow, at 4 p.m.*
>
> *I hope you have some promising information to share so this current adventure can be brought to a satisfying conclusion. Then, we can finally be united forever, never to part again.*
>
> *With all my heart,*
> *Your Beloved*

Verity wept tears of joyful anticipation as she re-read the note. She did have promising information, very promising information to share with her Beloved. For a second, she entertained the thought that the note wasn't genuine. But having re-read every letter he had ever sent her, Verity knew every loop, every jot of Chesney's handwriting. Just as Chesney could never disguise himself to her behind a Lorraine Innis façade, neither could his handwriting or his prose style be imitated. She was going to see her Beloved tomorrow! And she would share Martina's letter with him. Hopefully, that would be the beginning of the end of, what did he call it? "This current adventure." Yes, this would bring them to the end of this current adventure, after which they would embark on new adventures, together forever.

– 86 –
Remote Possibilities

Robert Valvano sat in the rental car cattycorner to the bank. He looked in the rearview mirror at Shorty Long seated in the backseat.

"This is neat," said Shorty, "I feel like I got a chauffeur."

"Shut up," replied Robert, "and don't go getting used to it. I got to drive so you can press the button."

"Cause I made the bomb, right?"

"That, and so if we get caught, you're the one responsible," said Robert.

Shorty laughed and then suddenly stopped. "You ain't kiddin', are you?"

"Partially," said Robert. "No one's getting caught, but if they are, I won't be the one going down. Since Miss Fierro…"

"She's Mrs. Eckner now," Shorty interrupted.

"Shut up. Soon she won't be anything but a pile of ashes and an unpleasant memory. As I was saying, Miss Fierro is no longer the heir of the family business, so I don't have a motive to kill her."

"I don't got no motive either," said Shorty. "Do I?"

"Only your reputation in the area of explosive devices."

Shorty shook his head. "You blow up a couple of cars, and that's all anyone thinks about you. It ain't fair. I'm more than that."

"Yeah, you've expanded into exploding lipstick cases."

"Mascara," corrected Shorty.

"Shut up."

The pair fell silent as they waited for Valerie to emerge.

"Why didn't we just do it at the hotel," asked Shorty. "Or sitting in a café drinking a beer?"

Robert growled. "For several reasons, which is why you'll never be anything more than a *gavone* who blows up things. First, if you do it in

353

the hotel, there could be collateral damage. That runs into money, making the joint owners want more answers from the cops. The cops then have to work harder on the case, which increases the chances of finding you. Which raises the chances that'll you'll talk, which increases the likelihood that you'd have an unfortunate accident before you can finger anyone else.

"Same goes for doing it from a café. We'd be sitting out in the open, which increases the chances someone will remember you sitting there pushing a button just as some broad gets her ass blown off.Finally, aside from being concealed, we can drive down the street, following her, and wait for the right moment. That means you don't blow her up when she's in a crowd. Innocent passersby getting hurt increases the chance that they'll dig deeper. You got that?"

"Yeah," said Shorty.

"And finally, we can drive away in a car," noted Robert. "You can't drive a café."

"Not unless it was like a food truck," said Shorty.

"Yeah, well, the rental place didn't have any food trucks," said Robert. "What's the range of your thing?"

Shorty looked puzzled for a moment. "Oh, you mean this?" He held up the detonator. Robert's eyes grew wide with panic, and Shorty quickly hid the device from view. "I just need to be within ten yards."

"And how powerful is the blast?" asked Robert. "How far does she have to be, so no one else gets hurt?"

Shorty rolled his eyes upward in thought. "Oh, I say about five feet, ten feet to make sure no one gets hurt by flying body parts. But there won't be much of that. I really packed it with good stuff. It's gonna be beautiful. She won't know what hit her."

Robert nodded. "Too bad. I wish she had a split second when she knew who was doing it."

"Me?"

"Me, you *strunze*! If it goes well. Otherwise, you're on your own."

They sat in silence for another ten minutes.

"What if she don't come out?" said Shorty.

"She's got to sooner or..." Robert sat up. "Make that much sooner. There she is."

Valerie Fierro walked out of the bank alone.

"So far, so good," said Robert as he started the engine.

"How far?"

"Shut up," said Robert. "I mean, she's alone, not that I wouldn't mind that little prick Eckner getting it, too."

"I could do another one for him if you want," offered Shorty. "Only he don't use makeup or carry a handbag."

"Don't be so sure," muttered Robert. He waited to make sure Valerie was going on foot. It was only a few blocks to her hotel. Then when he was certain, Robert put the car in gear and started slowly up the street.

"Okay," he said to Shorty. "We're coming to an intersection." The light turned red and they stopped. "Perfect, no one else is crossing."

"We're close enough," said Shorty.

"Let her get halfway across," said Robert. "NOW!"

Valerie crossed the road.

"Press the f**kin' button," growled Robert.

"I am, I AM!" squealed Shorty Long.

"We're not close enough," snapped Robert.

Shorty looked to the side. He could see evidence that the radio signal was working to their right and left. A door on a parking garage lowered, and the automatic security lights over a shop flicked on and off.

"We're close enough," said Shorty looking at the device.

"You f**ked up," said Robert. "I'll get her at the next corner."

Valerie Fierro walked on, unaware that she was being followed or that she was in any danger at all. At the next block, she was again by herself as she paused to look at a display in the window of a shoe store.

"Okay, keep down," said Robert. "We'll be less than five yards away. NOW!"

Again, Shorty pressed the button for all it was worth, but again there was no explosion. He did notice the lights in the shoe shop window coming on and off.

Robert only noticed that his half-cousin was entirely unexploded. He made up for it by having his own controlled detonation as he stepped on the gas and drove off.

"What did I bring you halfway around the world for, you *stunad?* You can't do a simple job."

"Maybe she didn't have it on her," reasoned Shorty. "She could have taken it out of her handbag, ya know."

"Broads don't clean out handbags," said Robert.

"Maybe she did," countered Shorty. "If she did, maybe it's in her room at the hotel. We could wait until she's in there and try again."

"And blow up the hotel without knowing if she's even near enough to it!" Robert continued voicing his disappointment in vivid Sicilian.

Shorty just stared at his remote. When they stopped at another light, he pressed it again. The traffic light turned green. Robert started. Shorty pushed it again. The light went back to red. He pressed it a third time, and green returned.

"I'll be glad to get out of this f**ked up country," snapped Robert. "Even the traffic lights are f**kin' goofy."

Shorty smiled to himself. He had an idea.

− 87 −
The Kindest Cut of All

Lorraine Innis hung the "do not disturb" sign on the doorknob and then bolted the door. Drawing the drapes, she turned on the light and undid the double locks on the smaller of her two suitcases. The first one had already been unpacked. That one had contained all Lorraine's clothes and the accouterments of her womanhood. There was so much to being a girl, she thought. Lorraine promised that Chesney Potts would never complain about any feminine regimens Verity might go through. She remembered Chesney's father fuming at how long it took Mrs. Potosky to get ready. Now, thanks to his time as Lorraine, Chesney greatly appreciated all that. Lorraine had an even greater anticipation for leaving all that behind, and very soon. Valerie promised she had delivered the note to Verity. They would meet up on the Rock, in one of the tunnels, just below one of the old gun emplacements. It would be tomorrow afternoon, but Valerie said Verity asked to move the time back an hour. According to Valerie, Verity had proof of who was responsible for Martina's death. With that mystery solved, Chesney could stop being Lorraine. They would get justice for Martina, and then Verity and Chesney would get married and live the rest of their lives in peace.

The second suitcase held all she needed to be Chesney. Li Gao had gotten her some men's clothes, and he had also bought her a good wig. Thankfully, Lorraine Innis' fame had made her signature shag hairstyle very popular and, consequently, much copied, even in hairpieces. Lorraine took the wig and shook it to fluff it out. Then she held it up to her own head.

"A perfect match," said Lorraine. "How ironic that Lorraine Innis would need a Lorraine Innis wig."

She put the wig down and pulled out two more acquisitions of Gao's: an electric clipper and a pair of barber scissors.

Then she took off her dress and slid out of her bra, letting her prosthetic breasts flop onto the bed.

"I won't need you two much longer," Lorraine muttered. The fake hips also came off. Lorraine slipped on her robe and took the clippers and scissors into the bathroom.

She disrobed and stared at the mirror above the sink. Aside from the times when she had been under hypnosis and programmed to accept it, Lorraine had never gotten used to seeing a woman's head atop Chesney's male body. As much as she hated the incongruity, it was comforting to see the resemblance to Aunt Elinor.

"Well, from now on, Aunt El," said Lorraine, "I'll have to be satisfied with your picture."

Lorraine cleaned the makeup from her face, then picked up the scissors. She trimmed back her feathered bangs and then the longer hair atop her head. Next, Lorraine picked up the clippers, selected a depth-setting attachment, and snapped it over the blades. Turning it on, Lorraine trimmed the brown tresses from the sides and back. She paused every few swipes to check her progress.

When she was done, Lorraine rubbed her hands through her hair. Looking at the clippings in the sink and on the tiled floor, she pondered what she had done.

"Goodbye, Mrs. Innis," said Lorraine. Then she looked up. It had been over a year since that person had looked back at her in the mirror, and it was oddly unfamiliar. When she started growing her hair, Chesney Potts had been considerably heavier. The man mirror was almost a complete stranger,

"Hello, Mr. Potts," said Lorraine.

Nearly a complete stranger… but one most welcome.

– 88 –
The Temperamental Prospective Lover of Shorty Long

Michael Valvano and Alphonse entered the hotel lobby carrying their suitcases.

"Good thing we're back to a place that speaks English," said Alphonse. "Spain was okay. The food was good, but they all converse in Spanish, especially when they talk."

Michael laughed. "Well, soon, our travels will be over. I just wanted to stop back here in Gibraltar to see if there are any loose ends."

"With Miss Fierro, I mean, Mrs. Eckner?" said Alphonse. "Only the last time we seen her, she wasn't exactly commodious."

"No, she wasn't," said Michael. "But we have to be charitable to Valerie. She's been through a lot. I think she's very confused and not at all happy."

"I get that way on those spinning rides at the Italian Festival back home," said Al. "It starts out fun and exciting, but they make me dizzy and sick to my stomach."

"An apt description of how Valerie may be feeling right now," said Michael as they approached the front desk. He looked at the time. "Almost eleven. I thought we'd be here sooner. I hope they still have our reservation."

"I hope we get a room so we can get room service," said Al. "Something American, like a pizza."

The night clerk welcomed them.

"We'd like to check-in. The reservation is under Valvano," said Michael.

The clerk checked the registration terminal. "Yes, is that Michael or Robert? Oh, sorry, you must be Michael. Robert has already checked in."

Michael's eyes widened. "Robert? That's my brother. Is he here?"

The clerk confirmed that he was and gave Michael the room number.

"Let's put our cases in our room," said Michael after they'd checked in. "Then we'll visit my dear brother."

A half-hour later, they knocked on Robert's door.

The door swung open. "I've been trying to call you. Did you get your gizmo working? I told you..."

"Hello, Robert," said Michael.

"What the hell are you doing here?" said Robert.

"Just stopping by on our way back to the States," said Michael, pointing over his shoulder. "You remember, Alphonse."

"Yeah, sure, I should. I fed him long enough," grumbled Robert.

"Hi ya, Mr. V.," said Al. "You also remunerated me."

"I'd like to remunerate you permanently," said Robert.

Michael pushed into the room with Alphonse following. "Sure, we'll come in. Can't have a family reunion in the hall. Nice suite you got here. We just have a regular double room downstairs." Michael sat down on the sofa. Al sat down on the opposite end.

"Please," said Robert dripping with sarcasm, "make yourself at home."

"Thanks," said Michael. "I don't want to impose, but we just got in and haven't had a chance to eat. Mind if we call room service."

Robert growled but nodded toward the phone. Alphonse took that for a yes, and ordered a pizza.

"Hope you got a large," said Michael. "Enough for four."

"Four?" said Robert. "Who else are you bringing?"

Michael shrugged. "No one else. I thought you were expecting someone. You've been calling them. Something about their gizmo?"

"What? Gizmo?" Robert fumbled. "No, no, I was calling the hotel maintenance. The, uh, the TV remote don't work."

Alphonse picked up the remote from the coffee table and pointed it at the television. It immediately came on.

"Your technical difficulties seemed to have been remedied, Mr. V.," said Al.

"Great, thanks," muttered Robert.

Michael smiled. "Good thing we dropped in. We were surprised to see you here, Robbie. On a little vacation? No, that couldn't be it. Meghan and the kids aren't here. Oh, right, the family has that bank here in Gibraltar. Of course, we're not full-blooded Valvanos anymore. I bet you're helping cousin Valerie."

"Something like that," said Robert.

"That's very nice of you, Robbie," said Michael, knowing his brother hated to be called "Robbie." "Maybe we can all get together for a big family party. And I read Valerie's other cousin, Lorraine, is in town, too. That would be fun to all have a big reunion."

Robert forced a smile on his face. "Yeah, yeah, good idea. You got to take advantage of those opportunities when you can. You never know how long everyone will be around."

The telephone rang. Robert picked up the receiver. "Where are you? ... where? ... What the hell are you doing there? Arr..." He stopped and looked at Michael. "How did that happen? ... Don't say anything to anybody? ... Okay, okay..."

Robert hung up. There were tiny beads of sweat on his forehead.

"Bad news?" asked Michael cheerfully.

"No, no," said Robert, "I just gotta go out."

Michael looked at his watch. "At this time of night? Can't it wait until morning?"

"Yeah, and the pizza is coming," said Alphonse.

Robert gave him an icy stare.

"That's okay, Al," said Michael rising. "You wait here for the pizza. I wasn't hungry. I'll go with my brother."

Robert began to protest.

"Nonsense," said Michael, "it will give us a chance to have a private chat on the way."

"On the way to where?"

"To wherever we're going," said Michael.

There was very little chatting as they caught a cab at the hotel entrance. Robert gave directions to the driver out of Michael's earshot. Within a few minutes, they stopped outside a two-story building fashioned of irregular stones. Two blue lamps on either side of the entrance identified it as the police station.

"Nothing serious, I hope," said Michael as they got out of the cab.

Robert grunted, paid the driver, and they went inside.

After some words at the front desk, they were buzzed through to an interview room; there sat Shorty Long looking very forlorn.

"Hi, Shorty," chirped Michael. Robert gave him a dirty look, though not as filthy as the one he reserved for Shorty.

"What did you do?" growled Robert.

A detective sergeant in plain clothes standing in the corner spoke. "D.S. Lines, sir, are you this man's attorney?

"Me? Do I look like a mouthpiece?"

"I'm representing Mr. Long," interrupted Michael. "I'm not licensed in Gibraltar. We're just visiting. This is Mr. Valvano. My name is Zimmer. What exactly has Mr. Long been accused of?"

D.S. Lines extracted a small remote from a manilla envelope and held it up. "Mr. Long was observed walking down Main Street, pointing this device at various business establishments, after hours, and generally causing various disruptions."

"Various disruptions?" asked Michael.

"Yes, Sir," said the D.S. "Lights going off and on, security gates raising and lowering, and alarms being set off."

"It was a misunderstanding," pleaded Shorty.

Michael gestured for him to be quiet. "May I see the device?"

360

D.S. Lines handed it to Michael, who examined it and nodded. Given Shorty Long's chosen profession, Michael had a good idea this was some sort of detonator for a bomb.

"Thank you," said Michael, returning the item. "Was there any actual property damaged?"

"No, Sir."

"I think I can clear this up, Detective Sergeant," said Michael. "If I can have a word with you in private." He glanced at Robert. There was panic in his brother's eyes.

Twenty minutes later, all three of them were being escorted out of the police station.

"What did..." Robert began.

Michael raised his hand. "I'll explain it back at the hotel."

They entered Robert's room to find Alphonse finishing the last piece of a large pizza.

"Shorty Long," said Al, wiping an anchovy from his mouth. "What are you doing here? I haven't encountered you since the night I almost precipitated your untimely demise."

Shorty nodded.

"This ain't no meeting of the *gavone's* social club," growled Robert. He grabbed Shorty by the lapels. "What the hell were you doing with that remote, looking for a..." He turned, remembered Michael, and fell silent.

"A bomb?" suggested Michael.

Shorty and Robert both feigned surprise.

"Sit down," said Michael. They did so on the sofa beside Alphonse. Michael paced back and forth for several laps, stroking his chin. Then he stopped. "Alphonse, what is Shorty Long's forte?"

"Forte? Oh, wait, I had that one a few weeks back," said Al. "That means what's he good at? Everyone knows that. It's blowing stuff up."

"Right," continued Michael. "And we know my brother here is good at making plans. So, when you put the two of them together, what do you get, Al?"

Alphonse scratched his head. "Planning... to blow something up!"

"Right, and what could they blow up in Gibraltar?"

Al's mouth dropped open, and he looked toward the window. "The Rock!"

Michael smiled. "No, I don't think so. There's no profit in that. Well, we'll just leave their target aside for now. I have a very good idea of what it was, but that's not important at the moment. Now, Shorty, if you would tell me what you were doing walking up and down the shopping district after hours with that detonation device? I know your little excursion came as a complete surprise to Robert."

Shorty Long explained how he had discovered that his remote emitted a radio frequency that seemed to control various security devices.

Robert slapped the back of Shorty's head. "You dumb bastard. It didn't work for… well, for something else, so you thought you'd try breaking into stores?"

Shorty nodded sheepishly. "It wouldn't be breaking in if I unlocked the store. There were some jewelry places…"

"Shithead!" said Robert delivering another slap. "You're not a burglar. You're not smart enough for burglary. You do explosives, and even that not very good."

"Very well," corrected Alphonse. Robert shot him a censorious look.

"Fortunately, it wasn't very well," said Michael. "As it is, I got you out of it. I told the police you were an inventor in the states working on a new car remote. I explained that you only discovered your remote was setting off those devices while taking your evening stroll."

"Thanks, Mike," said Shorty. "This is the second time you pulled me out of it."

"You're welcome," said Michael. "But I promised them you were going home tomorrow, on the next flight out."

Robert snorted. "I suppose you told them I own the car company."

Michael chuckled. "No, they wouldn't have believed that. I didn't think you wanted to be identified as Shorty's employer, especially if they didn't accept the first story. So, unfortunately, I lied. I told them you two were lovers."

"Me? With that little shit?" bellowed Robert.

Michael shrugged. "They believed it. Oh, by the way, you have to take the next plane, too."

Robert Valvano stormed into the bedroom, leaving a trail of expletives in his wake and slamming the door behind him.

Shorty stood up. "I think I'd better pack," he said. He looked at the bedroom door and shook his head. "It would never have worked out. He's too temperamental."

– 89 –
A Charwoman from the Knees Down

Verity Goodhue's hand trembled slightly as she did up the buttons on the blue shirtwaist dress. Blue was Chesney's favorite color. She didn't know how well lit the tunnels up on the Rock of Gibraltar were, but still, she hoped he would be able to appreciate it. Atop the blue background was a delicate floral pattern that made her feel soft and demure. She wasn't exactly sure who would be meeting her, Lorraine or Chesney. If it was the former, Verity wanted to be more feminine than Lorraine. If it was Chesney, she just wanted to look her best.

Brushing her long brown hair, Verity debated using a clip to pull back her tresses. Or should she wear a hat? She had a pretty straw hat. Or...

"Oh, for pity's sake," she said, catching herself, "you're not going on your first date. You're going up there to give him the letter."

Verity told herself that but still carefully applied the light cosmetics she wore, finishing with a spritz of perfume.

She turned to the closet for her shoes. At first, Verity selected the cute white pumps but then stopped. Though they only had a two-inch heel, the pumps probably wouldn't be the best for clambering around on a tunneled-out rock.

With a sigh, Verity returned the shoes to the closet and picked up the blue plimsolls she wore when cleaning the bank. Their rubber soles were better suited to the terrain of the Rock. After lacing them up, Verity stood and looked at herself in the full-length mirror on the closet door. From the knees up, she felt perfectly presentable to meet her Beloved. From the knees down, with her white ankle socks and blue sneakers, Verity felt like a charwoman.

While she wanted to look good for her Beloved, Verity was more concerned about that letter, or more specifically, how Chesney would react to it. She feared that he had a huge blind spot the exact size and shape of Valerie Fierro. What would he think when he read in Martina's own handwriting what Valerie had done? According to Chesney, Albrecht Eckner had made the change in plans that sent Martina to Chicago and her death. The fact that the letter had been in Eckner's safe tied the two circumstances together. Was this enough proof to lay the blame at Valerie's feet?

Verity looked at her watch. It was time to go. She would take the cable car up the Rock. In her purse, along with the letter, was a map of the tunnels. Verity had circled the place where they would meet. Closing the door, she said a silent prayer for the meeting.

– 90 –
A Question Concerning Microwaved Hamburgers

The veranda outside the hotel was filled with reporters. Lorraine Innis peeked through the curtain in the anteroom. She had promised Purvis Twankey an impressive stage for his announcement. With the Rock of Gibraltar rising behind the lectern, it couldn't get much more dramatic.

Lorraine glanced at her watch. She would have just enough time to introduce Purvis, then hurry back to her suite, change clothes, and remove any vestiges of Lorraine Innis. Then, as Chesney, she would rush to meet Verity up on the Rock. Once she had the proof that Valerie assured her was there, she could lay aside Lorraine for good.

It was perfect that the media was already there. Later, Lorraine Innis would have one last press conference. There she would tell the truth. Lorraine wasn't real. She had debated the subject and had discussed it with Li Gao. The easiest thing would be for Lorraine to disappear. Then Chesney and Verity could go away and live their lives in peace. But how long would that last? If Lorraine Innis just vanished, it would cause a worldwide frenzy. She recalled how crazy everyone had been to locate the imaginary Martin Innis. The madness would double if Lorraine was missing. Someone might figure it out. Or, Valerie or Clodagh might let the truth slip out, not deliberately, of course. He would trust either of them with his life. No, it would be better in the long run to admit it all. There would be a clean break. No one would be looking for Lorraine. There would probably be anger, but it would eventually die down when the media found a new shiny subject upon which to fixate. Despite the difficulty it might cause Chesney in the short term, Lorraine Innis had to be laid to rest once and for all.

"Howdy, Miss Lorraine!"

Lorraine turned around to see Purvis entering with Patsy.

"Hi, Lorraine," said Patsy. "Are we late? Sorry if we're late. I went to a bookstore to get a Spanish phrase book, but after I bought it, I realized that everyone here speaks English... almost as good as we do in America."

Lorraine smiled and nodded at Patsy. She looked at them, standing there, just beaming at her. A melancholy feeling swept over her. She wondered if she'd ever see them again after today. She would miss them.

"You okay, Miss Lorraine," said Purvis. "Only you look like I felt after I lost my darling Darlene. It was on a ghost train at Blackpool."

Patsy gasped. "A train with ghosts?"

"Shucks, they warn't real ghosts," said Purvis.

"It's an amusement ride, Patsy," explained Lorraine. "It's sort of like a ride through a haunted house."

"Oh, that's a relief," said Patsy before her expression darkened. "Wait a minute, who's this Darlene, and why was she your darling?"

Purvis smiled wistfully. "I loved her with all me heart."

"All your heart!" said Patsy.

"Darling Darlene, my pet rat," said Purvis. "I thought she'd like the ride, but she hopped off in the dark and left me flat. And I never found her again."

Patsy relaxed. "Oh, I guess that's okay. I mean, we won't be having any pet rodents around the house after we get married, will we?"

Purvis put his arm around her. "Who needs a pet rat when I've got you?"

Patsy looked up into his smiling overbite and returned it with her own toothy grin.

Maybe, thought Lorraine, maybe she wouldn't miss them that much after all.

"Yes, okay," said Lorraine, glancing at her watch, "are we ready to get started?"

Purvis reached into his pocket and pulled out a ragtag sheath of papers. "Got me words and stuff right here."

"Fine," said Lorraine. "I'll introduce you, and then I'll have to leave."

"Will we see you later," asked Patsy. "At the reception? They're having a really nice party. We'll even have..." Patsy leaned forward and whispered: "cocktail wienies!"

Lorraine stared at her, wondering why cocktail wienies were worthy of hushed awe. She looked at Purvis.

"Yeah, on them little sticks!" He added.

Lorraine shook her head. "No, probably not, sorry. I have to attend to some business. It's of a personal nature. I need..."

There was a knock on the door, and an event assistant stuck in her head.

"Excuse me, Mrs. Innis," she said. "But there are some people here who say they know you."

"We're about to begin," said Lorraine. "Who are they?"

The woman started to answer but was pushed aside.

"It is us!" The door swung open, and Nikolai Kropotkin entered.

The arrival of Kropotkin was surprising enough, but the appearance of Clodagh Clott on his arm was even more shocking.

"President Kropotkin... CLO!" Lorraine rushed to embrace them both.

"What are you two doing here and together?" exclaimed Lorraine. "Clo, where have you been. I thought..."

"We had a little adventure," admitted Clodagh.

"And about to embark on another," said Kropotkin, "on the sea of matrimony."

Lorraine's jaw went slack. Clodagh raised her hand to display an impressive diamond ring.

"We owe it all to you, Lorruska," laughed Kropotkin. "All of it, from saving my life to getting my little Clott kidnapped."

"Kidnapped? I didn't have her kidnapped..."

"They thought I was you," shrugged Clodagh, "even though I'm half-an-inch taller."

"Pah! Bulgarians," said Kropotkin. "They can't tell one beautiful woman from another. Fortunately, I can." He squeezed Clodagh's shoulder. "We wanted you to be the first to know. And I knew you would not mind."

"Mind?" laughed Lorraine. "I'm delighted!"

Kropotkin winked. "I know now why you found me so resistible," he said in a low voice. "Clodagh has told me your little secret."

Lorraine's eyes widened, and she looked at Clodagh.

Clodagh leaned forward and whispered in Lorraine's ear. "That you like girls."

Lorraine breathed a sigh of relief. Then she realized she was about to reveal the truth about herself anyway.

"Oh, well," said Lorraine, "I'm sorry if I misled you, Nikki."

Kropotkin waved dismissively and laughed.

Lorraine looked at her watch. "I'm sorry, but we really have to begin this press conference for Purvis. And then I have an urgent appointment. I should be back in an hour or so, and then we'll all sit down for a proper reunion and a long chat."

"That'll be nice," said Purvis, "we'll have a reunion, 'cept I don't know them. So for me, it'll just be a union."

Lorraine rolled her eyes and took Purvis by the elbow. "Come on, Purvis. Everyone else can watch on those monitors."

Lorraine and Purvis stepped out onto the veranda into a barrage of flashes and shutter clicks. She approached the podium and adjusted the microphone for her height.

"Thank you all for coming," she began. "We're here in the shadow of one of nature's great landmarks to hopefully unveil one of humanity's landmarks: the quest for renewable energy. I'm here to introduce the man who will explain his discovery that has far-reaching potential and ramifications.

"Most of you only know Purvis Twankey as a recording artist. Purvis is a friend and one of the most imaginative individuals I've ever met. If it were not for his inventiveness, I probably wouldn't be here today. Before he ever climbed the record charts, Purvis was an amateur inventor. Admittedly, some of his creations have been a bit far-fetched. But then progress is often made by those who dare to try the outlandish and unique. I don't know the specifics of Purvis' latest invention. He will introduce that and answer your questions. So, without further delay, I am honored to present my friend, Purvis Twankey."

There was a smattering of applause and several shouted questions directed toward Lorraine. She simply turned and made her way to a staff exit.

Purvis Twankey stepped to the microphone.

"How do, all," he said. "Thank you, Miss Lorraine. I hope I can live up to that swell introduction." Purvis looked at the media throng staring at him. "Did you ever microwave a hamburger?"

– 91 –
Rock, Leather, Plimsolls

Valerie Fierro checked her watch.

"She should be here in a few minutes," said Valerie. "You know what to do?"

Albrecht Eckner rolled his eyes. "I find that question quite insulting. Do I know what to do? I've been clever..."

"Underhanded," she interrupted.

"We'll compromise and call it conniving," he said without a trace of remorse. "I've been conniving way before you got your first training bra, which I would guess was about the age of seven."

Valerie gritted her teeth. She couldn't wait until the divorce.

"You need that letter back," Albrecht continued. "Taking it from Little Miss Cleaning Woman will be easy. I just don't know why we had to come up to this tunnel to do it. I could have done it as easily at the bank."

"But you forget," she said, "that Miss Goodhue thinks she meeting someone else. Someone she likes. Her guard will be down."

"Who does she think will be here?"

Valerie stood with her mouth agape. She didn't know whether to say Lorraine or Chesney since she didn't know which version would show up. Not that it mattered. Valerie told Lorraine to come later. That would give Valerie enough time to settle everything.

"Never mind," said Valerie, "just as long as she doesn't know it's you. Stand over there, in the shadows."

◆

As the cable car left the station, a recorded narration was reciting statistics about the Rock. It also warned about interactions with the apes that would be encountered at the top.

Verity Goodhue barely paid any mind. She didn't have any food with her, nor was she interested in simian encounters. The only interaction she craved was with her Beloved.

The car was empty, aside from her. The operator down at the station mentioned that it was usually more crowded. He attributed the absence of fellow passengers to the time of day, the dinner hour, and the event taking place at sea level.

"There's that big do," said the man at the station. "I expect that's where everyone is."

Verity knew the event to which he was alluding but feigned ignorance.

"Not only is that singer going to be there, you know, Purvis Twankey," said the man, "but Lorraine Innis, too. *The* Lorraine Innis!"

Verity nodded and smiled.

"Some announcement or something," continued the man. "Maybe they're going to announce they're getting married."

Verity stifled a giggle.

"No, straight up," said the operator. "It's been done before. John Lennon and that Japanese woman got married here. I mean Gibraltar. They didn't get married in the cable car station. That Twankey fellow is a pop star, too."

"But Lorraine Innis isn't Japanese," noted Verity facetiously.

The man's expression fell. "No, you're right; she isn't. Must be something else they're going to announce. Still, that's where everyone must be. The Rock isn't going anywhere; you can visit it anytime. But it's not every day you can see two celebrities in Gibraltar."

Hopefully, Verity thought, as the car neared the top station, there would soon be one less celebrity in Gibraltar. That press conference was going on now. Verity assumed Lorraine would slip away for their rendezvous. She lifted the flap on her purse. There was the copy of the letter Martina had written to Valerie Fierro. Verity prayed it would be all Chesney needed to solve the mystery of Martina's death and put Lorraine Innis to rest forever.

The recording was true to its word. Apes were hanging around the cable car's terminus. Verity clutched her purse close to her side as an attendant opened the door. The last thing she needed was fight with a monkey for her handbag, especially with the letter inside. As a precaution, Verity made a copy of the letter and left it back in her room.

Verity asked for directions to the top of the Rock. That was a disused military post called O'Hara's Battery. She was to meet Chesney halfway there. He would be waiting for her in one of the tunnels along the way. The attendant pointed the way. Verity thanked him and made her way up the steps, taking care to avoid the apes nearby.

The wind was much stronger atop the Rock, especially as it jetted through the paths carved out through the ancient limestone. The air, warm at sea level, was chilly up here. Verity's summery print dress, which had been so comfortable in the town, was a trifle thin now, especially with the breezes billowing around her skirt. At least she had had the sense to wear her plimsolls.

As she approached a bend in the tunnel, Verity could see a figure in the shadows. She had wondered in what guise her Beloved would be. It would be difficult for someone as famous as Lorraine Innis to appear in a public spot, even one as remote as a cave in a rock. Probably, given Chesney's need to continue as Lorraine, if just a little while longer, he would attempt some androgynous disguise.

A trousered leg stepped from the darkness. Verity was glad. She knew Lorraine Innis always wore skirts, but it was nice to meet her Beloved in trousers.

"I hope I'm not late," said Verity.

The figure emerged fully into the light. "Actually, you're right on time. I admire punctuality in my employees, even the cleaning woman."

"Mr. Eckner?" Verity stepped back. "I... I didn't expect, that is, I was supposed to meet someone here. Someone else."

Albrecht Eckner smiled, though it was far from a friendly expression. "I guess I'll have to do."

"No," she said, "you don't understand, my... my Beloved is coming. They'll be here any minute."

Albrecht Eckner drew closer. "No, you don't understand. No one else is coming, but I'll collect what you were going to give them."

"I don't know what you're talking about," said Verity, backing up against the tunnel wall.

Eckner came closer. "Oh, I think you do. I could have turned you over to the police, breaking into my safe like that. But if you return what you've taken, I'll let you off with a warning. Just don't do it again."

"I didn't break into your safe," said Verity. "I don't know what you're talking about."

Albrecht Eckner had her cornered against the rock. He adopted a nonchalant pose. "Oh, I think you know. You have a letter that was in my possession."

"That's not yours," said Verity.

"Well, it's certainly not yours," he said. "I'm holding it for a, well, let's say, a friend."

Verity almost said it was for his wife but kept her mouth shut. She glanced around. Albrecht Eckner was taller than her but didn't appear very strong. Also, he was wearing designer loafers. If she could get past him, Verity was confident she could outrun him back to the cable car depot in her rubber-soled shoes. "I... I.. don't have it," said Verity. "I left it in my room."

Eckner smirked. "I know you have it," he said. "You were told to bring it with you."

The sneaking fear that had played through Verity's mind came to the fore. Chesney had written that note to her. It was in his handwriting. But he had been duped into it by Valerie Fierro. She had to get back to the cable car.

"Okay, okay," said Verity opening her purse, "I'll give it to you."

"Good girl," said Albrecht. "I knew you'd listen to reason."

Verity reached in her purse and grabbed the envelope containing the bill for her room rent. She held it out to Albrecht Eckner, but as he reached for it, she dropped it. When he stooped to pick it up, Verity shoved him with all her might, pushing him over. She made a dash back the way she'd come. Verity had only gone ten yards when she came up short. There, standing in her way, was Valerie Fierro.

"I thought so," said Verity.

Valerie stared at her. "But still you came," she said.

"You changed Martina's plans," said Verity. "But why?"

Valerie sighed. "I'm not going to explain all that. Besides, it doesn't matter now. I had hoped you'd be sensible and go off and have a boring little life with him."

"He wouldn't let it go," said Verity. "Not after all he went through. And you let him go through this whole charade knowing the truth all along."

Valerie Fierro reached up and fingered her necklace. "You've got to look out for yourself first. He should have worried about himself and not a girl who was dead. Now give me my letter."

"I'm glad you've admitted that aloud," said Verity looking past Valerie. "Did you hear all that, Chesney?"

Valerie Fierro spun around, but there was no one there. Verity turned and ran back up the tunnel. Ahead, she could see Albrecht Eckner getting to his feet. Just in front of him was a side tunnel that went higher. Verity dashed up it, past the sign that read: "O'Hara's Battery."

Behind her, Verity could hear Valerie Fierro shouting. "After her!"

– 92 –
The Discovery That Will Last a Lunchtime

They say inspiration comes from the strangest places," began Purvis Twankey as he addressed the assembled media. "Mr. Newton had an apple fall on his head, and we got gravity. I don't mean we got it. They had gravity a'fore that. I mean, folks weren't floating around in the air. They just didn't know what it was that stuck stuff to the Earth.

"And that Greek fellow, him what took a bath and got his water displaced. He didn't expect when he stepped into the tub that he'd get inspired. He just did.

"Like I said, great ideas come from the oddest places," continued Purvis, "and this one came from my own head. As I was saying, I was eating a hamburger. That is, I bought hamburgers for me and my finance, that's her over there, the pretty gal doing a blush. Hamburgers is Patsy's favorite. That's her name… Patsy, not hamburger. Anyway, I got her a hamburger, and it went cold afore she could eat it. She don't like cold hamburgers, nor do I, so I said, 'don't worry, I'll put them in the microwave, y'know, to warm them up.

"Well, I did, and when I took the first bite, I had my apple on the head moment. The meat was just right, but the pickle… she likes extra pickles, does our Patsy… the pickle was too hot. It nearly burned me mouth. That's when I made the discovery what was there all along, sitting on top of the hamburger!"

Purvis flung his arms open wide. He expected the press corps to burst into applause. Instead, they were just staring at him with bewildered looks.

"Uh, on of top the burger…" repeated Purvis quietly. He scratched his head. "Don't you see? The burger was warm, but the pickles were hot! The pickels held the heat! That's the answer to the world's energy problem."

373

A woman reporter in the first row raised her hand. Purvis nodded to her.

"Hot pickles, Mr. Twankey?"

"Right," cried Purvis. "Everyone wants to run cars and things on batteries, but until now, it takes lots of metal, and then, when the battery's clapped out, you got a hunk of useless metal."

Purvis walked over to a table with several items under separate cloths.

"See here…" he pulled the cloth off the first item to reveal a car battery casing. The top was removed, and the case was filled with pickles. The media representatives giggled. "Right, see, you're laughing, and rightly so. It's just a battery box of pickles. But it t'aint the pickles, but that what they're made of! So, I figured what was needed was a bigger pickle."

He removed the next cloth to reveal a cucumber the size of a desert cactus. Gasps could be heard from the crowd.

"I graphed that to make it so big," said Purvis. "I expect I'd win a few prizes at the county fair with this fella. But that's not why I did it. I figured we could make batteries out of this. A gherkin this size would yield three regular car batteries. See?"

He removed the last cloth to reveal a clear plastic battery casing filled entirely with a green slab of pickle.

"With this, we got an endless supply of battery power. When it's used up, we got more growing."

"Batteries from cucumbers?" asked a reporter.

Purvis pointed at his battery. "Not just cucumbers. It works because of the combination of cuke and salt, like what's in pickle brine. I not only grew 'em big, but I also grew 'em already pickled!"

Purvis Twankey held out his hands in triumph.

The assembled media just stared.

– 93 –
Lorraine Innis Under New Management

Lorraine Innis hurried up the back stairs of the hotel. Her suite was on an upper floor, but she avoided the elevator to reduce the chances of being seen. She reached the top floor and paused a moment to catch her breath. Her heart was pounding, not just from climbing the stairs but from the adrenalin racing through her body. Opening the door, Lorraine peered out into the hallway. It was empty. She rushed to her suite, unlocked the door, and slipped inside.

Lorraine looked at her watch. She had only a few minutes to change and make her way up the Rock to meet Verity. She just had to wash the makeup off her face and change into men's clothes to emerge as Chesney.

Entering the suite's bedroom, Lorraine kicked off her flats and turned toward the closet. For a second, Lorraine thought she was looking at the mirror. Then she realized the figure standing before her looked like her but was wearing a different outfit. It was one of her skirt suits, but she wasn't in it.

"Hello, Mrs. Innis," said the figure.

The voice was similar to her own but different. It reminded Lorraine of her own early attempts to master a feminine timbre. Despite appearances to the contrary, Lorraine suspected the person was a man.

"Who are you?" said Lorraine, "and why are you wearing my clothes?"

The figure smiled. "The better to impersonate you, my dear."

"Impersonate? You're a man, aren't you?"

The figure nodded. "I know I couldn't fool you," he said. "What gave me away?"

Lorraine pointed at her own throat.

"Ah," said the man, "yes, the voice. I've been working on it. Good enough to fool most people, but then you're not most people. Granted, when you encounter someone in your suite, wearing your clothes, you're halfway there. You know I'm not you, so it raises many questions in your sharp little mind. Fortunately, most people won't have that advantage when they meet me."

"Meet you?" said Lorraine. "Do you intend on going out dressed as me?"

"Not just dressed as you," he said. "I'm going to be you. You see, Mrs. Innis, I've worked too hard to create you, to allow you to retire."

"Create me?" Lorraine sat down on the edge of the bed. She wracked her mind. She had created Lorraine. It was done with Valerie's help, but no one else was involved. She had invented the details of Lorraine Innis' life and... Suddenly, she recalled the mysterious appearance of all those details the previous year; how all the fictitious elements of her backstory had materialized as fact in the public record. She recalled the conversation with...

"Paul Rocher," whispered Lorraine.

The man nodded. "Bravo, Mrs. Innis. You really are remarkable. I do admire your thought processes. I knew you were special from the many pleasant hours I spent strolling through your mind last year."

Lorraine pointed at him. "The lemonade. That truth serum. That was you."

He nodded. "Right again. I really have admired you. I've been on so many operations over the years, but you've made this one very special."

"So special that you wanted to wear my clothes?"

He looked down at his appearance. "Oh, this is just the outside. Though I admit, it was a challenge to adopt your outward appearance. I don't have your advantage of being born female."

Lorraine bit her lip. Then she glanced at the clock beside the bed.

"Yes, well, now you know how the other half lives," said Lorraine. "I'd love to talk about your gender dysphoria, but I have an appointment that I'm very anxious to keep."

The man eyed Lorraine as if he were trying to read her mind. She turned away.

"An appointment?" he said slowly. "Now, it wouldn't be about your quitting, would it?"

Lorraine looked up in surprise.

"Ah, of course, it would," he said, noting her reaction. "That seems to be your motivation. Thank you for not asking how I knew. I know a lot about your affairs."

Lorraine wondered who had talked or, more likely, who had been tricked into it.

"I would try to talk you out of your early retirement," he continued, "but as you can see, I've come to the conclusion that wouldn't do any good." He gestured down at his female disguise. "Though, I am a sport. I'll give you one last chance now that you understand my motivation."

Lorraine smirked. "Your motivation? I can't say I come close to understanding it."

He shook his head. "You disappoint me, Mrs. Innis... again. You've been set up as the most powerful woman; pardon me, that's sexist, the most powerful person in the world. I was content to stay in the background. I planned to watch with great interest to see how you would wield your power. You see, I trust your innate wisdom and goodness. The problem with goodness is that too much of it ruins everything. That's the fatal flaw of heroes. They're often too virtuous for their own good."

"So, your proposal," said Lorraine, "is that I continue as I am, or rather, that I wield my influence to usher in some new world order."

He shrugged. "That would have been it, Mrs. Innis, but I can tell from your tone that would be unacceptable."

"And so you plan to take over for me?" she laughed. "Won't it quickly become obvious there are two Lorraines running around? I plan to disappear, but won't someone notice the difference?"

"I doubt it," he hitched up the hem of his skirt to reveal a small holster strapped to his thigh. He pulled out a small pistol and pointed it at Lorraine. "You see, there will only be one Lorraine Innis."

Instructing Lorraine to put her hands behind her head, he retrieved her purse from the bed. Keeping one eye on her, he rifled through her bag.

"Forgive me for violating the sanctity of your handbag, Mrs. Innis. Ah, here it is. Quite obvious... another downfall of goodness."

He held up the ticket Lorraine had purchased for the cable car, along with the map of the tunnel.

"What do you want that for?" asked Lorraine.

"This? This tells me where your meeting is," he said. "And I appreciate that you circled the location and even wrote the time on it." He glanced at the clock. "Yes, you were in a bit of a hurry, weren't you. I take it this appointment was integral to your plans to disappear. Something to do with a letter. Oh, please, don't ask me how I know. Your friend, Mr. Verve, told me about it."

"Verve? But I haven't seen him since he was in London," she said.

"Ah, yes, the dinner," he laughed. "The garlic capsule was a cute ploy you used to avoid his romantic advances."

Lorraine looked surprised.

"Oh, don't worry," he said. "Verve was a gentleman. He didn't kiss and tell. I was there as the waiter."

"Verve *was* a gentleman? You mean..."

He nodded. "Yes, I killed him. I don't usually admit as much, but I feel a special affinity with you. That plus, no one will know after I kill you."

Lorraine looked at the pistol.

"Don't worry," he said. "It's not that kind of a gun. That would be too messy and too noisy. No, this, like the special lemonade, is another of my designs. It's a poison dart. Once it hits you, you'll die instantly."

"What about the body?" she asked. "Two Lorraines, one alive and one dead, is even more of a problem than two live ones."

He smiled. "Now, don't worry your pretty head over that, dear heart. I've got it all worked out. After I keep your, or shall I say, my little rendezvous, I'll dispose of your body properly. Trust me. It will be done neatly and discreetly. This isn't my first cha-cha, though I've never assumed the identity of the deceased."

"I am honored."

"Believe me," he said, "I wish you were a little less virtuous." He closed Lorraine's purse and slung it over his shoulder. "Now, if you please, lower your arms and sit on the edge of the bed."

Lorraine did so, staring him in the face.

"Please," he said, "don't look at me like that."

"It makes it more difficult for you, does it?"

"No, not at all," he said. "I've done this so often it's quite easy. I'd rather remember you as you always were, the way I'll carry on for you. It's not like Lorraine Innis is going away."

"Just under new management?" said Lorraine.

"Exactly," he aimed the gun at her. "Say cheese."

Lorraine just looked at him, expressionless.

"Okay," he said, "have it your way."

He fired the poison dart into Lorraine's chest. Her eyes rolled upwards, then shut, as she fell backward onto the bed.

– 94 –
The Cab That Didn't
Go to Africa

Agent Margie Mackay sidled up to Paul Rocher as they stood at the rear of the press conference.

"Everything seems orderly," said Rocher. "Mrs. Innis introduced Twankey a few minutes ago."

Margie watched as Purvis Twankey continued to speak.

"What's he doing with that big pickle?" she asked.

Rocher shook his head. "Beats me. As long as he's not hitting someone over the head with it, I don't care. That's not why we're here. Is Mrs. Innis okay?"

Margie nodded. "I assume so."

Rocher turned to her. Concern was etched on his face. "You assume?"

Margie immediately felt her throat tighten. "Well, yes, she spoke, then left the stage. You saw that."

"And where did she go?"

"I, uh, she went back to the area just behind the stage, to the room she walked out of, the room with the others... I, uh, assume."

Rocher rubbed his hand across his face. "There's that word again. So, you didn't actually see her back in that room?"

"I saw her go in that direction... generally," said Margie.

Rocher grabbed her by the elbow and started off toward the staging area. "Come on!"

"I'm sure she's okay," said Margie, hoping that was true.

"I'll be sure when I see her," said Rocher.

Rocher flashed his credentials to the security guards at the door to the area. He looked around the room. Several people were watching the television monitor, including Nikolai Kropotkin.

"Mr. President," said Rocher showing his ID, "I'm Rocher, Secret Service."

"Yes," said Kropotkin, coolly, "I remember you, from Delaware."

Rocher felt the blood rush to his face. He had been detailed to Kropotkin the night Lorraine thwarted the assassination attempt.

"Is Mrs. Innis here?" asked Rocher.

Kropotkin smirked and pointed at the TV. "If Lorruska was here, do you think we'd be standing here listening to this imbecile boasting about his vegetables?"

"Nick," said Clodagh Clott, "don't be such a Russian bear!" She noticed the agent with Rocher. "Margie, it's me, Clodagh. Nick, this is Agent Mackay."

"Glad to see you're still with us, Miss Clott," said Margie. "But have you seen Lorraine? Maybe she went to the ladies' room?"

Clodagh informed them they hadn't seen Lorraine Innis since she left the podium.

Rocher thanked them and pulled Margie aside. "We've got to contact the Gibraltar police if we can't verify the location of Mrs. Innis."

"Relax," said Margie, not feeling particularly calm. "I'm sure it's nothing..."

"You saw that news report," he said. "Verve didn't kill himself, and if Lily..."

"He's in Nairobi," said Margie.

"Nairobi?" said Rocher. "How do you know? Did you get some intelligence I didn't see? I read the briefings."

Margie bit her lip. "It wasn't in a briefing. He told me."

Rocher grabbed her by the shoulders, then realizing he was manhandling a subordinate, quickly released her.

"You saw Vyvan Lily?"

She nodded.

"Why didn't you inform me?"

"Because," she paused. She had never broached the subject of a superior's personal life. He stared at her. "Because of your college girlfriend. Lily told me about it."

Rocher's face went through a series of emotions. Margie wasn't sure if she'd just talked her way out of a career.

"Obviously," said Rocher, after taking a deep breath, "Lily told you that. What else did he say?"

"He wanted to make sure Mrs. Innis was planning to retire," she said. "And once he determined that was her plan, he left for Africa."

Rocher rubbed his hands through his thinning hair. "And you saw him leave?"

"Yes, I did," said Margie.

"You saw him get on a plane or a boat?"

"It was a cab."

Rocher gritted his teeth. "Agent Mackay, you cannot take a cab to Africa."

"He said he was going to the airport," she said.

"Unless you saw him get on the plane, had full view of all the exits, and then watched until the plane took off and disappeared over the horizon, you cannot trust Vyvan Lily. Come on."

He jogged off toward the hotel lobby.

"Where are we going, Sir?" she said, running behind.

Rocher ignored her question and stopped at the front desk. He flashed his badge, though he was outside of his jurisdiction.

"Mrs. Innis' room," said Rocher. "Call Mrs. Innis' room."

The clerk dialed the number.

"There's no answer, Sir," said the clerk.

"Damn," spat Rocher.

"Because the phone is off the hook," added the clerk.

"The room number, man!" barked Rocher.

The clerk replied, and Rocher and Mackay rushed toward the elevator. On the way to the top floor, Margie observed that Rocher kept reaching inside his jacket. She surmised this was purely out of habit since neither of them was licensed to carry a gun in Gibraltar.

"I'm sure she's fine," said Margie, hoping against hope.

Rocher grunted and kept staring at the indicator buttons as if he could will the elevator to speed up.

When the elevator stopped on the top floor, Rocher instinctively dashed to the right. Margie looked at the sign containing the room number.

"This way, Sir," she said, pointing down the long corridor to their left.

They started down the hallway, when there, at the end, a woman emerged from the last door. It was Lorraine.

"Lorraine, I mean, Mrs. Innis," Margie called.

Lorraine paid them no notice and walked toward the stairwell. Her stride was quick, without appearing hurried.

"Lorraine, wait," said Margie. "It's me, Margie Mackay!"

Lorraine had already disappeared through the door.

Margie turned to Rocher. "She must have heard me. Maybe she didn't recognize us. She didn't know we'd be in Gibraltar."

Rocher said nothing but ran toward the stairwell with Margie in tow. When they reached it, they looked down the stairs, which were empty.

"What now," said Margie. "She must have gone to another floor."

Without responding, Rocher ran down to the opposite end of the hall, near the elevators. There, there was a window overlooking the hotel entrance.

"Wait," said Rocher looking down. In a moment, a motor scooter emerged from the hotel garage.

"It's her," said Margie. "Where's she going?"

Rocher ignored the question and watched. In another moment, he said: "She's heading up the Rock!"

– 95 –
Assault on O'Hara's Battery

Verity Goodhue ran up the rocky path towards O'Hara's Battery, the summit of the Rock of Gibraltar. She put one sky-blue plimsoll in front of the other, scrambling to keep ahead of Albrecht Eckner and Valerie Fierro. As she ran, Verity thought of a conversation she had had with Chesney years before. They were watching a program on TV, and the pretty heroine was being pursued by the villains. The heroine entered an abandoned warehouse and immediately rushed up the stairs.

"Don't go up," Verity recalled shouting at the TV.

"What?" said Chesney.

"This drives me barmy," said Verity pointing at the girl running up the stairs. "They invariably do this in these chases. Why would you go up? Eventually, they will reach the top and then be cornered! It makes no sense. It's just foolish!"

"You could say it was the height of foolishness," laughed Chesney.

Now Verity was being pursued by villains, and she was going up. She had no choice, but still, Verity chided herself for being so foolish.

"Don't let her get away!" Verity heard Valerie Fierro shout, but she dared not turn around to see how close her pursuers were.

"She... she can't get... away," she heard Eckner puff.

Unfortunately, Albrecht Eckner was right. Despite having footwear better suited to the challenge and in better physical condition, Verity was trapped. She wondered if Chesney was coming or if they had done away with him before taking his place at the rendezvous.

Emerging from the last tunnel, Verity found herself on a narrow concrete path with just a thin rope railing on one side and the rock face on the other. Forced ever higher, Verity scaled the rough Mediterranean Steps, chiseled out of the Rock, and leading toward the top. Her heart pounded in her chest.

Verity climbed the steps to the entrance of the abandoned gun emplacement. There was a stairway going down. A sign indicated it led to the engine rooms and storage magazines. For a moment, Verity considered going down there but realized that would afford her no escape. Up top, at least, she had a chance. She looked around the flat concrete pad. There were steps to a large gun that pointed out over the Straits of Gibraltar toward Africa. Opposite, toward Europe, steps led up to a blockhouse surrounded by a chain link fence, behind which was a radio tower. While she weighed her options, the doughy frame of Albrecht Eckner came puffing up the steps.

"Why… why did you have to run… away," wheezed Eckner.

Verity just looked at him as he leaned on the railing, catching his breath. She stood along the opposite rail, five yards away.

"Do you really have to ask such a silly question," said Verity.

He took another gulp of air. "Give me that letter."

"And then what?" she said. "Then you'll let me go? You'll take me out to dinner?"

"You can give us that letter," said Valerie Fierro climbing the stairs.

"Or what?" said Verity. "You'll kill me."

Valerie tossed her head to one side. "That is entirely your decision."

Verity took the letter from her handbag and held it above her head. "I could just toss it over the edge."

"Please, don't be a drama queen," said Valerie.

"Like you?" said Verity.

Valerie smiled and took a step toward Verity. "Oh, you could never be like me. A plain girl like you? To an ordinary girl like you, excitement is having an extra spoonful of jam on your crumpets. Even the late Miss Fergus was more exciting than you."

"She was certainly more forgiving," said Verity waving the letter. "Martina forgave you, but obviously, you haven't forgiven yourself. Whether I hand you this letter or not, you will still have to live with yourself."

Valerie smirked and caressed the pendant around her neck. "You wouldn't understand. Needs must…"

"…when the devil drives," said Verity completing the quote.

"Oh, it's easy for you to moralize on my behavior," said Valerie. "You, who's never had a worry thanks to your rich father. My father wasn't rich, but he taught me to look out for number one."

"No matter how you do it?" said Verity. "Chesney told me this one," she pointed at Albrecht Eckner, "changed Martina's plans, but he didn't understand why."

"And now you know," said Valerie. "Shame you won't have the opportunity to tell him."

Verity backed up against the railing and looked down the sheer rock cliff overlooking the sea. Albrecht Eckner and Valerie had her cornered.

Verity's mind raced. She couldn't threaten to jump. That would suit their goals. If she handed them the letter, they would probably throw her off the Rock, anyway. She would have to fight.

"Wait," cried Verity as they crept within feet of her. "What if I made copies of the letter?"

Valerie shrugged. "We know where you live. I was the one who delivered Chesney's note. I won't even have to break in. I can just offer to help poor distraught Chesney clear out your room."

"Like you did after you killed Martina?"

Valerie sneered. "I did not kill her. That was an accident."

"And I'm sure you'll make this look like an accident, too," said Verity. She clutched the letter to her bosom as Albrecht Eckner lunged at her.

As Albrecht Eckner dove, Verity tried to dodge him, only succeeding by half. Albrecht's shoulder struck hers, pushing Verity over the railing.

Fortunately, the drop was only about eight feet to a concrete ledge. After that, there was a steeper, rockier fall. Verity pressed her back against the wall. She looked up to see Albrecht and Valerie peering down at her.

"Give us that letter," said Valerie, "and we'll help you up."

Verity looked down. Going down the Rock wasn't an option. The concrete ledge extended along the wall. She could stay there, but she couldn't climb up without help. Verity looked up again. Valerie wore a kind smile.

"Come on," said Valerie. "Give me the letter. We'll pull you up."

"And what will I tell Chesney?" said Verity.

"Who cares? Tell him whatever you want," said Valerie, "he'll believe it from you. He believed it from me, didn't he?"

"You're an accomplished liar," said Verity. "I can't lie to him. And he won't stop until he learns the truth."

"So what," said Valerie, "he'll just go on being Lorraine."

Albrecht Eckner did a double take. "Lorraine Innis is dumpy Cheesy Potts?! And you worried about a letter when you're holding the trump cards on the blackmail opportunity of the century! You really are an amateur sneak, Valerie."

"I'd rather not..." said Valerie.

"You'd rather not what?" laughed Albrecht. "Ruin your reputation in the eyes of a loser like Cheese Potts? You can always buy a new reputation, but chances like this are once in a lifetime."

As they argued, Verity could hear the sound of a motorbike approaching. It had to be Chesney. She had to distract them.

"Wait, wait," cried Verity. "I'll give you the letter."

The pair looked over the railing. "You know it makes sense," said Valerie. "Hand me the letter."

"Okay, okay," shouted Verity. "Here's the letter! Here!" She reached up, waving the letter.

"Get it," Valerie ordered Albrecht.

Albrecht leaned over and reached for the letter. "Steady me," he told Valerie.

From her vantage point, Verity saw a wicked grin overspread the face of Valerie Fierro as she reached down and lifted Albrecht Eckner's feet off the ground tipping him over the railing and onto the ledge with Verity.

"What the hell did you do that for?" Albrecht said as he scrambled to his feet. "You could have killed me!"

"Get the letter," said Valerie.

Albrecht snatched the letter from Verity's hand. She heard the sound of the motor stop. Chesney would be coming up the stairs in a moment. She didn't struggle, given the hope that Chesney was almost there.

"I've got it," said Albrecht, shoving it into his breast pocket. "Now get a rope and pull me up!"

– 96 –
Never Send a Macaque to Do a Woman's Job

Valerie Fierro peered over the railing at Albrecht Eckner and Verity Goodhue below her on the lip of concrete. A few steps beyond them was a sheer drop off the top of the Rock.

"Get me up," shouted Albrecht.

Just a few feet away, thought Valerie. Just a few feet, and they both would fall to their deaths. She would be rid of Albrecht. And the evidence about Martina would die with Verity.

No, thought Valerie, she wasn't a murderer. But if they weren't careful, well, that would be an accident. Valerie looked around. There were several gatherings of those small apes, the macaques, around. The narration on the cable car discouraged contact with them as they could become aggressive if frightened or annoyed. They also warned against displaying food around them as they would steal it.

"Are you going to get me out of here?" yelled Albrecht.

Valerie looked through her handbag. She had some chewing gum. Wait, she thought; Lorraine gave her some candy. Yes, there it was toward the bottom, a large bag of M&Ms.

"Get me a rope," called Albrecht.

Valerie looked over the edge. "Yeah, I'm looking."

"In your handbag?" he yelled.

About twenty feet away, on a railing up on the gun emplacement, were two of the apes. Valerie took the bag of M&Ms and waved it over her head. "Yoo, hoo!" she shouted, "who wants some candy?"

"Candy? Are you nuts," yelled Albrecht. "Get help!"

"M&Ms! Come and get your candy!" called Valerie.

The macaques perked up at the sight of the bag and started toward Valerie.

"Come on and get it!" cried Valerie. As they approached, she tore open the bag and sprinkled M&M's on the ledge below her.

"What the hell are you doing!" yelled Albrecht.

"Yes, stop that!" said a voice.

Valerie turned. The voice was coming from a familiar body. It was Lorraine Innis, or at least they looked awfully like Lorraine.

"What are.. who are... HEY!" Valerie cried.

Distracted by this Lorraine lookalike, Valerie didn't notice that while several of the macaques had gone for the candy, one went for the bag she had raised over her head. While another ape, coming from the opposite direction, jumped on her shoulder. Valerie screamed and tried to shake the monkey off her back. She succeeded, but only after the ape ripped off the necklace her father had given her.

"Hey, give me that!" Valerie swung her handbag at the macaque now sitting atop the railing. The blow sent the ape diving off the rail while her precious necklace flew off in the other direction, landing below on the Rock.

Valerie peered over the edge. Albrecht and Verity had scrambled away, each going in opposite directions on the ledge while the macaques greedily devoured the M&Ms.

"Damn," spat Valerie. "You can't trust a f**kin' monkey!"

"Valerie, what's going on?"

Standing aside her on the railing was the person dressed like Lorraine.

"I don't know how you know me, but..."

The person smiled. "Know you? I'm your cousin Lorraine."

"You look like Lorraine, and you almost sound like Lorraine," said Valerie. She stared at the imposter. There was a deranged look in their eyes. Valerie stepped back. "Oh, yes, oh, right, you're Lorraine, sorry. I'd didn't recognize you at first... Lorraine."

"That's right, we're good friends," said the new Lorraine, "and we're going to be even closer."

"Hey, what's going on up there," shouted Albrecht.

The ersatz Lorraine peered over the railing. "Oh, my, that's a dangerous place to be. How ever did they fall over the edge?"

"Uh, it was an accident," said Valerie.

"I see," said the fake Lorraine. "And I believe there's a letter I'm supposed to get."

Valerie's eyebrows raised. Was this imposter sent by Chesney? Or were they working on their own? And why did they want Martina's letter? Then an idea flashed into Valerie's mind.

"Oh, yes, the letter," said Valerie. "He has it." She pointed at Albrecht. "Could you get it?"

"Yes, that's a good idea," said the fake Lorraine. She leaned over the railing above Albrecht and dangled her handbag toward him. "Grab hold of my bag, and I'll pull you up."

Albrecht reached up and clutched at the purse.

As "Lorraine" leaned over, Valerie saw her opportunity. She grabbed the imposter's ankles and pushed her over the side.

"Never send an ape to do a woman's job," muttered Valerie.

With Albrecht pulling from the other end, the momentum carried the fake Lorraine and Albrecht over the side, off the concrete ledge, and tumbling down the Rock. The pair struggled with each other and the force of gravity. They rolled with increasing velocity when suddenly there was an explosion, blowing them to bits. The apes scrambled away, screeching in terror. And what was left of Albrecht and the imposter tumbled off the Rock in flames into the sea far below.

Valerie stood with her mouth agape. They were gone. Albrecht was dead. She looked down. Verity Goodhue was still standing on the ledge staring at the point of the explosion. Then she looked up at Valerie.

At least, thought Valerie, the letter was gone. She knew this other Lorraine was an imposter. Had Verity realized it? If she thought Chesney was dead, Valerie could still get away with it. After all, Valerie had to look out for herself, especially now that she was a widow. Look out for herself? She instinctively reached for her necklace and then remembered. The ape had torn it off of her. She peered down and saw it glistening on the Rock about ten yards below the concrete lip.

"Hey," Valerie called down, "a little help."

"What?" said Verity.

"My necklace," said Valerie pointing down to where it lay. "That ape threw it over there. Be a sport and get it for me. And I'll get a rope to pull you up."

Verity stared at her. "You've got to be joking."

"No, really, it's not that far," said Valerie. "And you've got the right shoes for it. It'll be easy with your sneakers on."

"No," said Verity.

"C'mon, don't be a selfish little bitch all your life," said Valerie.

Verity just stared with her mouth agape.

"Fine," said Valerie, "I'll do it myself!"

Slipping off her shoes, Valerie lowered herself over the railing and dropped the remaining three or four feet to the ledge. Verity stood on the opposite end. Valerie glowered at her. And went to retrieve her necklace. It wasn't too steep, at least at first.

Valerie inched her way down. The necklace was there on a point just before a sharp drop. She got on her belly and crawled toward it. The jagged rocks tore at her blouse and slacks. They were haute couture, but they could be replaced. Daddy's necklace was priceless.

The necklace was now just inches away. Holding on to a small branch with her right hand, Valerie reached as far as she could toward the necklace with her left hand. She almost had it. Almost. Then the branch came loose, and she rolled over and down the Rock. She grasped for the necklace as she tumbled past it. Clutching it for a second, then losing it. The necklace went over the precipice and disappeared.

"DADDY!" screamed Valerie.

She fell further, the sharp rocks ripping her face as she rolled. Just as she was about to go over the edge, Valerie grabbed an outcropping of rock. She dangled there, alive, but with her clothes in tatters, her face bleeding, and her Daddy's necklace gone.

– 97 –
A Death Verified

Verity Goodhue stood on the ledge looking down at Valerie Fierro, clinging to a rock. If she had a rope…

"Verity!"

Verity looked up. There, looking over the railing, was Chesney. Not Lorraine, but her Beloved!

"Chesney!"

"Are you all right?" he asked.

"I'm fine," she said.

"I heard an explosion," said Chesney.

"Yes, there was…"

"Wait," he said, "I'll get a rope or a ladder."

Chesney turned around. Policemen and soldiers were coming up the stairs to the battery. He called them over.

"My fiancée is down there," said Chesney. "I just got here. There was some explosion or something. She can tell you about it."

An army sergeant stepped forward and directed his men to bring up Verity. A policeman asked Chesney his name.

"Potts, I am Chesney Potts," he said with a deep exhale.

"Yes, sir, Mr. Potts," said the policeman.

The soldiers were pulling Verity over the railing. She and Chesney embraced and kissed.

"Did you see it, ma'am," said the policeman. "Did you see Mrs. Innis die?"

"Die?" said Chesney. "Lorraine Innis is…"

"It just came over the radio," said the policeman. "It was picked up on one of the security cameras posted around the summit. Did you see it, ma'am?"

"Yes," said Verity. "I fell over the side there," she pointed. "Then a man, Mr. Eckner, fell over trying to help me, and then a woman…"

"Lorraine Innis," said the policeman.

"Yes, it certainly looked like her," said Verity. "She was pulled over the side. Then suddenly there was an explosion. It was horrible, but I'm sure it killed both of them."

The policeman nodded. "And you saw it."

"Yes," said Verity looking into Chesney's eyes. "I saw Lorraine Innis die."

"Then," said Chesney, "it appears that Lorraine Innis is dead." He hugged Verity tightly and whispered in her ear: "Finally."

"I saw her die, as well," said an American voice.

They turned around, and an older man flashed his identification. "I'm with the United States Secret Service. My associate, Agent Mackay, and I were part of Mrs. Innis' security detail. We were following her up here. We saw the explosion, too."

Chesney looked into Rocher's eyes and then looked away.

"HELP! WILL SOMEBODY HELP ME DAMNIT!"

Verity turned to the soldiers. "There's a woman down there." She pointed down the face of the Rock.

"We'll get her up," assured the Sergeant as he ordered his men into action.

– 98 –
A Much Better Place

Within an hour, the news had reached around the world with wall-to-wall coverage on all media outlets. The public's grief was unanimous over the death of Lorraine Innis. Fortunately for Purvis Twankey, the tragedy overshadowed the announcement of his bizarre plan for solving the search for renewable energy with giant pickles.

Clodagh Clott saw the first reports at the hotel along with Nikolai Kropotkin, Purvis Twankey, and Patsy Einfalt. They all watched in stunned silence at the replay of the footage taken from security cameras of Lorraine tumbling down the mountain, struggling with a man, and then both being blown to bits.

The international media crews that had been there to cover the press conference quickly departed to make their way up to the location of the incident at O'Hara's Battery. In addition, several helicopters began swarming around the site with the first live pictures from the scene.

While the others watched with tears in their eyes, Clodagh suddenly recognized a figure among the rescuers. It looked like Chesney. His hair was short, wearing male clothing, and looking terribly thin, but it was definitely Chesney. As the helicopter video zoomed in and out, Clodagh could see him with his arm around the young woman who had just been pulled over the railing. She had only seen photographs of the girl, but Clodagh would have sworn that it was Verity Goodhue.

"Are you all right, my dear?" asked Nikolai Kropotkin, nudging Clodagh's shoulder as she sat shaking her head.

"I don't believe it," Clodagh muttered.

"It is a great tragedy," agreed Kropotkin. "Not only for her friends but for the entire world."

She looked up into his grief-stricken face. Whoever was blown up, it wasn't Chesney. And somehow, Verity was alive, too. Clodagh didn't understand how they did it, but they did, or someone did.

"What?" she said. Clodagh realized she couldn't explain it to Kropotkin, nor would she ever try.

"I said," he repeated, "It is a tragedy. I know Lorruska believed in an afterlife. I only hope she is in a better place now."

Clodagh looked back at the TV screen. Chesney and Verity were embracing.

"Oh, yes, Nick," said Clodagh nodding her head, "a much better place."

– 99 –
Hijinks Often End in Tragedy

Chesney and Verity lost themselves in the crowd of rescuers at O'Hara's Battery. Thus they eluded the media now swarming over the site. Even without the corroborating news reports, the authorities all assumed that it had been Lorraine Innis who had been blown up. Valerie Fierro was pulled up on a stretcher and dispatched in an ambulance. Verity was the focus of the investigation, as the only other witness who had been there.

Verity was ushered into the back of a police van, insisting that Chesney, her fiancée, be allowed to come along. Fortunately, Chesney had brought a bucket hat that he pulled down over his eyes. That deranged intelligence agent had taken Lorraine's place. And now that Lorraine was believed to be dead, Chesney wanted nothing more than to keep her that way.

Verity told the police the truth, though not all the truth. She explained that she had gone there to meet her fiancée, Mr. Potts. Before Chesney arrived, she ran into Valerie Fierro and Albrecht Eckner.

She described leaning over the railing, and the police assumed she was trying to get a better view. Verity then said that Mr. Eckner fell over after her. Again, the police reasoned that he was attempting to help her. Verity kept silent. Then she mentioned the apes getting involved and Lorraine Innis showing up.

"So, to sum up," said the detective inspector, "you went up to meet your fiancée, but before he arrived, you ran into Miss Fierro and Mr. Eckner, whom you knew from the bank. Then you fell over the side, and Mr. Eckner fell over trying to help you?"

Verity agreed.

"That seems consistent with the video," said the inspector. "We don't have any sound, and from the camera angle, you barely show up. Now, you haven't been entirely honest with us, Miss Goodhue, have you?"

Verity looked at Chesney and then agreed with the inspector.

The detective inspector shook his head. "As I mentioned, we couldn't see you very clearly, but it appears that you were involved in horseplay. Fooling around with your friends. Those sort of hijinks often end in tragedy."

Verity nodded her head sadly. "I was rather foolish," she said.

"Still, I don't think you're responsible for whatever happened with Mrs. Innis."

"No, I wouldn't have had Lorraine Innis harmed for anything," said Verity. She squeezed Chesney's hand. "After all, Lorraine brought us together. But what caused that explosion?"

The inspector closed his notebook. "We don't know yet. With public figures like Mrs. Innis, for every hundred admirers, there will always be one or two individuals motivated by jealousy or hatred. Anyway, we'll have that statement typed up, and then you can sign it. We appreciate your help, Miss Goodhue."

Unaccustomed to using his male voice, Chesney had kept silent, but on the way out, he asked where Valerie was taken. They were told she was sent to St. Bernard's hospital. Chesney thanked them, and they were escorted out of the police station.

"It's only a short distance to the hospital," said Chesney. "Let's walk. It may sound odd, but I feel as if I haven't been outside for the longest time. It's like being released from prison."

Verity smiled and put her arm through his as they walked.

"I hope Valerie is okay," said Chesney. "Did you see her fall?"

Verity bit her lip. "Yes, I did. She was trying to retrieve her necklace. She lost it fighting with the apes."

"I hope she's not hurt too badly," he repeated.

Verity kept silent.

"Valerie said you had the information about Martina," he said.

"Yes, I do," she said. "But I don't want to go into it here, in public."

Chesney looked around. "Yes, this is probably not the best place. We can go back to my hotel…" He stopped and laughed. "I don't have a hotel. In fact, I don't even have a passport."

"You can visit the American consulate," she said. "They can issue you a replacement."

They arrived at the hospital and asked at the desk about Valerie. They were told she had been admitted and went up to the floor she was on. At the nurses' station, Chesney explained he was a friend of Valerie's.

"Oh," said the nurse, "what a tragedy about her cousin."

Chesney stared at the nurse for a moment until he realized she was referring to Lorraine. He agreed.

The nurse said Valerie was sedated, but they could see her for a minute. She led them to a private room down the hallway. The curtain was drawn around the bed.

"You have some visitors," said the nurse cheerfully as she drew back the curtain. "Just a few minutes; she needs her rest," whispered the nurse to Chesney and Verity.

Valerie was in the bed. Her face was heavily bandaged. Her eyes had a glassy appearance.

"Valerie, it's me," he said, "Chesney."

Valerie moaned in a groggy voice. She turned her head toward them, and suddenly her eyes grew wide.

"Verity's here," said Chesney. "You didn't know. She's alive. I mean, she's the girl from England. The one I was going to marry. We both thought the other was dead."

Valerie tried to look away.

"It's okay," he said. "Verity has the information about Martina. I haven't seen it yet, but I want to thank you."

Valerie looked at him and then at Verity. Her eyes seemed in a panic.

The nurse came back in and saw Valerie's agitation. "I think you'd better go."

"Yes," he said, "you're probably right." He turned to Valerie. "You rest, and we'll stop in later. Everything is going to be okay now. Thank you for all you did for us…"

Valerie began moaning loudly through the bandages.

"Really, you'd better leave," said the nurse.

Chesney agreed and left, turning to look at Valerie as they went.

"She was upset about something," said Chesney as they left the hospital.

Verity wore a look of concern. "I made extra copies of the letter, just in case. There's a little restaurant nearby. We can talk there."

– 100 –
Requiem for
Two Remarkable Ladies

Chesney and Verity sat in the corner booth of a small restaurant in Gibraltar. Chesney finished reading the letter a third time. He looked up and shook his head.

"So, Valerie had that letter all along," he said.

"I don't think so," said Verity. "It was locked in Albrecht Eckner's safe."

"Yes, so you said. Well, it's authentic. That's definitely Martina's handwriting. I just can't believe Valerie would do all that."

"People do strange things to hold on to items that ultimately don't matter," said Verity. "Fear is a strong motivator. Look at what Father put us through. Perhaps Valerie was afraid of losing your good opinion of her. Insecurity can make us do strange things. I remember a boy who jumped on a train in the middle of the night and ran away to London due to insecurity."

Chesney nodded and stared at the letter. "Martina understood that. She understood a lot. She extended forgiveness to Valerie. I suppose I can't do anything less."

Verity leaned over and kissed him tenderly on the cheek.

"Valerie isn't directly responsible for Martina's death," he continued. "But she almost buried me under Lorraine Innis. Ultimately, I have to agree with Li Gao. There is a sovereign power that has the final say in our lives. Gao once told me that God works things out for our ultimate good and His glory. Still, I'm glad Lorraine's dead."

"Lorraine Innis did a lot of good," said Verity, holding his hand. "She brought you back to me. So, I'll always hold a special place in my heart for her."

A man approached their table. "Pardon me," he said. "I couldn't help overhearing you talking about Lorraine Innis." It was Paul Rocher. "May I sit down?"

Chesney fumbled a bit but agreed.

"Did you know Lorraine?" Rocher asked.

Chesney and Verity admitted they had met her.

"A remarkable woman," said Rocher. He looked at Chesney directly. "I wouldn't really call her a woman. She was more of a lady."

They nodded in agreement.

"She reminded me of a remarkable woman I knew back in college," said Rocher. "I guess you could call her my first real love and the one who got away."

Verity squeezed Chesney's arm. "This one almost got away."

Rocher nodded. "You're very fortunate. Hold on to each other tight."

"Tightly," said Chesney softly. "Oh, sorry."

Rocher smiled. "I understand. Very well, I understand." He fixed his gaze on Chesney. At first, Chesney squirmed, and then seeing the warmth in Rocher's eyes, he relaxed.

"I did a lot of work for Mrs. Innis," said Rocher. "Some before she even met me."

"I'm sure she appreciated it," said Chesney.

"Yes, I know she did," said Rocher. "She was a singular creation, was Mrs. Innis. Many people loved her; some allowed that to lapse into obsession. I've read of people so obsessed with a celebrity that they want to become that person."

Verity looked at Chesney.

"Yes, I've heard that, as well," said Chesney. "I know of such a case. They actually impersonated the object of their obsession and tried to kill them."

"How did they do that?" asked Rocher.

"By shooting them in the chest with a poison dart," said Chesney.

"Fascinating," said Rocher, "and lethal, I would think."

"Yes," agreed Chesney, "fortunately, in that case, they were wearing a gel-filled... well, sort of a chest protector. They just pretended that it was fatal until the attacker left."

Rocher nodded. "Well, then, that worked out very well for them, didn't it? What happened after that?"

"Oh, the impersonator met with an accident, and the celebrity, well, they just retired to a quiet life," said Chesney. "Neither were ever heard from again."

"Sounds like the best possible outcome," said Rocher. "Oh, incidental to nothing in particular, the forensic report said the explosion was caused by a bomb concealed in Mrs. Innis' handbag."

Chesney's mouth dropped open.

"Yes, apparently, it was designed to be triggered remotely," continued Rocher.

"So, someone atop the Rock set it off?" said Verity.

"No," said Rocher, "the British Army demolition people believe it was put together by a clever amateur. Those sorts of devices are susceptible to radio frequencies."

"Those radio towers," said Verity, "there are all those towers up at O'Hara's Battery."

"Precisely," said Rocher. "It was lucky that none of us were carrying that purse."

Chesney's face went pale.

Rocher patted him on the shoulder. "Of course, neither you nor I would carry a handbag, let alone one with a bomb in it, would we?"

Chesney's mouth hung open. "Uh, no, I don't think I'll ever carry a handbag again... I mean, no, why would I."

Rocher nodded. "Yes, a quiet life, that's what I'm going to have. Well, it was nice chatting with you both." He started to rise.

"Uh, wait, Agent Rocher," said Chesney. "You talked about the one that got away."

Rocher stopped. "Yes, son?"

"It's just that it reminds me of a story my aunt told me," continued Chesney, "my Aunt Elinor. She had a similar experience. She said she always regretted it. She never got married, and until her dying day, I'm sure she held a place of fondness and highest esteem for that young man. I'm sure somewhere, wherever she is, she's pleased to know what a fine gentleman he turned out to be."

Rocher's eyes moistened. He held out his hand, and Chesney shook it.

"Well, I'm sure that fellow would be happy to hear that," said Rocher. "I'll leave you two to the rest of your lives. It's been a distinct honor, all of it."

They watched as he left the restaurant.

"He never said his name," said Verity after Rocher exited, "but you called him by name. Do you think he recognized you?"

Chesney nodded. "I'm sure he did. I certainly hope so."

– 101 –
The Genuine Long Island Girl

The paperwork was done, finally. Chesney got a replacement passport from the Consulate General in Gibraltar. Then after completing the license and the waiting period, Chesney and Verity were married at the Registry Office. As they came out, a soft rain was falling.

"I didn't bring an umbrella," said Chesney.

Verity looked into his eyes and smiled. "I'm glad. It's perfect. It reminds me of that night when we were first dating. We had been to the pictures, and it was pouring. We didn't have an umbrella then, either. And rather than running like mad, you took my hand, and we walked as if it was a beautiful night."

"We got soaked, I recall," said Chesney.

"Yes, we did," she said, "soaked and sopping wet. It was lovely."

"Lovely?" he laughed.

"Whether it's fair or stormy," said Verity, "it doesn't matter, as long as we're holding each other's hand, Beloved."

And they strolled through the rain, only pausing every few moments to kiss.

♦

The next morning Chesney was reading the paper while waiting for Verity to get ready.

"Sorry I'm taking so long," said Verity sticking her head out of the bathroom.

"I will never complain about how much time you take," said Chesney.

Verity rushed out and kissed him on the forehead.

He laughed. "What was that for?"

"That was for a certain lady, recently departed," said Verity. "She has made the perfect husband even more understanding. I just need to finish my hair."

Chesney was about to reply when there was a knock at the door. He opened it to find Clodagh standing there.

"Clo," said Chesney. He looked out in the hallway. She was alone. "Come in. Is everything okay?"

"I just wanted to see you before I leave," she said.

Verity entered, and Chesney introduced her.

"We're leaving, too," said Chesney. "Going for a proper honeymoon."

Clodagh smiled. "I thought so. I snuck away, hoping to get the full story of what happened."

"That wasn't me that blew up," said Chesney.

Clodagh shook her head. "Same Chesney Potoski. You always had the capacity to be so smart and so dumb in the same day. I knew it wasn't you. I saw you in the news footage. I couldn't tell Nick, President Kropotkin, or anyone else, but I knew it was you. I went to the consulate and then to the registry office." She turned to Verity, "oh, and congratulations. I feel I know you."

"Yes, I told Verity about the hypnotherapy," said Chesney. "You didn't tell Nikolai about it, did you?"

Clodagh snorted. "You're still alive, aren't you? I'm only kidding. He didn't suspect a thing, but I thought it was easier for him to mourn Lorraine than find out the truth. Either way, Lorraine is dead. May she rest in peace."

They invited Clodagh to sit down as she related the story of how she was kidnapped in Lorraine's place and then the rocky road to romance she and Kropotkin traversed.

"He really is very sweet," said Clodagh. "I love him, and he loves me. It must be something about Long Island girls he can't resist."

"I just glad he found a genuine one," said Chesney. "When will you get married?"

"Right after he resigns," said Clodagh. They expressed surprise. "Nick got the evidence on his old rival from the KGB. He's been arrested and should be locked away for good. Nick decided to retire from politics."

"To do what?" asked Verity.

"He wants to do charitable work," explained Clodagh.

"What about the Cross of Lorraine," said Chesney. "Would he like to take over that?"

"I was sort of thinking along those lines," said Clo, "but I didn't want to be presumptuous. I mean, there's you...'

Chesney and Verity both shook their heads. "I want to be as far away from anything Lorraine," he said. "I can't run the risk of anyone figuring it out. I was going to confess everything, but that lunatic rogue agent took care of that for me."

Chesney related the story of the Lorraine imposter and the events leading up to the incident on O'Hara's Battery.

"I can see why you don't want to run the charity," said Clodagh. She paused. "What about Valerie?"

Chesney hung his head. Verity rubbed his shoulder.

"It was Valerie's fault," said Chesney quietly. "I found out she wasn't a very good friend, after all."

Clodagh patted him on the knee. "I'm so sorry, Ches," she said. "I had my suspicions. I wanted to tell you."

Chesney shook his head. "I wouldn't have believed you."

"That's where I was going," she said, "when I was kidnapped. I was going to try and get proof."

"It's like you said, so smart and so dumb," Chesney said with a shrug.

Verity kissed him. "We all have blind spots, my Beloved. But I think it's a wonderful idea to turn the Cross of Lorraine over to President Kropotkin and Clodagh."

"Can we do that legally?" said Clodagh. "I mean, it's not like Lorraine had a will."

Chesney looked up and smiled. "Not yet."

Verity and Clodagh exchanged puzzled looks as he rose and went to the writing desk. Taking out a piece of stationary, Chesney began writing. He cleared his throat and announced: "For her final trick...." Then he cleared his throat again and spoke in Lorraine's register as he wrote: "I Lorraine Innis, being of sound mind...."

Chesney continued to write, and after about ten minutes, he signed the document as Lorraine.

"There," said Chesney. "I dated it a few days before the accident. I've distributed all of Lorraine's worldly goods and responsibilities to the people who will best appreciate each. I can't see anyone who would contest it."

"Not even Valerie?" asked Clodagh.

"Now that I know Valerie is more concerned with her reputation," he said. "She probably more afraid of me than I am of her."

– 102 –
The Strassburg Collection

The leaves had fallen from the trees in Strassburg, Pennsylvania, as Chesney and Verity drove the rental car into the picturesque little town.

"I hope she kept it," said Chesney as he parked in front of Denise Zane's law office.

"It's an old barn," said Verity with delight. "It reminds me of the mews cottages back home."

"I hope she still has it," he said as he held the door for his wife. "It will definitely help us get started."

Behind the railing that constituted the waiting area, Denise Zane was busily packing a briefcase. She looked up.

"You just caught me," she stopped and looked at her desk calendar. "Oh, no, you didn't have an appointment, did you? I don't have one written down, but it's been quite frantic the last few days. I'm going out of town for a wedding."

"Yes," said Chesney, "I know, your sister Clodagh."

"That's right," said the attorney and then stopped. "Wait, how did you know?"

Chesney smiled. "Denise, it's me, Chesney Potts, that is, Chesney Potoski, and this is my wife, Verity Goodhue."

"Verity Potts," said Verity. "I'm more used to it than he is."

Denise Zane stared at them for a moment, and then a look of surprise overspread her face. "Little Chesney Potoski! What are you doing here?"

"Actually, Denise," he said, "I'm here on official business. You have something for me, I hope."

Denise looked puzzled. "I don't know what you're talking about."

"Something left in your care by Lorraine Innis," said Chesney.

The look of puzzlement dissolved into one of shock. "You knew her?"

"I did," said Chesney. "She told me that if she didn't come to see you, I was to come and collect something. I hope you still have it, only it's more than a year. Things happened. A lot of things."

Denise crossed to the large office safe and began entering the combination. "You won't tell on me, but I didn't follow the instructions to the letter."

"Who would I tell?" Chesney laughed. "Lorraine Innis?" Then realizing Lorraine was supposed to be dead, he became serious. "I mean, rest her soul."

"That was a tragedy," said Denise. "When she came to see me, I had no idea she was about to become world famous."

"Neither did I," said Chesney.

"Good thing she did," Verity whispered in his ear.

"I meant you wouldn't tell the bar association," said Denise. "But aside from all that happened with Lorraine, our family had a lot going on. First, Clodagh started working for her, then Clodagh disappeared, and finally, she showed up to announce she was getting married to the President of Russia. I'm sorry to say I was distracted." Denise opened the safe and pulled out an envelope. She handed it to Chesney. "Mrs. Innis told me that someone I knew would pick it up. I never imagined that mysterious someone would be you. If that person didn't appear, I was supposed to deliver part of this to Valerie Fierro."

"You didn't read the letter inside?" asked Chesney.

"As you can see, the seal hasn't been broken," she said. "What about Valerie Fierro?"

"We're on the way to see her now," said Chesney. "Well, tell Clodagh to have a wonderful wedding. I wish we could be there, but we've already spoken to her about that. Bon voyage."

– 103 –
Pop and the
Fatal Pucker

The plane touched down at Heathrow Airport.

"And, now, we're home," said Chesney.

Verity squeezed his hand. "You're sure about living in England, Beloved?"

"Anywhere you are is home," he said. "Besides, it's as if Aunt Elinor was preparing me for this ever since I received her first letter. Being in Britain is like being closer to her, and your grandfather. Then there's Li Gao and Mr. Postlewaite."

"I wonder if dear Mr. Postlewaite will realize you've been gone. He didn't even know who Lorraine Innis was."

"Thankfully, there was one person in the civilized world unaware of her existence."

"Don't forget, Father is in England, too," said Verity. "I sent him a telegram that I was married. I thought it was more dramatic than a letter," she explained. "And if I had telephoned, it would have given him the opportunity to ask questions. All he knows is that I was married in Gibraltar, and I'm bringing my husband to England."

"How do you think he'll react when he sees me?" said Chesney.

"I hope he faints and is out for a week," said Verity. "No, make that a month. Eventually coming to is more than he deserves."

Chesney looked at her with one eyebrow raised. Her expression softened.

"Yes, I know, you're right," said Verity. "Leave retribution to a higher authority."

He smiled. "Good. I wouldn't want you to adopt a different persona just to get back at your father." As soon as he said it, Chesney's grin disappeared. Verity stroked his cheek.

"It's not your fault," she said. "You tried to see Valerie."

405

"She wouldn't even let me in," he said. "I wanted to forgive her. That's what Martina would have wanted. After everything I went through, do you know how difficult it was to forgive her?"

Verity nodded. "Yes, Beloved. I do. But it was even more difficult for her to be forgiven."

"Sorry, I keep bringing it up," he said, hanging his head.

Verity kissed his cheek. "It will get better. And it's all done. And it was a lovely trip. I got to meet your mother and your brother, not to mention your babysitter. Your mother was very sweet. She pulled me aside and told me the secret of being a good wife."

A wary look crossed his face. "Oh, yes?"

Verity smiled and, approximating an American accent, announced: "Always change your shelf paper at least once a year."

"And there you have it," he laughed.

"Now there's just Father," she said. "And that will be interesting."

After going through customs, they were met in the baggage claim by Mr. and Mrs. Carstairs, the servants at Lord Bagnold's London home. There were hugs and introductions and more hugs.

Mrs. Carstairs monopolized Chesney wrapping her arms around him.

"So you're the lucky fellow who captured our little wren," said Mrs. Carstairs.

Chesney looked at Verity. "Little wren, I like that!"

"Ooh, but you're not much more than bird yourself," exclaimed Mrs. Carstairs, observing his slim physique. "Don't they feed you? You need a little home cooking."

"I like Yorkshire Pudding," he said.

"You shall have it," she said. "My specialty."

"She has a lot of specialties," warned Carstairs as he escorted them to the car. "I have to watch my waistline."

"You've managed to keep trim, Mr. Carstairs," said Verity.

"It's all the exercising he gets," said his wife, "hopping around every time your father says 'jump!'"

"Now, now," said Carstairs, "mustn't bite the hand that feeds us. You'll give his new son-in-law a bad impression before he meets His Lordship."

Chesney smirked as they climbed in the back of Lord Bagnold's Rolls Royce.

"He's already met him," said Verity, "only Father doesn't know it."

"Then His Lordship will have another surprise," said Mrs. Carstairs with a shake of her head. "Two in one day!"

Verity looked concerned. "What's the other one?"

"The news has broken in just the last few hours," said Carstairs pulling a tabloid from the front seat and handing it to Verity.

She opened it to reveal the front page banner headline: "Lord Bogroll... FLUSHED!" The subhead read: "Paper Peer's Green Product Sees Red."

"What is it?" asked Chesney.

"It's that new toilet paper," said Mrs. Carstairs, climbing in the front seat. "He staked the company on its success."

"The one that I, I mean, that I saw Lorraine Innis advertising," said Chesney.

"The very same," said Carstairs as he started the car and pulled away.

"It's a blot on that poor woman's memory," said Mrs. Carstairs. "I don't know whatever compelled her to do those ads."

Verity looked up from her reading. "She had no choice, Mrs. Carstairs."

"Just a consolation then that she's dead," said Mrs. Carstairs. "She'd be spinning in her grave... if she hadn't been blown to bits, poor dear."

"What's wrong with the tissue?" asked Chesney.

"According to this," said Verity, "it was made from a new, more sustainable process. It was vegetable based."

Chesney's mind raced back to when Purvis Twankey had visited the commercial studio. Lorraine had decked Purvis, and when he came to, he was looking for his formula. Lord Bagnold handed it back to him.

"Giant pickles," muttered Chesney.

"The story said it was cucumber-based," said Verity. "According to this, Father rushed it into production. In actual use, the tissue proved to be strangely irritating."

"Read further," said Carstairs from being the wheel. "It puckered your bum."

His wife slapped his arm. "Don't be so cheeky!"

"Cheeky, she says," laughed Carstairs. "You know how your lips pucker up when you eat a sour pickle? Imagine that effect but down in the southern hemisphere!"

Verity modestly declined to read aloud but pointed out parts of the article to Chesney. The more severe reactions included constricted sphincters and chronic constipation.

"It concludes," said Verity, "by saying he's being sued."

"Again," added Chesney.

Soon they arrived at Lord Bagnold's London home on Eaton Square. Carstairs parked the car out front and opened the door for Verity.

"I'll bring your bags up to your room, Miss, I mean, Ma'am," said Carstairs.

"And I'll put on the kettle," said Mrs. Carstairs, "and I've made a fresh cake."

They thanked the Carstairs and climbed the marble steps to the front door.

"I've been looking forward to this moment," said Verity, fishing the key from her handbag. "Though now, I don't know what sort of a mood Father will be in with this lawsuit."

Chesney shook his head. "You'd think after that beard-growing perfume, your father would know better to pinch ideas from Purvis Twankey. I hate to say it, but it serves him right."

"That's the problem," she said, "it more than serves him right. I just don't know what seeing you is going to do. You're supposed to be dead."

"He knows I'm not dead," said Chesney. "Still, we can't put it off any longer."

Verity opened the front door and stepped into the foyer.

"Father," she called out.

A moan emanated from the library. Verity tapped softly on the library door, provoking another tortured lament. Taking this as a signal to enter, Verity opened the door a crack and looked in. Lord Bagnold was slumped in a leather wing chair, his shoulders where his rear should have been, his long legs stretched across the floor. The day's newspapers were strewn around him.

"Oh, daughter," he whimpered, "you's come just in time. If ever I needed the family bosom, it's now."

"Yes, Father," she said, "I saw the news today…"

"Oh, boy!" he moaned.

"I'm home from my honeymoon," said Verity. "I brought someone to meet you."

"Your 'usband, I expect," said His Lordship. "Please tell me you 'ad the foreword to marry a lawyer, a solicitor, or a banister."

"Sorry, Father," she said. "He's none of those things, but he is the most wonderful man in the world."

Lord Bagnold grunted. "I needs a lawyer, and you brings 'ome Superman."

Verity opened the door wide, and Chesney stepped into the doorway.

"Hi," said Chesney with a grin and a wave.

Lord Bagnold's mouth dropped open. He clambered to his feet and stared at Chesney. Then he blinked several times, rushed to his desk, reached for a pair of pince-nez glasses, and propped them on his Roman nose. Then he took them off and kept staring.

Verity and Chesney just stood smiling and holding hands. After shaking his head several times to confirm he was actually seeing what his eyes were conveying, Lord Bagnold began looking around the room, anywhere but at the happy couple. It was as if he were searching for an excuse.

Finally, he raised his brow as if he had a rationale.

"Why, why, you is dead," said Lord Bagnold pointing at Chesney. He looked to Verity. "Daughter, 'e's dead. We went to 'is funeral. Didn't we?"

Verity smiled. "Yes, Chesney's dead."

Lord Bagnold snorted. "Yes, I thought so. That would h'explain why 'e's so skinny. Well, you can't not marry a corpse."

"Actually, Father," said Verity, "it turns out that not only is Chesney dead, but so am I. And there's no law we could find against two corpses getting married. You could say it's a perfect combination."

"Dead?" said Bagnold, "you h'ain't not dead, daughter, not no 'ow."

"Sure she is," said Chesney. "Remember, you and I attended her funeral, Lord Bagnold, or may I call you 'Pop?'"

Lord Bagnold clenched his fist and his teeth. "Pop? I'll pop you, you scrawny little whelk!"

"Alive or dead," said Verity, "that scrawny welk is my husband now. Till death us do part."

"And since you had the forethought to kill us both off," added Chesney, "we won't have to part now."

Verity kissed Chesney. "Isn't my Beloved clever, Father?"

Lord Bagnold went through a series of apoplectic gyrations before finally throwing up his hands. "I suppose you expect some sort of h'explanation an h'apology of sorts."

Verity smiled. "You can do as you wish, Father. An explanation isn't necessary. We know why you did your dastardly deed. As Joseph told his brothers after they sold him into slavery: 'You meant it for evil, but God meant it for good.' An apology, if sincere, would do you more good than it would us. I hope you've learned that are some things you can't defeat."

"Gah!" snorted His Lordship. "Fine, 'ave your sticky mush. I 'opes you enjoy it. You might as well. Me own life's work is down the 'opper!"

"An apt metaphor, Pop," said Chesney. "Given your line of work."

Lord Bagnold sneered at the "Pop" reference. "You is all against me. First that Innis woman, then that dopey inventor friend of 'ers from Lancaster, then that Innis woman...."

"You've named Lorraine Innis twice," said Verity.

"Aye, well, if she warn't so flippin' popular, that pickled toilet paper wouldn't 'ave sold so well. I'm ruined! I've already got competitors wanting to buy me company. It's probably the only way out. Lorraine Innis! Curse the day I h'ever seen 'er. Just as well, she was blown up. Saves me the trouble!"

Chesney embraced Verity. "And with that, I heartily agree, Pop."

– 104 –
The Self-Sufficient Orthopedic Heir

Michael Valvano drove up to the entrance of *Bella Culo*. Gone were the henchmen and hangers-on with which his brother had adorned the home. Robert and his family had moved out. Rose Fierro owned the house now, though she didn't live there.

The most pleasant surprise of the entire Valvano-Fierro-Zimmer affair had been Rose Fierro. She was a generous woman. Not as flashy as her younger sister. In fact, she wasn't flashy at all but had that wonderful gift of being happy in her own skin and content with an ordinary life.

When she was informed by Julius Rosen that she was the sole heir of the Valvano estate, Rose immediately set to divide up the remaining assets between all of Nonnia's survivors. The fortune wasn't nearly as large as it had been. It was never discovered who transferred the bulk of the money to The Cross of Lorraine. Had it been up to Robert, he would have hired computer experts to decipher it. Rose, however, was satisfied that the dishonest gains had gone to charity. Everything else was distributed equally, except for *Bella Culo*, which Rose kept for her mother, and one other inhabitant.

Michael knocked on the door. Unlike in the past, Alphonse's hulking figure didn't answer it. Alphonse was off at college, training to be a kindergarten teacher. Robert had used his share of the inheritance to help pay the tuition for Al's dream. Instead of Al, a petite figure greeted Michael.

"Hello, Michael, come in," she said.

"Aunt Connie," said Michael as he kissed her cheek.

She led him back to the kitchen. "Sit down," she said, pouring him a cup of coffee. She placed a decorative tin in front of him and opened it.

"I just made some pizzelles."

Michael smiled as he reached into the tin and pulled out one of the waffle cookies. "I'd never say no to a pizzelle."

After some small talk, Connie's face grew serious.

"She still spends most of her days in that room," she said.

Michael shook his head. "It's almost a year. I had hoped..."

"Valerie's always been a stubborn girl," sighed Connie. "I don't know how two daughters can be so different."

Michael nodded and thought of his own brother.

"How is she feeling?"

Connie threw up her hands. "Physically, she's fine. The scars are there," she ran her fingers across her face. "They're obvious, but not hideous, except to Valerie. And she has to wear that thing." She gestured across her torso.

Michael nodded. In addition to the facial scars, the fall on Gibraltar had left Valerie with the need for a heavy surgical support corset.

"So different," mused Connie. "If that had been Rose, she would have done what she needed to do, and got on with life, and barely missed a beat. Valerie still hasn't told me what she was doing climbing on that Rock."

"And she doesn't get out at all?" asked Michael.

"She comes out for meals," said Connie. "And even then, she barely eats. Rose visits us twice a week. She's getting married."

"Nice," said Michael.

"Valerie hardly congratulated her," said Connie.

"And there have been no other visitors?"

"There was that nice boy," said Connie. "He used to work with Valerie back in the day. He came here with his wife. A nice girl. She's from England. In fact, he moved to England. He had a different kind of a name, Chauncey, or something like that. He was over here on a visit and made a special point to come all the way to see her. He heard about the accident."

"That was nice," said Michael.

Connie raised her hands. "Nice of him, but a wasted trip. She wouldn't even see him; she locked the door and wouldn't come out. But you know about that. You come here every month, and you still haven't had an audience with her highness."

"May I try again?" he asked.

"You can try," said Connie. She leaned forward and whispered. "I didn't tell her you were coming this time. Just knock and then enter before she can answer. She'll think it's just me."

Michael was hesitant but agreed.

He climbed the stairs and paused outside the door. It was Nonnia's old room, the best bedroom in a house of many bedrooms. Then he knocked, waited a second, and opened the door.

"Valerie, I know you didn't want…" Michael stopped at the sight that greeted him. There, in a darkened room with the curtains drawn, sat Valerie. She turned toward the door and then, seeing who it was, quickly turned away.

"Go away," said Valerie.

Michael closed the door behind him. "I wanted to see you…"

She turned toward him. "See me? See the ugly girl's scars? Well, take a good look." Valerie rose and approached him.

Standing face-to-face with her, Michael could see the three wide scars running from her ear across her cheek to her mouth.

"I meant I wanted to talk to you," he said.

Valerie turned and walked back toward the chair. Michael noticed her steps were halting. It was the first time he had seen her wear low shoes. Also, her dress was long and plain. Valerie's hair, always meticulously done, was now pulled back. In the dim light, he couldn't help but notice the resemblance to their grandmother.

"Does it hurt much," asked Michael, pointing toward her legs.

"Hurt? Ha," she said. "No, not too much as long as I wear my glamorous corset and my oh, so stylish old lady orthopedic shoes. Of course, I get all those wonderful items wholesale."

"Oh?"

"Yes, as the widow Eckner," she snorted, "I inherited his parent's hideous surgical supply store." She sat back down. "I was supposed to inherit this family's estate: the bank, the power, all of it. Instead, I get a disgusting emporium for cripples. And why not? That's what I am now."

"You're not disgusting, Valerie," he said.

"No? Pull back the curtains, Michael," screeched Valerie. "Get a good look. There was no one better at applying cosmetics than me. But even I can't do anything with this face now."

Michael crouched by her chair. "The first time I saw you, you weren't wearing any makeup."

"Yeah, or any scars!"

He took her hand. "We all carry scars. The worst ones are those that are on the inside. And beauty, real beauty isn't applied with a brush; it comes from within. When it comes from within, nothing on the surface can mar it or take it away."

Valerie stared at him. For a moment in the darkened room, Michael thought he could see a tear forming in the corner of her eye. His own eyes widened in hope. Then Valerie's brows lowered into a scowl pushing back the tear.

"Let me help," he said.

Valerie reached up and touched her neck as if reaching for something. Then her fingers fumbled.

"Get out, Michael," she said. "I don't need you or any man. I don't need anyone."

Michael waited a moment, hoping her defiance was the momentary hitting of a nerve. Instead, Valerie's expression hardened even further. With a sigh, Michael rose to his feet and walked to the door. He turned for one last look, hoping against hope for a thaw. There was none.

Michael shook his head. *"Prima I dente, poi I parenti,"* he said as he closed the door.

– 105 –
Four Years Later:
The Return of a Heart
and a Tie that Binds

The cheery little bell danced on its metal bracket, and Chesney Potts rushed to the door of the caretaker's cottage.

"Gao!" said Chesney greeting Li Gao. "Please come in. Let me pay the cab."

"No need, my friend," said Gao. "It was such a pleasant day; I walked from the station."

"That's over two miles," said Chesney. "You should have called. I would have picked you up."

"When one has earned their living driving for many years," said Gao, "it is a pleasure to walk when one can."

Chesney nodded, escorted his friend into the living room, and gave him a seat of honor by the fire.

"And how are mother and child," asked Li Gao.

"Verity is just putting Elinor down for her nap," said Chesney as he leaned on the mantlepiece.

"Fatherhood agrees with you," said Gao, "even more so the second time. You are beaming, my boy."

A toddler cut through the room at a breakneck clip until Chesney grabbed him. His legs continued to scurry at a furious pace.

"Herbie," said Chesney to the boy in his arms, "you didn't say hello to Mr. Li."

The toddler looked at Gao and smiled. "'lo, Mr. Li."

Li Gao bowed his head slightly. "And greetings to you, young Master Potts."

The boy's grin widened. "Mr. Li, did you..."

"Herbert Goodhue Potts," said Verity entering the room. "You have better manners to ask what Mr. Li brought you."

"Oh, I am quite positive he was going to ask me if I had a pleasant train journey," said Gao. "But, as the boy's godfather, it is incumbent upon me to not show up without an earnest of my goodwill."

Herbie looked at his mother. She nodded. "Yes," said Verity, "that means he brought you something."

Gao reached into his pocket and pulled out a yo-yo. "This belonged to Elinor," he noted to Chesney.

The toddler laughed. "You're telling fibs, Mr. Li. Elinor's a baby."

"He means your great aunt Elinor, Herbie," said Chesney. "May I?"

The boy handed it to his father only after securing a promise that he would quickly return it.

"I sent this to Aunt El," said Chesney, "when I was about nine."

"A yo-yo," said Verity with a laugh.

"She was so fun-loving," noted Chesney with a shrug. "When you're a nine-year-old boy, you figure your favorite aunt needs a good yo-yo." He turned over the wooden toy. On the back, he could still make out his childish scrawl written in marker: "To Aunt El" and a drawing of a heart. His voice grew soft. "She kept it all those years."

Verity looked over his shoulder and hugged him. "She couldn't throw away your heart."

"And what of the estate house's new owner?" asked Gao.

"Another rich businessman," said Chesney. "His first move was to divert the main drive so his entrance wouldn't have to go past our caretaker's cottage."

"And we had the fake grave and headstone removed before he took ownership," noted Verity. "It was disturbing to visit your own grave, even if it was filled with bricks."

"Ah, yes, the bricks your father buried," said Li Gao, "to add weight to the coffin."

"I offered to return them to Lord Bagnold, one at a time," said Chesney, "but he wouldn't stand still."

Verity poked her husband. "He's kidding, Gao. We've smoothed things out with Father. It was punishment enough to lose his paper empire. Frankly, he's much happier now. Father retired and opened a little seaside stand in his beloved Skegness."

"I h'am the only peer," said Chesney imitating Lord Bagnold, "wot sells winkles in the 'ole of Skeggy!"

"And his grandson," said Verity, stroking little Herbie's hair, "loves to visit him."

"And I see the charity is doing good works with Mr. Kropotkin and his wife at the helm," said Gao.

"Yes," said Chesney, "I hope we'll be able to visit them someday when the memory of Lorraine Innis fades a bit more. I'd like to see Purvis and Patsy, as well. They have a baby now, too. And they've written a book about Lorraine Innis. Thankfully, they don't know the full story."

Chesney's expression dropped.

Verity, knowing he was thinking about Valerie, kissed his cheek. "You've tried, Beloved. That's all you can do."

Chesney nodded. "Yes, still, I've no complaints at all. We have a home. I have my writing that earns our daily crust. It's all worked out. I'm just glad that's all behind us. It's like you always told me, Gao, what Paul wrote to the Romans."

"'And we know that in all things God works for the good of those who love him,'" quoted Li Gao, "'who have been called according to his purpose.'"

A timer went off in the kitchen.

"Well, dinner's just about ready," said Verity rising, "I don't know where…"

As if on cue, there was a knock on the door. Chesney answered it and escorted in their errant visitor.

"Am I early?" said Mr. Postlewaite.

"Precisely where you should be at the present moment, dear friend," said Li Gao, "as always."

"We're just about to eat," said Chesney.

Postlewaite started to turn for the door. "Oh, well, I'm sorry. I didn't realize. I could come back later."

"But we invited you, Mr. Postlewaite," said Verity, "for dinner."

Postlewaite looked around. "Oh, well, then, if it's not an imposition."

"Never an imposition, Mr. Postlewaite," said Chesney guiding him towards the dining room. The others followed.

They all took their seats around the table. Young Herbert was lifted onto a booster seat between his parents. His infant sister slept peacefully in a nearby carrier. Chesney asked Li Gao to offer the blessing, which he did. Verity excused herself and came back in a moment with a large dish.

"Nothing fancy," said Verity, "it's Mrs. Carstairs' recipe."

"And one of my favorites," said Chesney. "Toad in the hole."

"What a remarkable coincidence," exclaimed Mr. Postlewaite. "That was the name of one of Laurel and Hardy's films. Of course, that was a play on words, T-o-w-e-d in a hole."

"How very interesting, my friend," said Gao.

"Yes, but here's the coincidence," said Postlewaite reaching into his pocket and pulling out a rectangular box. He lifted off the lid. "This is a bow tie actually worn by Stan Laurel in one of their films. I've been searching for this item for years. I bought it at auction, and then a young woman stole it from me and sold it to a competitor, a fellow name Rathman."

"A young woman," said Verity, as she served the toad in the hole, "how terrible."

"That's not the worst bit," said Postlewaite. "I had actually befriended this girl, practically rescued her. And then she stole my most prized possession from me. I know you could never imagine such a dastardly deed."

Chesney and Verity exchanged glances. "No, never," said Chesney. Verity agreed.

"And just how I managed to retrieve it," said Postlewaite, "well, I don't mind telling you, it was an adventure."

"An adventure, my friend?" said Li Gao.

Postlewaite took a bite of his dinner and nodded his head. "Average folks like yourselves don't understand the exciting world of memorabilia collecting. If I told you half of my adventures, it would make your hair stand on end!"

Chesney looked at Verity and smiled. "Yes, one can only imagine!"

The End of

The Girl in the Sky Blue Plimsolls

and the

Lorraine Innis Saga

S.D.G.

www.ingramcontent.com/pod-product-compliance
Lightning Source LLC
Chambersburg PA
CBHW030619250626
47154CB00006B/1844